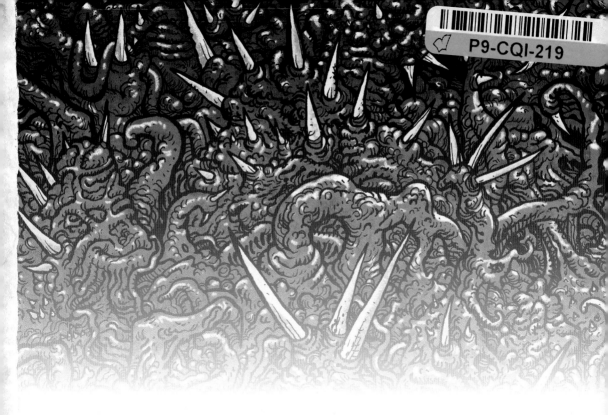

SPREAD

VOL. 3: NO SAFE PLACE

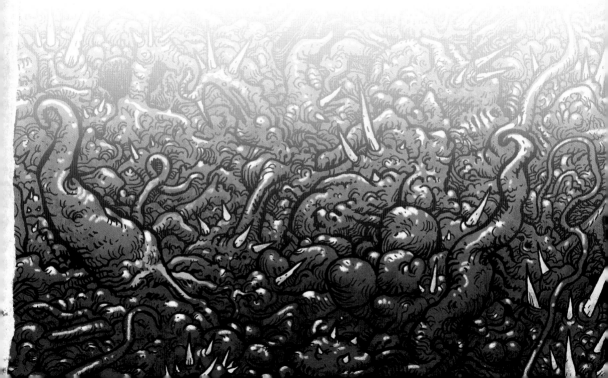

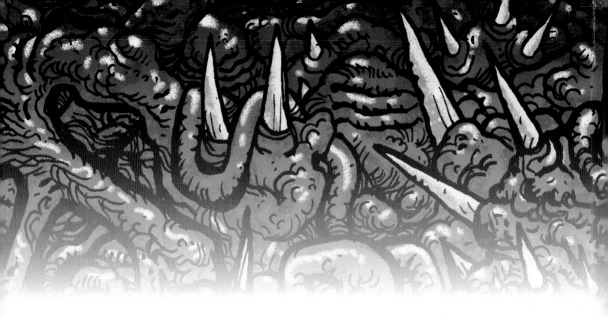

IMAGE COMICS, INC.

Robert Kirkman – Chief Operating Officer
Erik Larsen – Chief Financial Officer
Todd McFarlane – President
Marc Silvestri – Chief Executive Officer
Jim Valentino – Vice-President

Eric Stephenson – Publisher
Corey Murphy – Director of Sales
Jeff Boison – Director of Publishing Planning & Book Trade Sales
Jeremy Sullivan – Director of Digital Sales
Kat Salazar – Director of PR & Marketing
Branwyn Bigglestone – Controller
Drew Gill – Art Director
Jonathan Chan – Production Manager
Meredith Wallace – Print Manager
Briah Skelly – Publicist
Sasha Head – Sales & Marketing Production Designer
Randy Okamura – Digital Production Designer
David Brothers – Branding Manager
Olivia Ngai – Content Manager
Addison Duke – Production Artist
Vincent Kukua – Production Artist
Tricia Ramos – Production Artist
Jeff Stang – Direct Market Sales Representative
Emilio Bautista – Digital Sales Associate
Leanna Caunter – Accounting Assistant
Chloe Ramos-Peterson – Library Market Sales Representative
IMAGECOMICS.COM

SPREAD VOL. 3: NO SAFE PLACE. FIRST PRINTING. DECEMBER 2016.
ISBN# 978-1-63215-907-6

For international rights, contact:
foreignlicensing@imagecomics.com

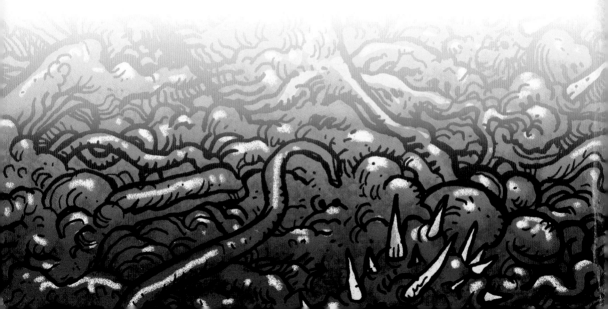

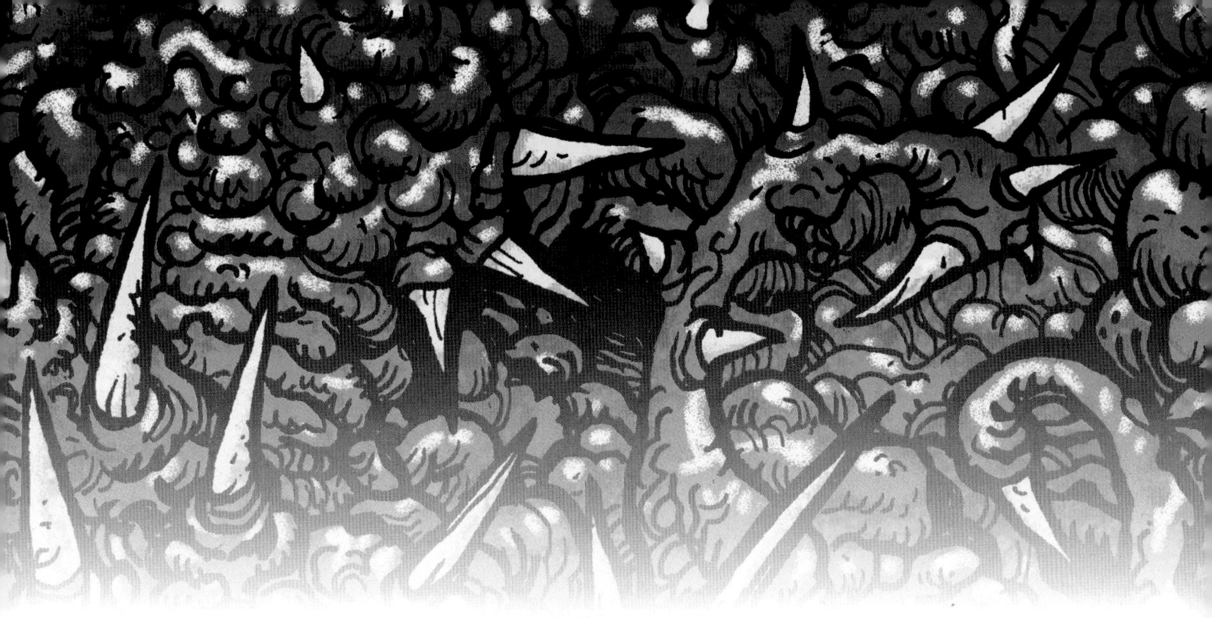

CO-CREATED BY

JUSTIN JORDAN and KYLE STRAHM

WRITTEN BY

JUSTIN JORDAN

ISSUE #12 ART BY
JEN HICKMAN

ISSUE #13 ART BY
FELIPE SOBREIRO

ISSUE #14-17 ART BY
JOHN BIVENS

COLORS BY
FELIPE SOBREIRO

LETTERS BY
CRANK!

EDITED BY
SEBASTIAN GIRNER

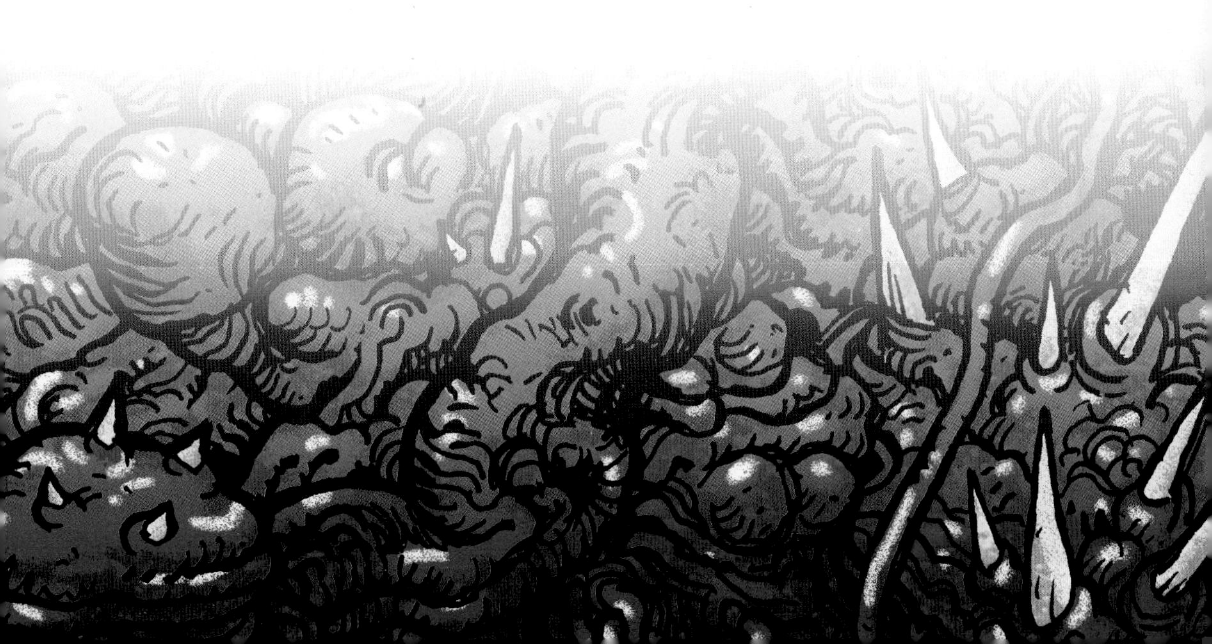

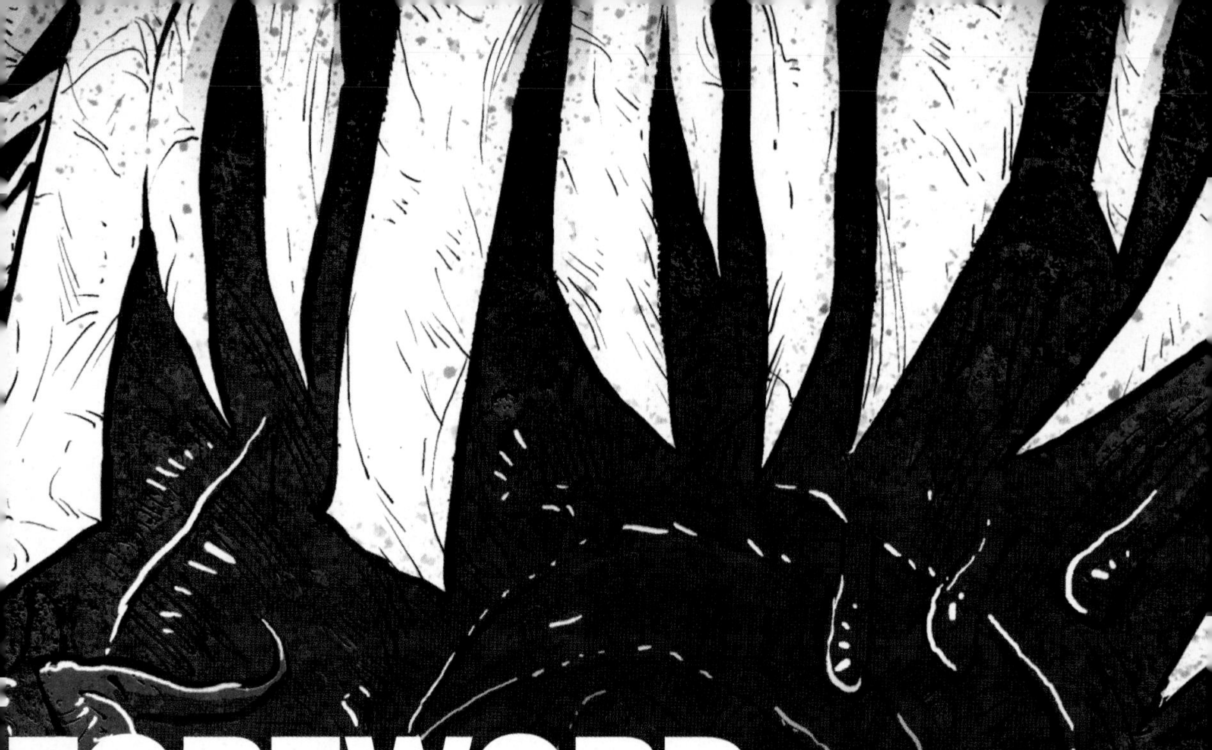

FOREWORD

Once More Into The Breach

Well, we're really cooking now. We've got the secret origin of Molly, courtesy of artist Jen Hickman. We've got the secret origin of Jack, drawn by our very own Felipe Sobreiro. And we've got a glimpse into a side of the Spread we haven't yet seen.

This is roughly the halfway point of our story, and man, I am glad we've made it. Doing a book like this isn't quite as difficult as getting a baby out of the Quarantine Zone, but it's not easy. Seventeen issues so far, and we wouldn't have been able to do it without the support of people like you. So thanks, and I hope you enjoy the rest of the ride.

John Bivens, my old-time buddy and artist on the Image series *Dark Engine* has joined us for this arc. He's a pretty dang good match for the book, and we're lucky to have him on. Kyle is planning on being back down the road, so no worries there.

-Justin Jordan

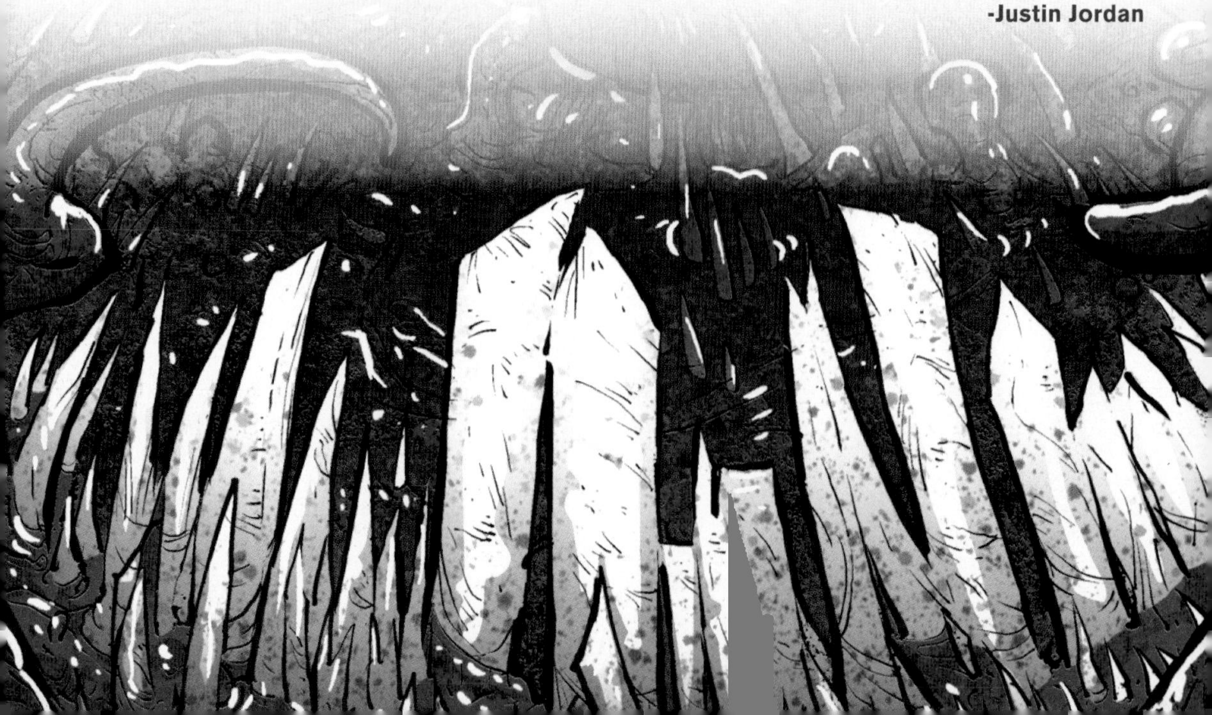

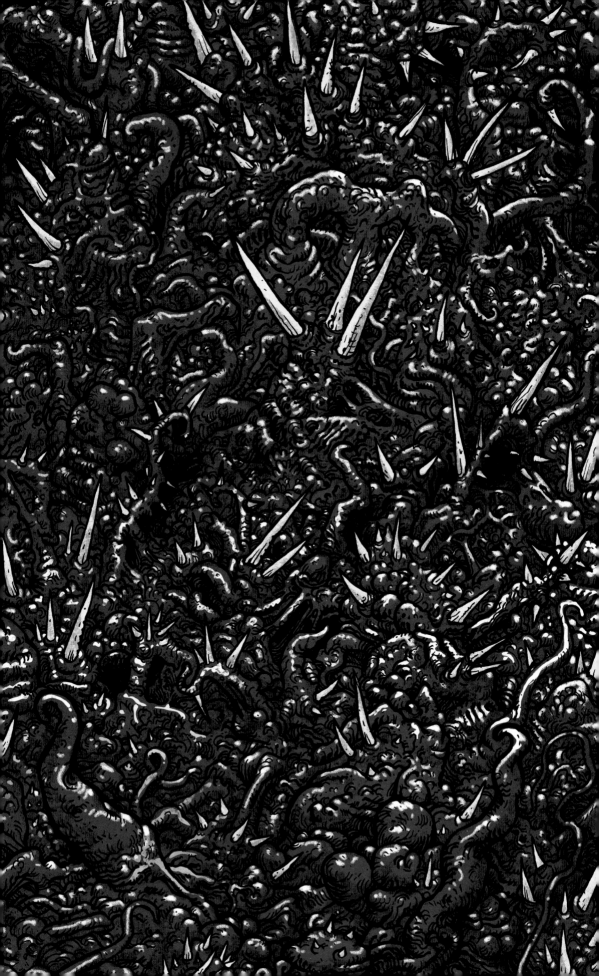

CHAPTER ONE

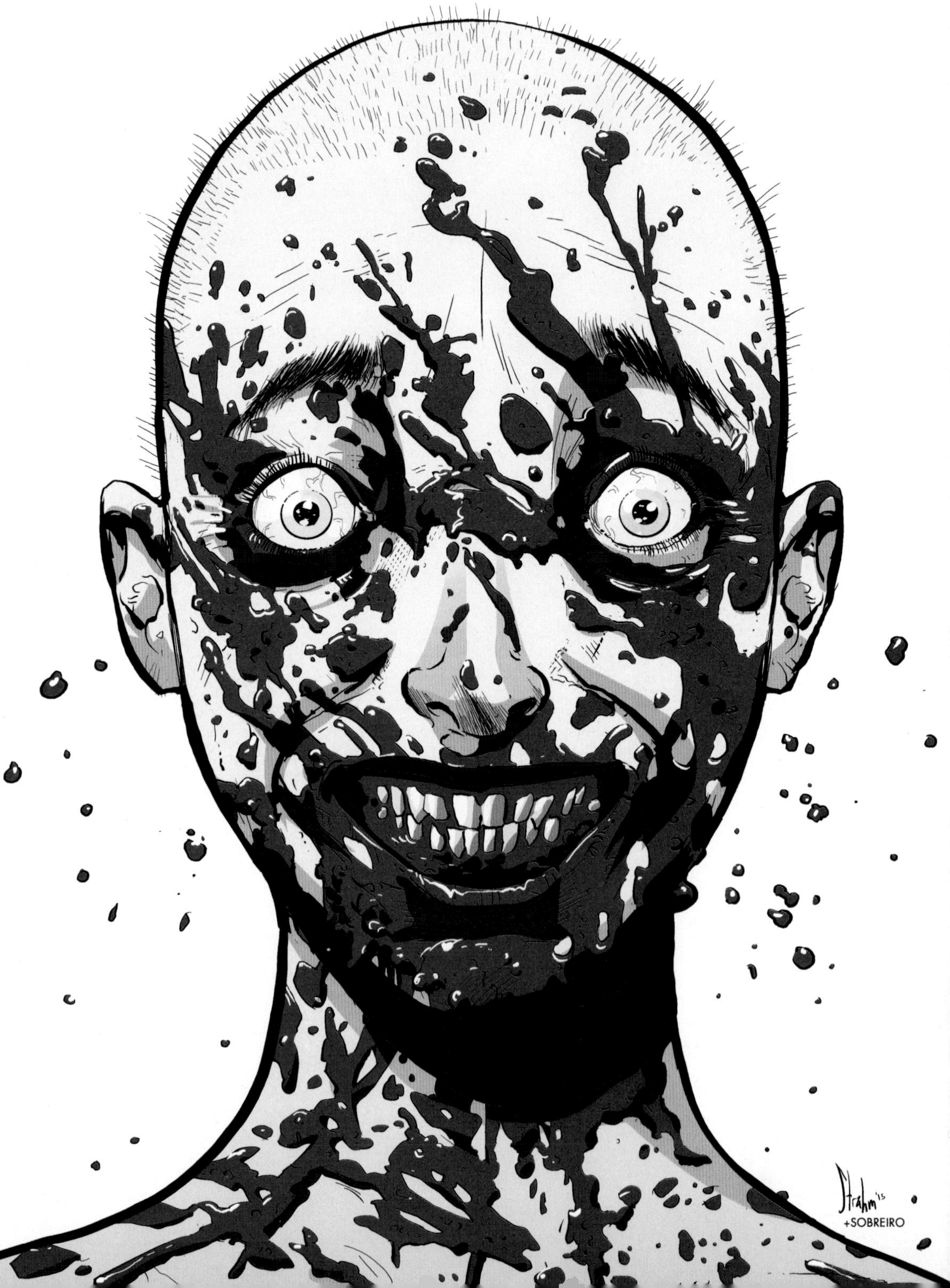

+SOBREIRO

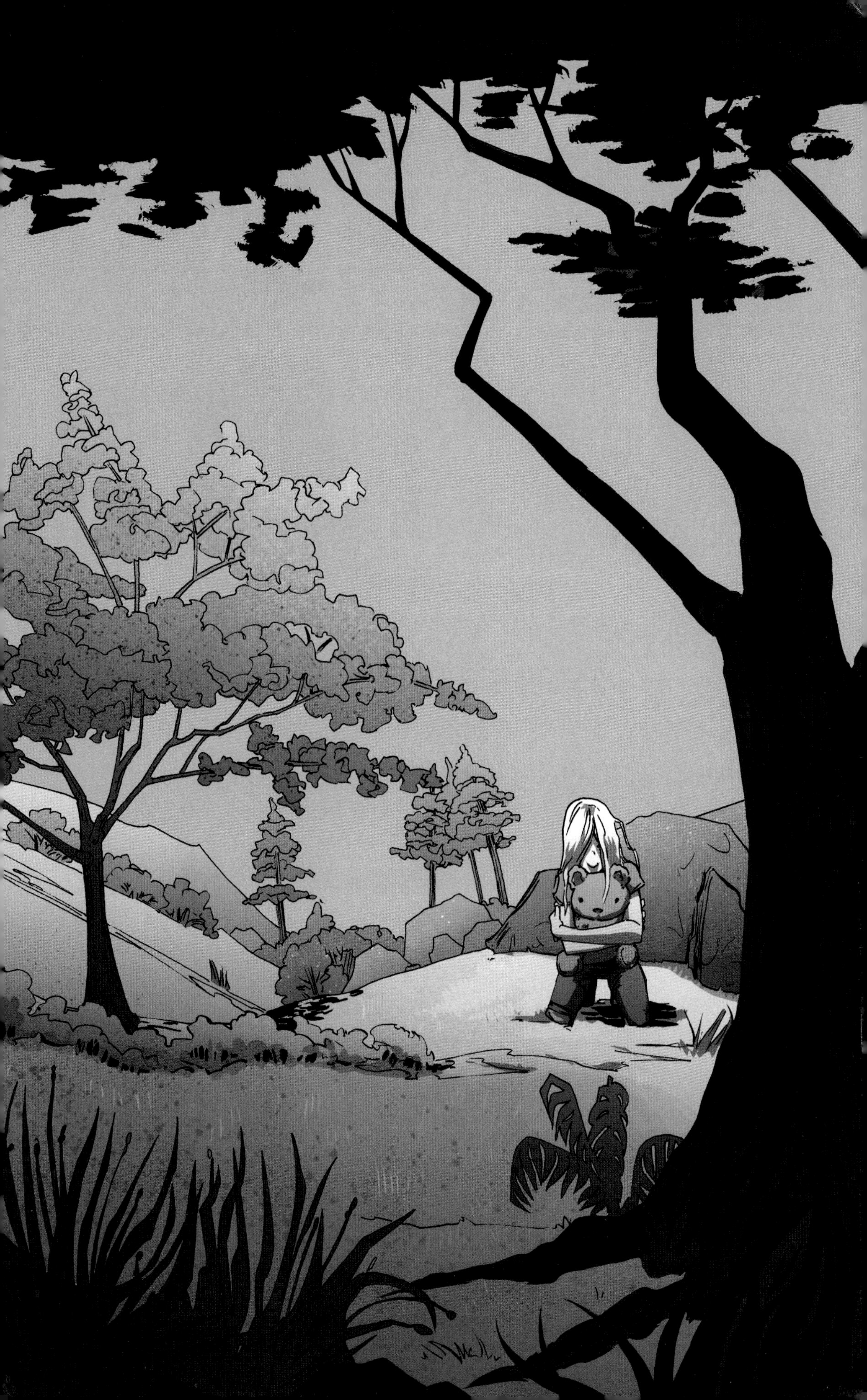

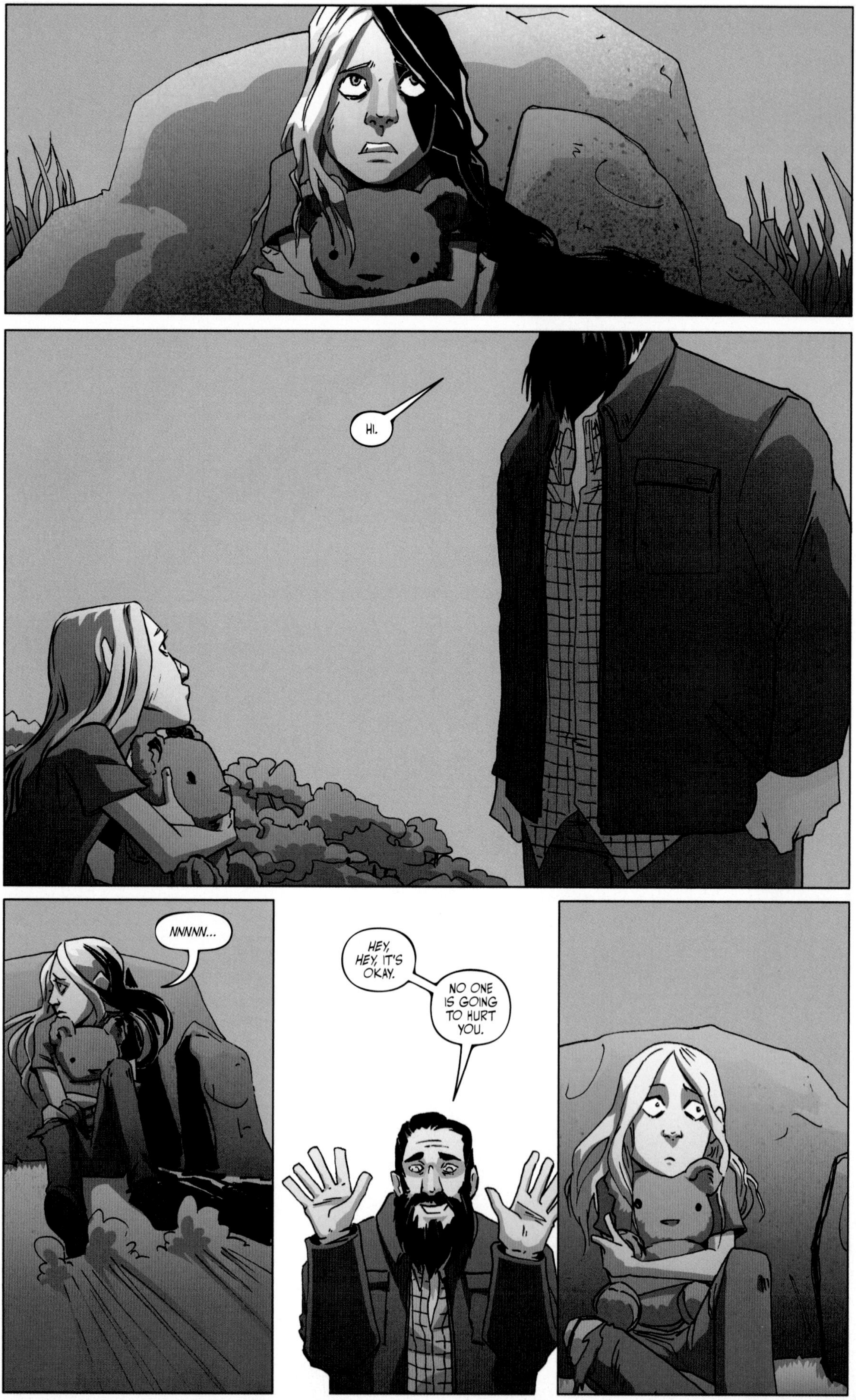
HI.
NNNNN...
HEY, HEY, IT'S OKAY.
NO ONE IS GOING TO HURT YOU.

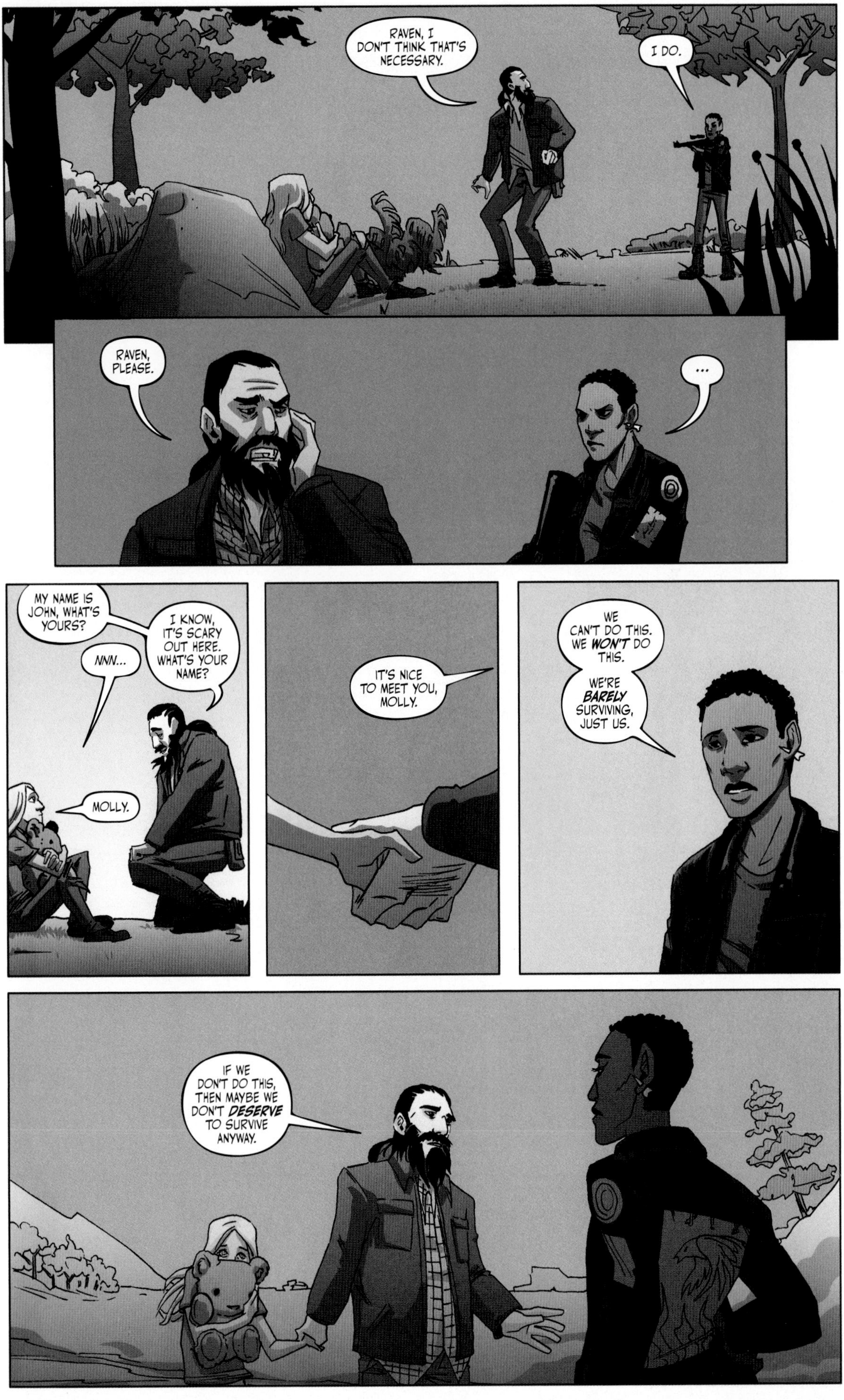
RAVEN, I DON'T THINK THAT'S NECESSARY.
I DO.
RAVEN, PLEASE.
...
MY NAME IS JOHN, WHAT'S YOURS?
NNN...
I KNOW, IT'S SCARY OUT HERE. WHAT'S YOUR NAME?
MOLLY.
IT'S NICE TO MEET YOU, MOLLY.
WE CAN'T DO THIS. WE WON'T DO THIS.
WE'RE BARELY SURVIVING, JUST US.
IF WE DON'T DO THIS, THEN MAYBE WE DON'T DESERVE TO SURVIVE ANYWAY.

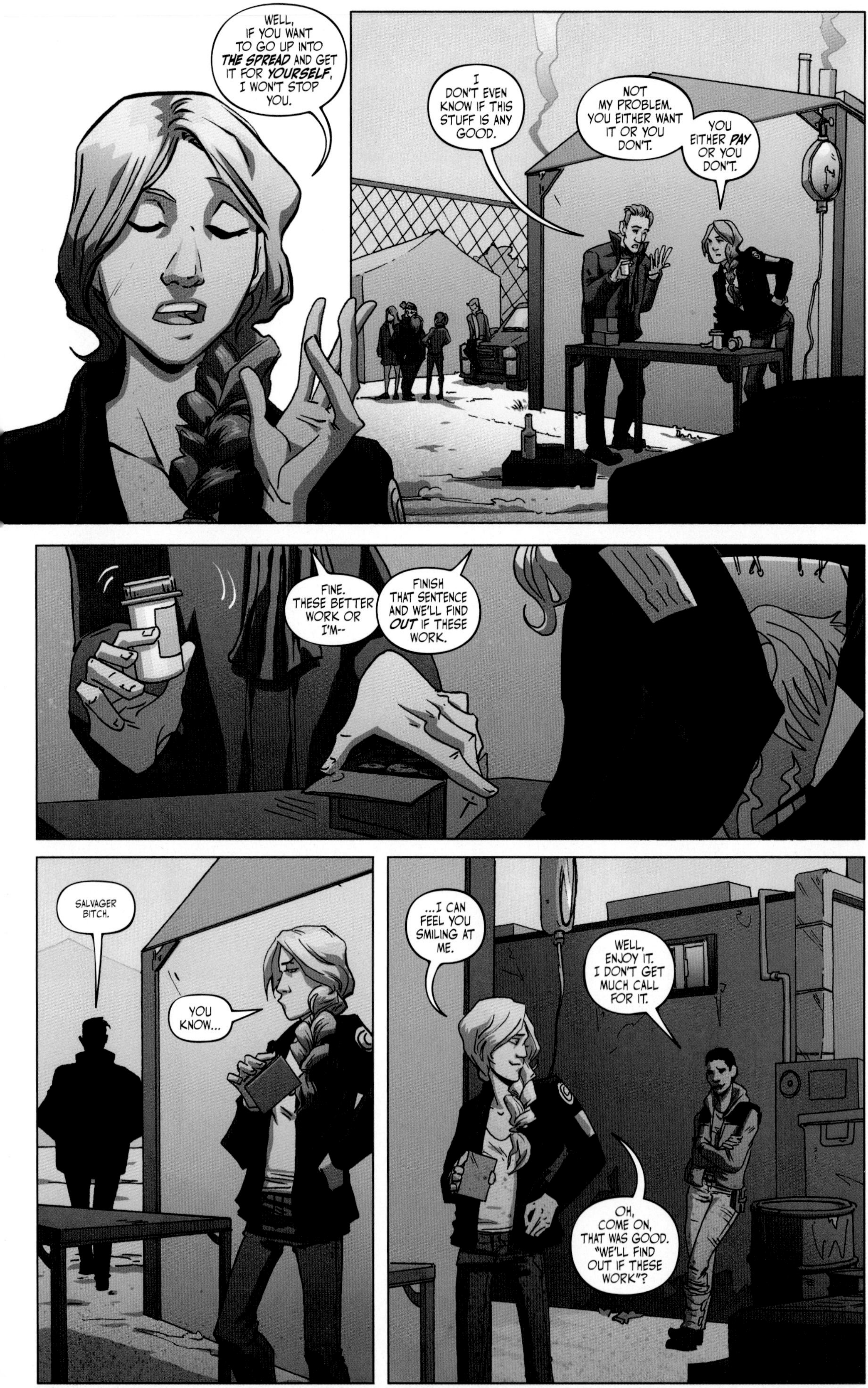
WELL, IF YOU WANT TO GO UP INTO THE SPREAD AND GET IT FOR YOURSELF, I WON'T STOP YOU.
I DON'T EVEN KNOW IF THIS STUFF IS ANY GOOD.
NOT MY PROBLEM. YOU EITHER WANT IT OR YOU DON'T.
YOU EITHER PAY OR YOU DON'T.
FINE. THESE BETTER WORK OR I'M--
FINISH THAT SENTENCE AND WE'LL FIND OUT IF THESE WORK.
SALVAGER BITCH.
YOU KNOW...
...I CAN FEEL YOU SMILING AT ME.
WELL, ENJOY IT. I DON'T GET MUCH CALL FOR IT.
OH, COME ON, THAT WAS GOOD. "WE'LL FIND OUT IF THESE WORK"?

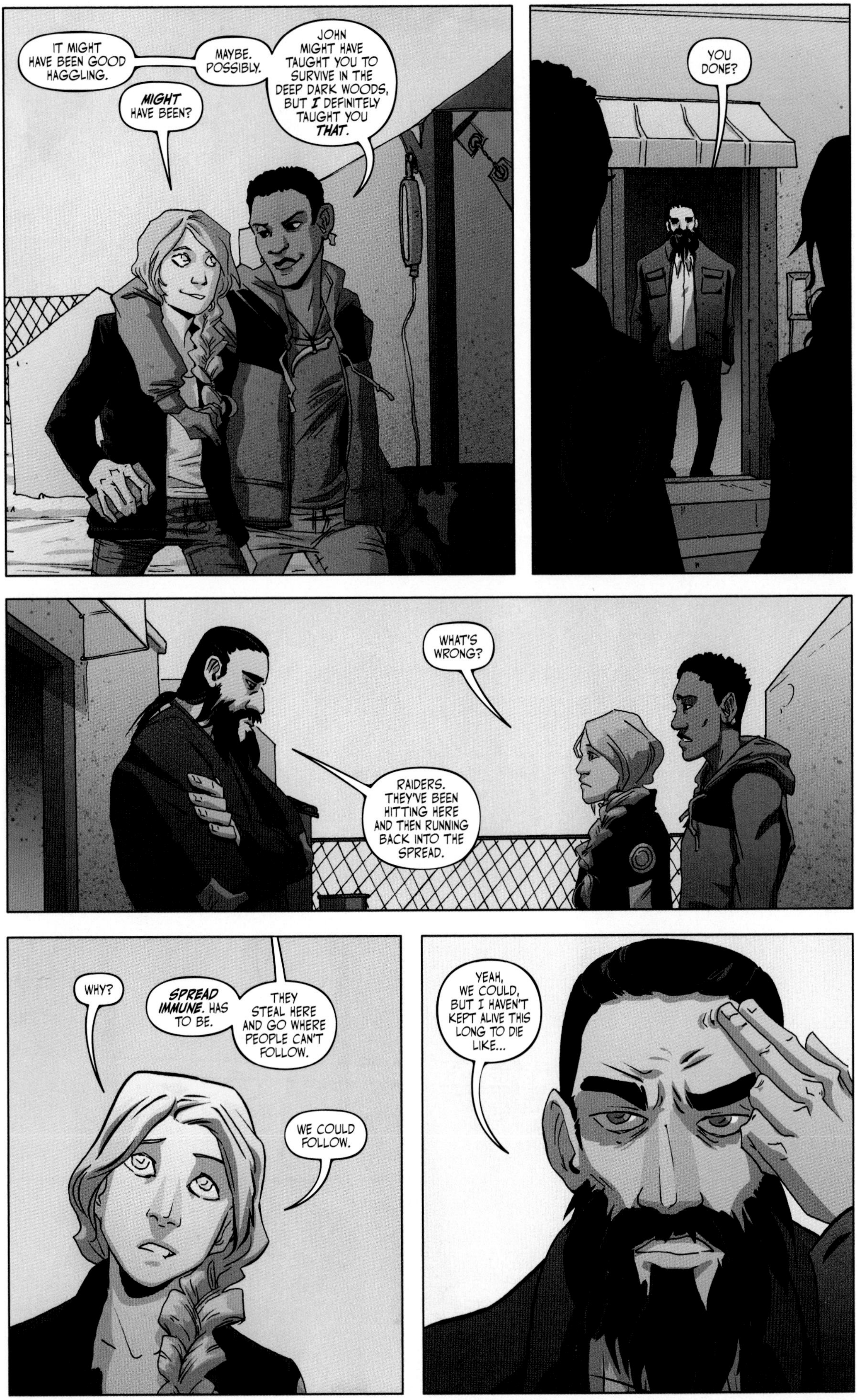
IT MIGHT HAVE BEEN GOOD HAGGLING.
MIGHT HAVE BEEN?
MAYBE. POSSIBLY.
JOHN MIGHT HAVE TAUGHT YOU TO SURVIVE IN THE DEEP DARK WOODS, BUT I DEFINITELY TAUGHT YOU THAT.
YOU DONE?
WHAT'S WRONG?
RAIDERS. THEY'VE BEEN HITTING HERE AND THEN RUNNING BACK INTO THE SPREAD.
WHY?
SPREAD IMMUNE. HAS TO BE.
THEY STEAL HERE AND GO WHERE PEOPLE CAN'T FOLLOW.
WE COULD FOLLOW.
YEAH, WE COULD, BUT I HAVEN'T KEPT ALIVE THIS LONG TO DIE LIKE...

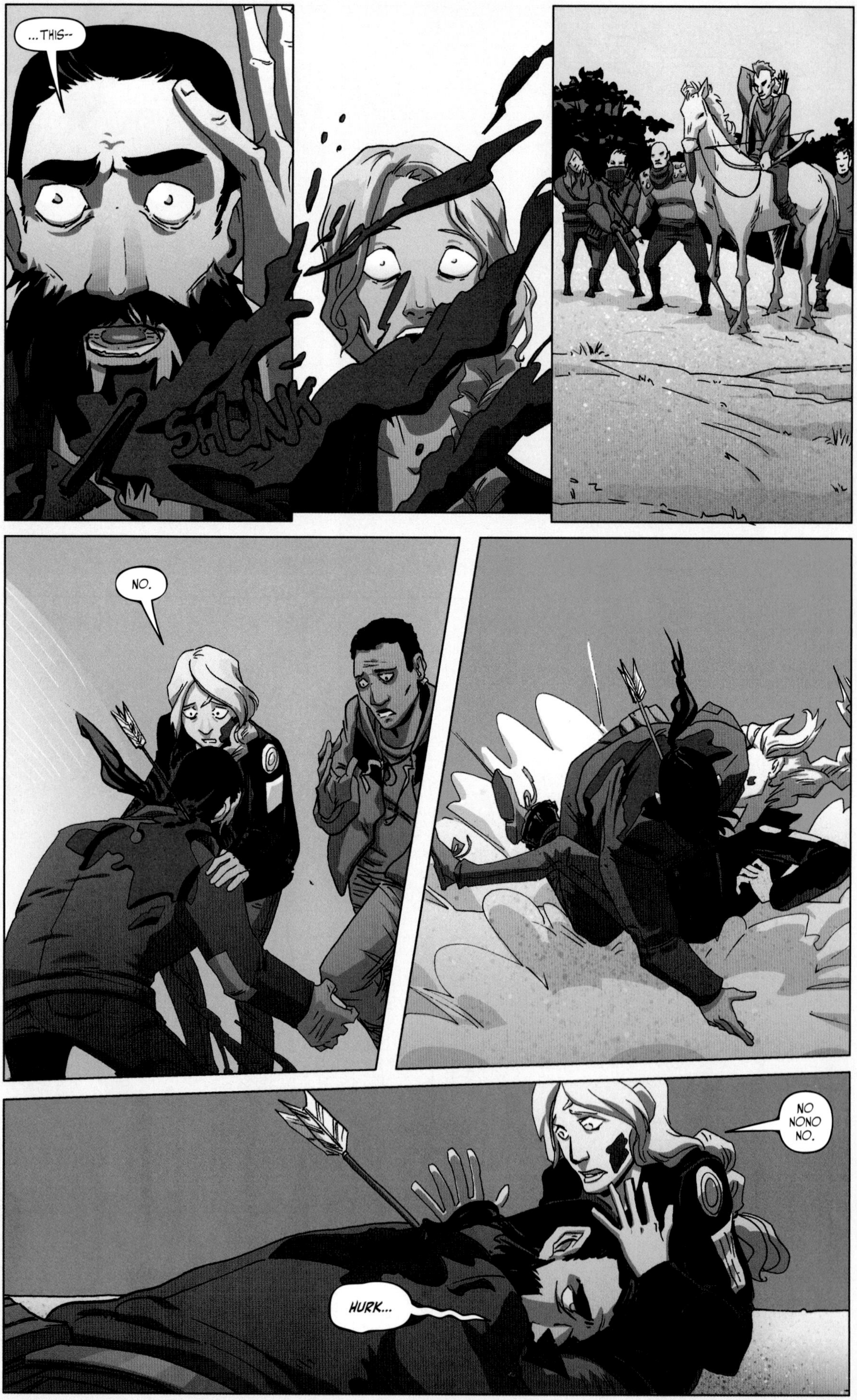
...THIS--
SHUNK
NO.
NO NONO NO.
HURK...

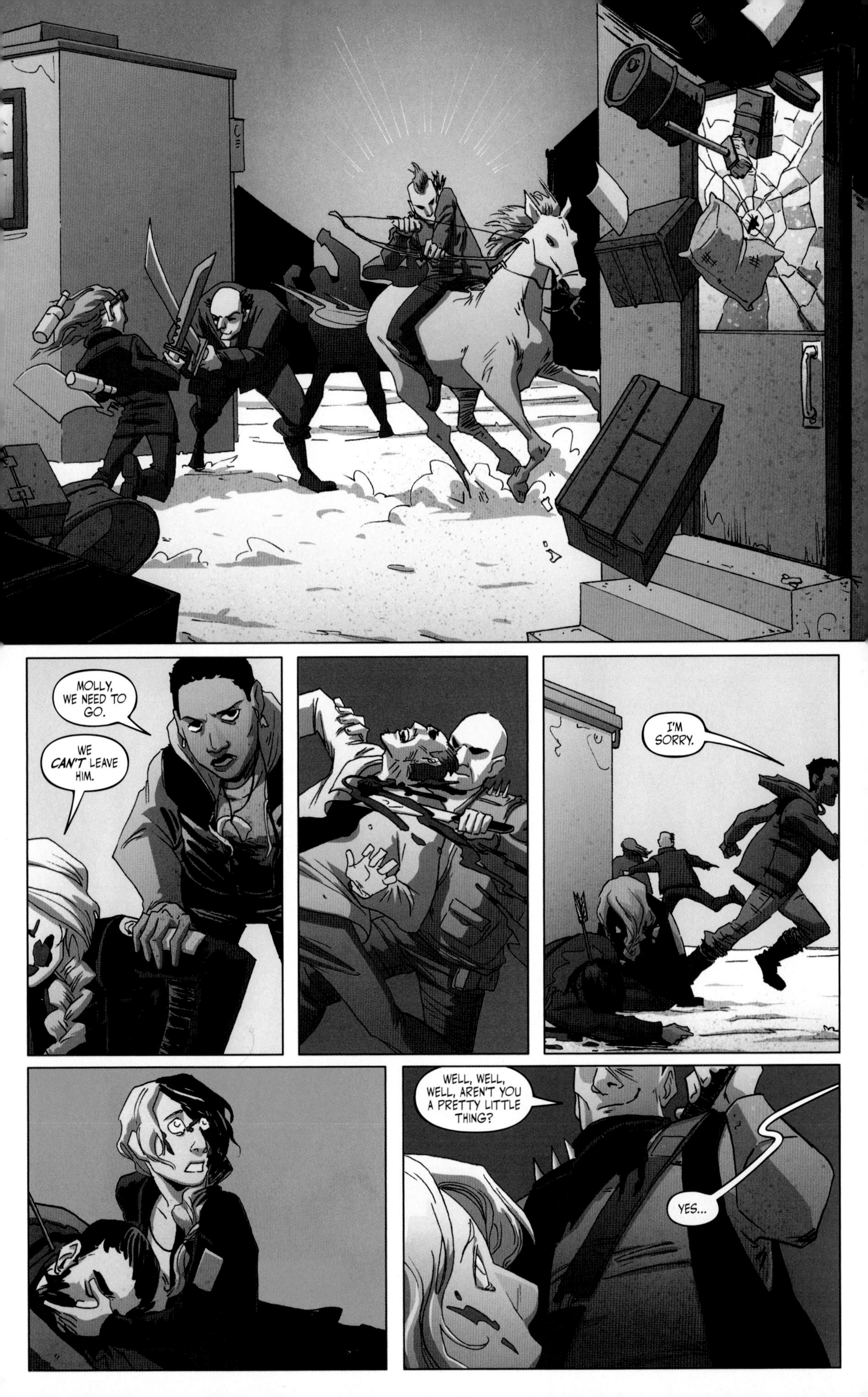
MOLLY, WE NEED TO GO.
WE CAN'T LEAVE HIM.
I'M SORRY.
WELL, WELL, WELL, AREN'T YOU A PRETTY LITTLE THING?
YES...

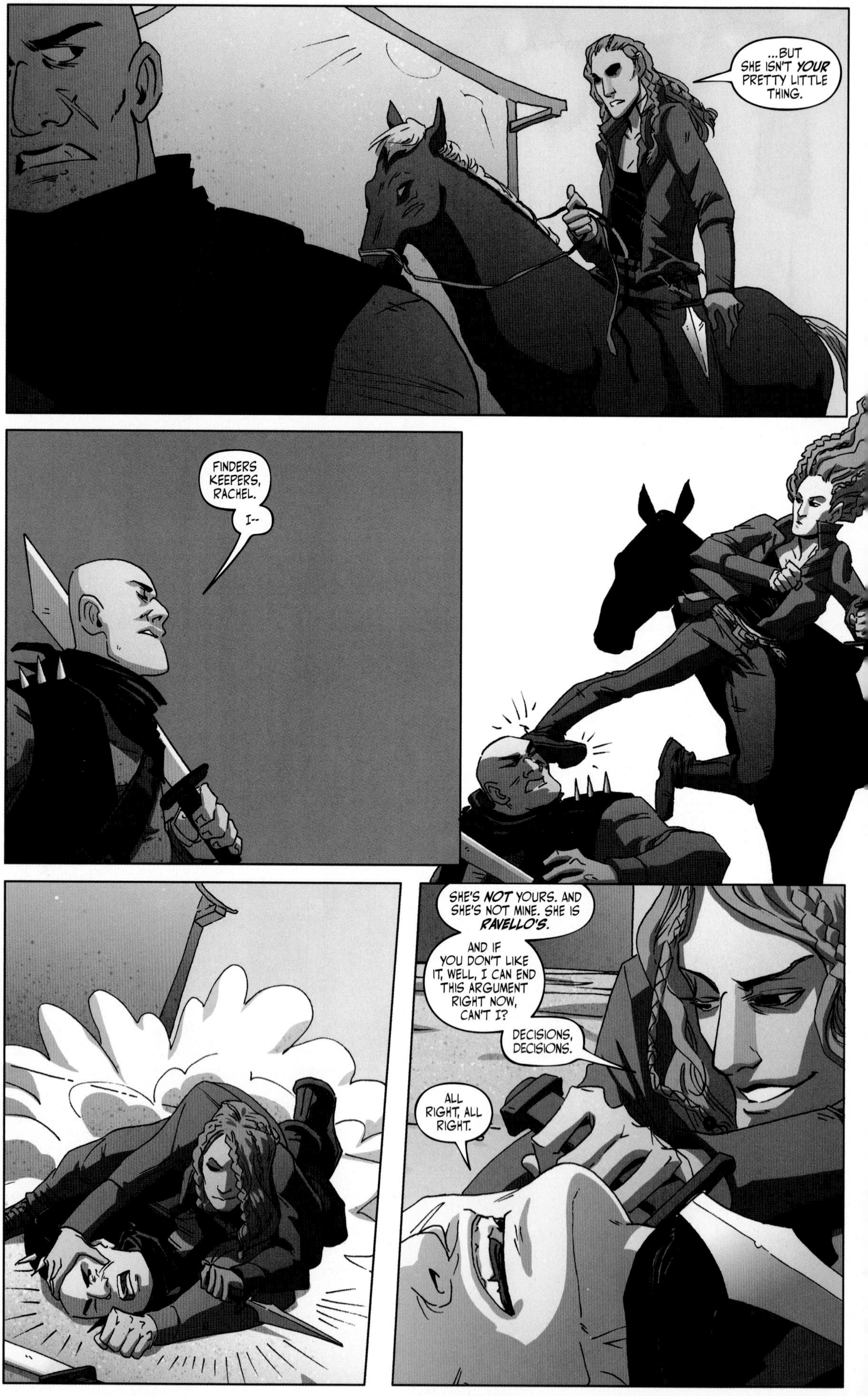
...BUT SHE ISN'T YOUR PRETTY LITTLE THING.
FINDERS KEEPERS, RACHEL.
I--
SHE'S NOT YOURS. AND SHE'S NOT MINE. SHE IS RAVELLO'S.
AND IF YOU DON'T LIKE IT, WELL, I CAN END THIS ARGUMENT RIGHT NOW, CAN'T I?
DECISIONS, DECISIONS.
ALL RIGHT, ALL RIGHT.

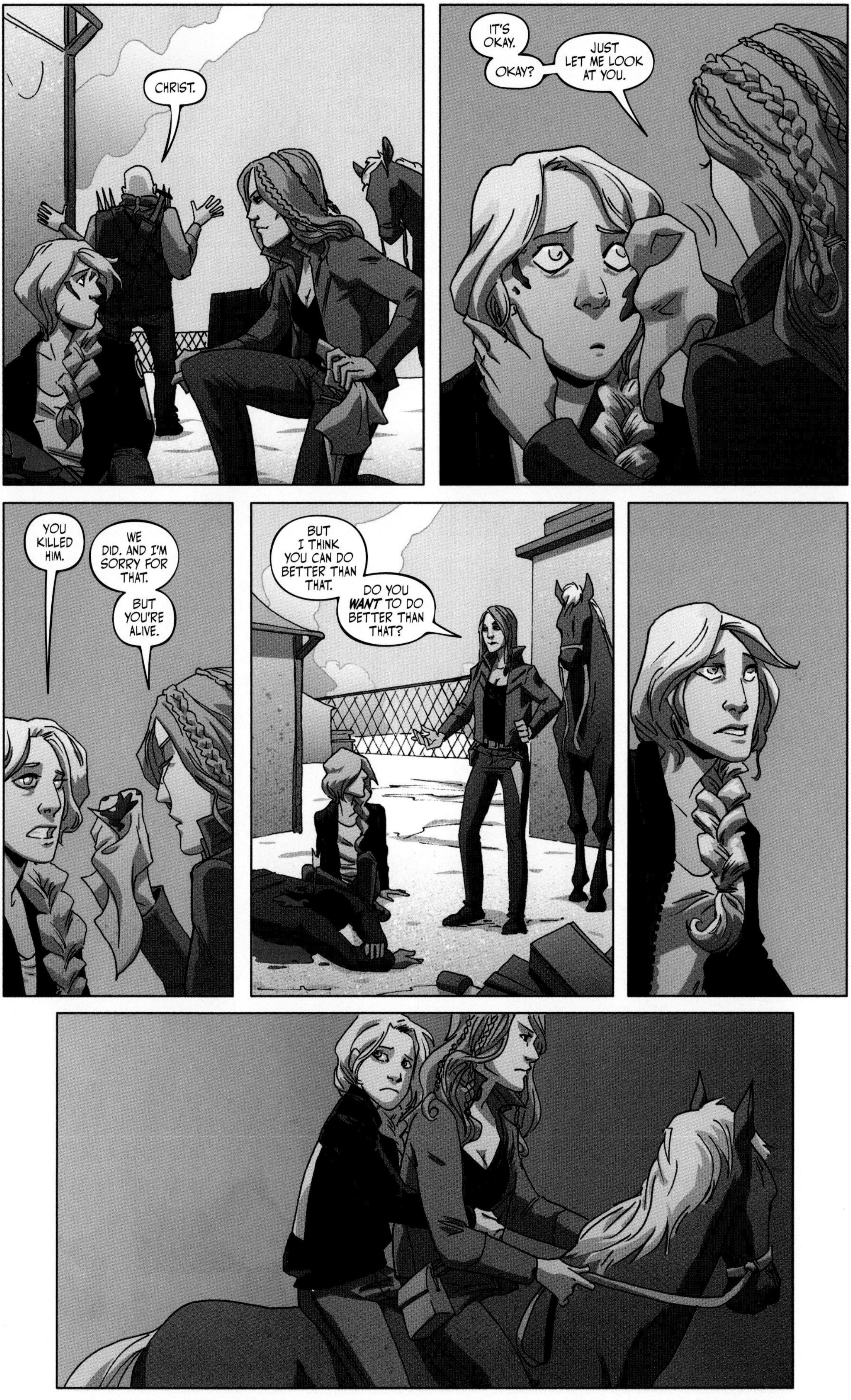
CHRIST.
IT'S OKAY.
OKAY?
JUST LET ME LOOK AT YOU.
YOU KILLED HIM.
WE DID. AND I'M SORRY FOR THAT.
BUT YOU'RE ALIVE.
BUT I THINK YOU CAN DO BETTER THAN THAT.
DO YOU *WANT* TO DO BETTER THAN THAT?

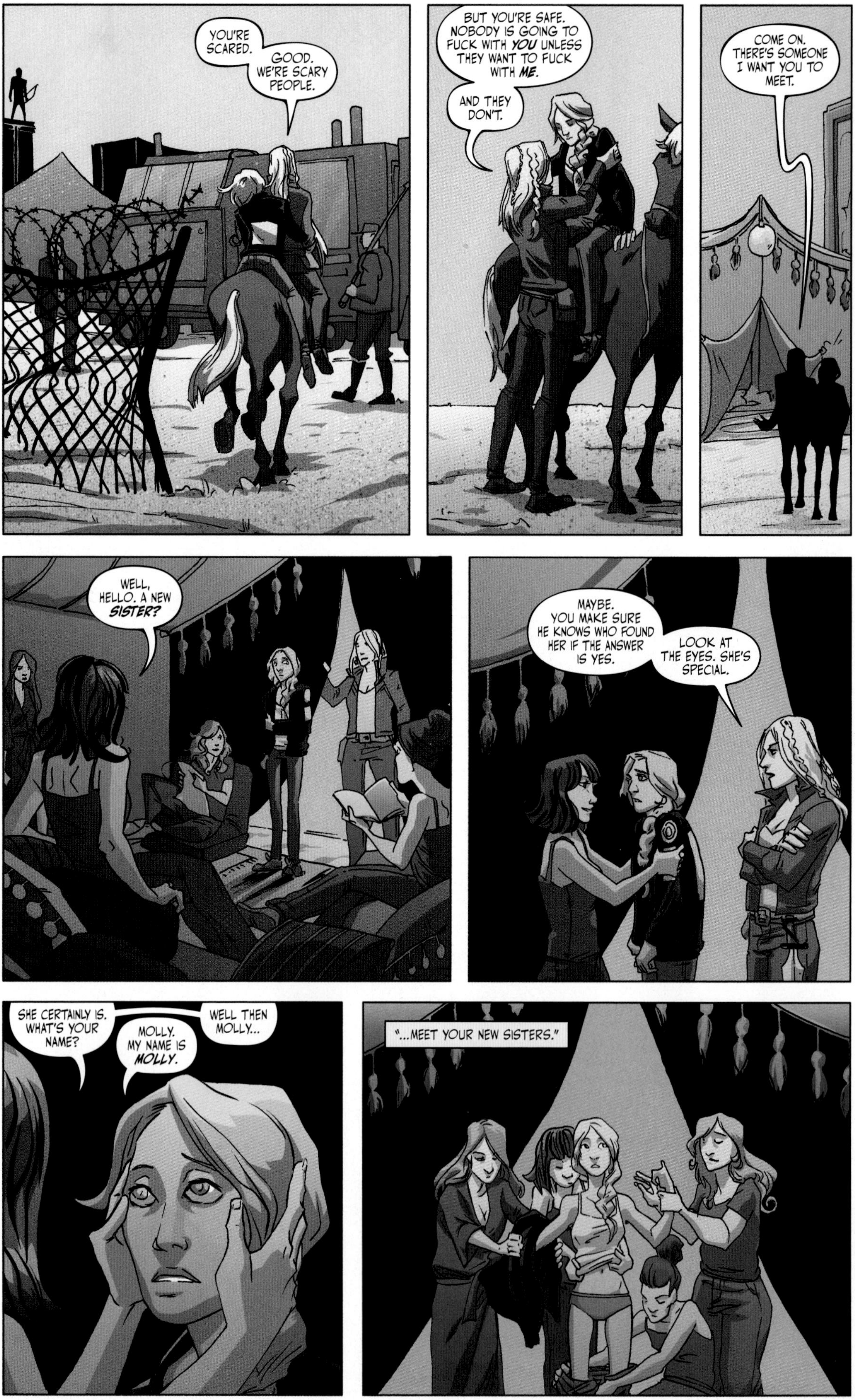
YOU'RE SCARED.
GOOD. WE'RE SCARY PEOPLE.
BUT YOU'RE SAFE. NOBODY IS GOING TO FUCK WITH *YOU* UNLESS THEY WANT TO FUCK WITH *ME*.
AND THEY DON'T.
COME ON. THERE'S SOMEONE I WANT YOU TO MEET.
WELL, HELLO. A NEW *SISTER?*
MAYBE. YOU MAKE SURE HE KNOWS WHO FOUND HER IF THE ANSWER IS YES.
LOOK AT THE EYES. SHE'S SPECIAL.
SHE CERTAINLY IS. WHAT'S YOUR NAME?
MOLLY. MY NAME IS *MOLLY*.
WELL THEN MOLLY...
"...MEET YOUR NEW SISTERS."

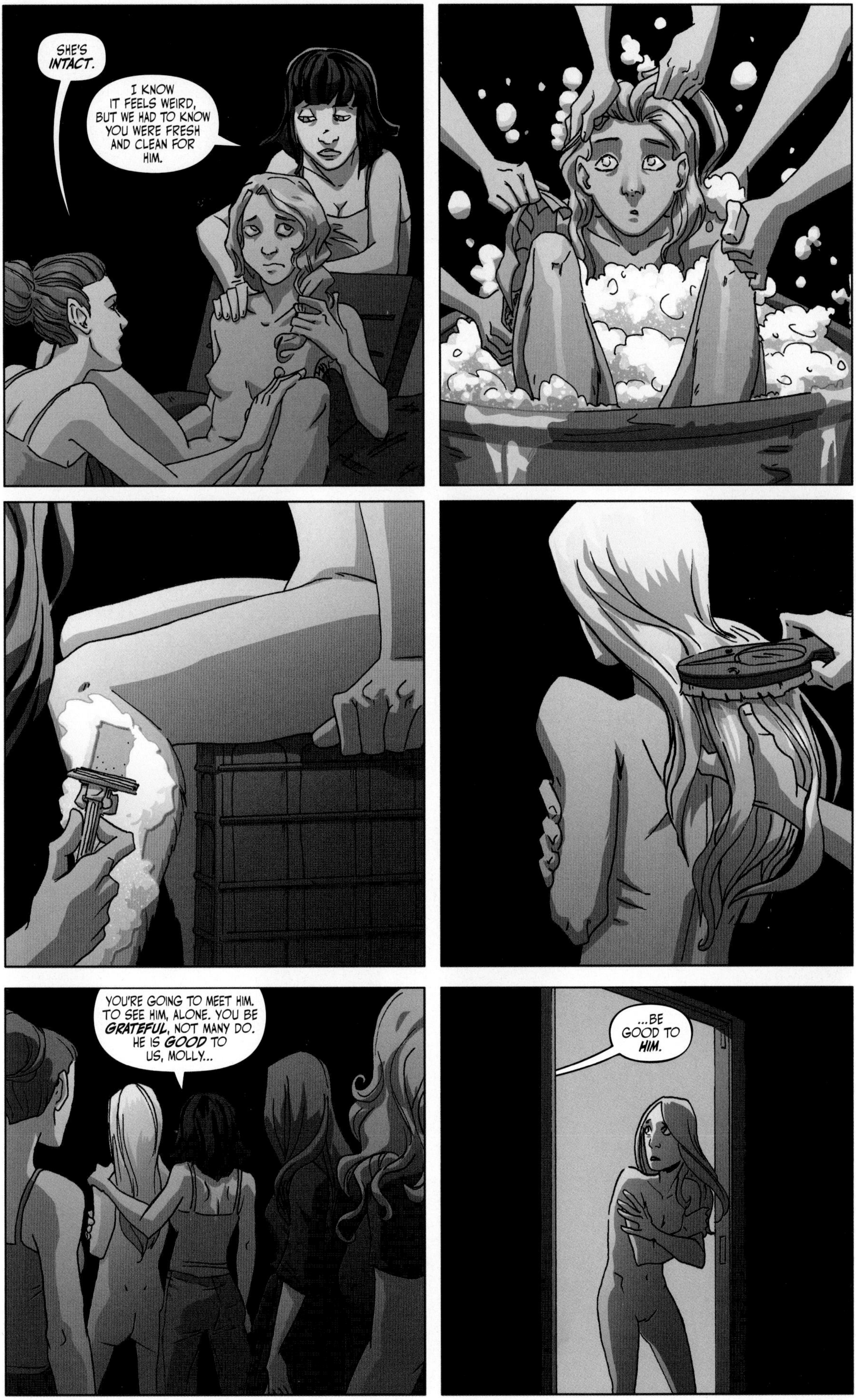
SHE'S INTACT.
I KNOW IT FEELS WEIRD, BUT WE HAD TO KNOW YOU WERE FRESH AND CLEAN FOR HIM.
YOU'RE GOING TO MEET HIM. TO SEE HIM, ALONE. YOU BE GRATEFUL, NOT MANY DO. HE IS GOOD TO US, MOLLY...
...BE GOOD TO HIM.

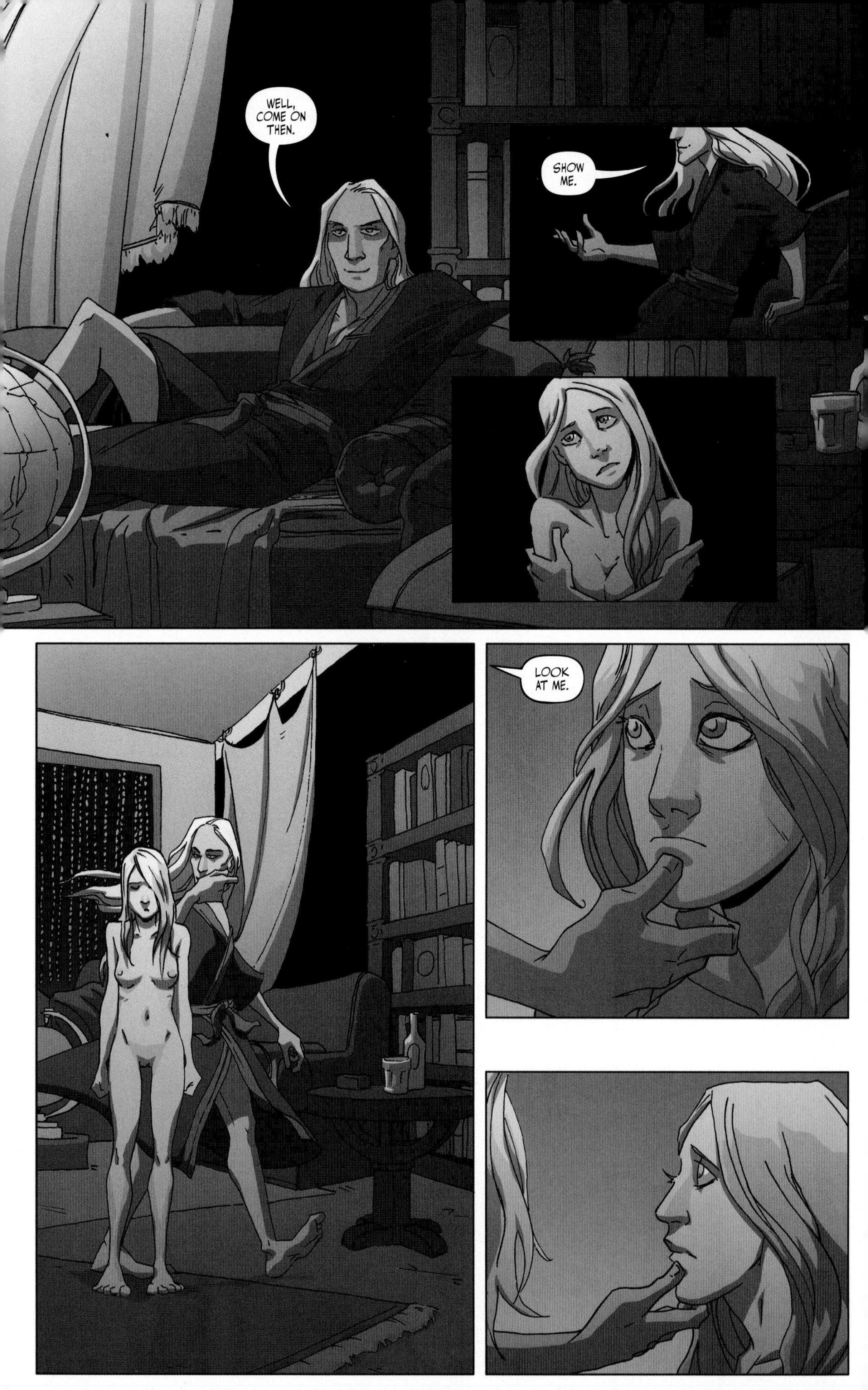
WELL, COME ON THEN.
SHOW ME.
LOOK AT ME.

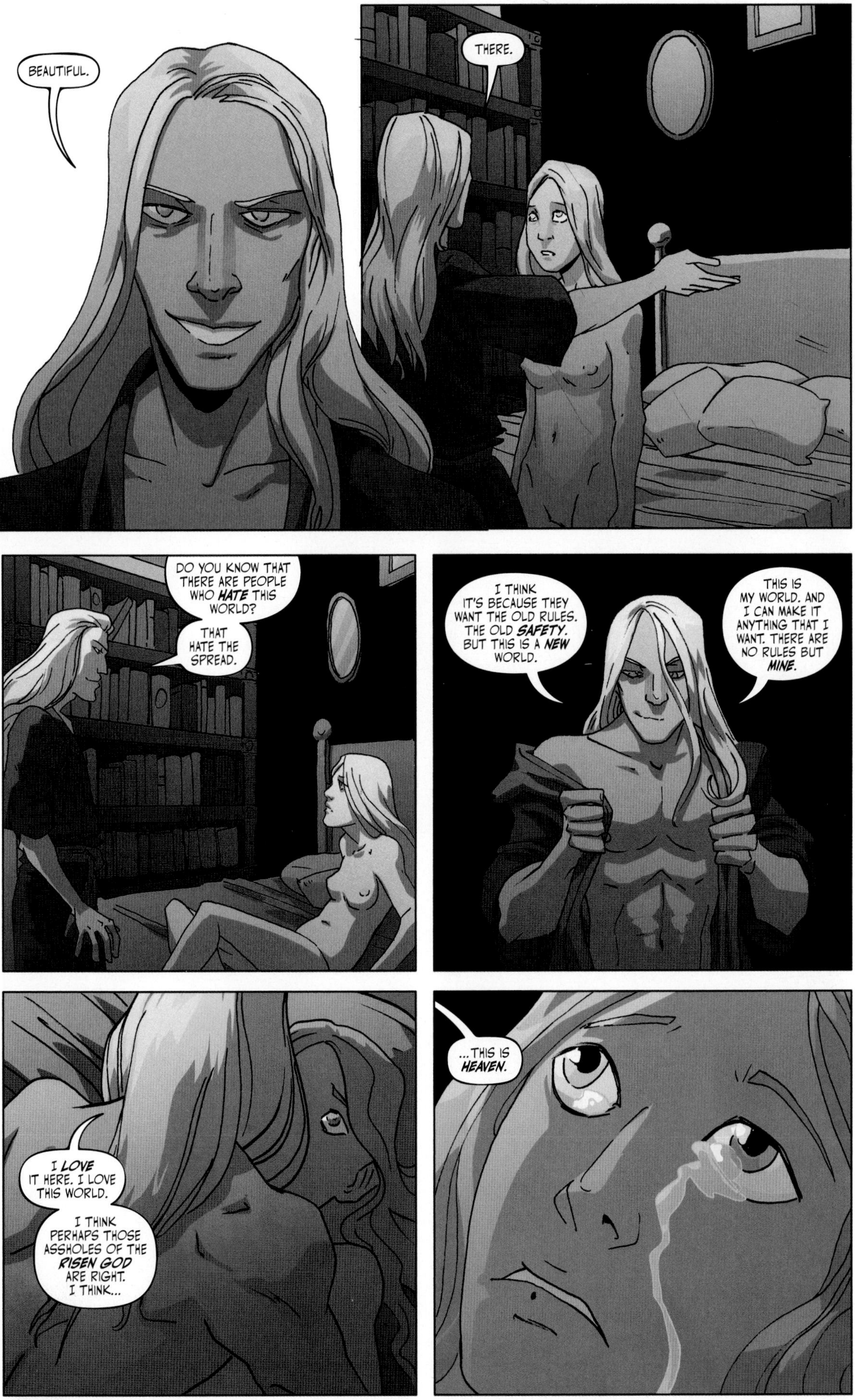
BEAUTIFUL.
THERE.
DO YOU KNOW THAT THERE ARE PEOPLE WHO HATE THIS WORLD?
THAT HATE THE SPREAD.
I THINK IT'S BECAUSE THEY WANT THE OLD RULES. THE OLD SAFETY. BUT THIS IS A NEW WORLD.
THIS IS MY WORLD. AND I CAN MAKE IT ANYTHING THAT I WANT. THERE ARE NO RULES BUT MINE.
I LOVE IT HERE. I LOVE THIS WORLD.
I THINK PERHAPS THOSE ASSHOLES OF THE RISEN GOD ARE RIGHT. I THINK...
...THIS IS HEAVEN.

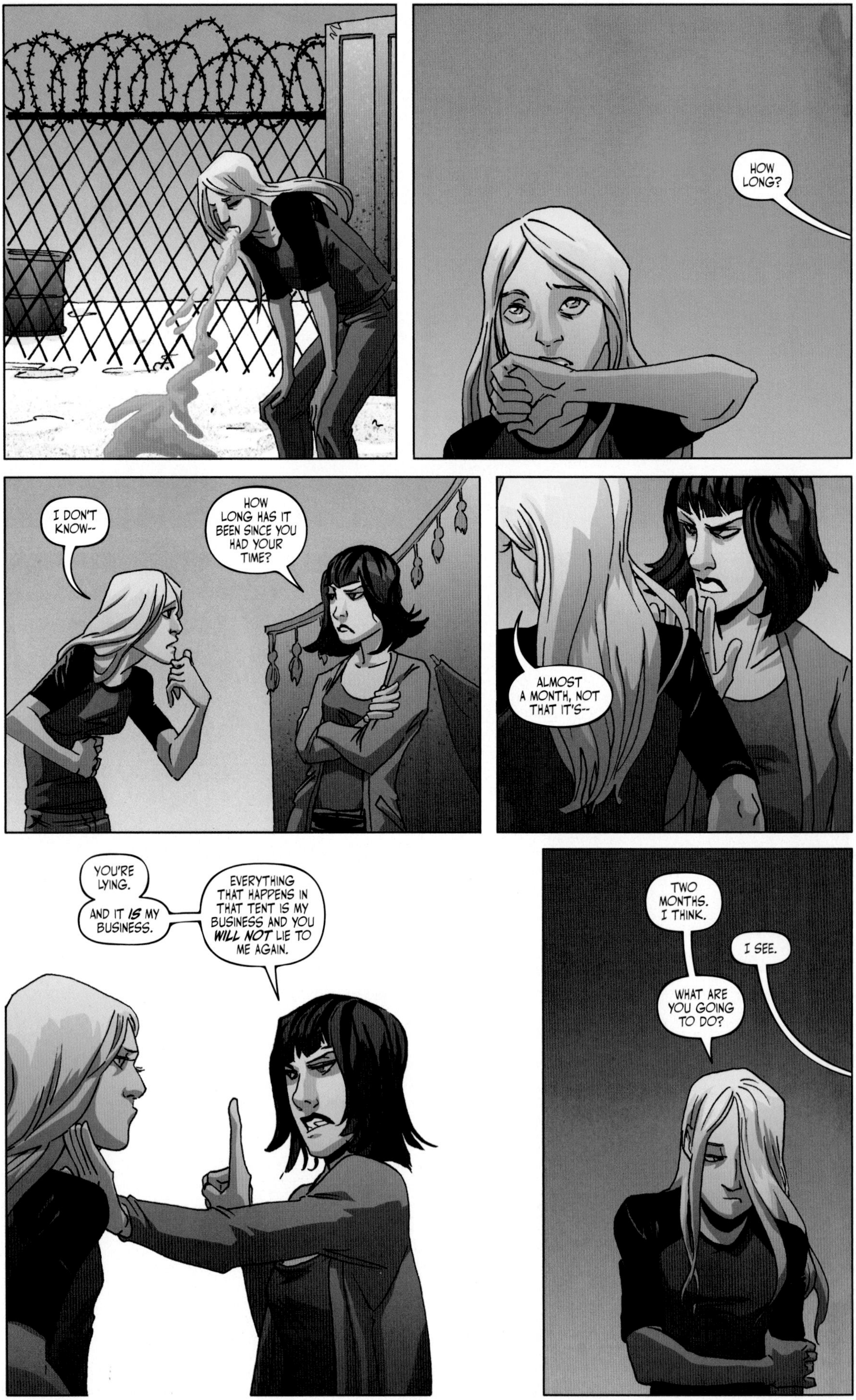
HOW LONG?
I DON'T KNOW--
HOW LONG HAS IT BEEN SINCE YOU HAD YOUR TIME?
ALMOST A MONTH, NOT THAT IT'S--
YOU'RE LYING.
AND IT *IS* MY BUSINESS.
EVERYTHING THAT HAPPENS IN THAT TENT IS MY BUSINESS AND YOU **WILL NOT** LIE TO ME AGAIN.
TWO MONTHS. I THINK.
I SEE.
WHAT ARE YOU GOING TO DO?

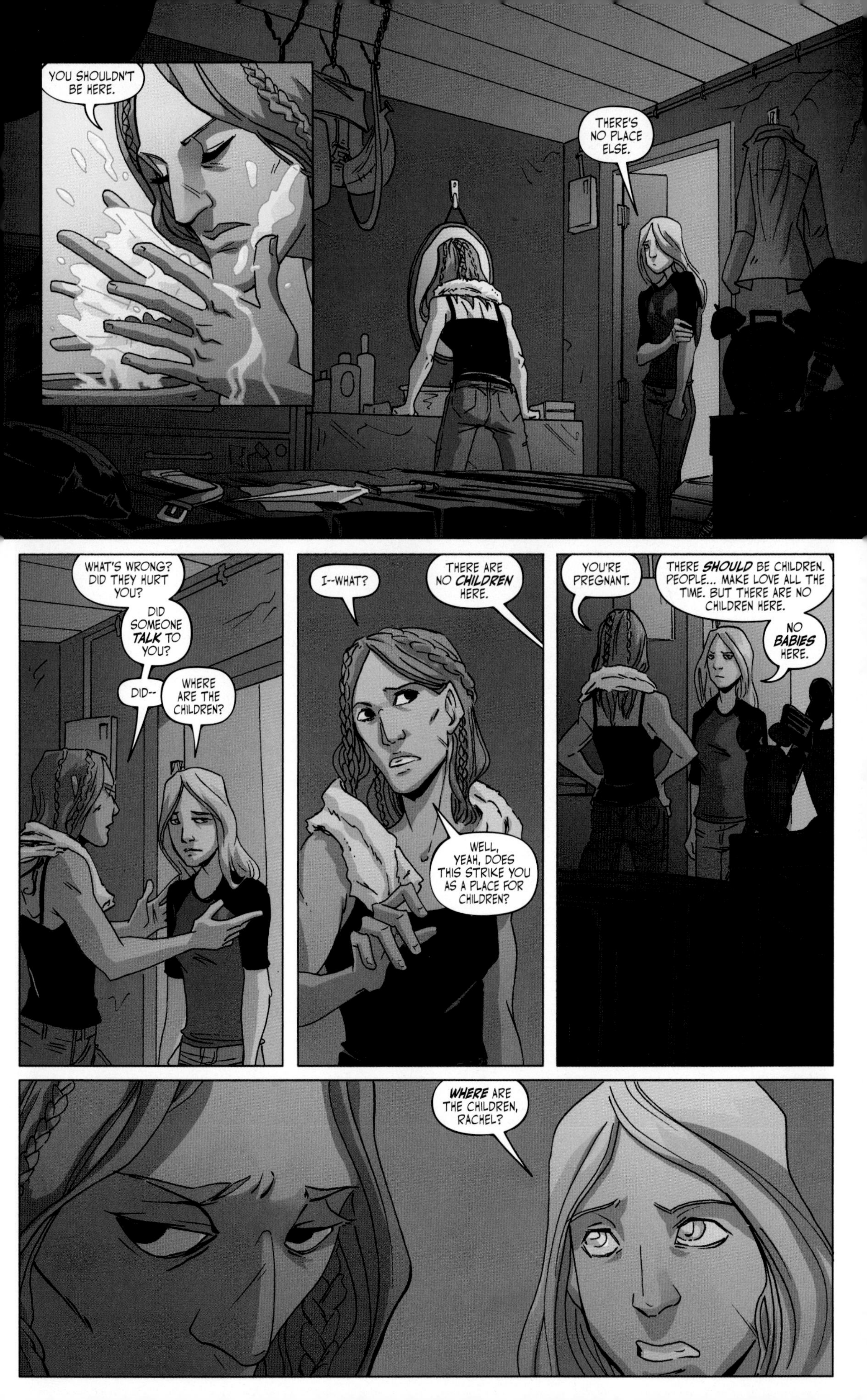
YOU SHOULDN'T BE HERE.
THERE'S NO PLACE ELSE.
WHAT'S WRONG? DID THEY HURT YOU?
DID SOMEONE *TALK* TO YOU?
DID--
WHERE ARE THE CHILDREN?
I--WHAT?
THERE ARE NO *CHILDREN* HERE.
WELL, YEAH, DOES THIS STRIKE YOU AS A PLACE FOR CHILDREN?
YOU'RE PREGNANT.
THERE *SHOULD* BE CHILDREN. PEOPLE... MAKE LOVE ALL THE TIME. BUT THERE ARE NO CHILDREN HERE.
NO *BABIES* HERE.
WHERE ARE THE CHILDREN, RACHEL?

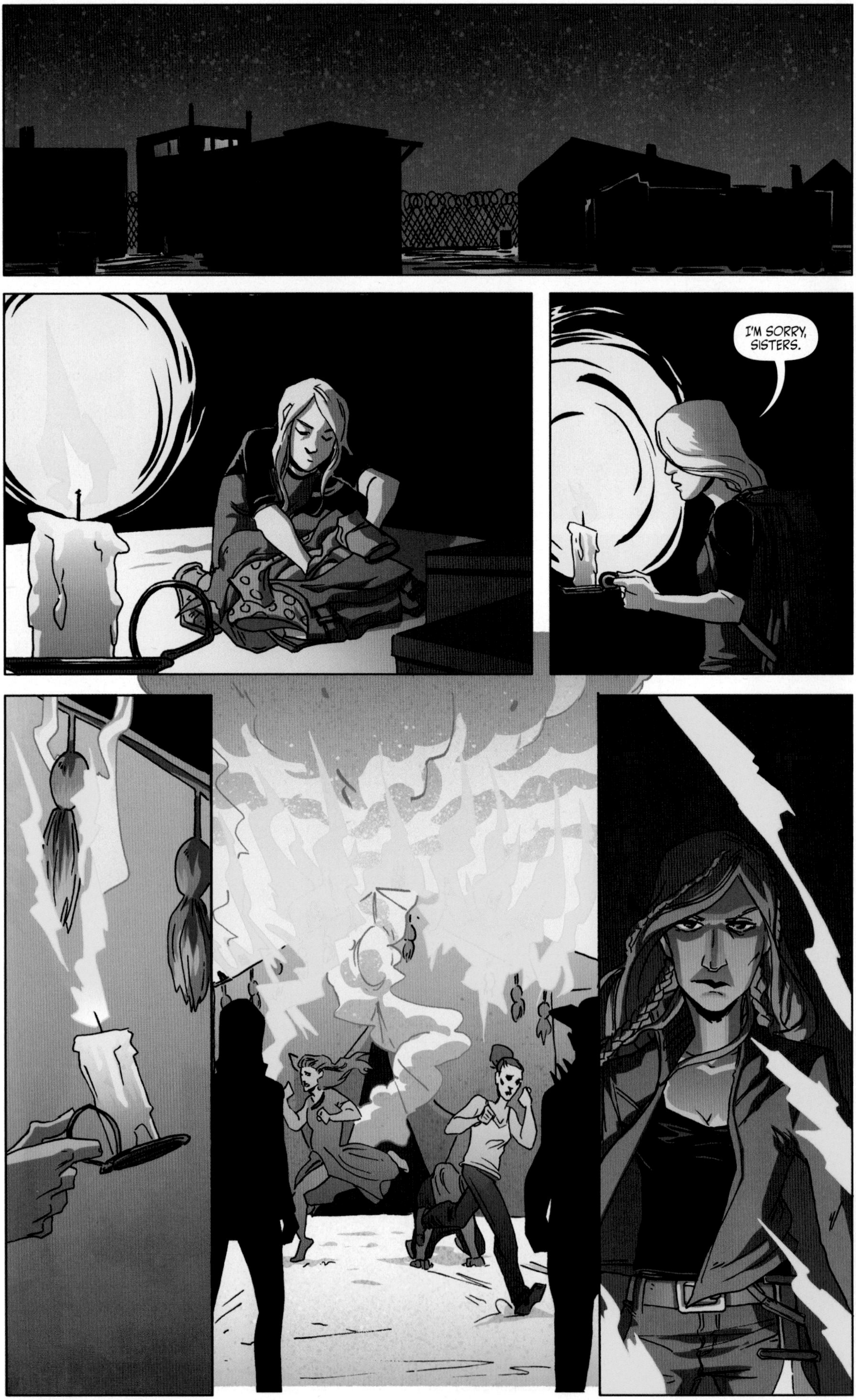
I'M SORRY, SISTERS.

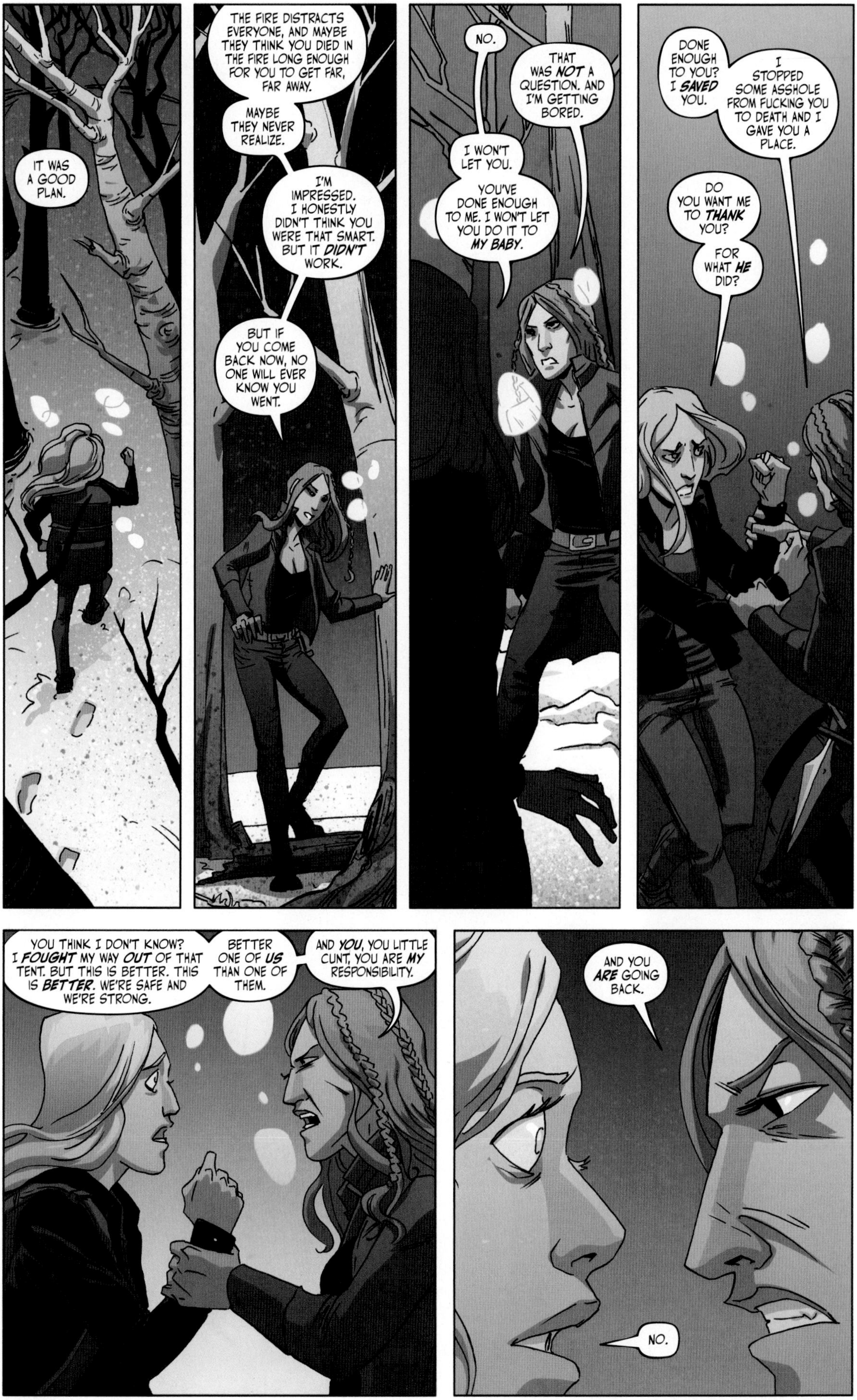
IT WAS A GOOD PLAN.
THE FIRE DISTRACTS EVERYONE, AND MAYBE THEY THINK YOU DIED IN THE FIRE LONG ENOUGH FOR YOU TO GET FAR, FAR AWAY.
MAYBE THEY NEVER REALIZE.
I'M IMPRESSED. I HONESTLY DIDN'T THINK YOU WERE THAT SMART. BUT IT DIDN'T WORK.
BUT IF YOU COME BACK NOW, NO ONE WILL EVER KNOW YOU WENT.
NO.
I WON'T LET YOU.
YOU'VE DONE ENOUGH TO ME. I WON'T LET YOU DO IT TO MY BABY.
THAT WAS NOT A QUESTION. AND I'M GETTING BORED.
DONE ENOUGH TO YOU? I SAVED YOU.
I STOPPED SOME ASSHOLE FROM FUCKING YOU TO DEATH AND I GAVE YOU A PLACE.
DO YOU WANT ME TO THANK YOU?
FOR WHAT HE DID?
YOU THINK I DON'T KNOW? I FOUGHT MY WAY OUT OF THAT TENT. BUT THIS IS BETTER. THIS IS BETTER. WE'RE SAFE AND WE'RE STRONG.
BETTER ONE OF US THAN ONE OF THEM.
AND YOU, YOU LITTLE CUNT, YOU ARE MY RESPONSIBILITY.
AND YOU ARE GOING BACK.
NO.

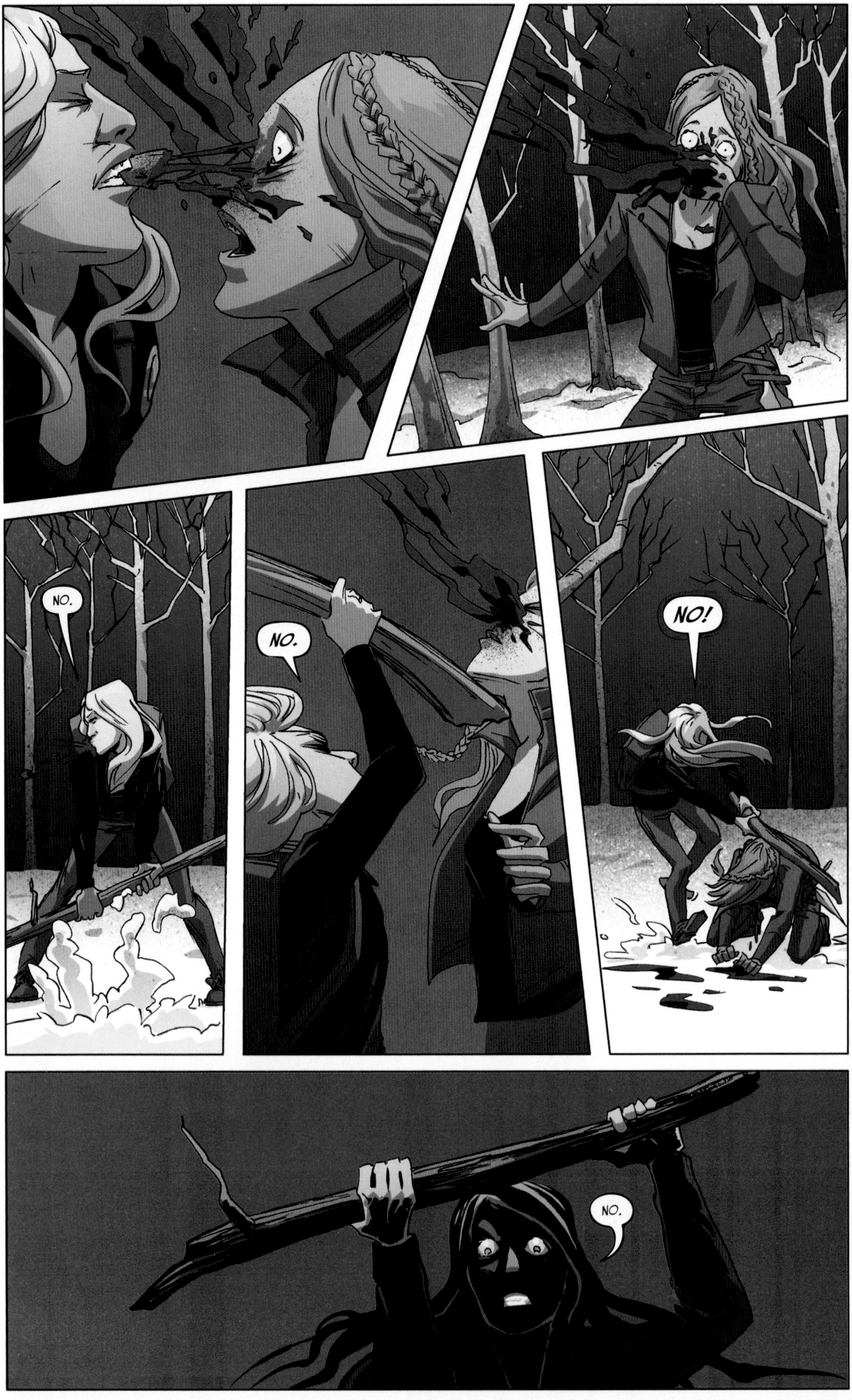
NO.
NO.
NO!
NO.

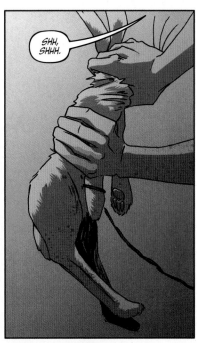

SHH, SHHH.

THANK YOU.

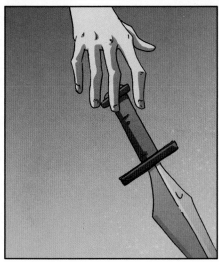

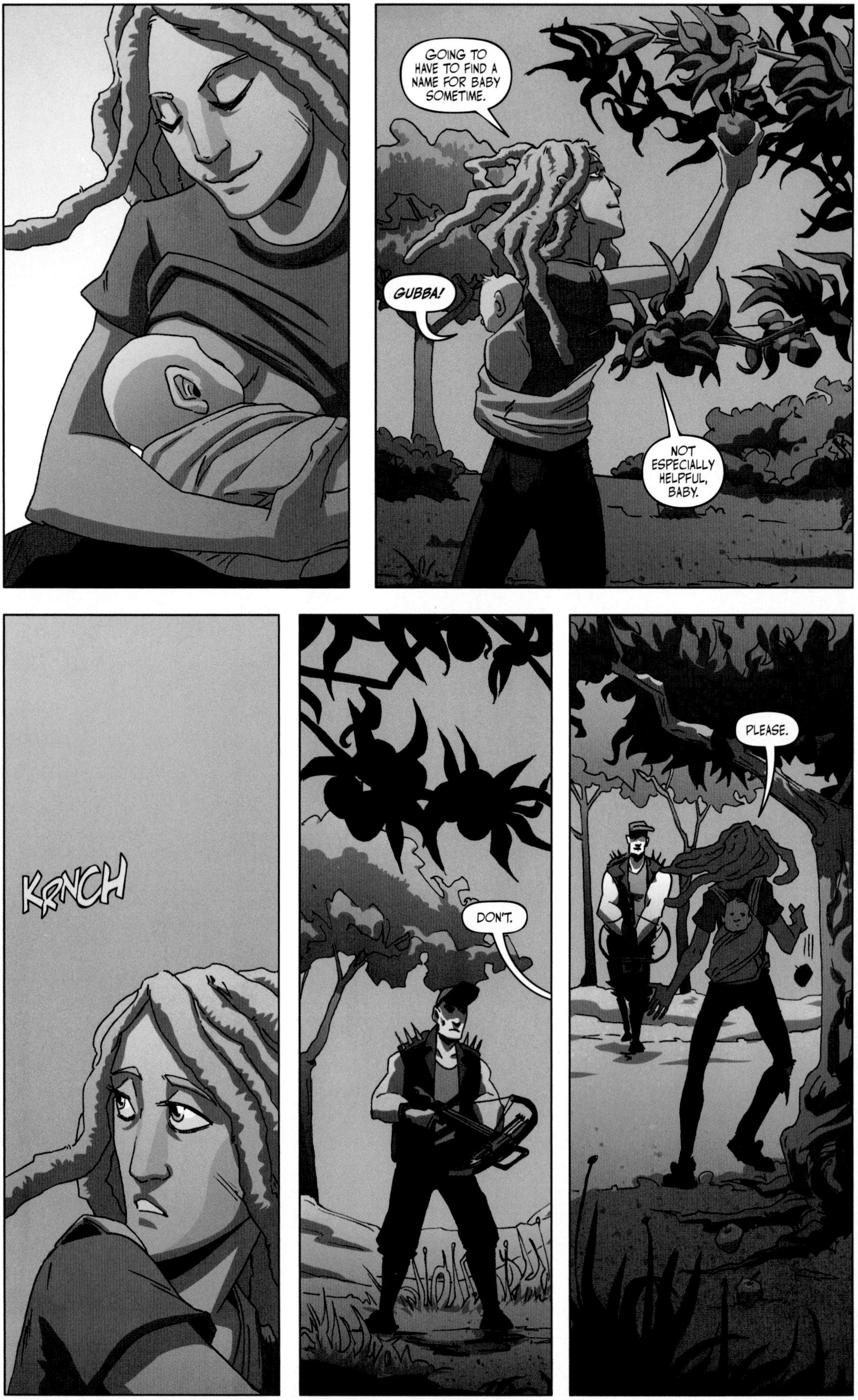
GOING TO HAVE TO FIND A NAME FOR BABY SOMETIME.
GUBBA!
NOT ESPECIALLY HELPFUL, BABY.
KRNCH
DON'T.
PLEASE.

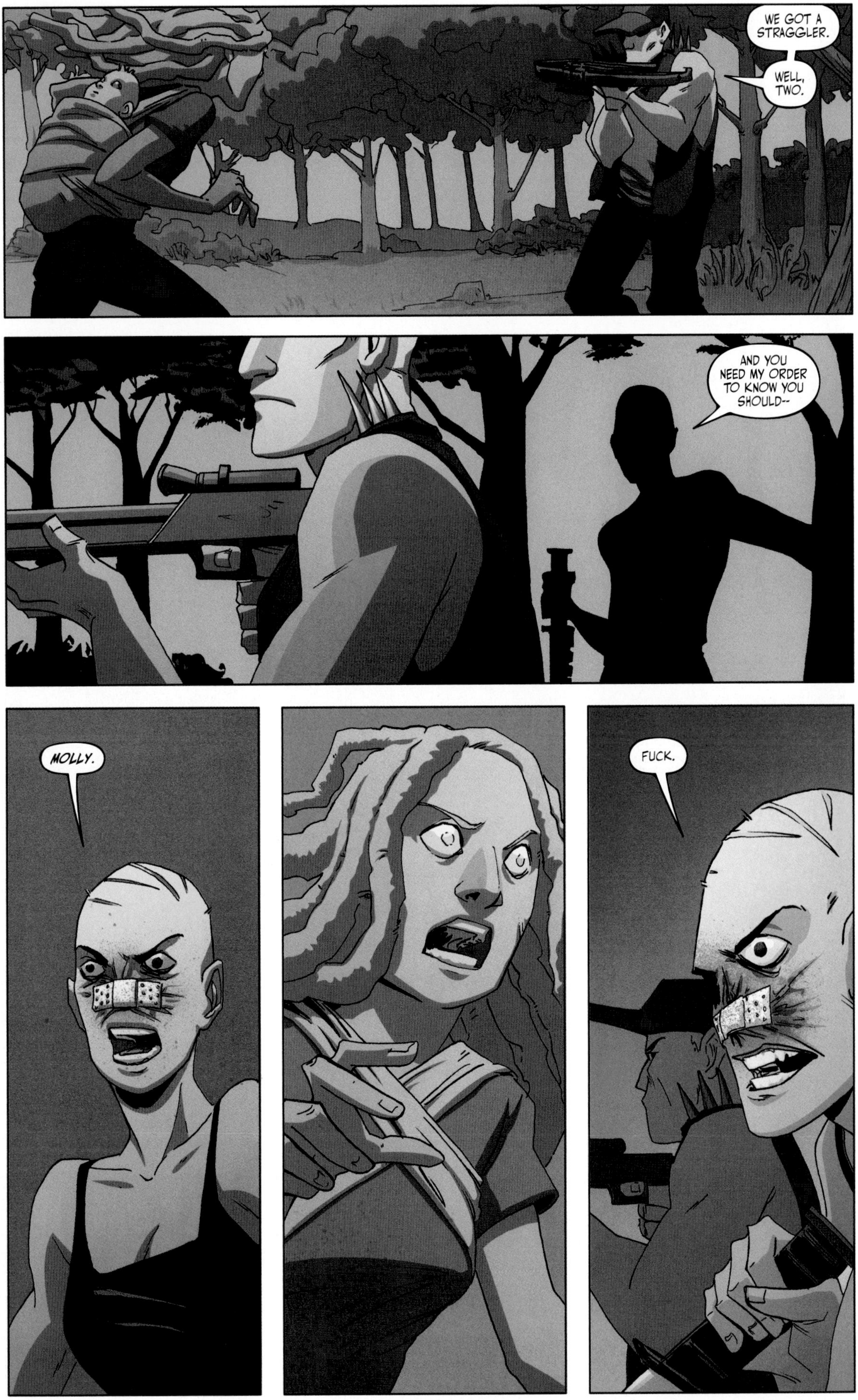
WE GOT A STRAGGLER.
WELL, TWO.
AND YOU NEED MY ORDER TO KNOW YOU SHOULD--
MOLLY.
FUCK.

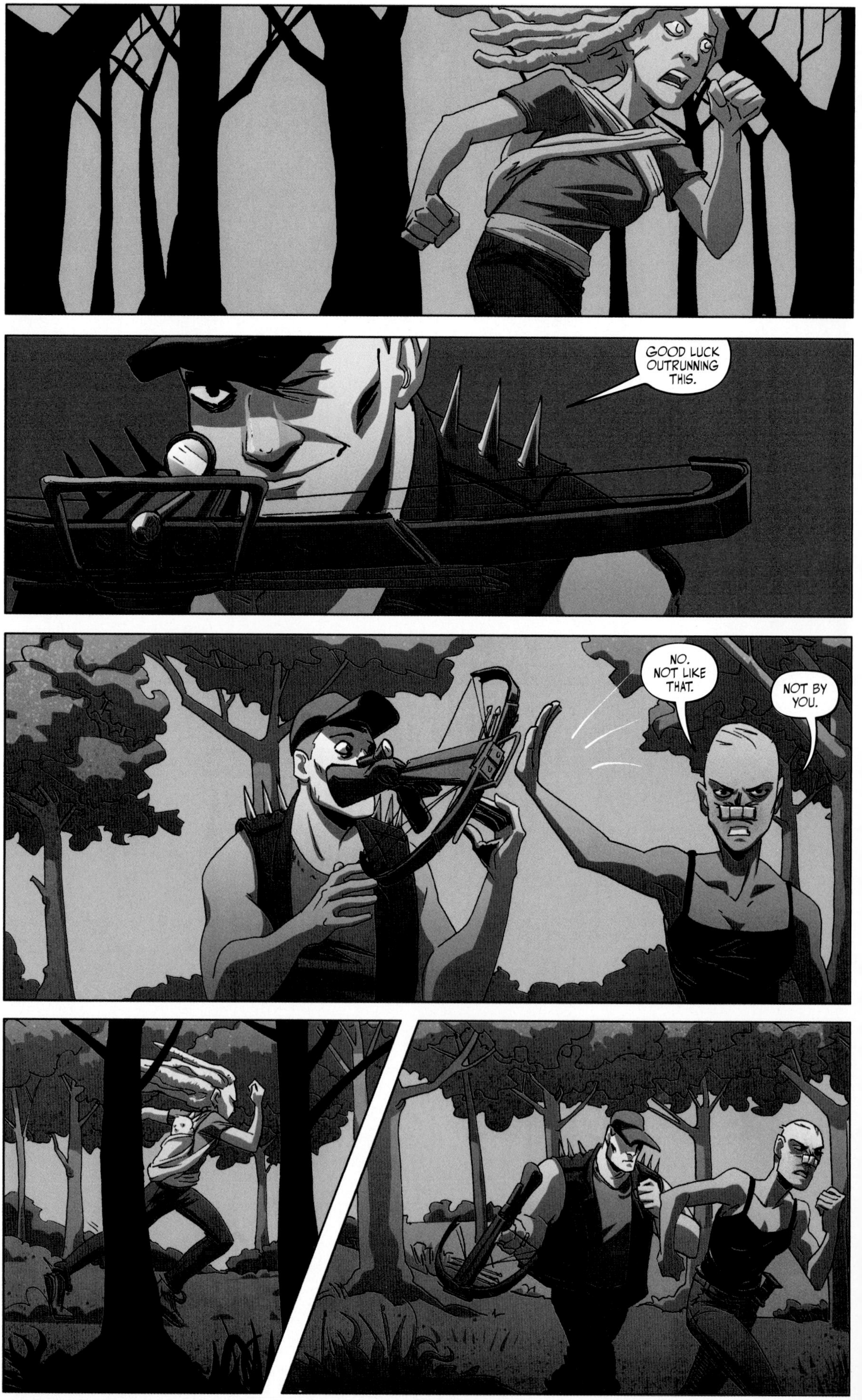
GOOD LUCK OUTRUNNING THIS.
NO. NOT LIKE THAT.
NOT BY YOU.

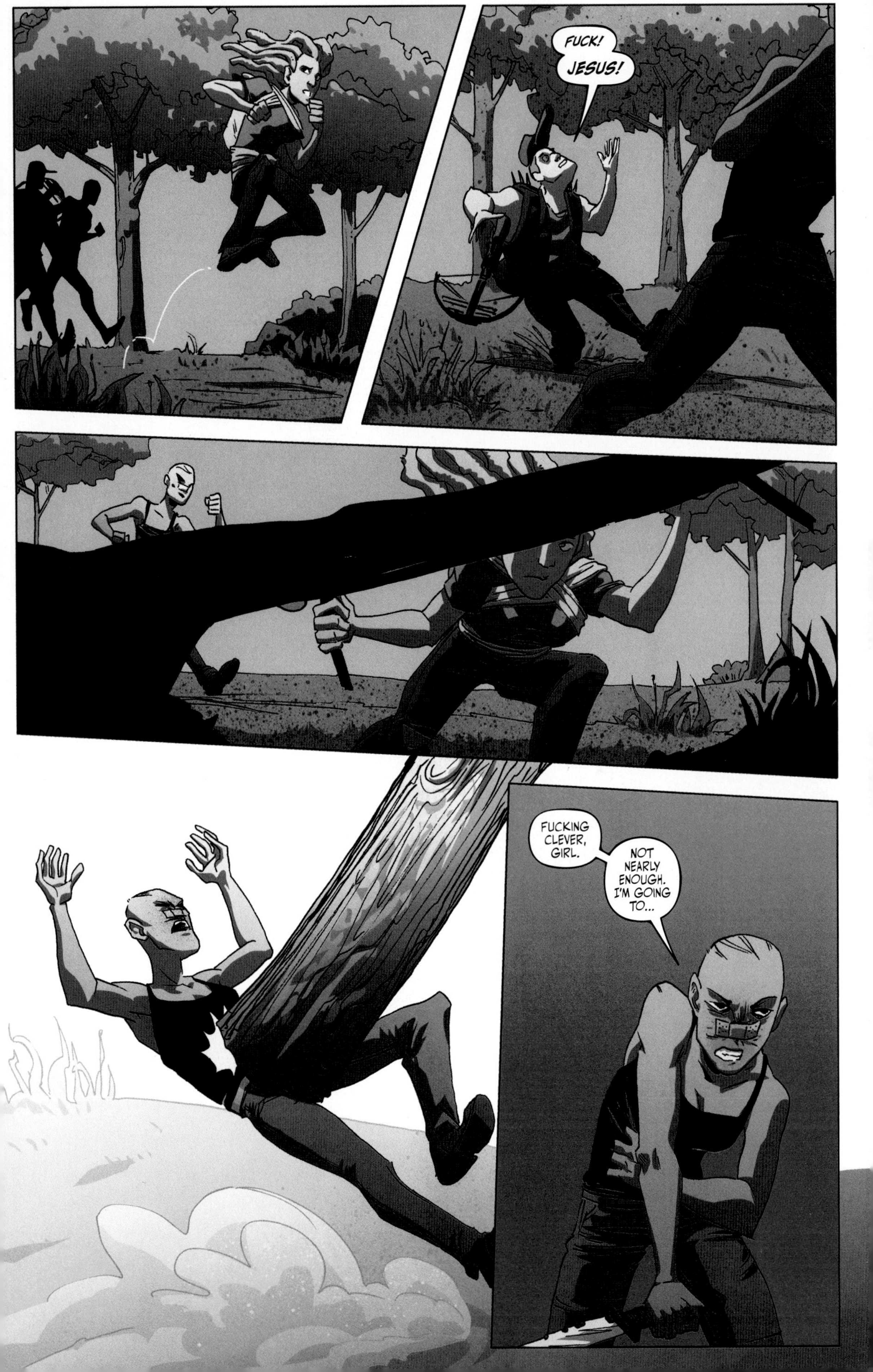
FUCK!
JESUS!
FUCKING CLEVER, GIRL.
NOT NEARLY ENOUGH. I'M GOING TO...

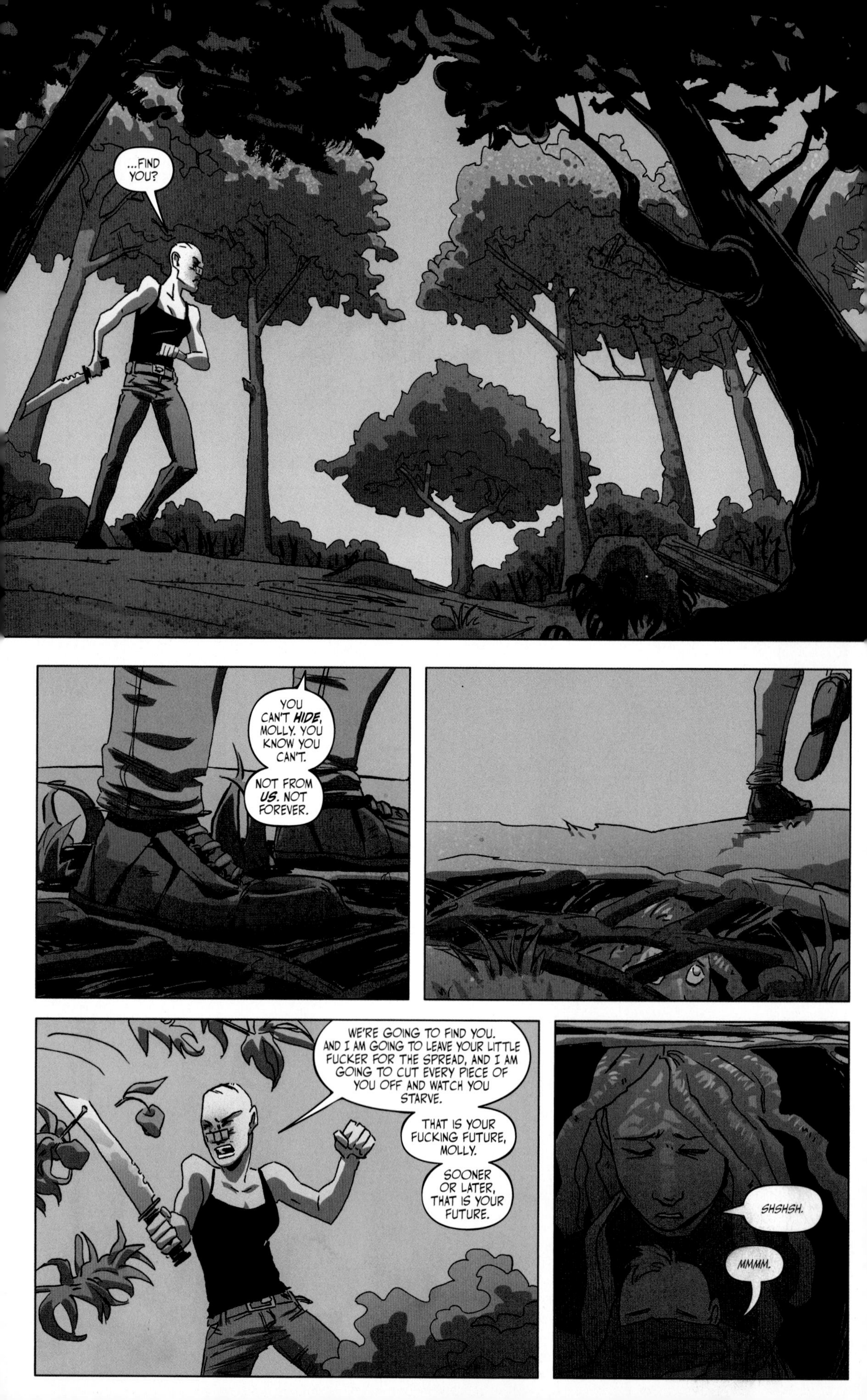

...FIND YOU?
YOU CAN'T ***HIDE***, MOLLY. YOU KNOW YOU CAN'T.
NOT FROM ***US***. NOT FOREVER.
WE'RE GOING TO FIND YOU. AND I AM GOING TO LEAVE YOUR LITTLE FUCKER FOR THE SPREAD, AND I AM GOING TO CUT EVERY PIECE OF YOU OFF AND WATCH YOU STARVE.
THAT IS YOUR FUCKING FUTURE, MOLLY.
SOONER OR LATER, THAT IS YOUR FUTURE.
SHSHSH.
MMMM.

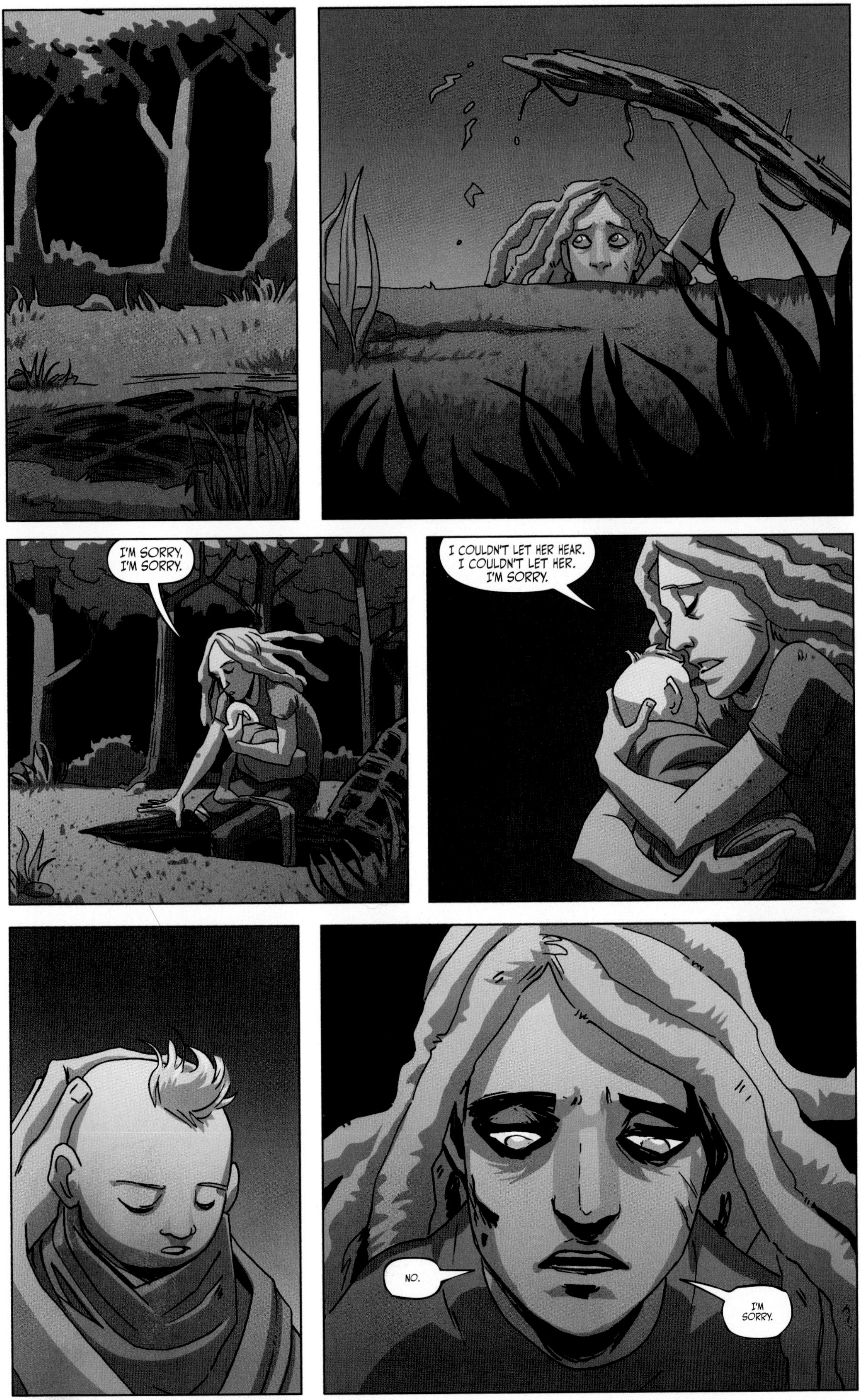
I'M SORRY,
I'M SORRY.
I COULDN'T LET HER HEAR.
I COULDN'T LET HER.
I'M SORRY.
NO.
I'M
SORRY.

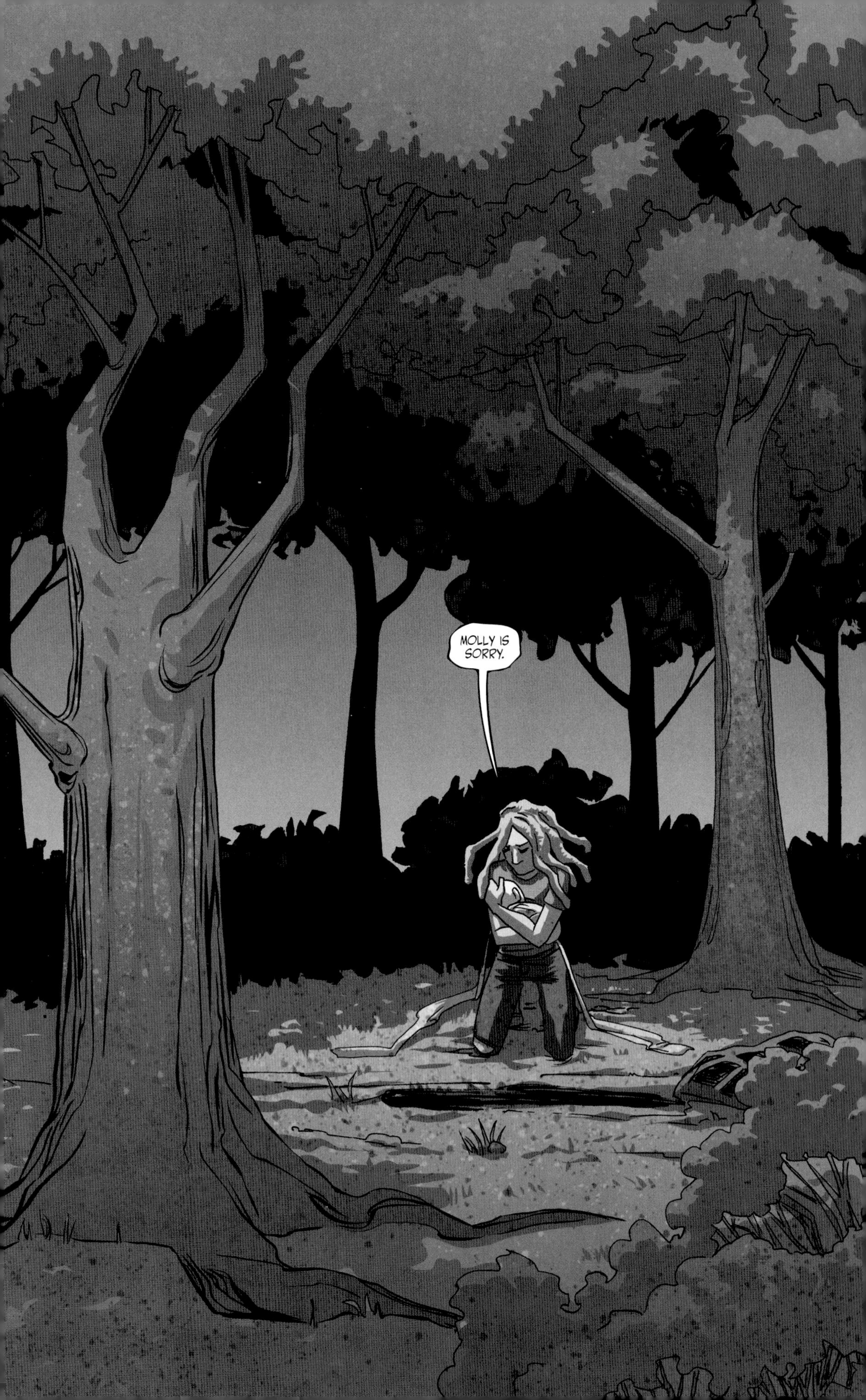
MOLLY IS SORRY.

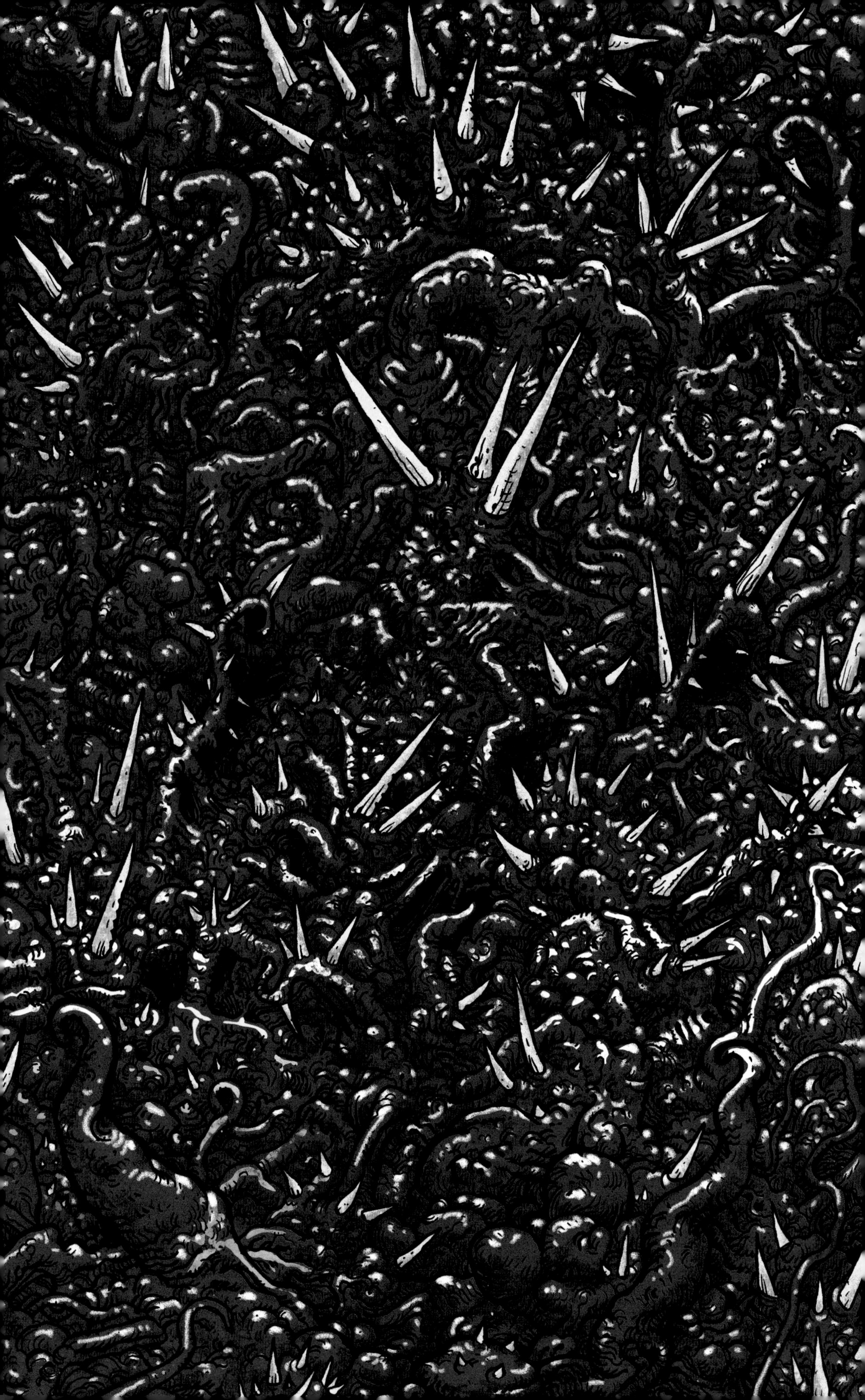

CHAPTER TWO

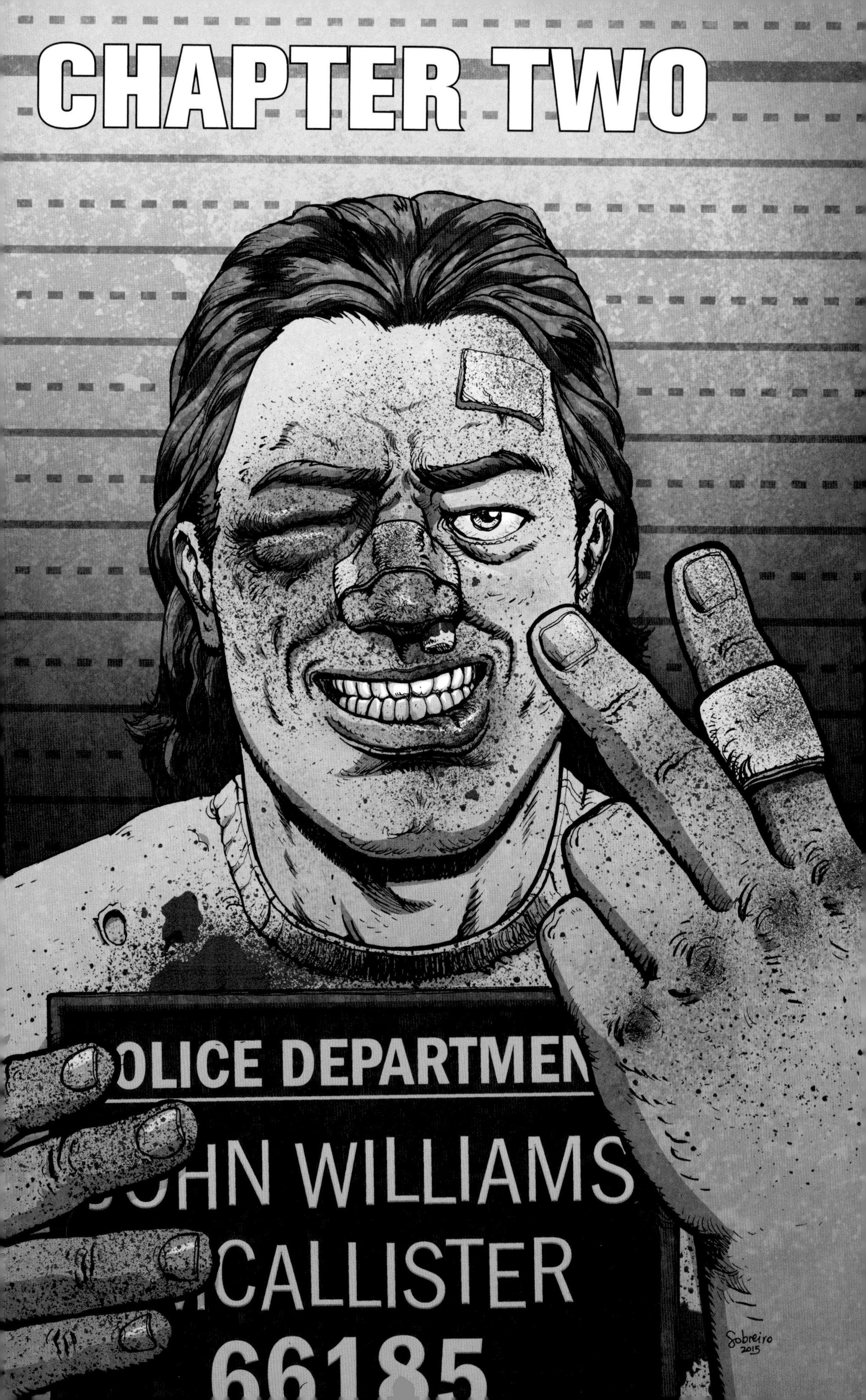
OLICE DEPARTMEN
OHN WILLIAMS
CALLISTER
66185
Sobreiro 2015

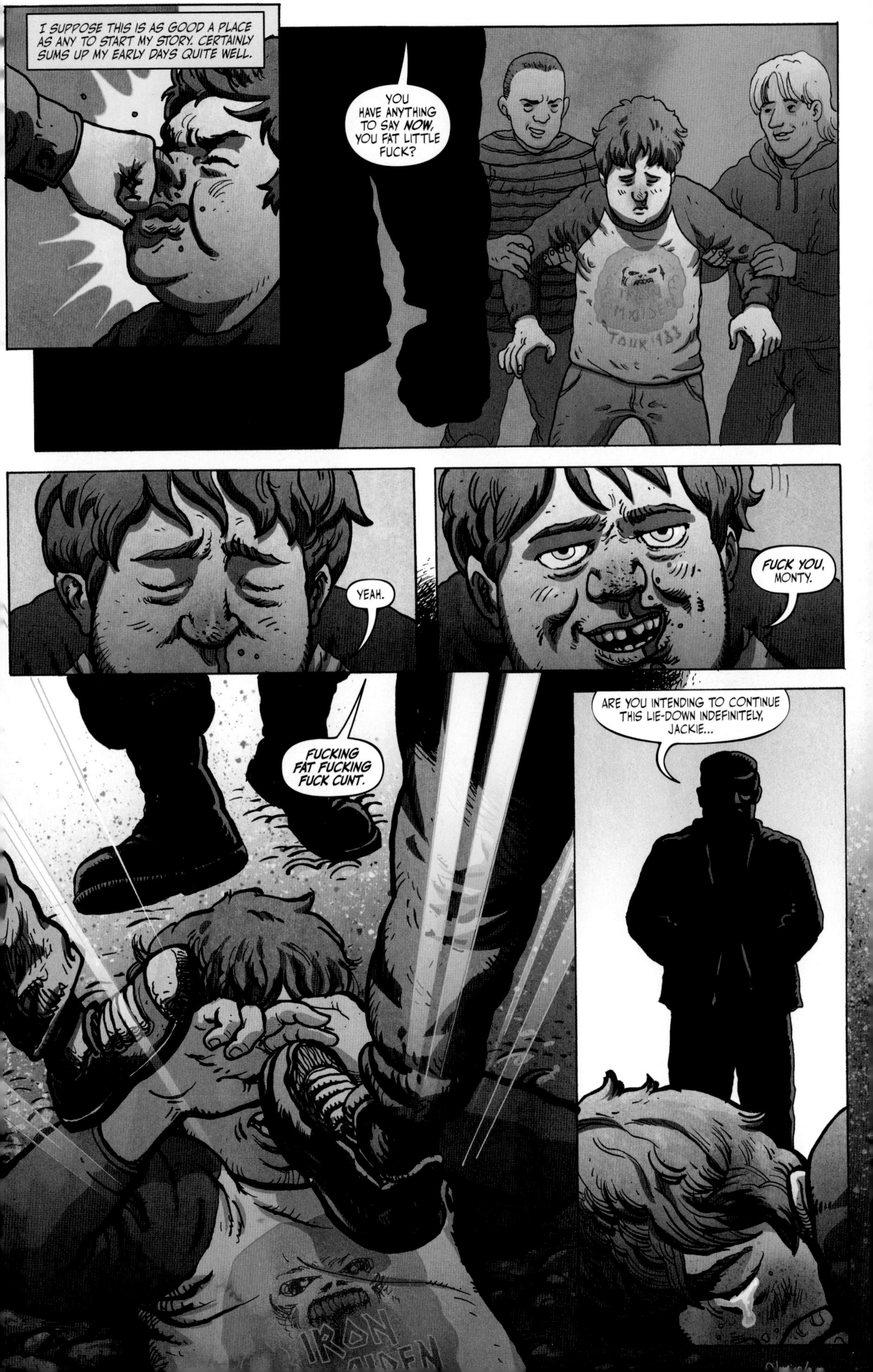
I SUPPOSE THIS IS AS GOOD A PLACE AS ANY TO START MY STORY. CERTAINLY SUMS UP MY EARLY DAYS QUITE WELL.
YOU HAVE ANYTHING TO SAY NOW, YOU FAT LITTLE FUCK?
YEAH.
FUCK YOU, MONTY.
FUCKING FAT FUCKING FUCK CUNT.
ARE YOU INTENDING TO CONTINUE THIS LIE-DOWN INDEFINITELY, JACKIE...

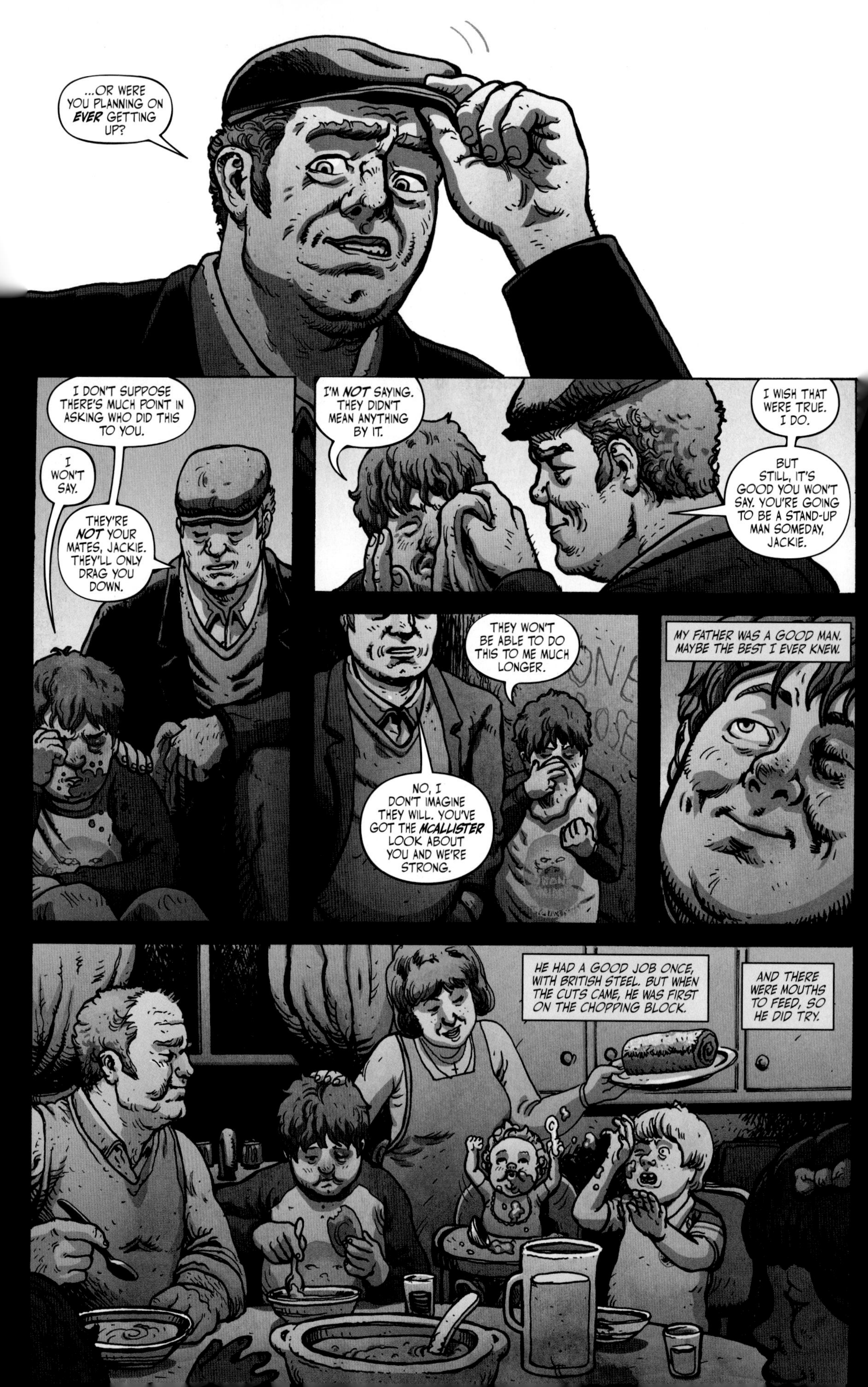
...OR WERE YOU PLANNING ON EVER GETTING UP?
I DON'T SUPPOSE THERE'S MUCH POINT IN ASKING WHO DID THIS TO YOU.
I WON'T SAY.
THEY'RE NOT YOUR MATES, JACKIE. THEY'LL ONLY DRAG YOU DOWN.
I'M NOT SAYING. THEY DIDN'T MEAN ANYTHING BY IT.
I WISH THAT WERE TRUE. I DO.
BUT STILL, IT'S GOOD YOU WON'T SAY. YOU'RE GOING TO BE A STAND-UP MAN SOMEDAY, JACKIE.
THEY WON'T BE ABLE TO DO THIS TO ME MUCH LONGER.
NO, I DON'T IMAGINE THEY WILL. YOU'VE GOT THE MCALLISTER LOOK ABOUT YOU AND WE'RE STRONG.
MY FATHER WAS A GOOD MAN. MAYBE THE BEST I EVER KNEW.
HE HAD A GOOD JOB ONCE, WITH BRITISH STEEL. BUT WHEN THE CUTS CAME, HE WAS FIRST ON THE CHOPPING BLOCK.
AND THERE WERE MOUTHS TO FEED, SO HE DID TRY.

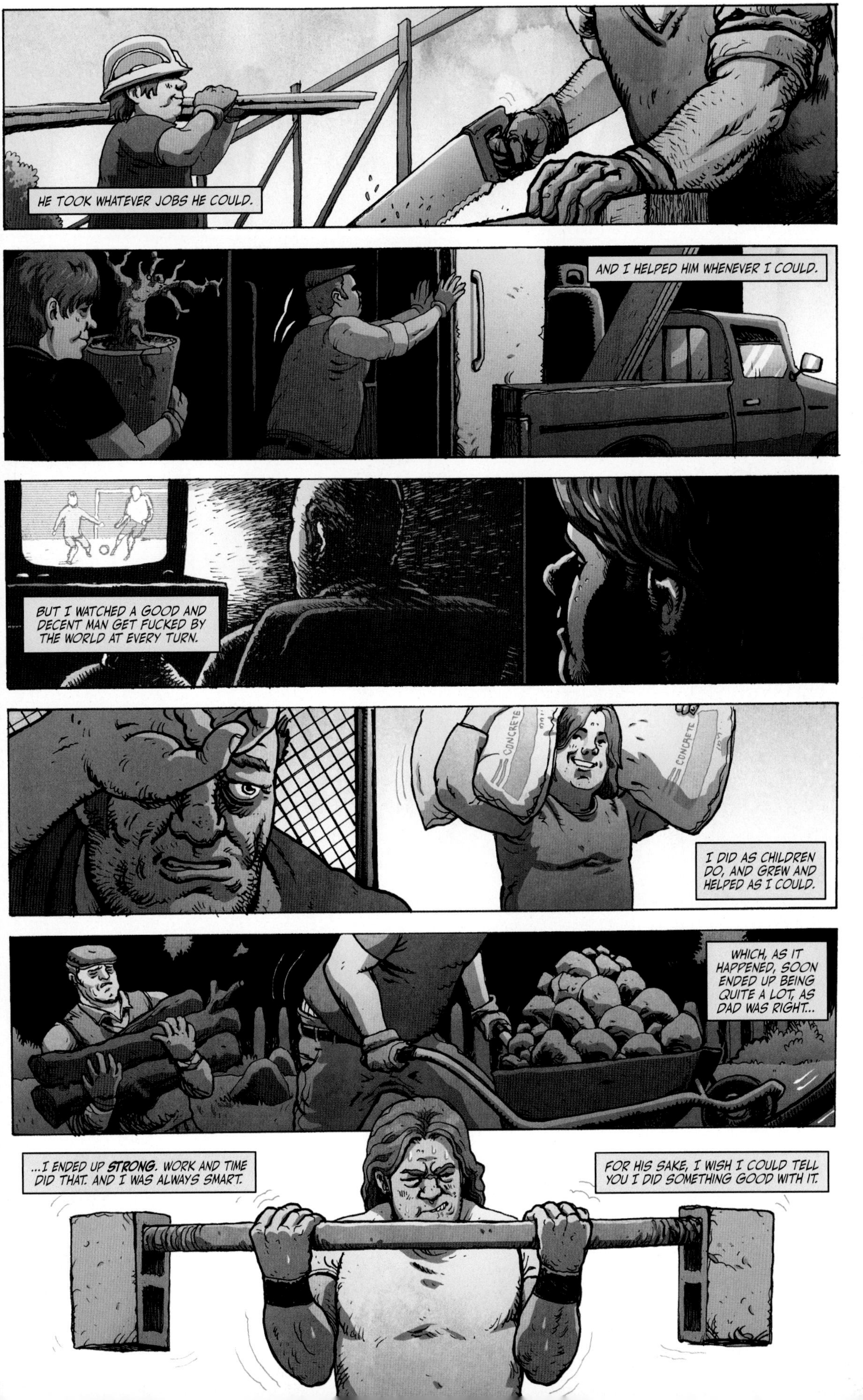
HE TOOK WHATEVER JOBS HE COULD.
AND I HELPED HIM WHENEVER I COULD.
BUT I WATCHED A GOOD AND DECENT MAN GET FUCKED BY THE WORLD AT EVERY TURN.
CONCRETE
CONCRETE
I DID AS CHILDREN DO, AND GREW AND HELPED AS I COULD.
WHICH, AS IT HAPPENED, SOON ENDED UP BEING QUITE A LOT, AS DAD WAS RIGHT...
...I ENDED UP **STRONG**. WORK AND TIME DID THAT. AND I WAS ALWAYS SMART.
FOR HIS SAKE, I WISH I COULD TELL YOU I DID SOMETHING GOOD WITH IT.

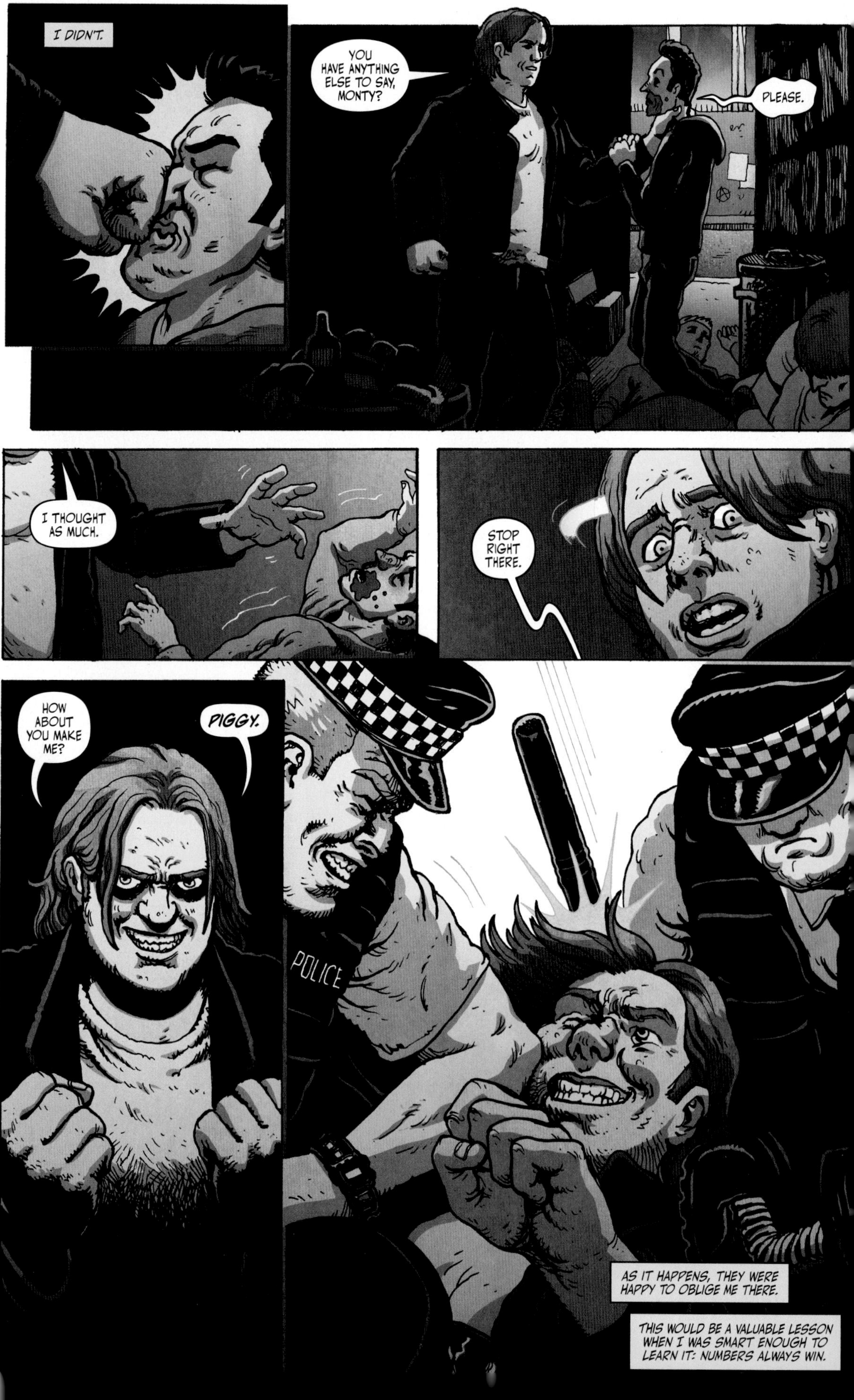
I DIDN'T.
YOU HAVE ANYTHING ELSE TO SAY, MONTY?
PLEASE.
I THOUGHT AS MUCH.
STOP RIGHT THERE.
HOW ABOUT YOU MAKE ME?
PIGGY.
POLICE
AS IT HAPPENS, THEY WERE HAPPY TO OBLIGE ME THERE.
THIS WOULD BE A VALUABLE LESSON WHEN I WAS SMART ENOUGH TO LEARN IT: NUMBERS ALWAYS WIN.

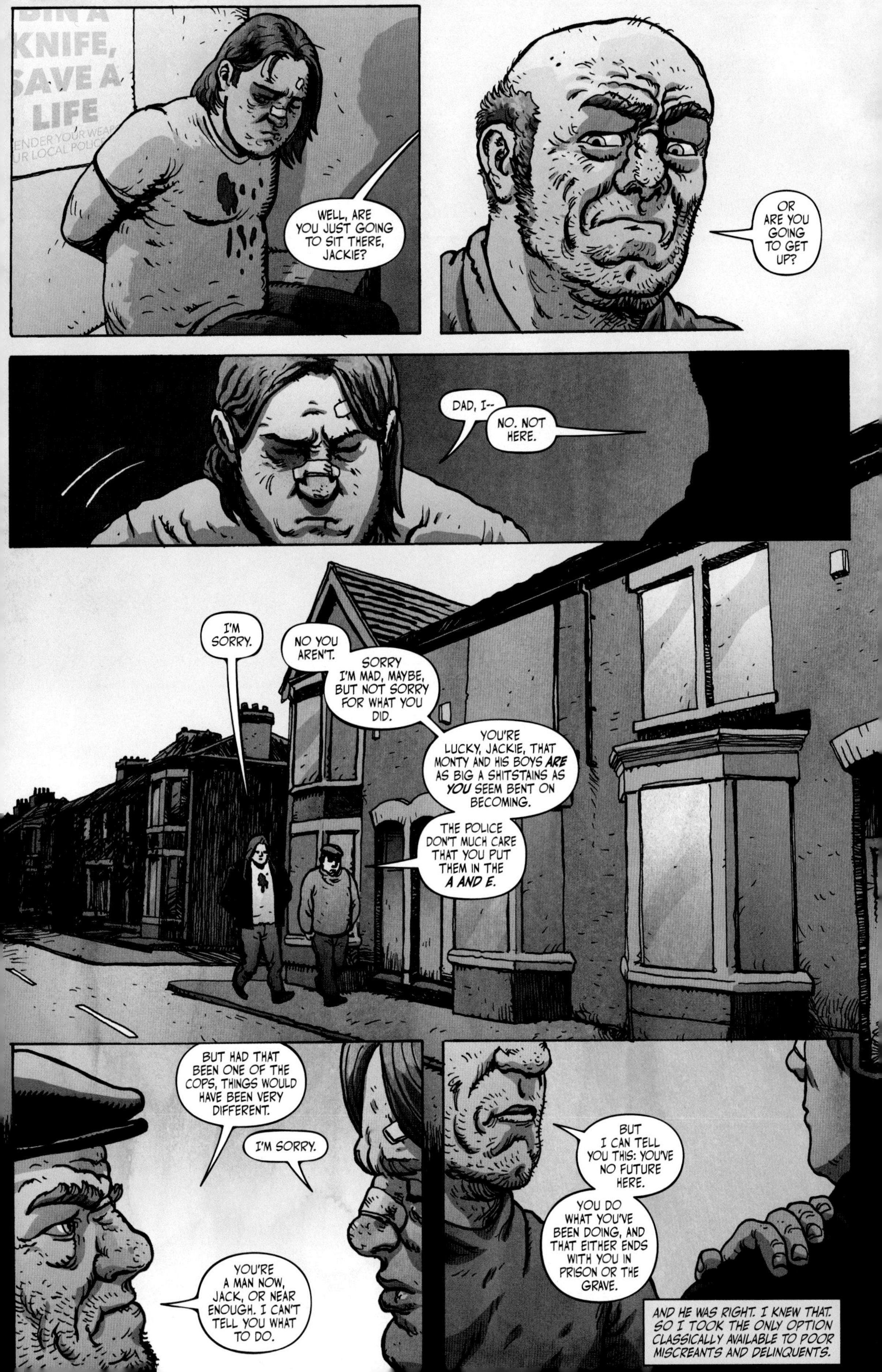
BIN A KNIFE, SAVE A LIFE
WELL, ARE YOU JUST GOING TO SIT THERE, JACKIE?
OR ARE YOU GOING TO GET UP?
DAD, I--
NO. NOT HERE.
I'M SORRY.
NO YOU AREN'T.
SORRY I'M MAD, MAYBE, BUT NOT SORRY FOR WHAT YOU DID.
YOU'RE LUCKY, JACKIE, THAT MONTY AND HIS BOYS ARE AS BIG A SHITSTAINS AS YOU SEEM BENT ON BECOMING.
THE POLICE DON'T MUCH CARE THAT YOU PUT THEM IN THE A AND E.
BUT HAD THAT BEEN ONE OF THE COPS, THINGS WOULD HAVE BEEN VERY DIFFERENT.
I'M SORRY.
YOU'RE A MAN NOW, JACK, OR NEAR ENOUGH. I CAN'T TELL YOU WHAT TO DO.
BUT I CAN TELL YOU THIS: YOU'VE NO FUTURE HERE.
YOU DO WHAT YOU'VE BEEN DOING, AND THAT EITHER ENDS WITH YOU IN PRISON OR THE GRAVE.
AND HE WAS RIGHT. I KNEW THAT. SO I TOOK THE ONLY OPTION CLASSICALLY AVAILABLE TO POOR MISCREANTS AND DELINQUENTS.

I JOINED UP.

I OUGHT NOT TO HAVE BEEN ABLE TO JOIN THE ROYAL MARINES, BUT I WAS SMART AND STRONG AND YOUNG, WHICH COUNTED FOR QUITE A LOT.

I'M NOT SURE FUN IS THE RIGHT WORD. BUT I LIKED IT.

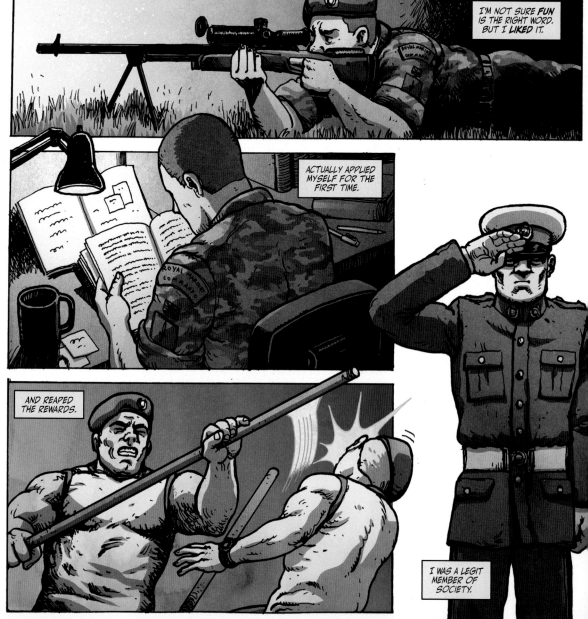

ACTUALLY APPLIED MYSELF FOR THE FIRST TIME.

AND REAPED THE REWARDS.

I WAS A LEGIT MEMBER OF SOCIETY.

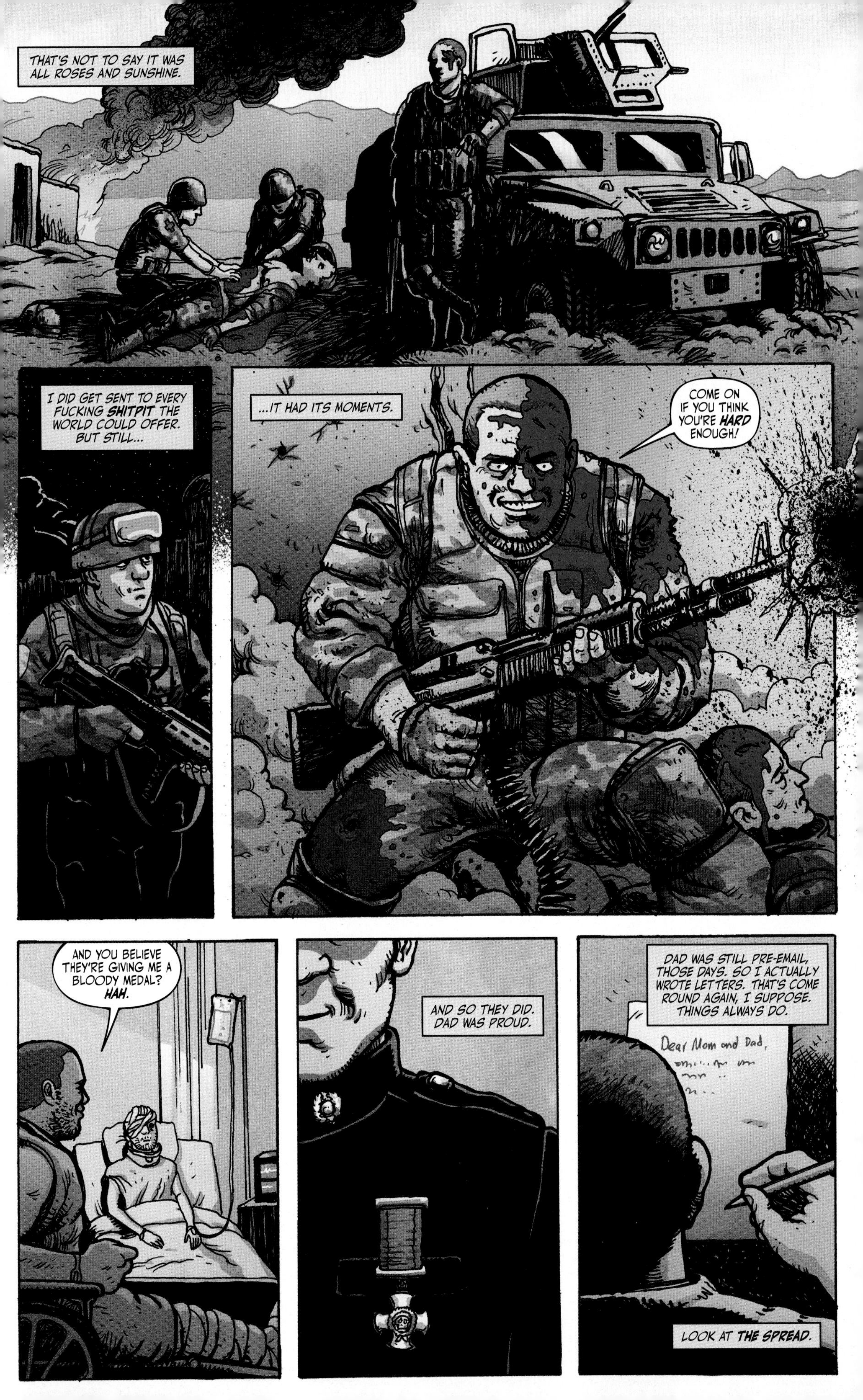
THAT'S NOT TO SAY IT WAS ALL ROSES AND SUNSHINE.
I DID GET SENT TO EVERY FUCKING SHITPIT THE WORLD COULD OFFER. BUT STILL...
...IT HAD ITS MOMENTS.
COME ON IF YOU THINK YOU'RE HARD ENOUGH!
AND YOU BELIEVE THEY'RE GIVING ME A BLOODY MEDAL? HAH.
AND SO THEY DID. DAD WAS PROUD.
DAD WAS STILL PRE-EMAIL, THOSE DAYS. SO I ACTUALLY WROTE LETTERS. THAT'S COME ROUND AGAIN, I SUPPOSE. THINGS ALWAYS DO.
Dear Mom and Dad,
LOOK AT THE SPREAD.

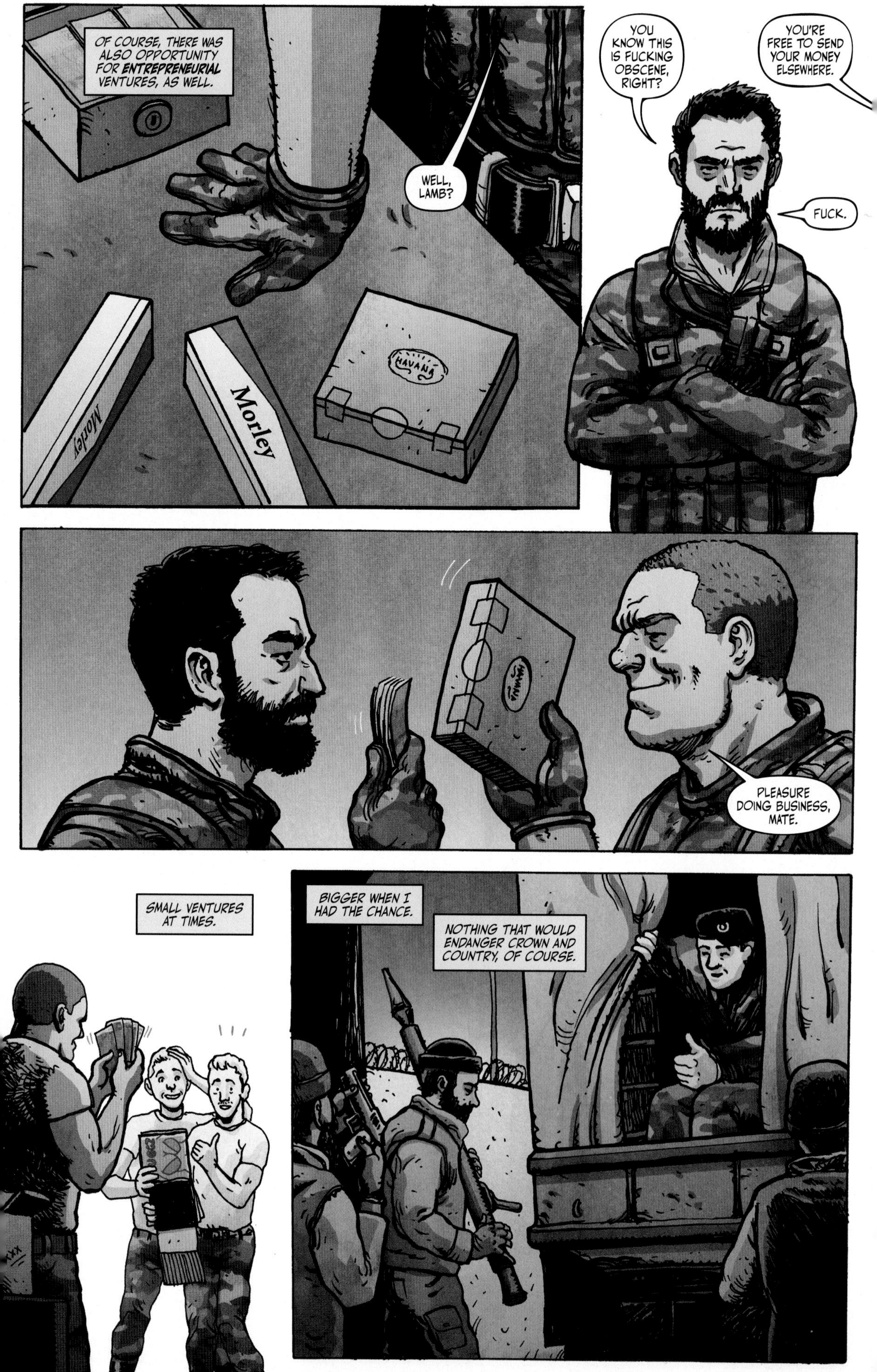

OF COURSE, THERE WAS ALSO OPPORTUNITY FOR **ENTREPRENEURIAL** VENTURES, AS WELL.
Morley
Morley
HAVANA
WELL, LAMB?
YOU KNOW THIS IS FUCKING OBSCENE, RIGHT?
YOU'RE FREE TO SEND YOUR MONEY ELSEWHERE.
FUCK.
PLEASURE DOING BUSINESS, MATE.
SMALL VENTURES AT TIMES.
BIGGER WHEN I HAD THE CHANCE.
NOTHING THAT WOULD ENDANGER CROWN AND COUNTRY, OF COURSE.

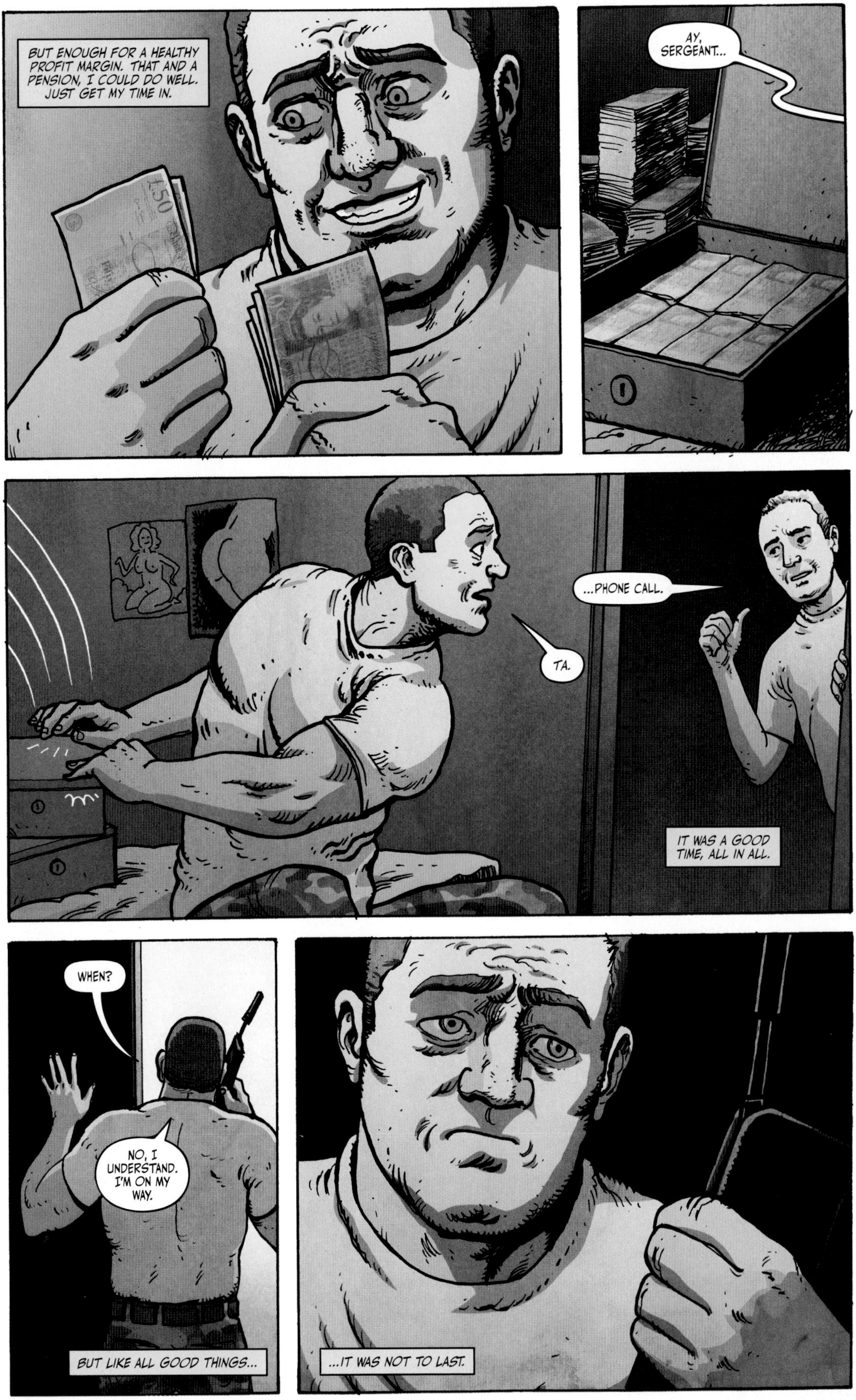
BUT ENOUGH FOR A HEALTHY PROFIT MARGIN. THAT AND A PENSION, I COULD DO WELL. JUST GET MY TIME IN.
AY, SERGEANT...
...PHONE CALL.
TA.
IT WAS A GOOD TIME, ALL IN ALL.
WHEN?
NO, I UNDERSTAND. I'M ON MY WAY.
BUT LIKE ALL GOOD THINGS...
...IT WAS NOT TO LAST.

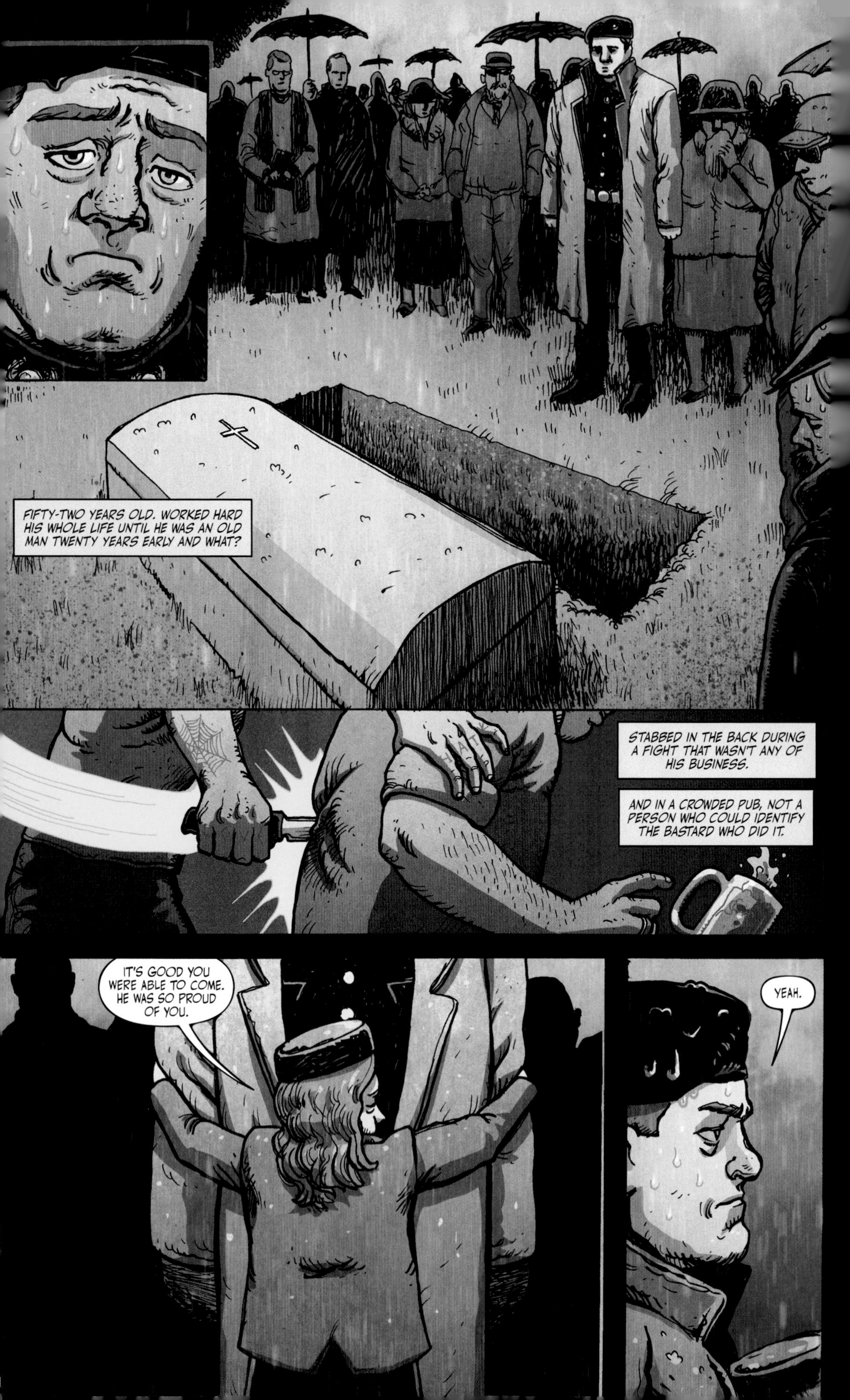
FIFTY-TWO YEARS OLD. WORKED HARD HIS WHOLE LIFE UNTIL HE WAS AN OLD MAN TWENTY YEARS EARLY AND WHAT?
STABBED IN THE BACK DURING A FIGHT THAT WASN'T ANY OF HIS BUSINESS.
AND IN A CROWDED PUB, NOT A PERSON WHO COULD IDENTIFY THE BASTARD WHO DID IT.
IT'S GOOD YOU WERE ABLE TO COME. HE WAS SO PROUD OF YOU.
YEAH.

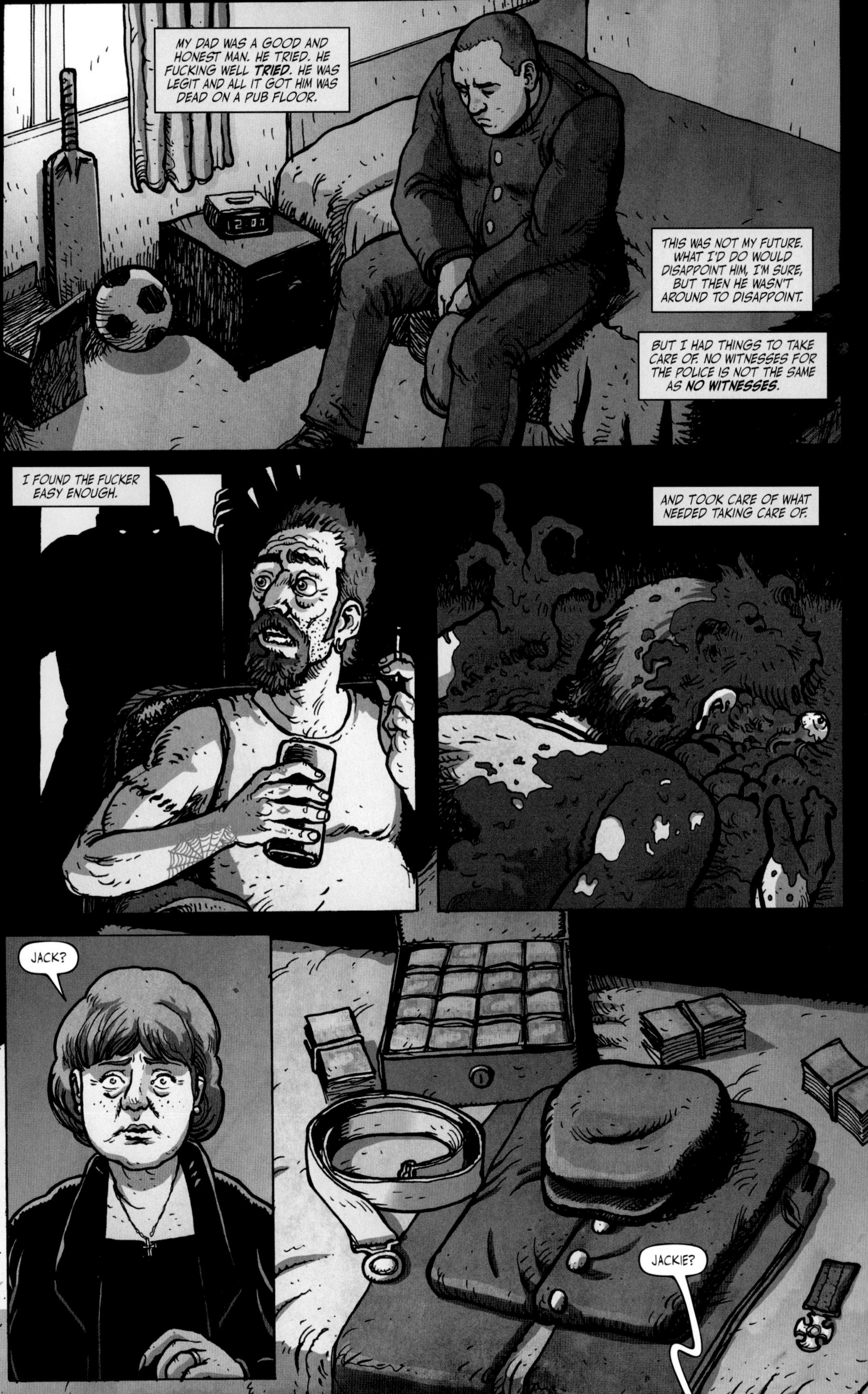
MY DAD WAS A GOOD AND HONEST MAN. HE TRIED. HE FUCKING WELL **TRIED**. HE WAS LEGIT AND ALL IT GOT HIM WAS DEAD ON A PUB FLOOR.
THIS WAS NOT MY FUTURE. WHAT I'D DO WOULD DISAPPOINT HIM, I'M SURE, BUT THEN HE WASN'T AROUND TO DISAPPOINT.
BUT I HAD THINGS TO TAKE CARE OF. NO WITNESSES FOR THE POLICE IS NOT THE SAME AS **NO WITNESSES**.
I FOUND THE FUCKER EASY ENOUGH.
AND TOOK CARE OF WHAT NEEDED TAKING CARE OF.
JACK?
JACKIE?

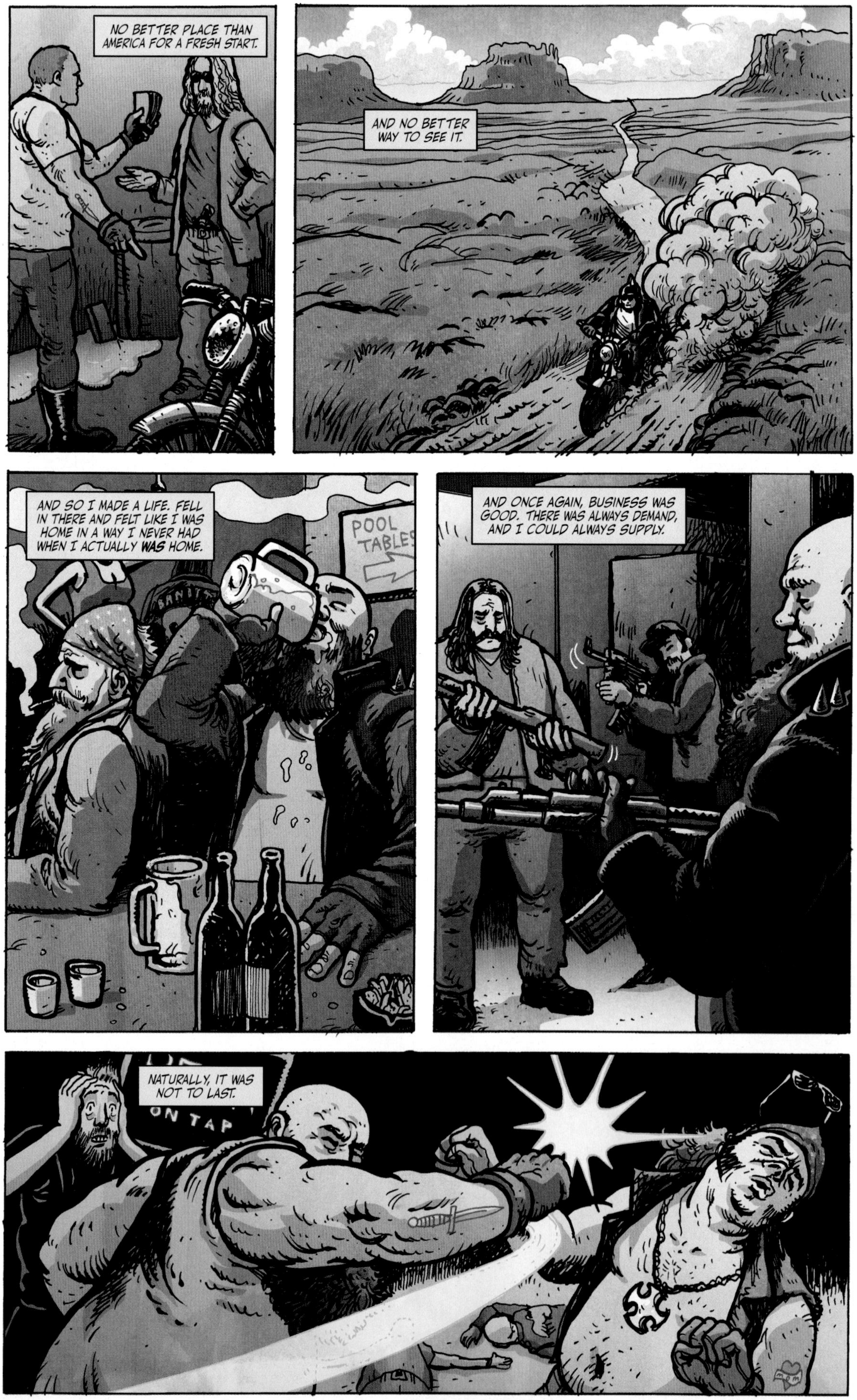
NO BETTER PLACE THAN AMERICA FOR A FRESH START.
AND NO BETTER WAY TO SEE IT.
AND SO I MADE A LIFE. FELL IN THERE AND FELT LIKE I WAS HOME IN A WAY I NEVER HAD WHEN I ACTUALLY **WAS** HOME.
POOL TABLES
AND ONCE AGAIN, BUSINESS WAS GOOD. THERE WAS ALWAYS DEMAND, AND I COULD ALWAYS SUPPLY.
NATURALLY, IT WAS NOT TO LAST.
ON TAP

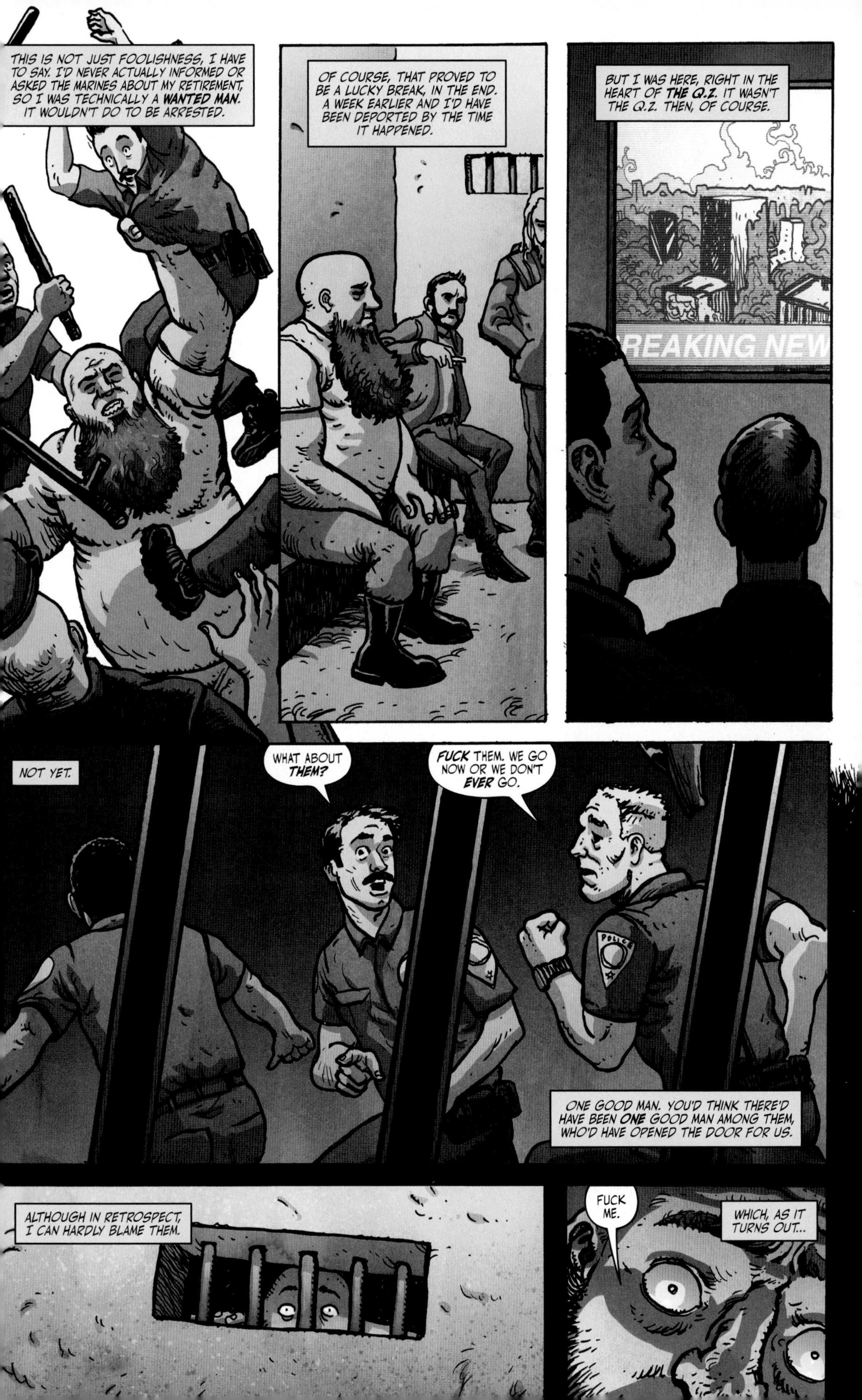

THIS IS NOT JUST FOOLISHNESS, I HAVE TO SAY. I'D NEVER ACTUALLY INFORMED OR ASKED THE MARINES ABOUT MY RETIREMENT, SO I WAS TECHNICALLY A **WANTED MAN**. IT WOULDN'T DO TO BE ARRESTED.
OF COURSE, THAT PROVED TO BE A LUCKY BREAK, IN THE END. A WEEK EARLIER AND I'D HAVE BEEN DEPORTED BY THE TIME IT HAPPENED.
BUT I WAS HERE, RIGHT IN THE HEART OF **THE Q.Z.** IT WASN'T THE Q.Z. THEN, OF COURSE.
REAKING NEW
NOT YET.
WHAT ABOUT **THEM?**
FUCK THEM. WE GO NOW OR WE DON'T **EVER** GO.
POLICE
ONE GOOD MAN. YOU'D THINK THERE'D HAVE BEEN **ONE** GOOD MAN AMONG THEM, WHO'D HAVE OPENED THE DOOR FOR US.
ALTHOUGH IN RETROSPECT, I CAN HARDLY BLAME THEM.
FUCK ME.
WHICH, AS IT TURNS OUT...

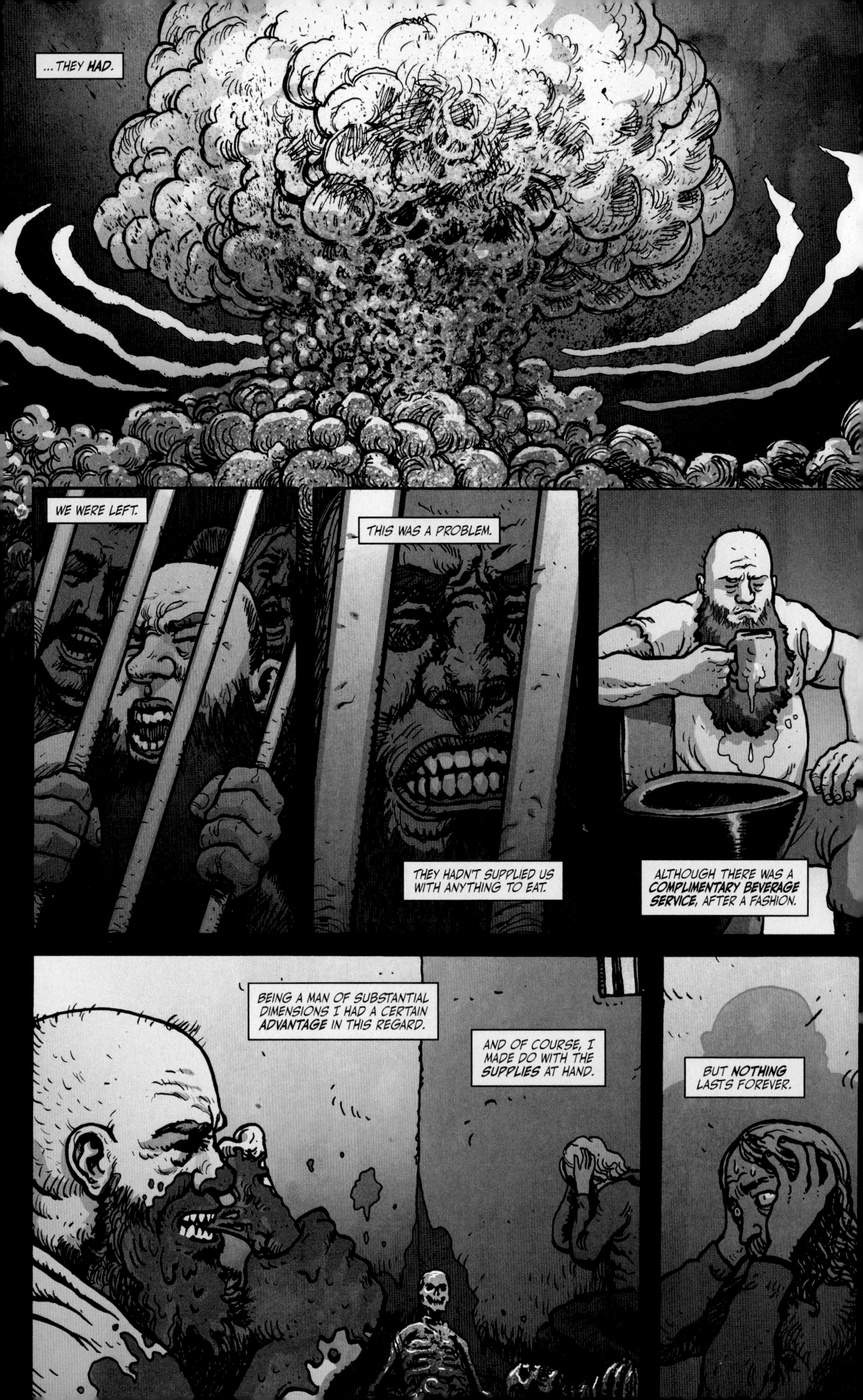
...THEY HAD.
WE WERE LEFT.
THIS WAS A PROBLEM.
THEY HADN'T SUPPLIED US WITH ANYTHING TO EAT.
ALTHOUGH THERE WAS A COMPLIMENTARY BEVERAGE SERVICE, AFTER A FASHION.
BEING A MAN OF SUBSTANTIAL DIMENSIONS I HAD A CERTAIN ADVANTAGE IN THIS REGARD.
AND OF COURSE, I MADE DO WITH THE SUPPLIES AT HAND.
BUT NOTHING LASTS FOREVER.

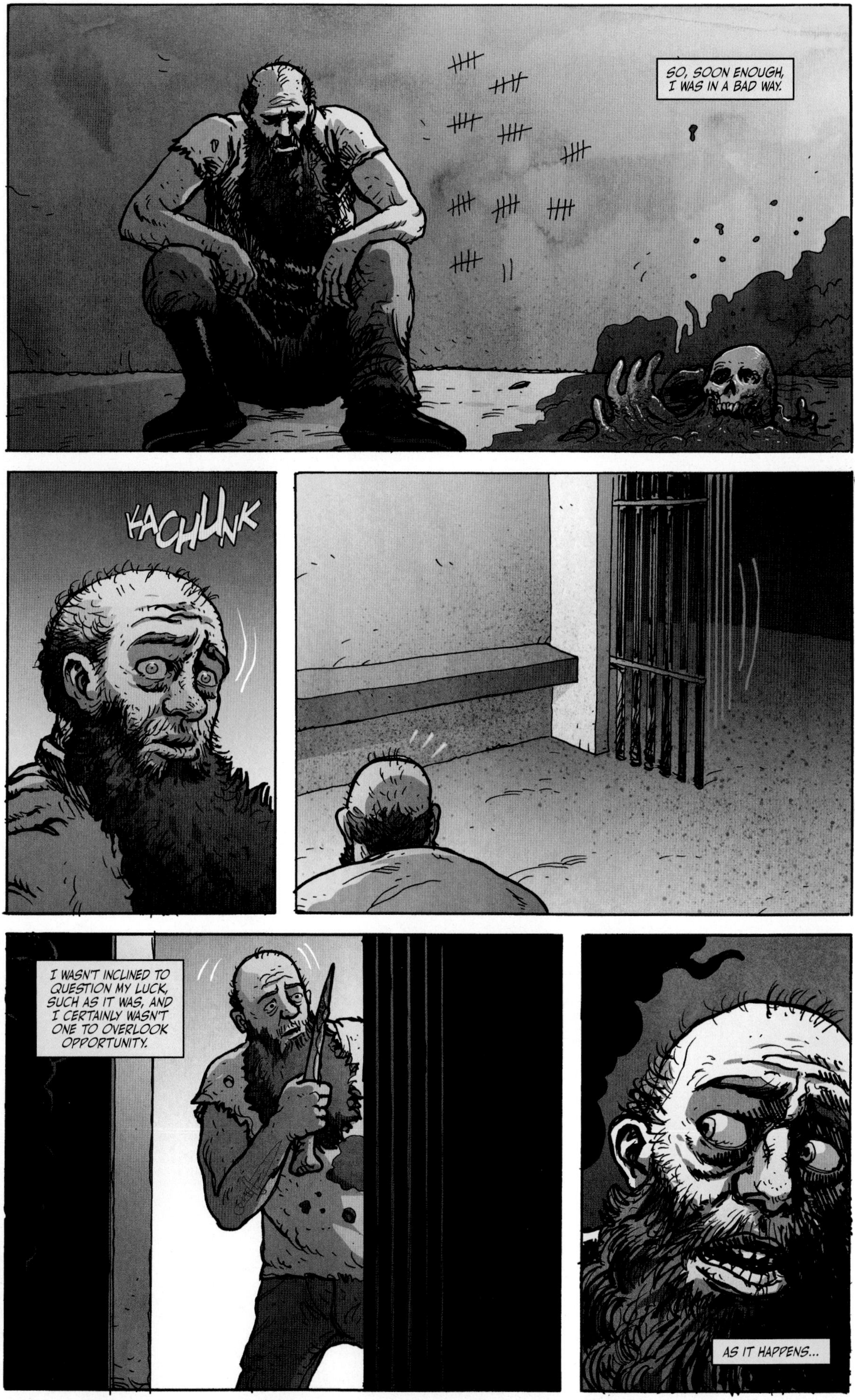
SO, SOON ENOUGH, I WAS IN A BAD WAY.
KACHUNK
I WASN'T INCLINED TO QUESTION MY LUCK, SUCH AS IT WAS, AND I CERTAINLY WASN'T ONE TO OVERLOOK OPPORTUNITY.
AS IT HAPPENS...

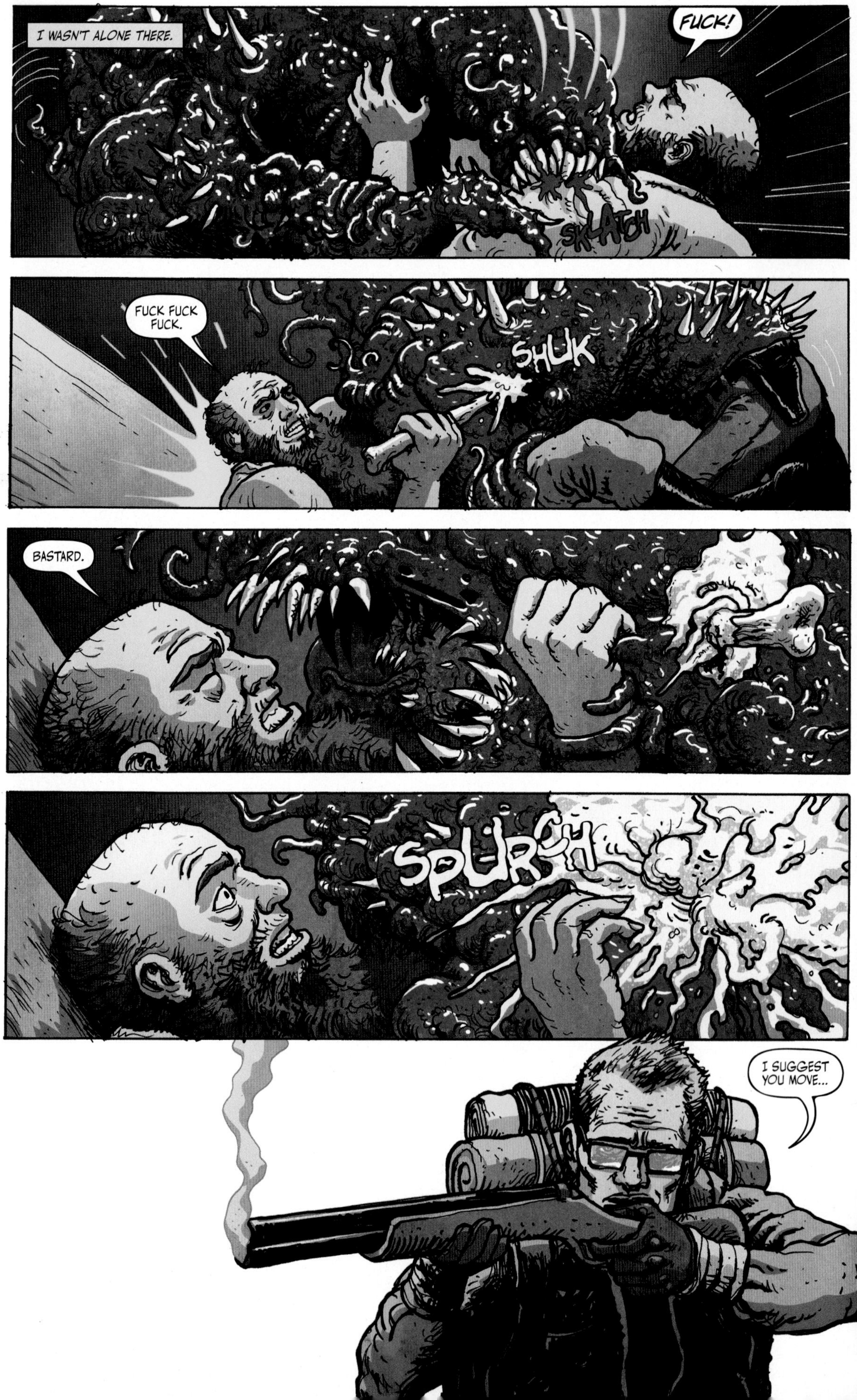
I WASN'T ALONE THERE.
FUCK!
SKLATCH
FUCK FUCK FUCK.
SHUK
BASTARD.
SPURCH
I SUGGEST YOU MOVE...

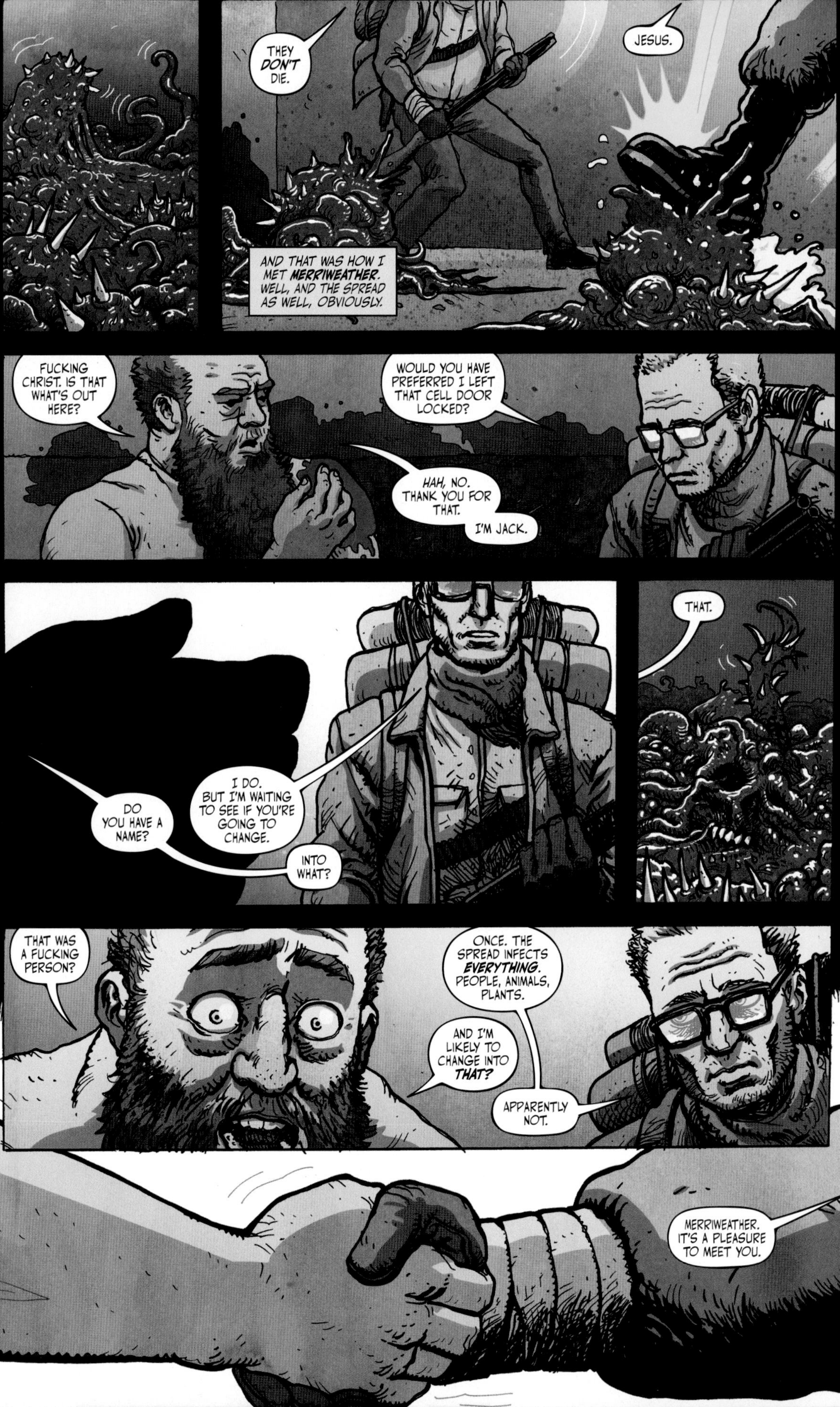
THEY *DON'T* DIE.
JESUS.
AND THAT WAS HOW I MET ***MERRIWEATHER***. WELL, AND THE SPREAD AS WELL, OBVIOUSLY.
FUCKING CHRIST. IS THAT WHAT'S OUT HERE?
WOULD YOU HAVE PREFERRED I LEFT THAT CELL DOOR LOCKED?
HAH, NO. THANK YOU FOR THAT.
I'M JACK.
DO YOU HAVE A NAME?
I DO. BUT I'M WAITING TO SEE IF YOU'RE GOING TO CHANGE.
INTO WHAT?
THAT.
THAT WAS A FUCKING PERSON?
ONCE. THE SPREAD INFECTS ***EVERYTHING***. PEOPLE, ANIMALS, PLANTS.
AND I'M LIKELY TO CHANGE INTO ***THAT?***
APPARENTLY NOT.
MERRIWEATHER. IT'S A PLEASURE TO MEET YOU.

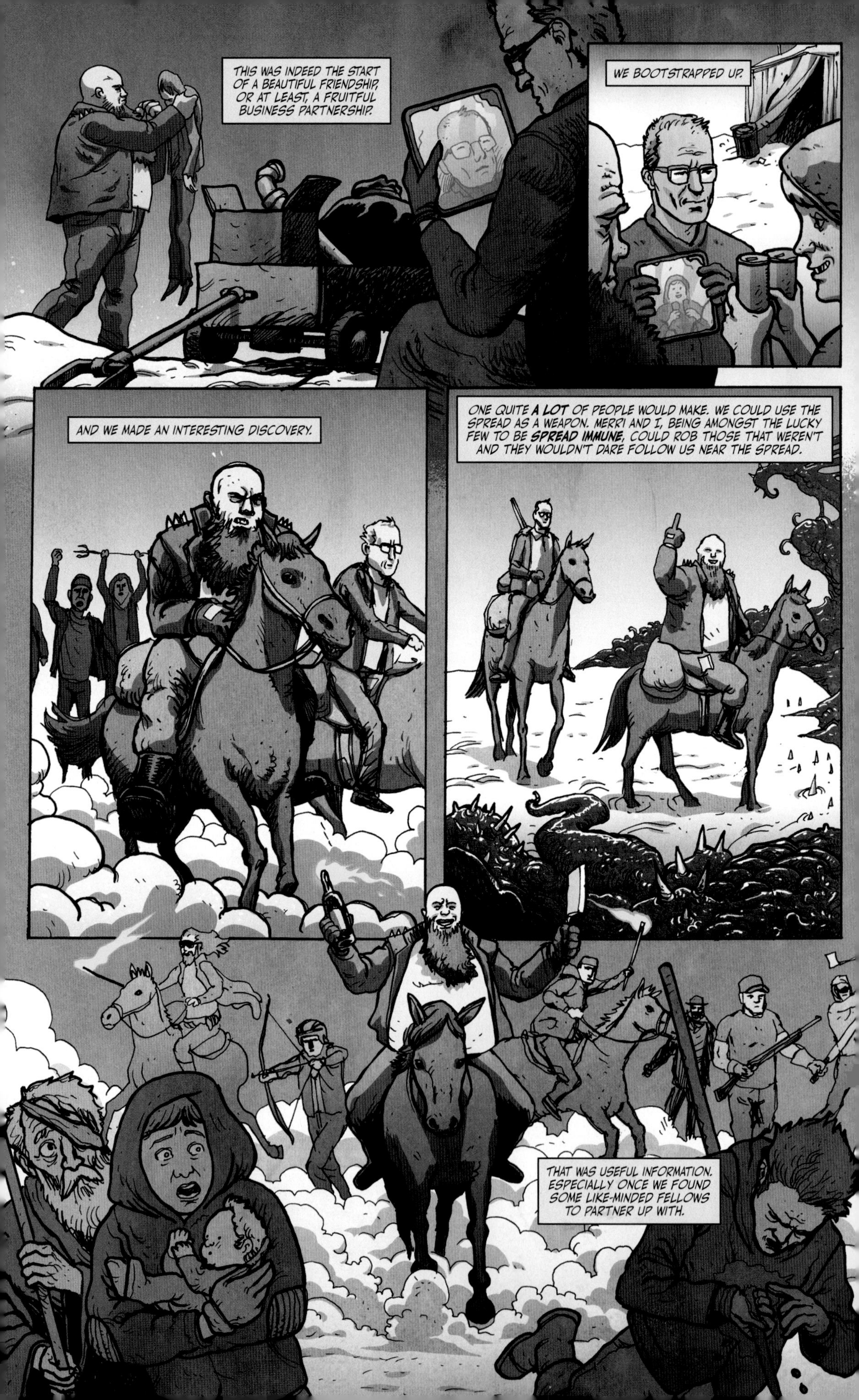
THIS WAS INDEED THE START OF A BEAUTIFUL FRIENDSHIP, OR AT LEAST, A FRUITFUL BUSINESS PARTNERSHIP.
WE BOOTSTRAPPED UP.
AND WE MADE AN INTERESTING DISCOVERY.
ONE QUITE A LOT OF PEOPLE WOULD MAKE. WE COULD USE THE SPREAD AS A WEAPON. MERRI AND I, BEING AMONGST THE LUCKY FEW TO BE SPREAD IMMUNE, COULD ROB THOSE THAT WEREN'T AND THEY WOULDN'T DARE FOLLOW US NEAR THE SPREAD.
THAT WAS USEFUL INFORMATION. ESPECIALLY ONCE WE FOUND SOME LIKE-MINDED FELLOWS TO PARTNER UP WITH.

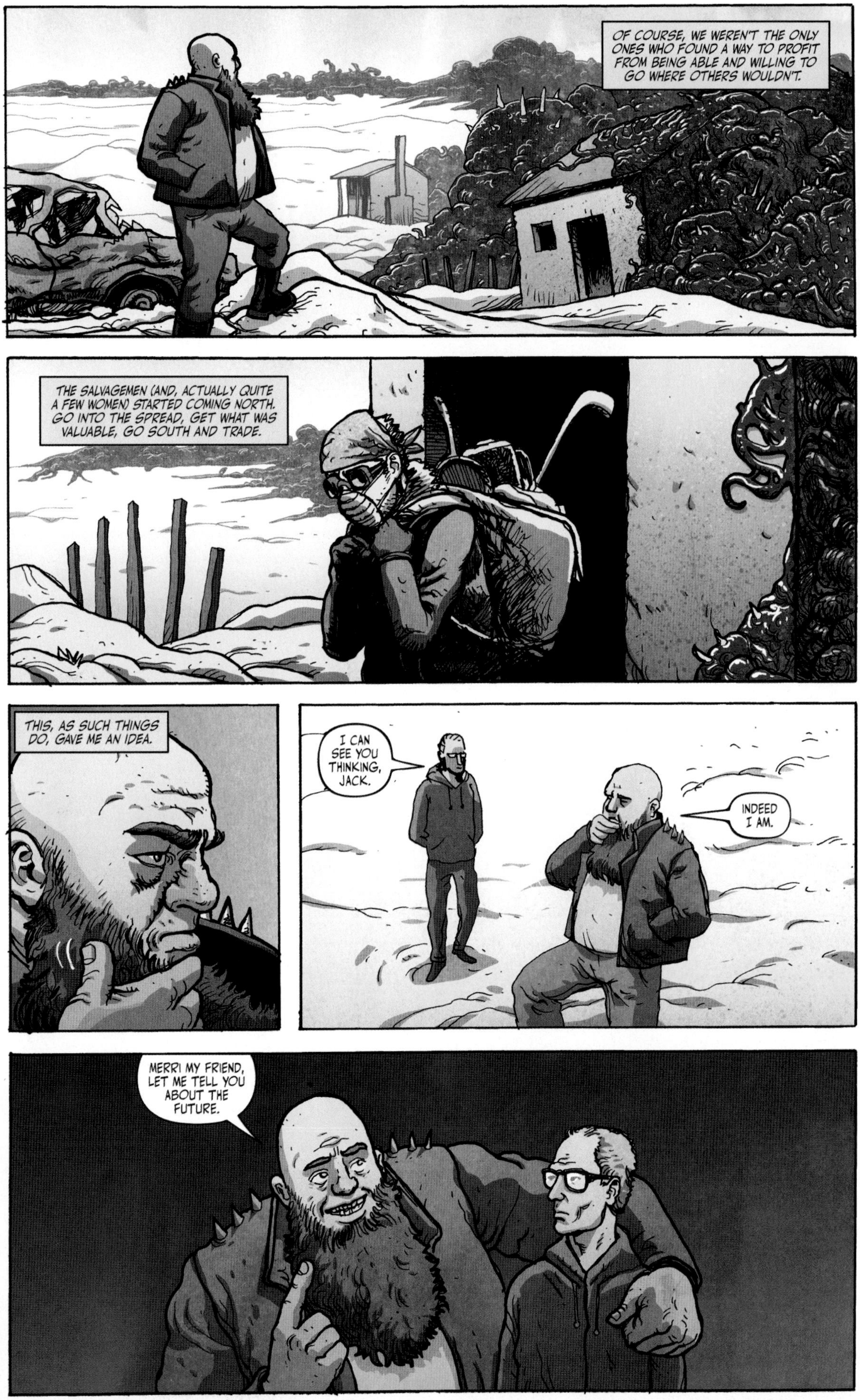
OF COURSE, WE WEREN'T THE ONLY ONES WHO FOUND A WAY TO PROFIT FROM BEING ABLE AND WILLING TO GO WHERE OTHERS WOULDN'T.
THE SALVAGEMEN (AND, ACTUALLY QUITE A FEW WOMEN) STARTED COMING NORTH. GO INTO THE SPREAD, GET WHAT WAS VALUABLE, GO SOUTH AND TRADE.
THIS, AS SUCH THINGS DO, GAVE ME AN IDEA.
I CAN SEE YOU THINKING, JACK.
INDEED I AM.
MERRI MY FRIEND, LET ME TELL YOU ABOUT THE FUTURE.

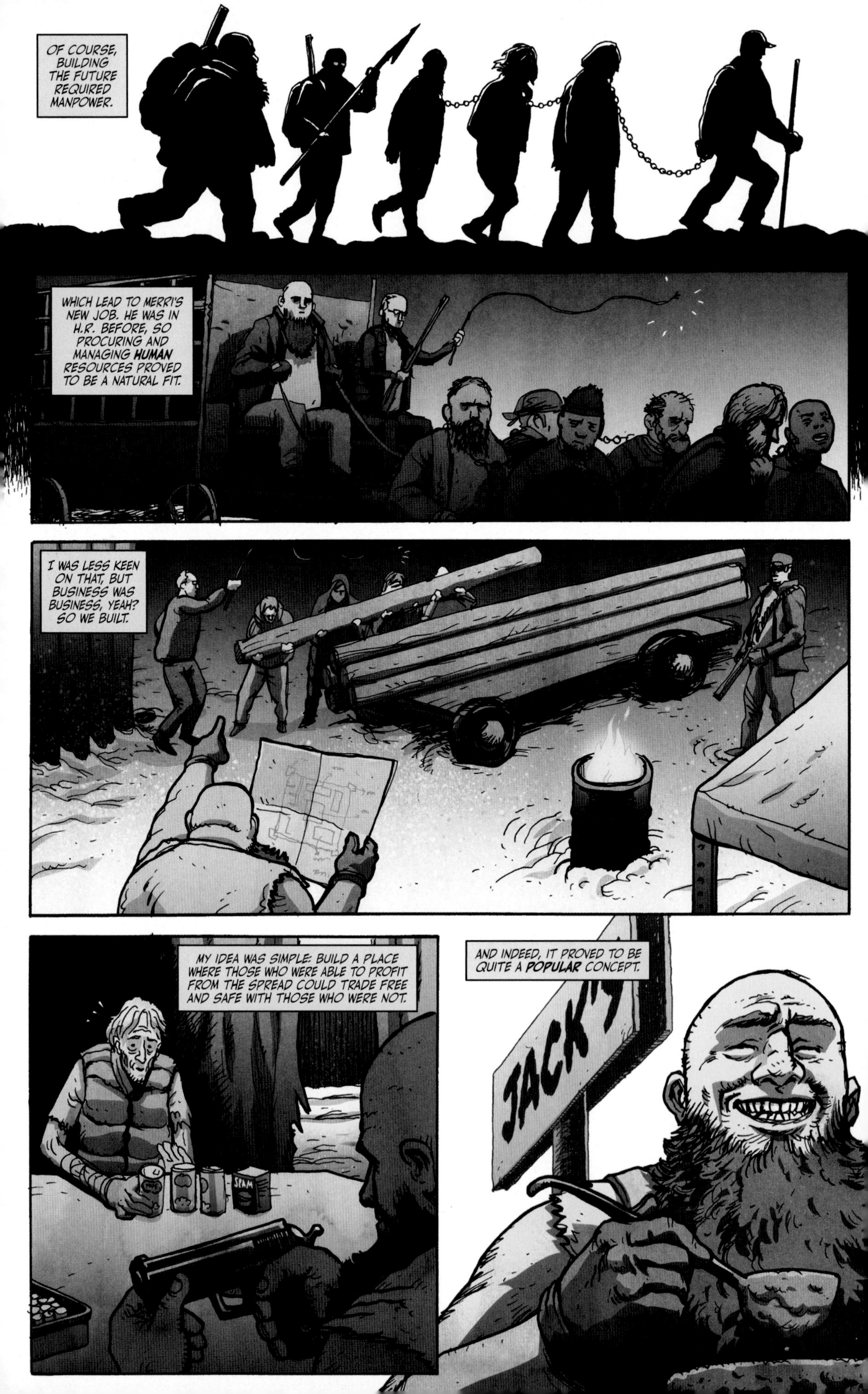
OF COURSE, BUILDING THE FUTURE REQUIRED MANPOWER.
WHICH LEAD TO MERRI'S NEW JOB. HE WAS IN H.R. BEFORE, SO PROCURING AND MANAGING HUMAN RESOURCES PROVED TO BE A NATURAL FIT.
I WAS LESS KEEN ON THAT, BUT BUSINESS WAS BUSINESS, YEAH? SO WE BUILT.
MY IDEA WAS SIMPLE: BUILD A PLACE WHERE THOSE WHO WERE ABLE TO PROFIT FROM THE SPREAD COULD TRADE FREE AND SAFE WITH THOSE WHO WERE NOT.
SPAM
AND INDEED, IT PROVED TO BE QUITE A POPULAR CONCEPT.
JACK'S

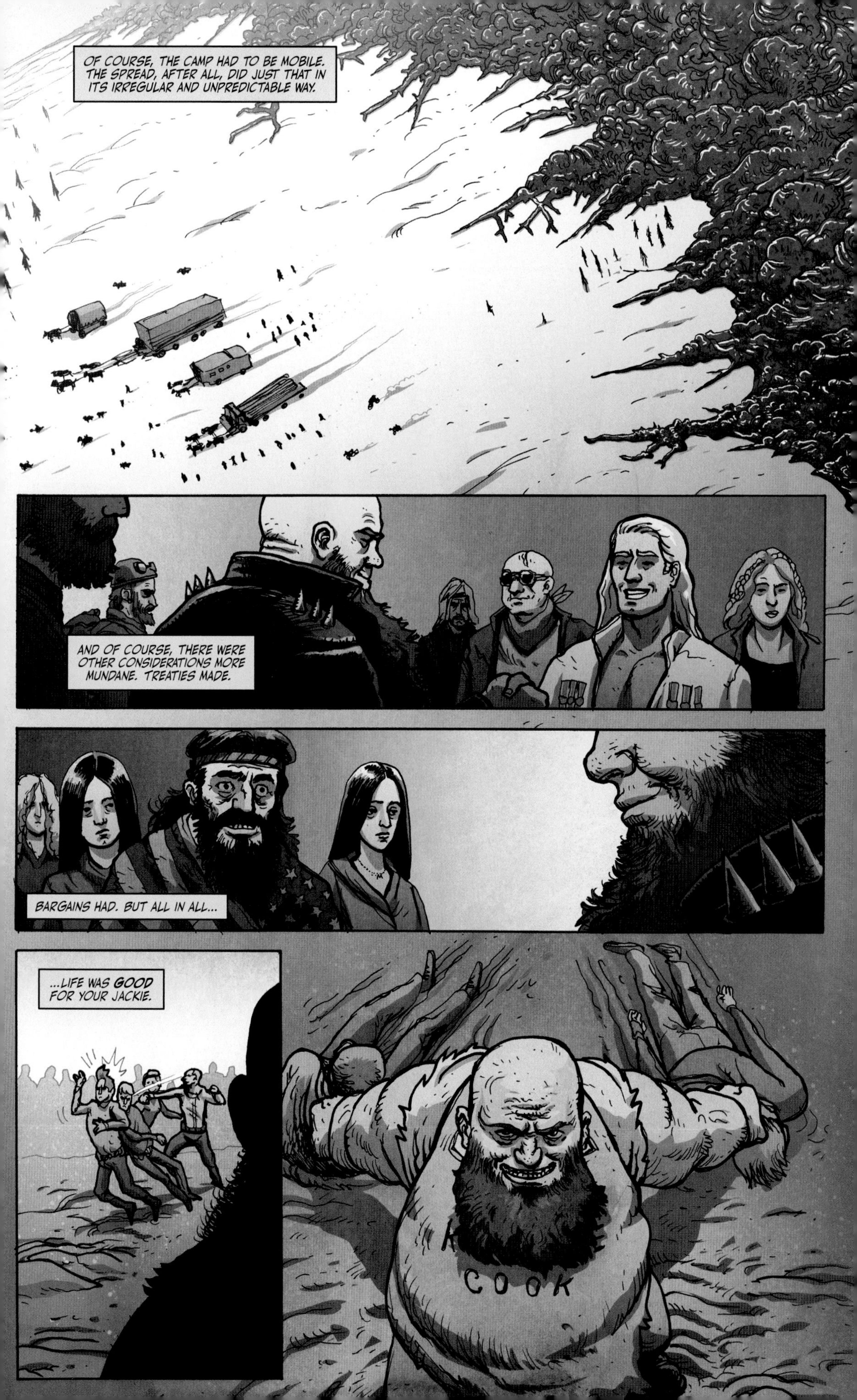
OF COURSE, THE CAMP HAD TO BE MOBILE. THE SPREAD, AFTER ALL, DID JUST THAT IN ITS IRREGULAR AND UNPREDICTABLE WAY.
AND OF COURSE, THERE WERE OTHER CONSIDERATIONS MORE MUNDANE. TREATIES MADE.
BARGAINS HAD. BUT ALL IN ALL...
...LIFE WAS **GOOD** FOR YOUR JACKIE.
COOK

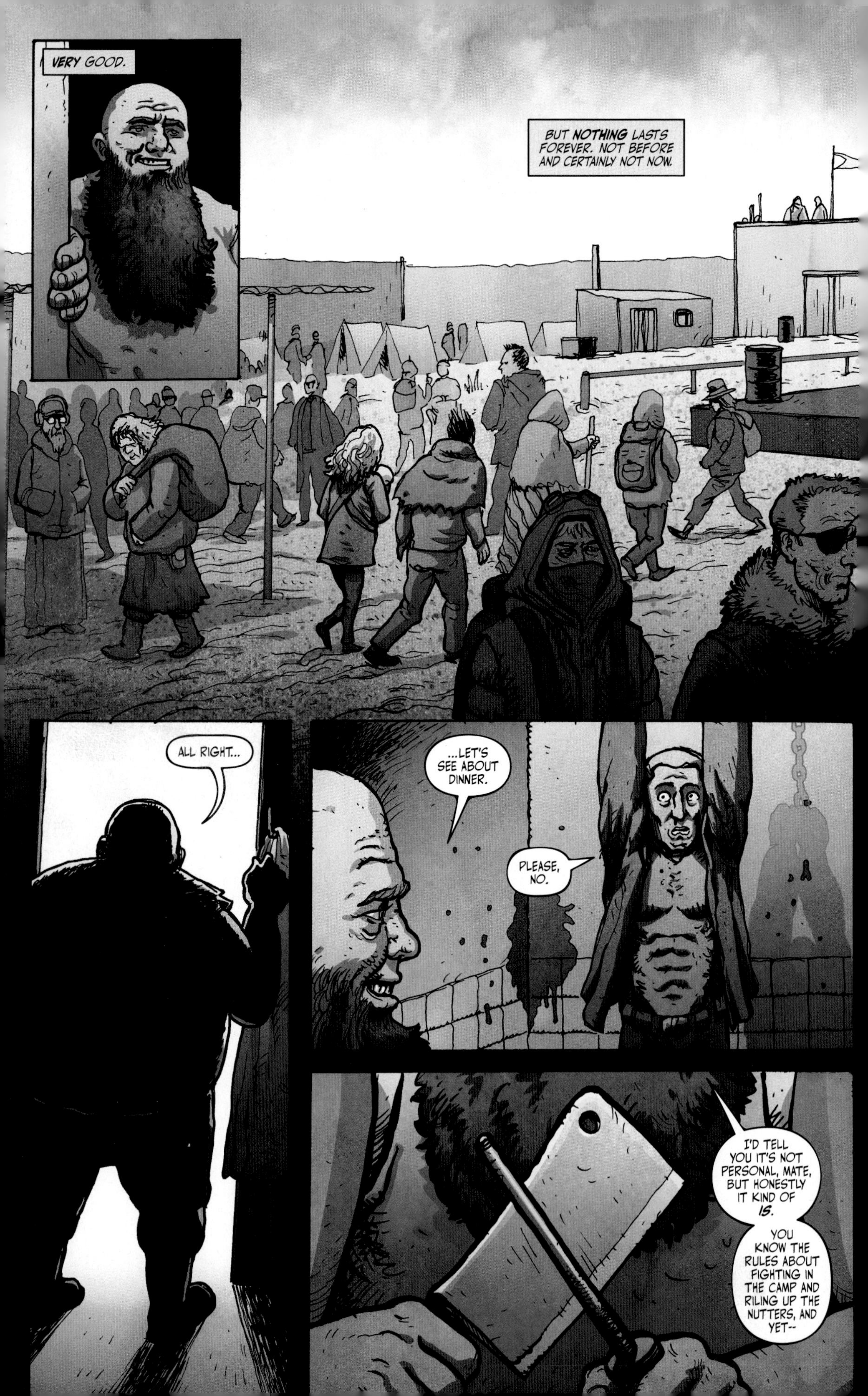
VERY GOOD.
BUT NOTHING LASTS FOREVER. NOT BEFORE AND CERTAINLY NOT NOW.
ALL RIGHT...
...LET'S SEE ABOUT DINNER.
PLEASE, NO.
I'D TELL YOU IT'S NOT PERSONAL, MATE, BUT HONESTLY IT KIND OF IS.
YOU KNOW THE RULES ABOUT FIGHTING IN THE CAMP AND RILING UP THE NUTTERS, AND YET--

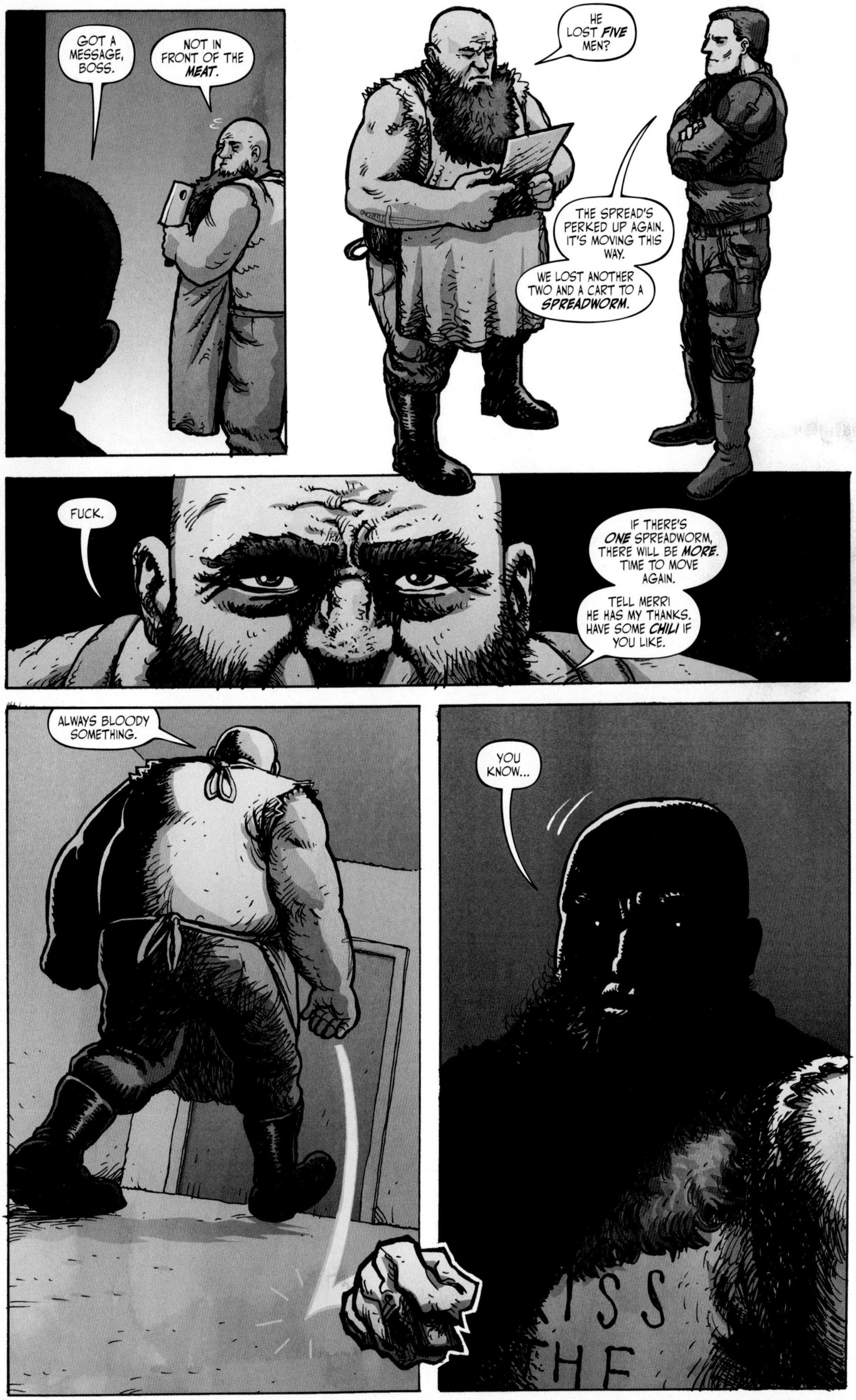
GOT A MESSAGE, BOSS.
NOT IN FRONT OF THE MEAT.
HE LOST FIVE MEN?
THE SPREAD'S PERKED UP AGAIN. IT'S MOVING THIS WAY.
WE LOST ANOTHER TWO AND A CART TO A SPREADWORM.
FUCK.
IF THERE'S ONE SPREADWORM, THERE WILL BE MORE. TIME TO MOVE AGAIN.
TELL MERRI HE HAS MY THANKS. HAVE SOME CHILI IF YOU LIKE.
ALWAYS BLOODY SOMETHING.
YOU KNOW...
ISS
HE

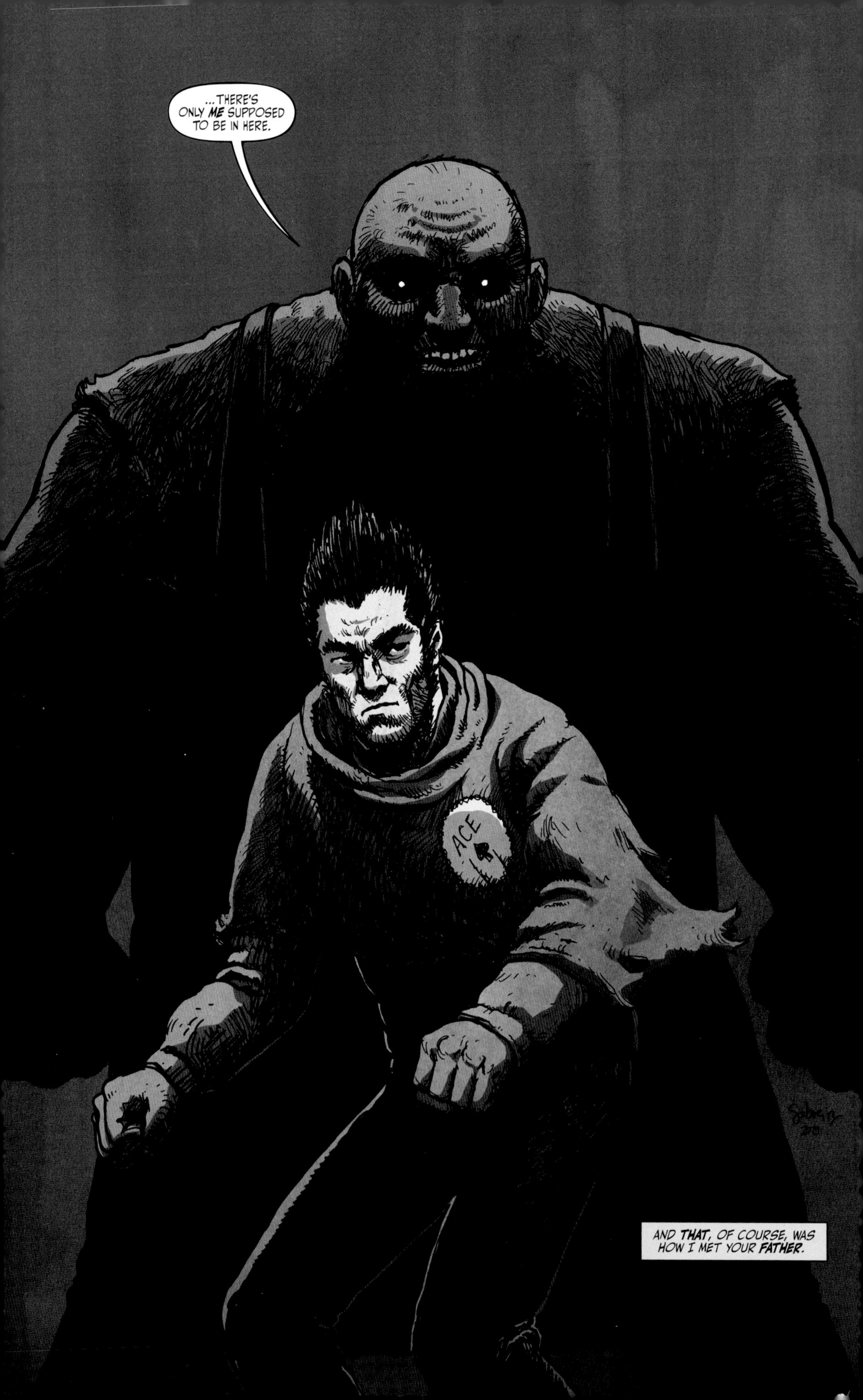
...THERE'S ONLY ME SUPPOSED TO BE IN HERE.
ACE
AND THAT, OF COURSE, WAS HOW I MET YOUR FATHER.

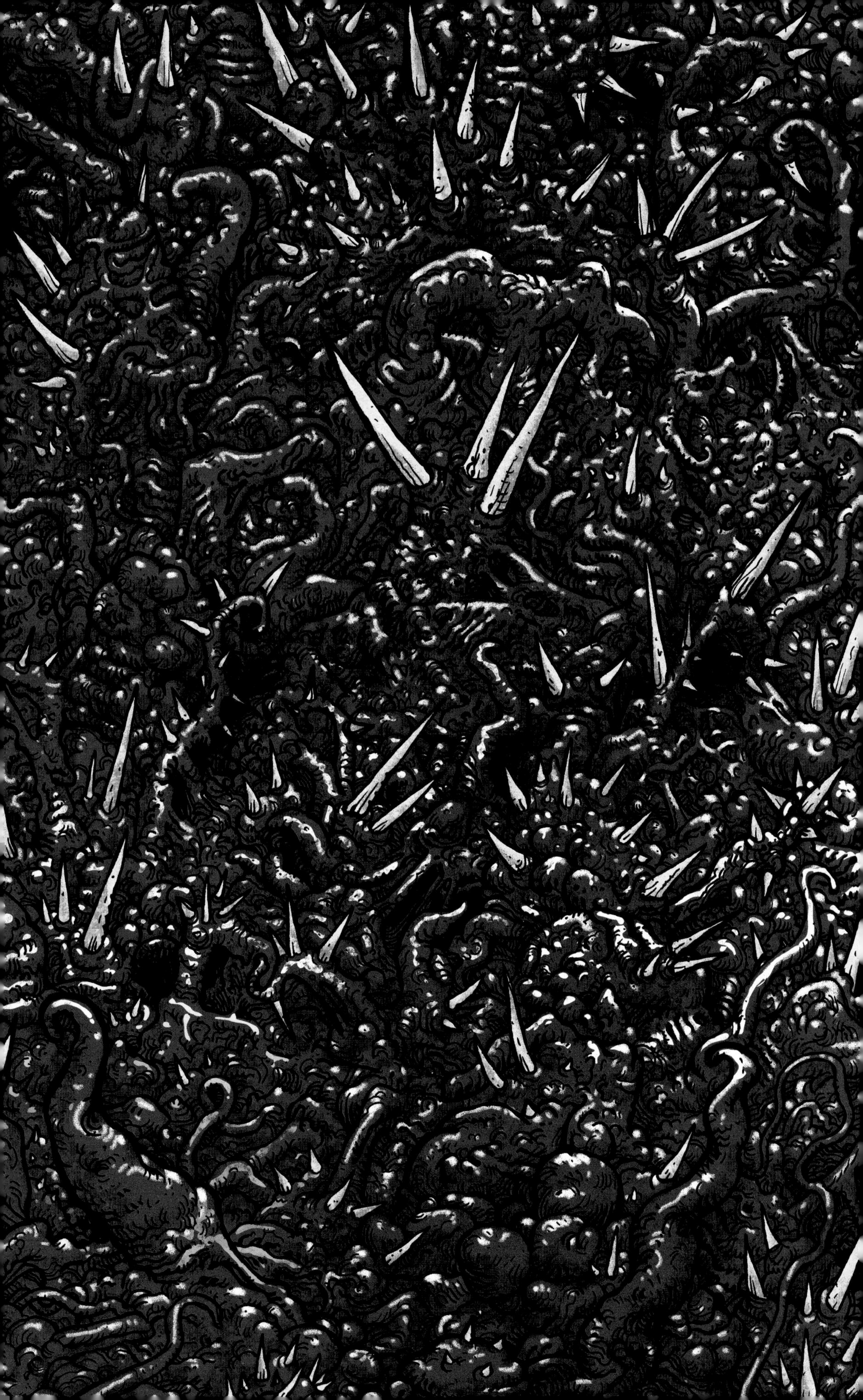

CHAPTER THREE

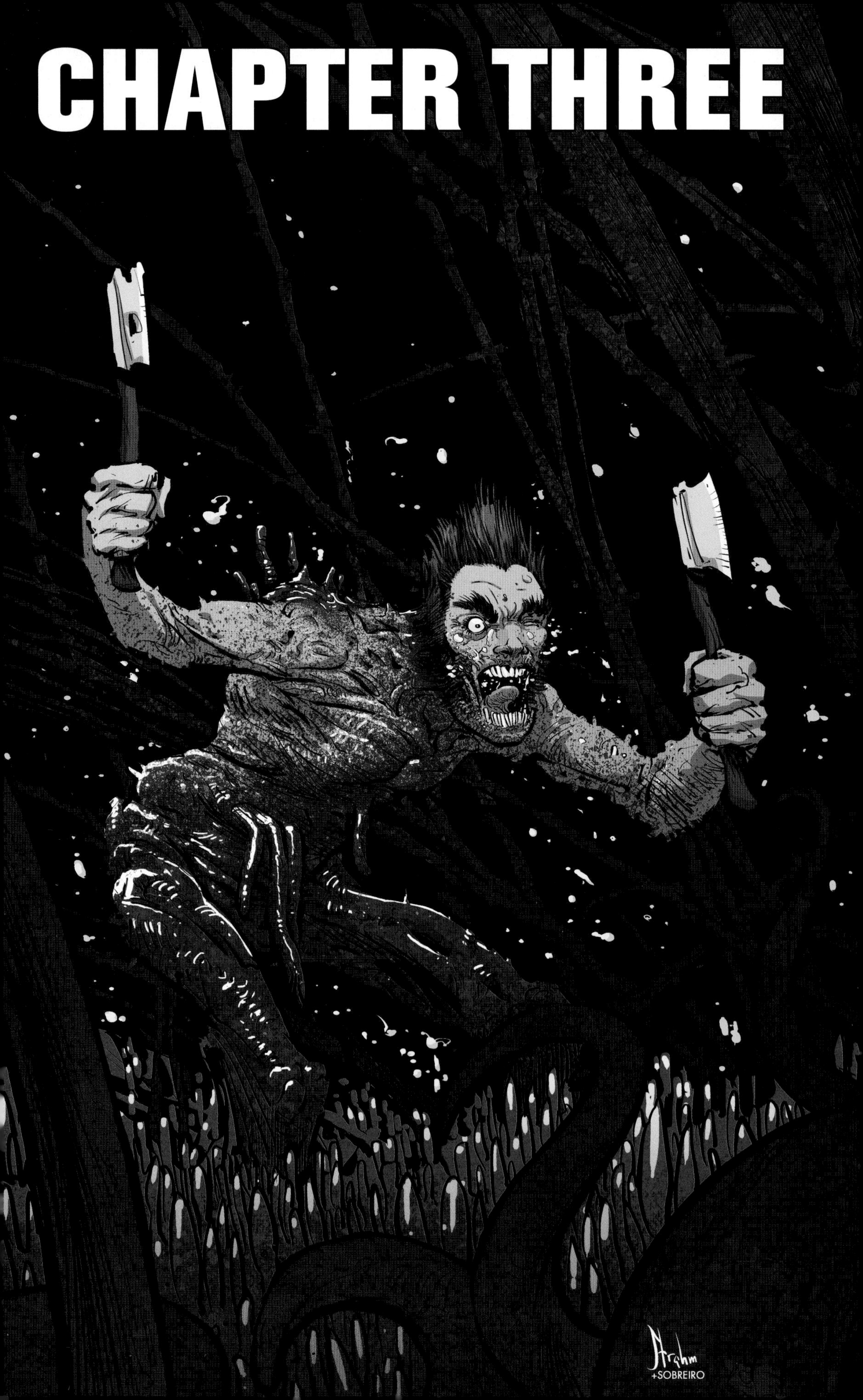
+SOBREIRO

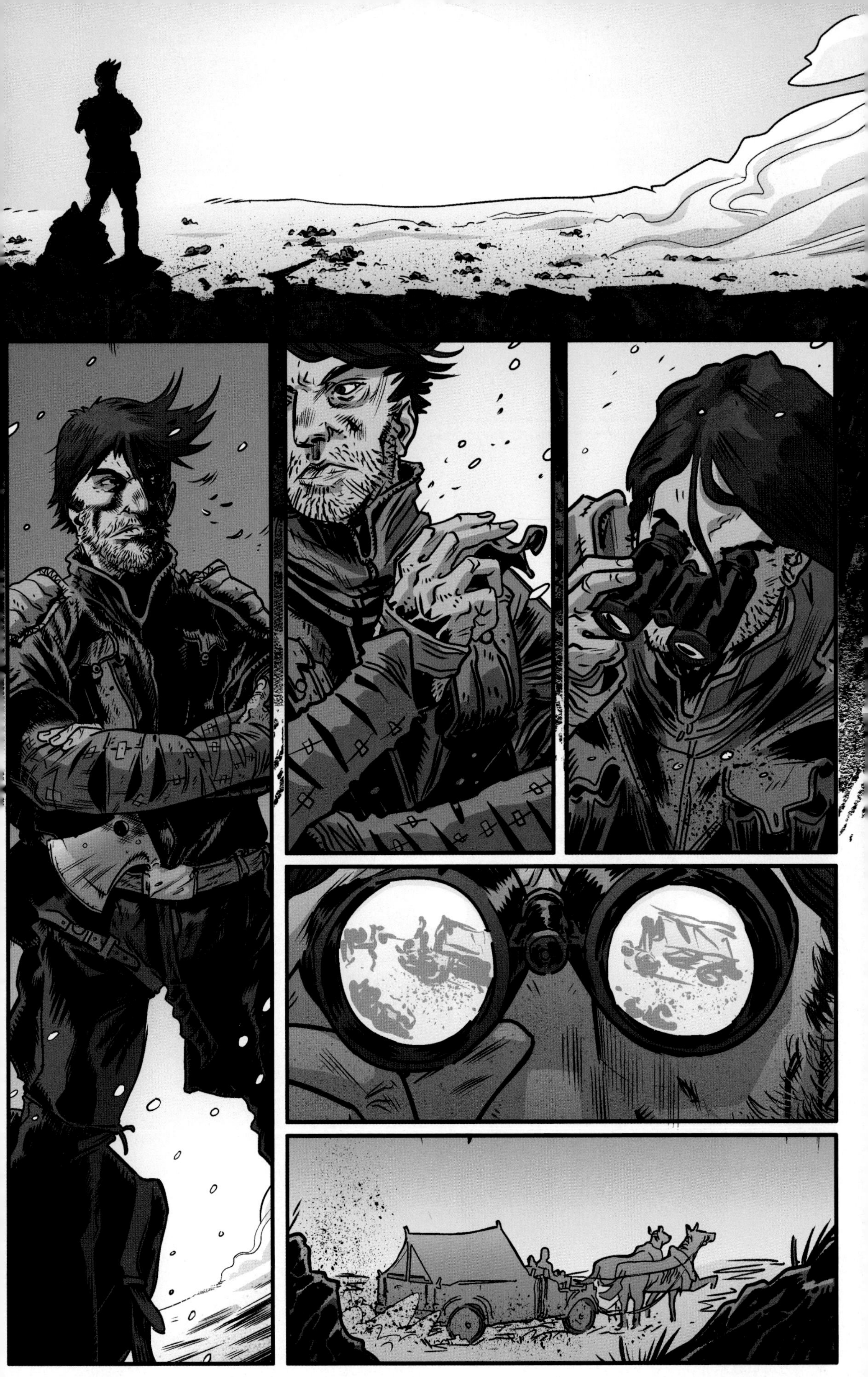

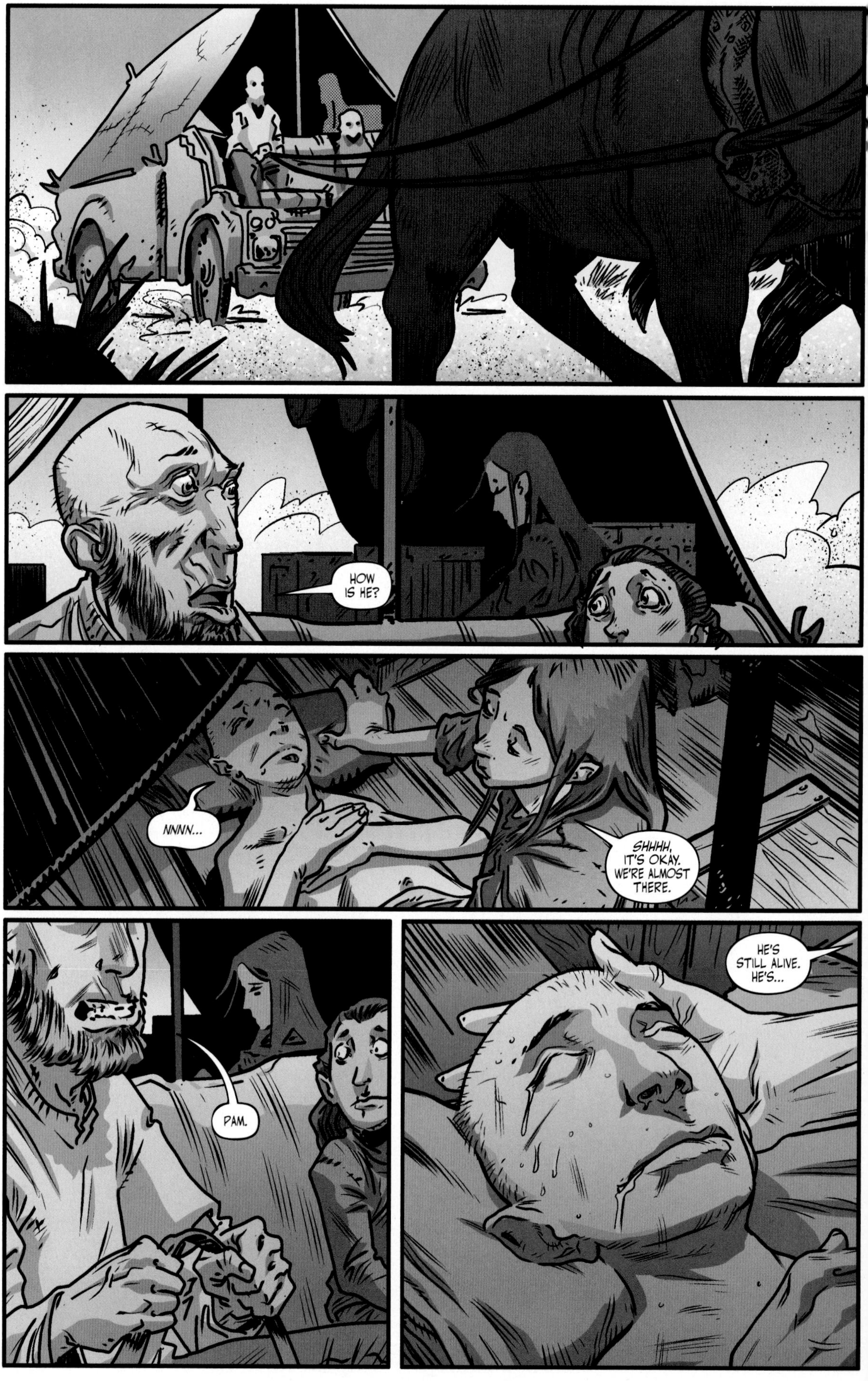
HOW IS HE?
NNNN...
SHHHH, IT'S OKAY. WE'RE ALMOST THERE.
PAM.
HE'S STILL ALIVE. HE'S...

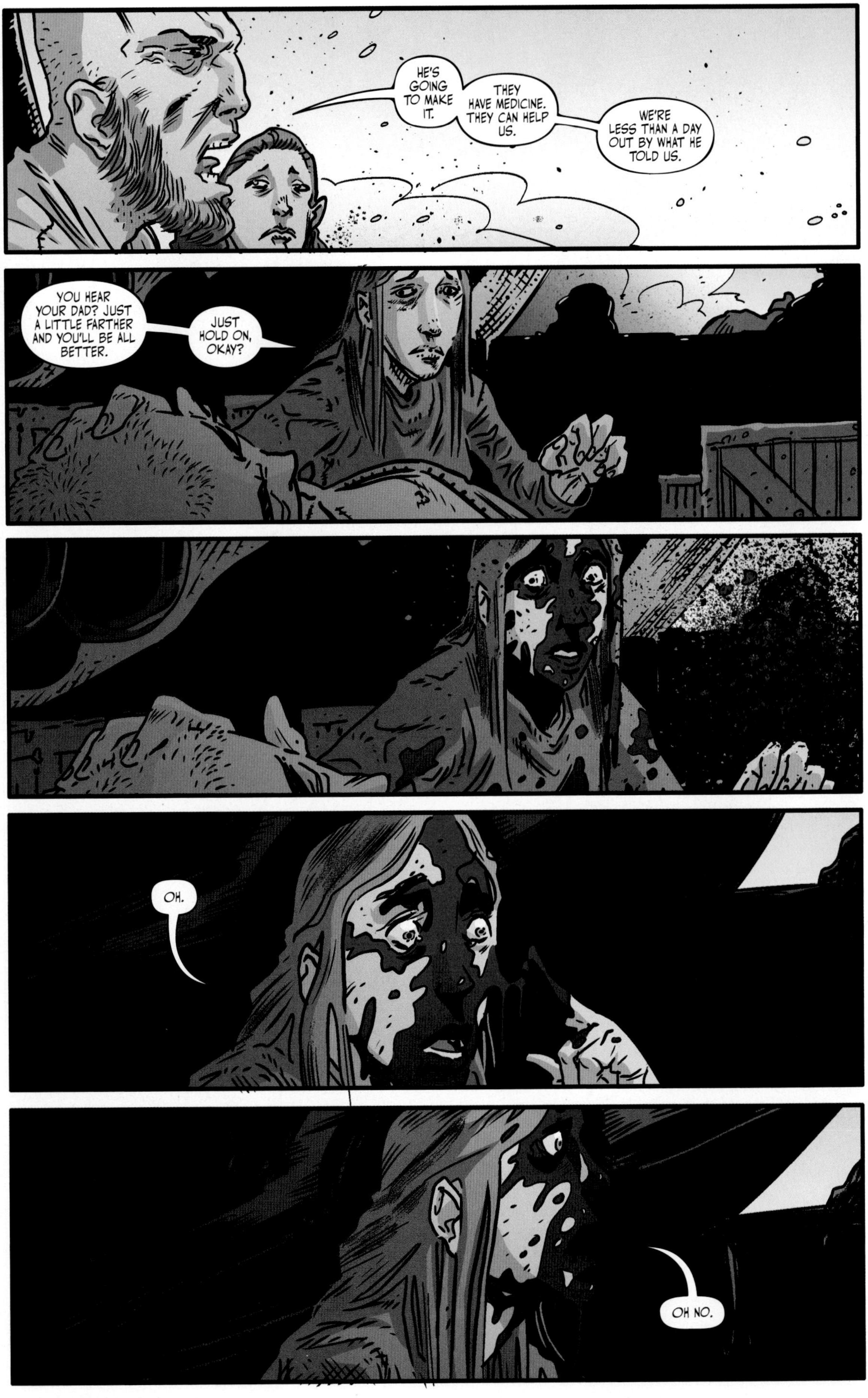
HE'S GOING TO MAKE IT.
THEY HAVE MEDICINE. THEY CAN HELP US.
WE'RE LESS THAN A DAY OUT BY WHAT HE TOLD US.
YOU HEAR YOUR DAD? JUST A LITTLE FARTHER AND YOU'LL BE ALL BETTER.
JUST HOLD ON, OKAY?
OH.
OH NO.

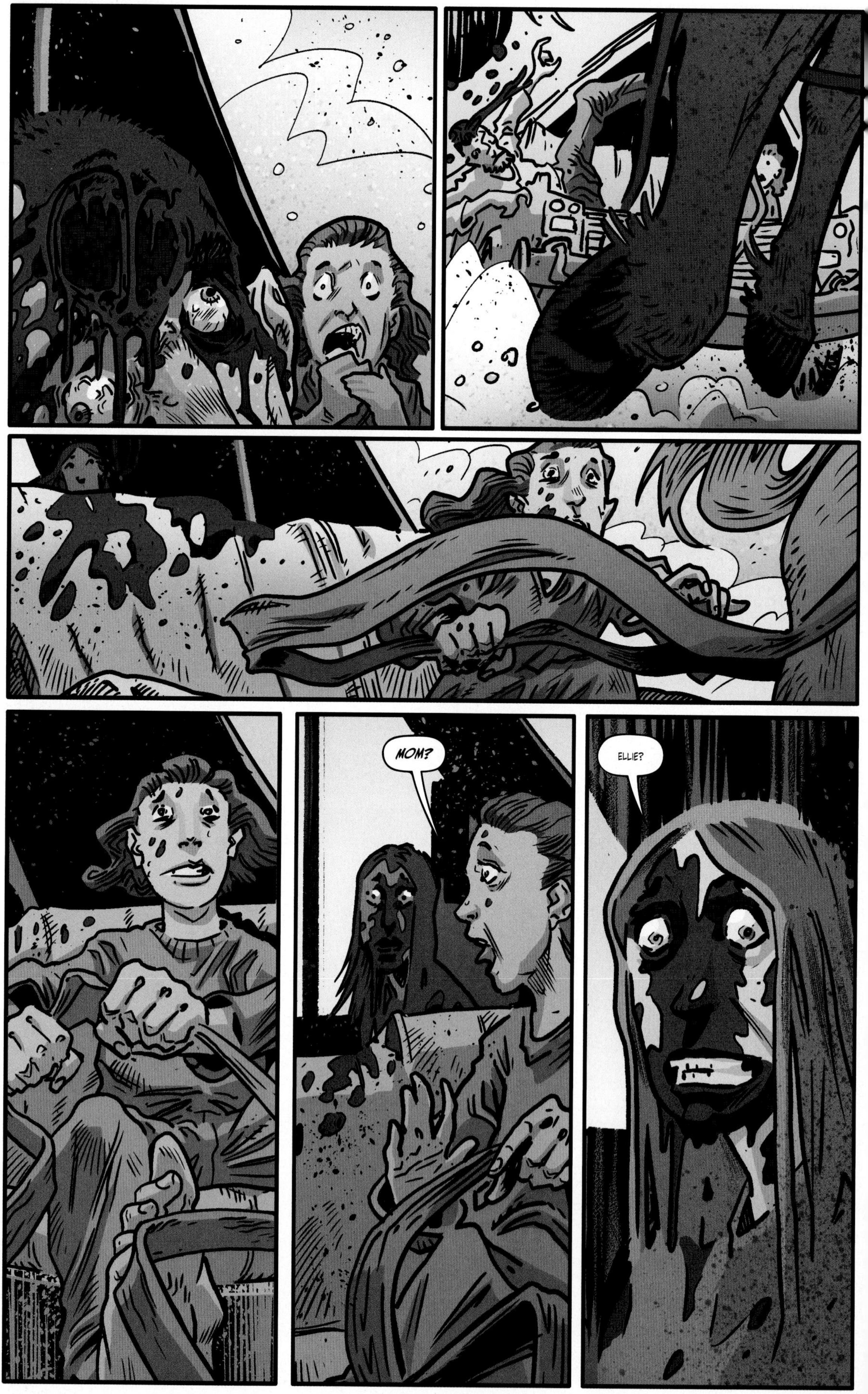
MOM?
ELLIE?

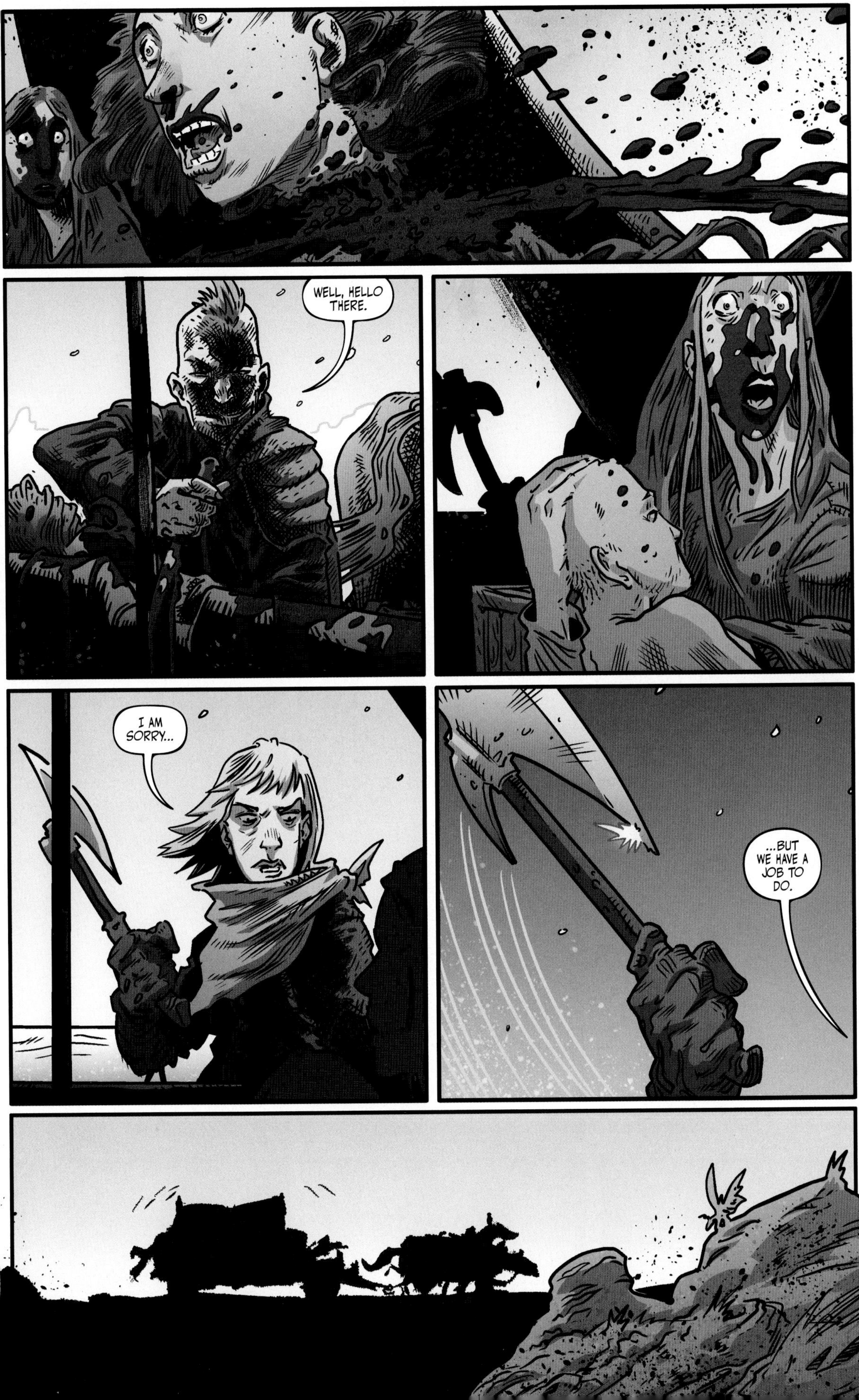
WELL, HELLO THERE.
I AM SORRY...
...BUT WE HAVE A JOB TO DO.

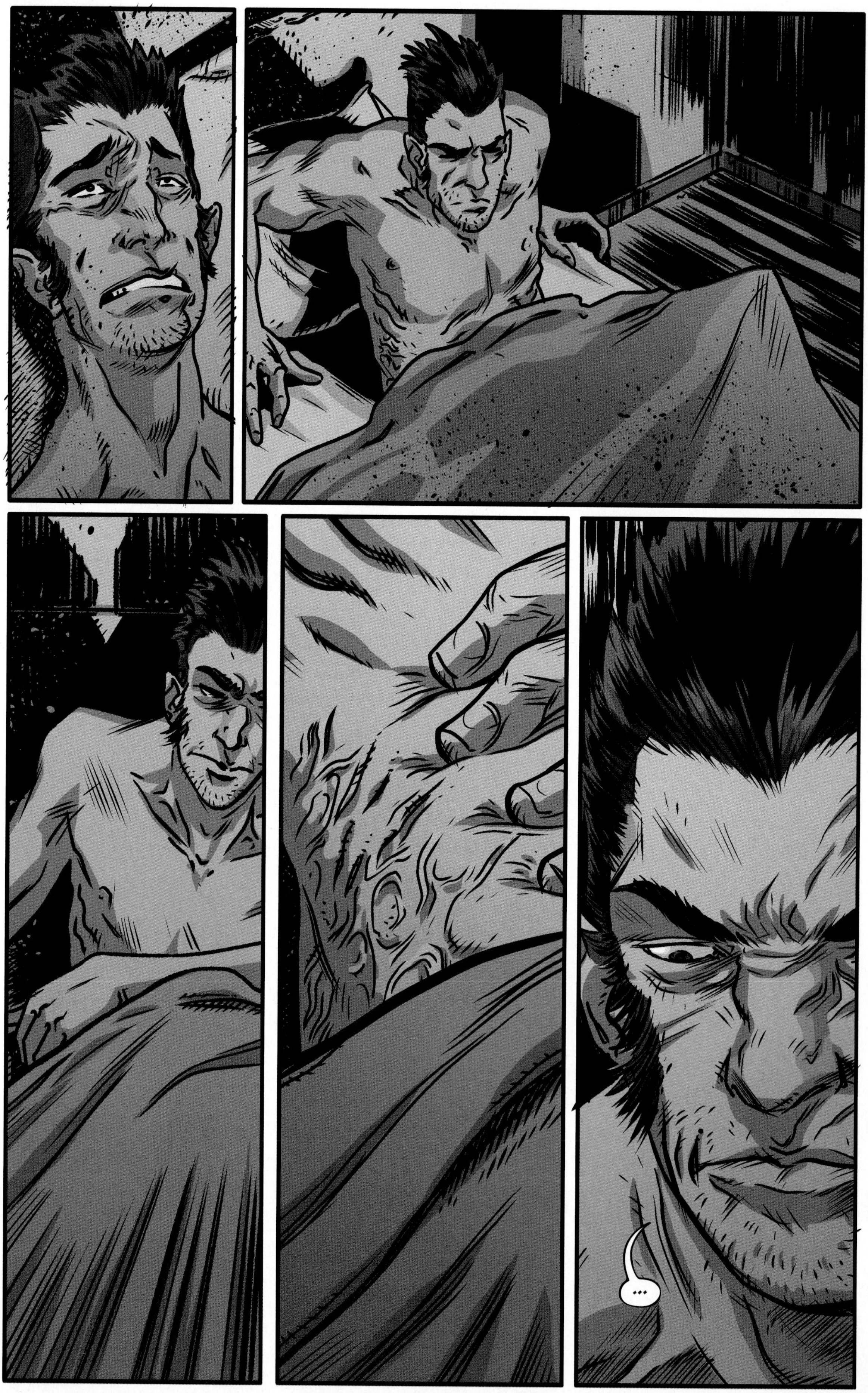
...

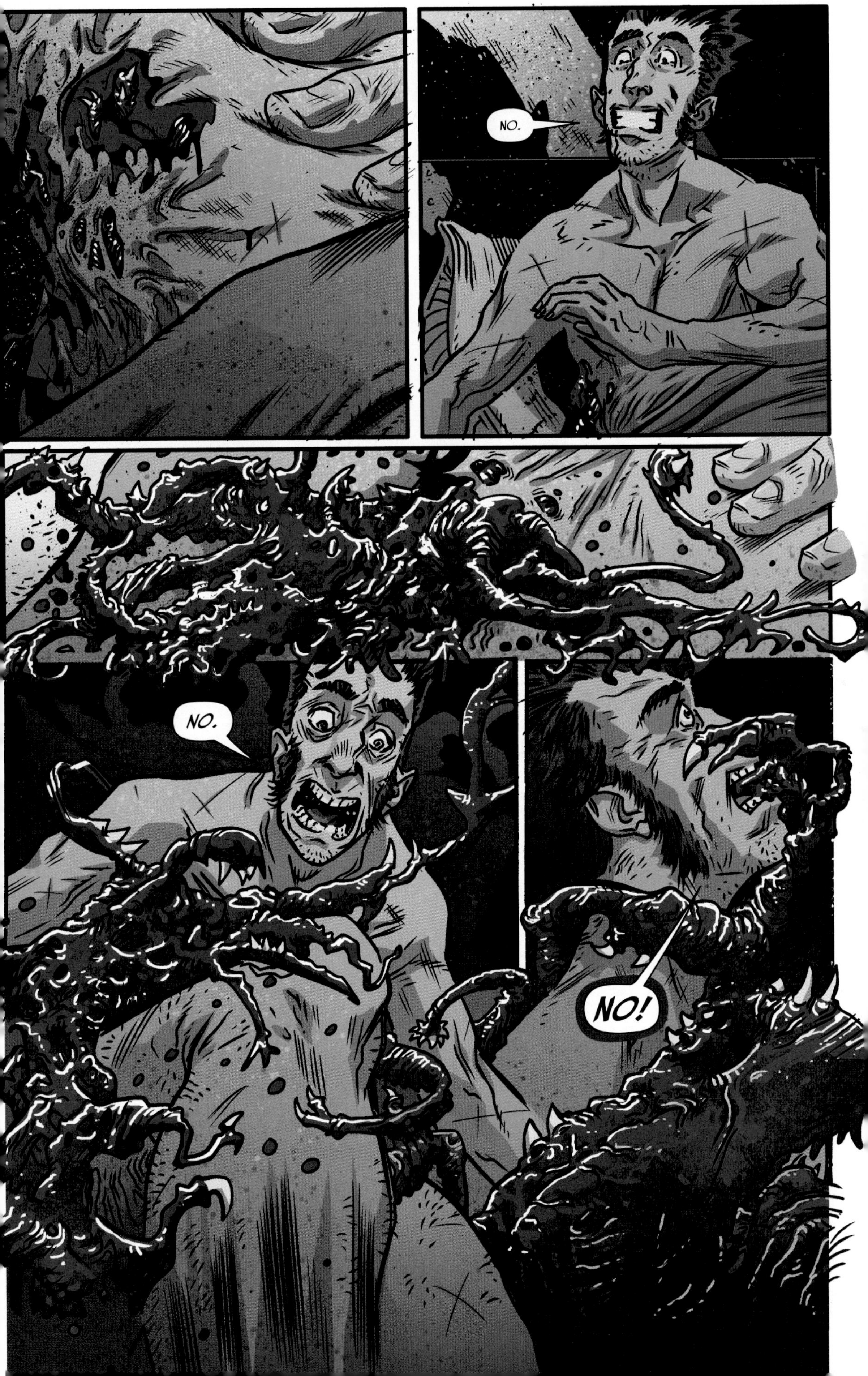
NO.
NO.
NO!

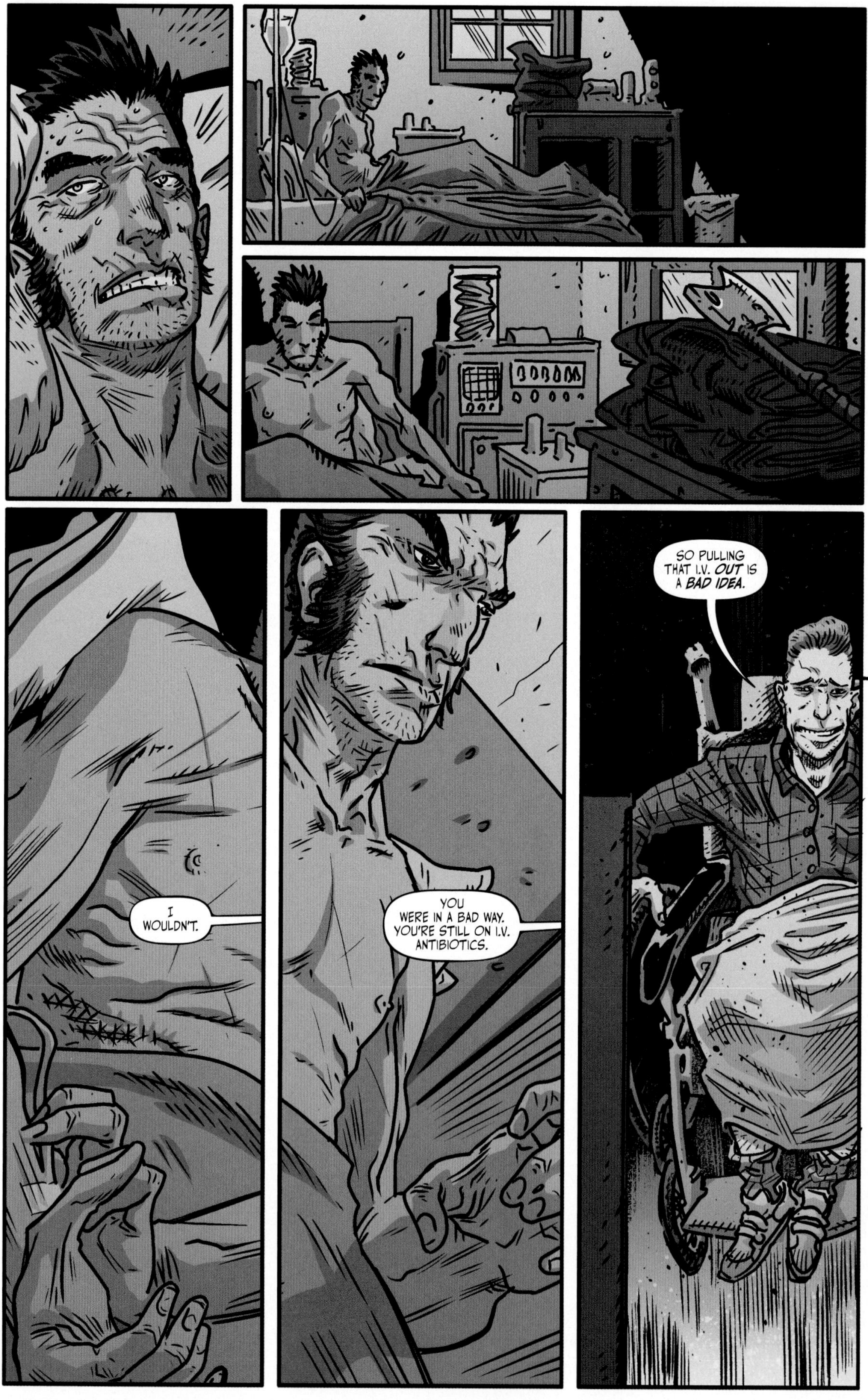
I WOULDN'T.
YOU WERE IN A BAD WAY. YOU'RE STILL ON I.V. ANTIBIOTICS.
SO PULLING THAT I.V. OUT IS A BAD IDEA.

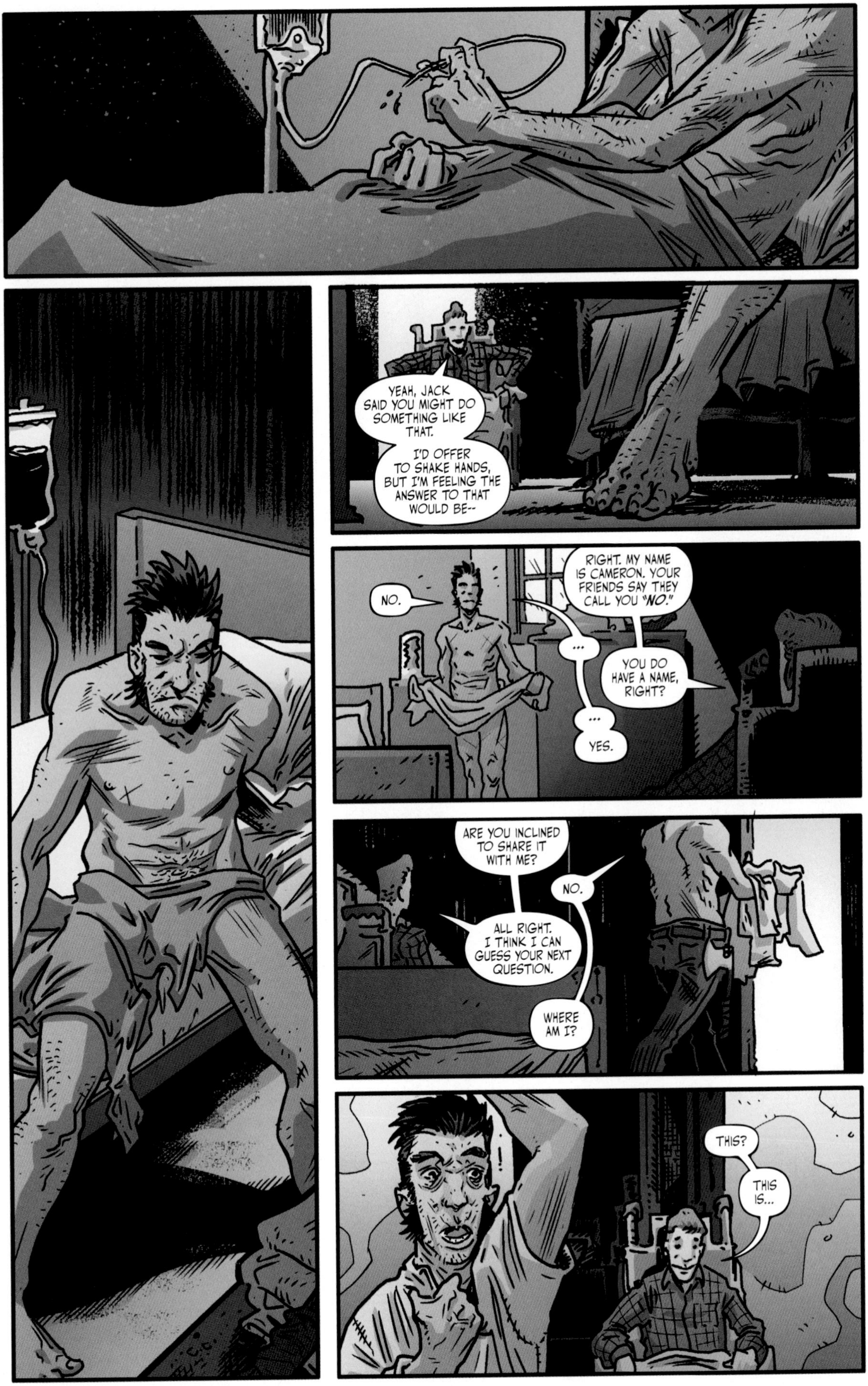
YEAH, JACK SAID YOU MIGHT DO SOMETHING LIKE THAT.
I'D OFFER TO SHAKE HANDS, BUT I'M FEELING THE ANSWER TO THAT WOULD BE--
NO.
RIGHT. MY NAME IS CAMERON. YOUR FRIENDS SAY THEY CALL YOU "NO."
...
YOU DO HAVE A NAME, RIGHT?
...
YES.
ARE YOU INCLINED TO SHARE IT WITH ME?
NO.
ALL RIGHT. I THINK I CAN GUESS YOUR NEXT QUESTION.
WHERE AM I?
THIS?
THIS IS...

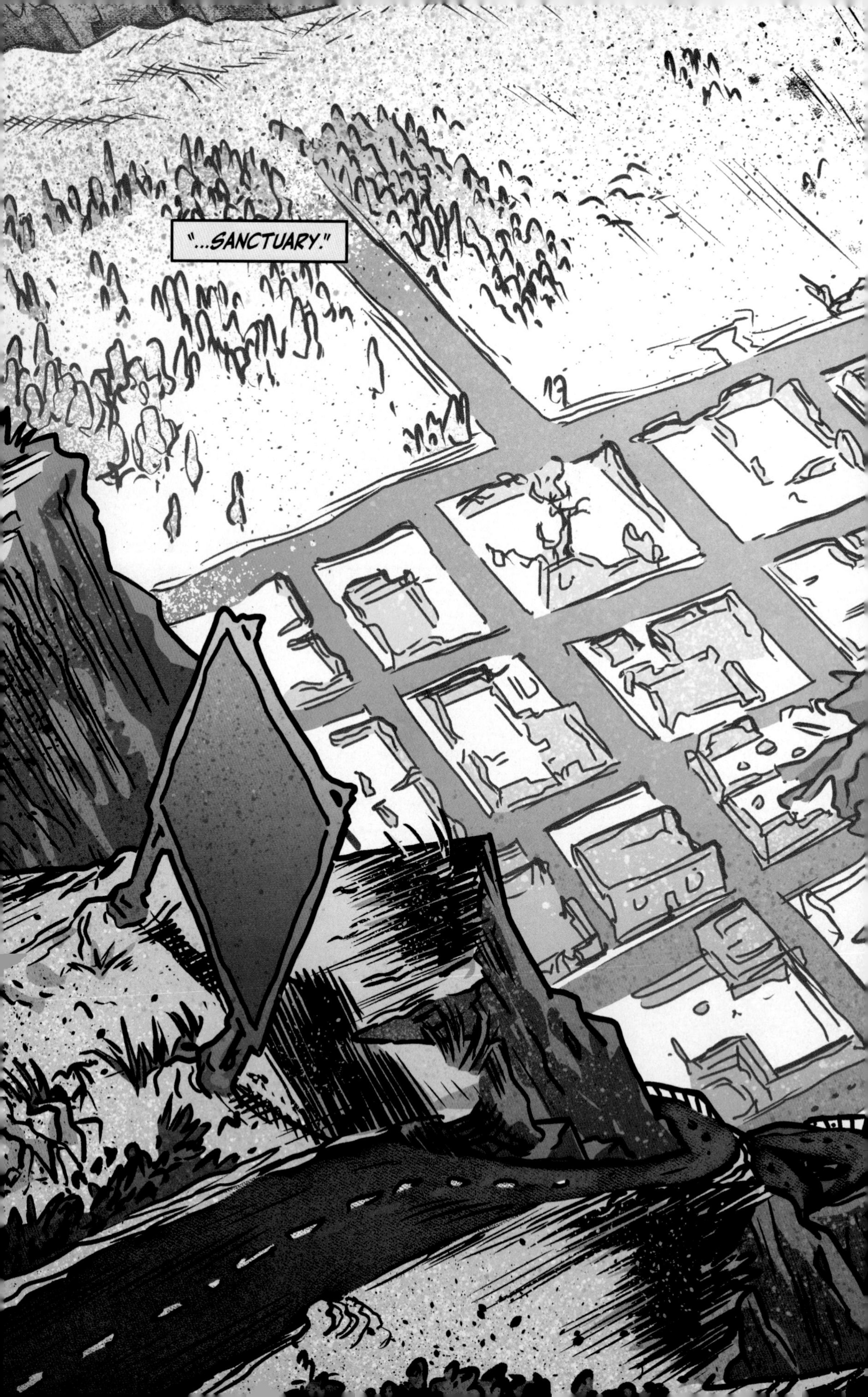
"...SANCTUARY."

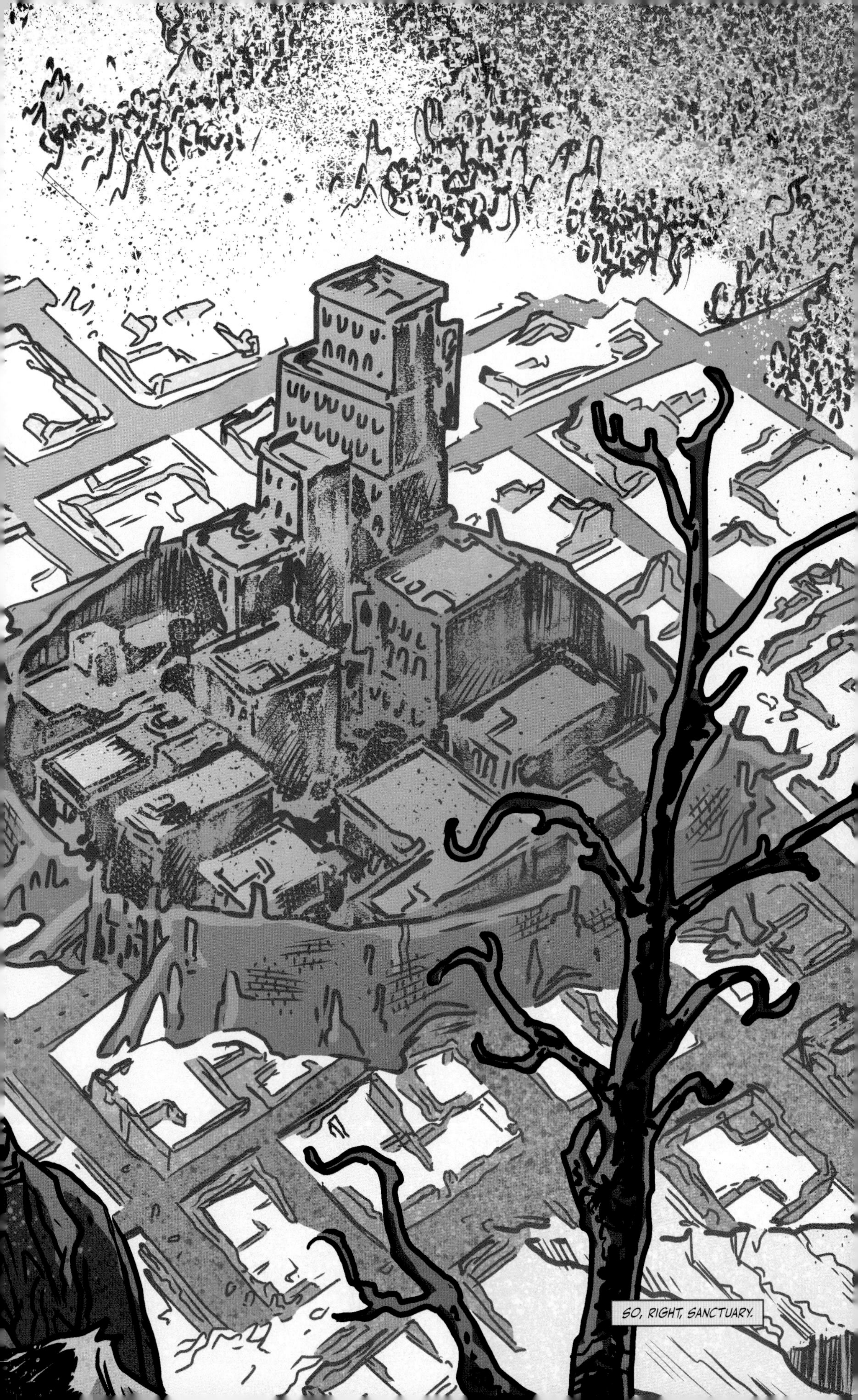
SO, RIGHT, SANCTUARY.

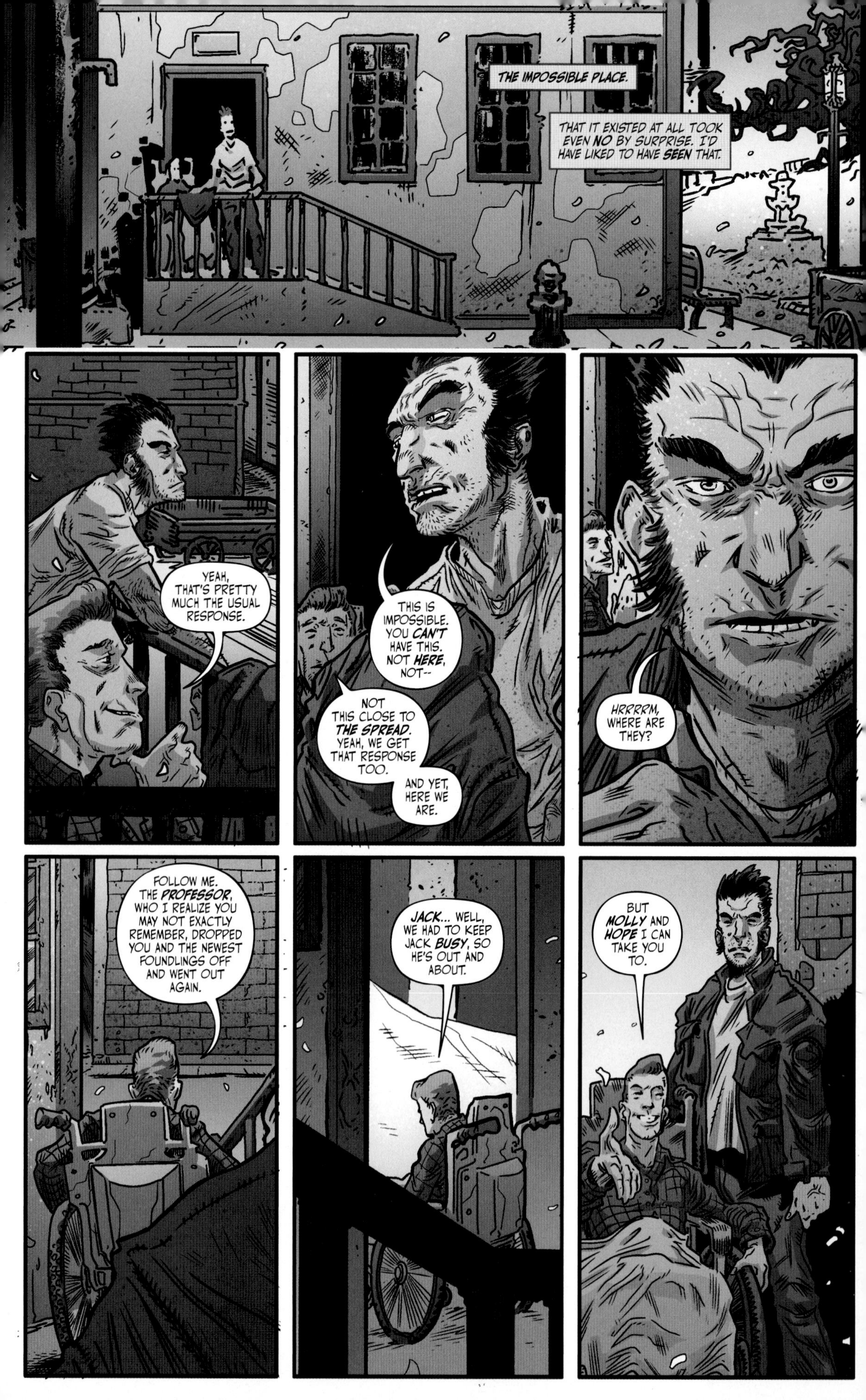
THE IMPOSSIBLE PLACE.
THAT IT EXISTED AT ALL TOOK EVEN NO BY SURPRISE. I'D HAVE LIKED TO HAVE SEEN THAT.
YEAH, THAT'S PRETTY MUCH THE USUAL RESPONSE.
THIS IS IMPOSSIBLE. YOU CAN'T HAVE THIS. NOT HERE, NOT--
NOT THIS CLOSE TO THE SPREAD. YEAH, WE GET THAT RESPONSE TOO.
AND YET, HERE WE ARE.
HRRRRM, WHERE ARE THEY?
FOLLOW ME. THE PROFESSOR, WHO I REALIZE YOU MAY NOT EXACTLY REMEMBER, DROPPED YOU AND THE NEWEST FOUNDLINGS OFF AND WENT OUT AGAIN.
JACK... WELL, WE HAD TO KEEP JACK BUSY, SO HE'S OUT AND ABOUT.
BUT MOLLY AND HOPE I CAN TAKE YOU TO.

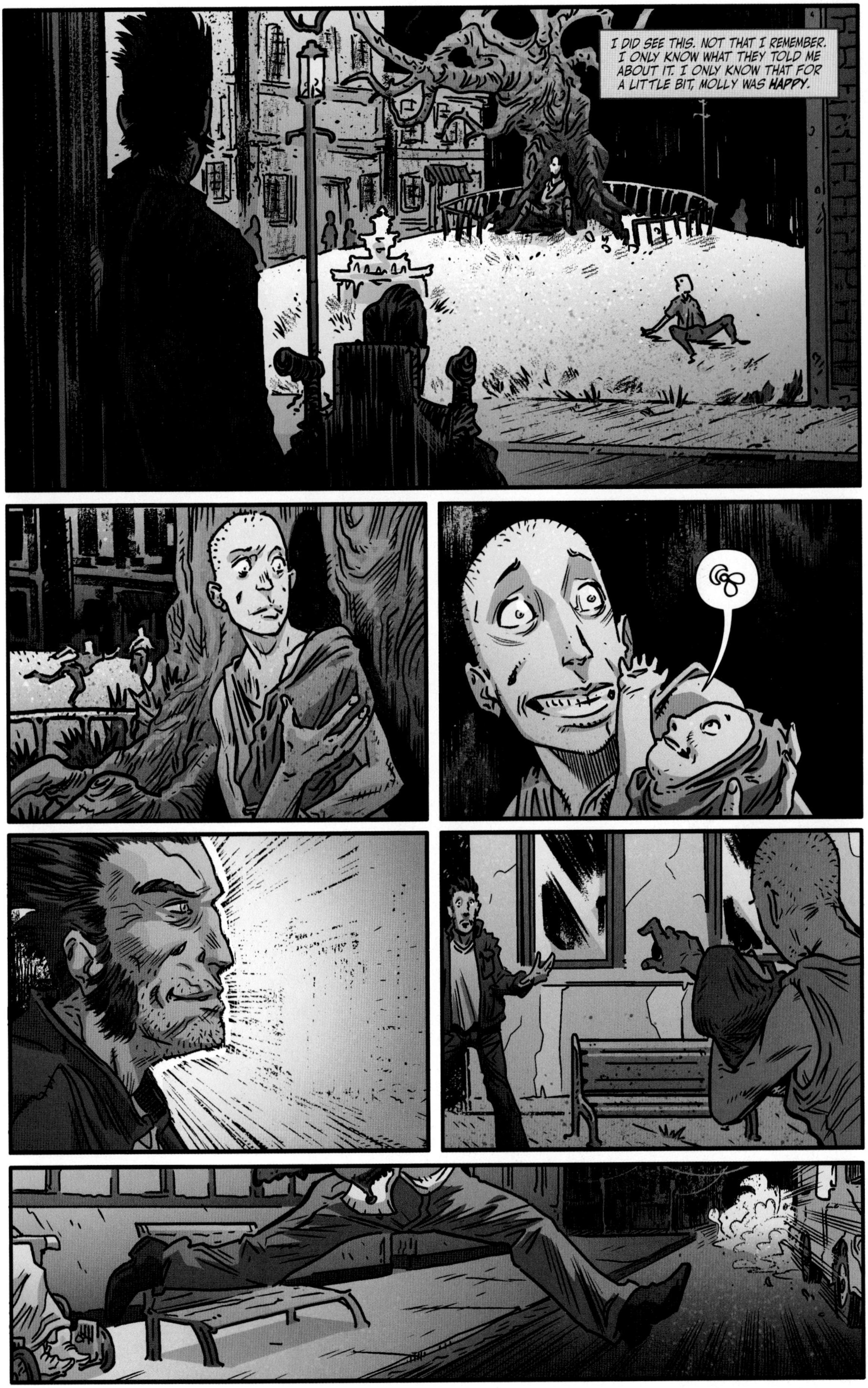
I DID SEE THIS. NOT THAT I REMEMBER. I ONLY KNOW WHAT THEY TOLD ME ABOUT IT. I ONLY KNOW THAT FOR A LITTLE BIT, MOLLY WAS **HAPPY**.

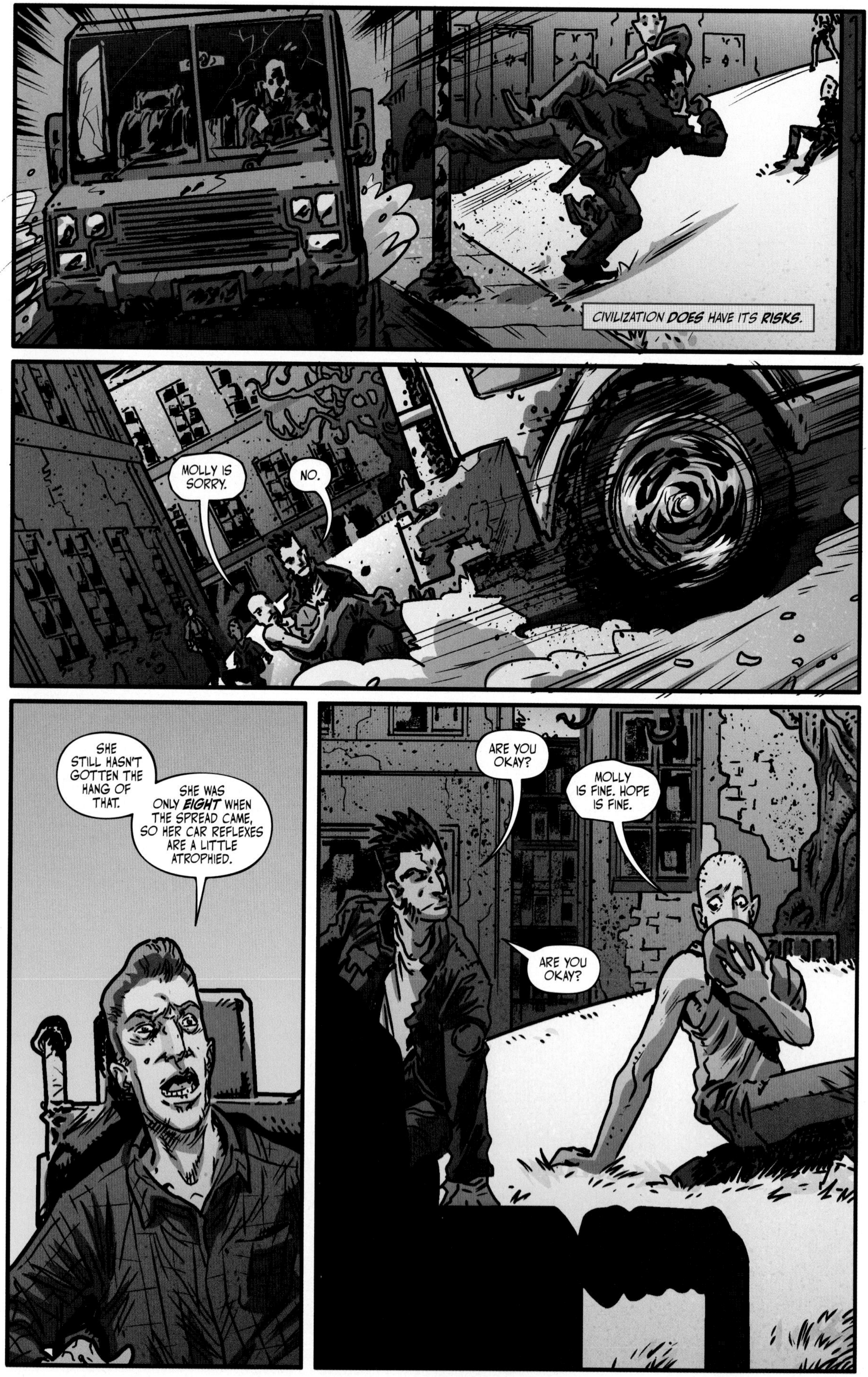
CIVILIZATION DOES HAVE ITS RISKS.
MOLLY IS SORRY.
NO.
SHE STILL HASN'T GOTTEN THE HANG OF THAT.
SHE WAS ONLY EIGHT WHEN THE SPREAD CAME, SO HER CAR REFLEXES ARE A LITTLE ATROPHIED.
ARE YOU OKAY?
MOLLY IS FINE. HOPE IS FINE.
ARE YOU OKAY?

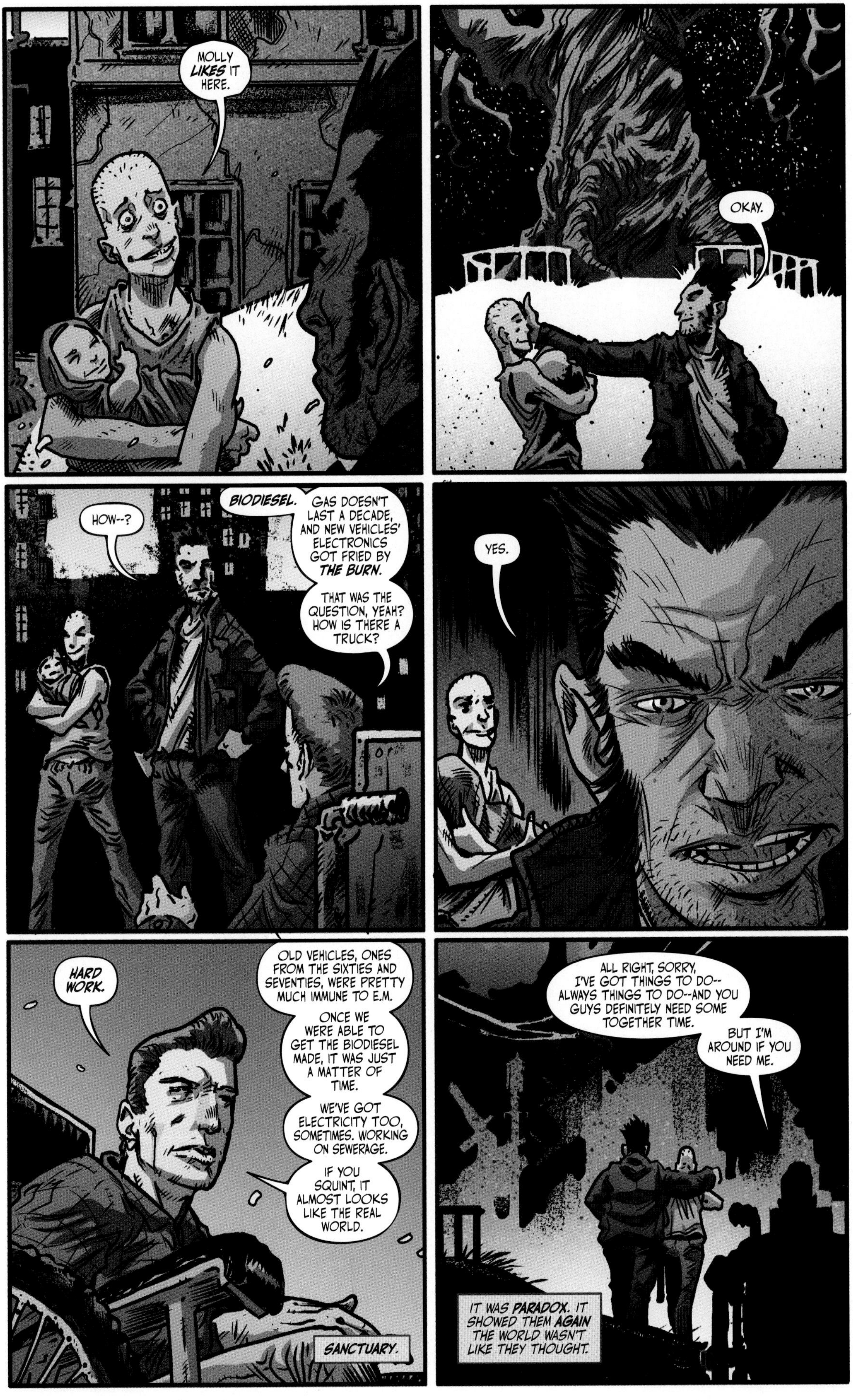
MOLLY LIKES IT HERE.
OKAY.
HOW--?
BIODIESEL.
GAS DOESN'T LAST A DECADE, AND NEW VEHICLES' ELECTRONICS GOT FRIED BY THE BURN.
THAT WAS THE QUESTION, YEAH? HOW IS THERE A TRUCK?
YES.
HARD WORK.
OLD VEHICLES, ONES FROM THE SIXTIES AND SEVENTIES, WERE PRETTY MUCH IMMUNE TO E.M.
ONCE WE WERE ABLE TO GET THE BIODIESEL MADE, IT WAS JUST A MATTER OF TIME.
WE'VE GOT ELECTRICITY TOO, SOMETIMES. WORKING ON SEWERAGE.
IF YOU SQUINT, IT ALMOST LOOKS LIKE THE REAL WORLD.
SANCTUARY.
ALL RIGHT, SORRY, I'VE GOT THINGS TO DO--ALWAYS THINGS TO DO--AND YOU GUYS DEFINITELY NEED SOME TOGETHER TIME.
BUT I'M AROUND IF YOU NEED ME.
IT WAS PARADOX. IT SHOWED THEM AGAIN THE WORLD WASN'T LIKE THEY THOUGHT.

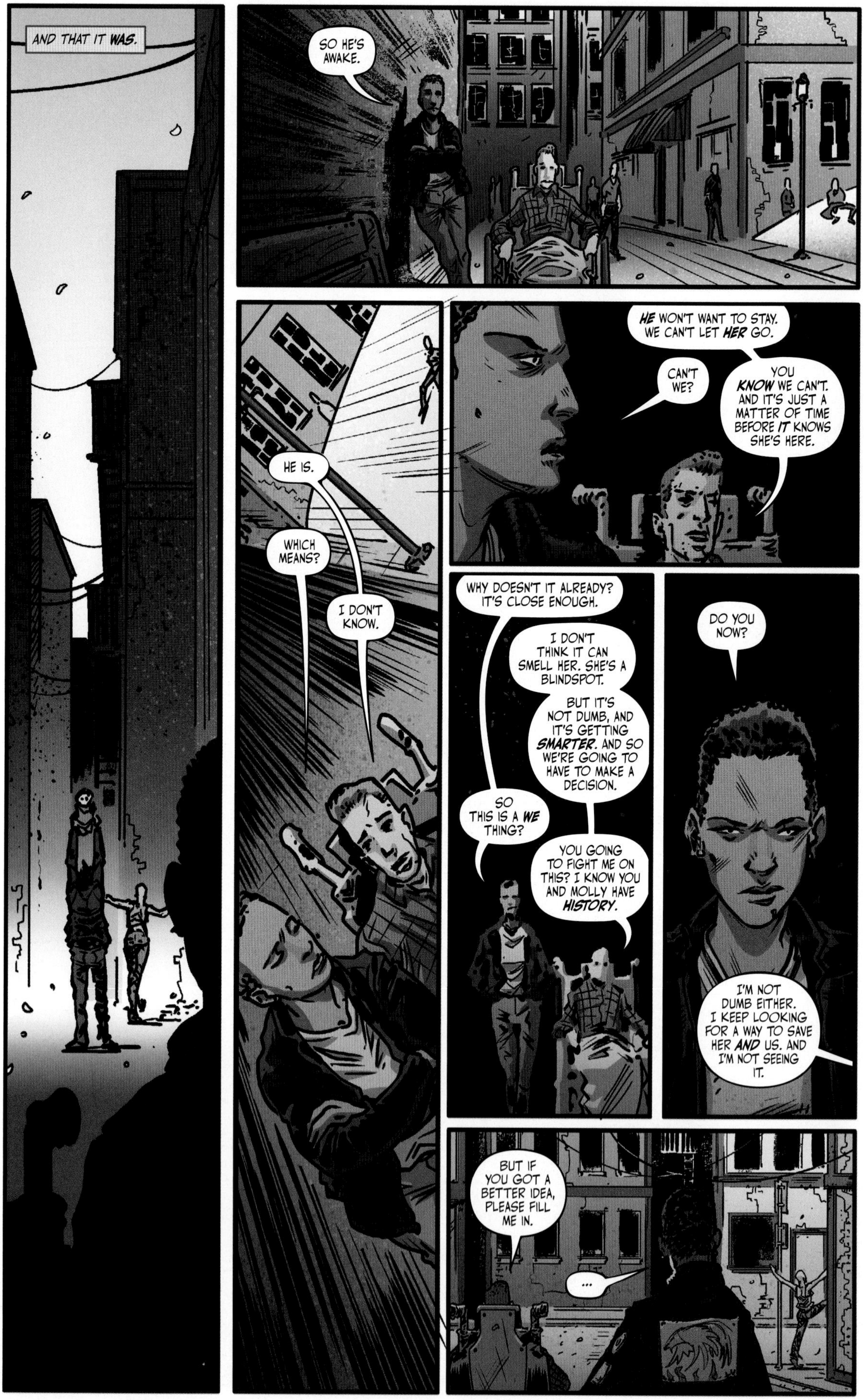
AND THAT IT **WAS**.
SO HE'S AWAKE.
HE IS.
WHICH MEANS?
I DON'T KNOW.
HE WON'T WANT TO STAY. WE CAN'T LET **HER** GO.
CAN'T WE?
YOU **KNOW** WE CAN'T. AND IT'S JUST A MATTER OF TIME BEFORE **IT** KNOWS SHE'S HERE.
WHY DOESN'T IT ALREADY? IT'S CLOSE ENOUGH.
I DON'T THINK IT CAN SMELL HER. SHE'S A BLINDSPOT.
BUT IT'S NOT DUMB, AND IT'S GETTING **SMARTER**. AND SO WE'RE GOING TO HAVE TO MAKE A DECISION.
SO THIS IS A **WE** THING?
YOU GOING TO FIGHT ME ON THIS? I KNOW YOU AND MOLLY HAVE **HISTORY**.
DO YOU NOW?
I'M NOT DUMB EITHER. I KEEP LOOKING FOR A WAY TO SAVE HER **AND** US. AND I'M NOT SEEING IT.
BUT IF YOU GOT A BETTER IDEA, PLEASE FILL ME IN.
...

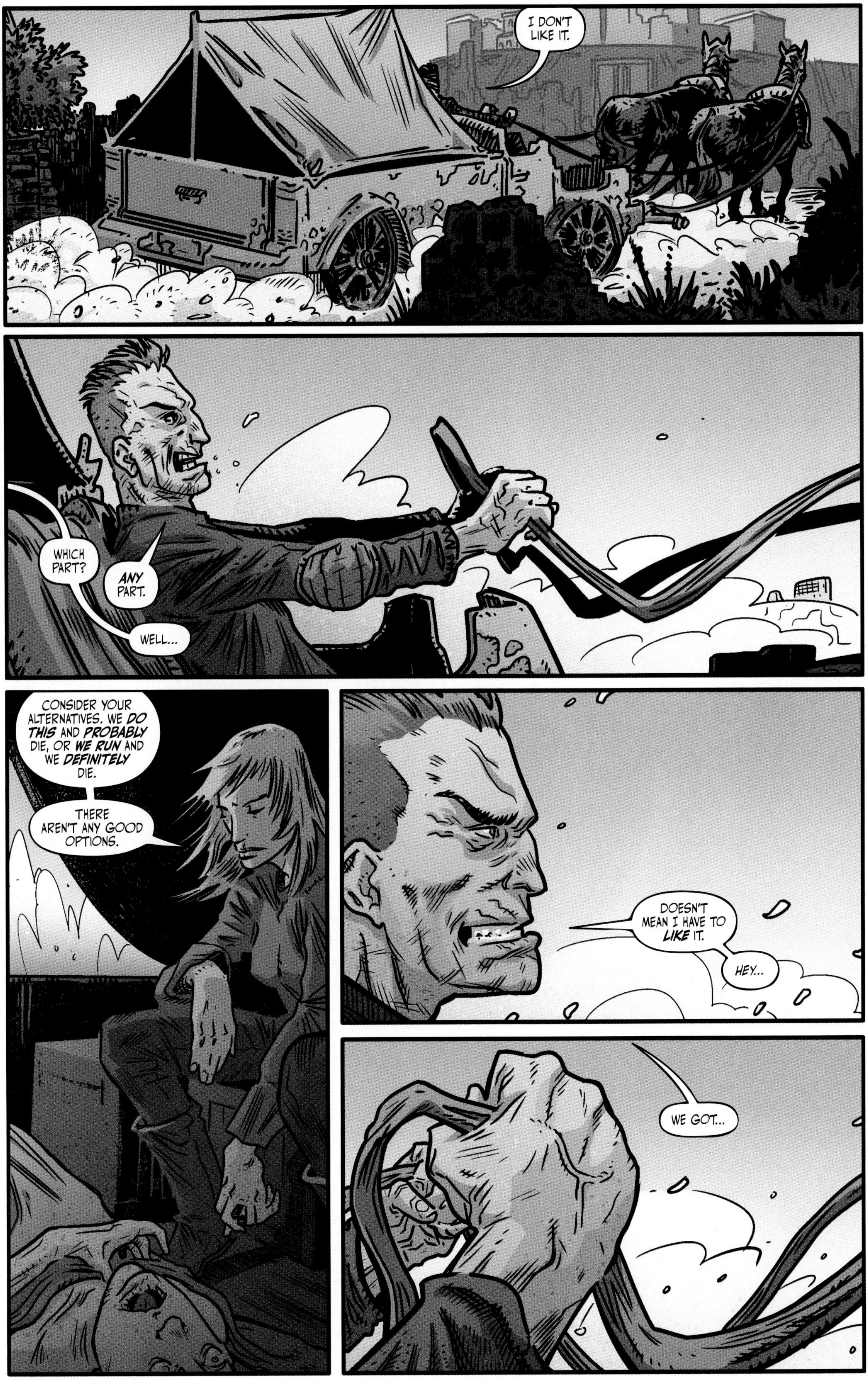
I DON'T LIKE IT.
WHICH PART?
ANY PART.
WELL...
CONSIDER YOUR ALTERNATIVES. WE DO THIS AND PROBABLY DIE, OR WE RUN AND WE DEFINITELY DIE.
THERE AREN'T ANY GOOD OPTIONS.
DOESN'T MEAN I HAVE TO LIKE IT.
HEY...
WE GOT...

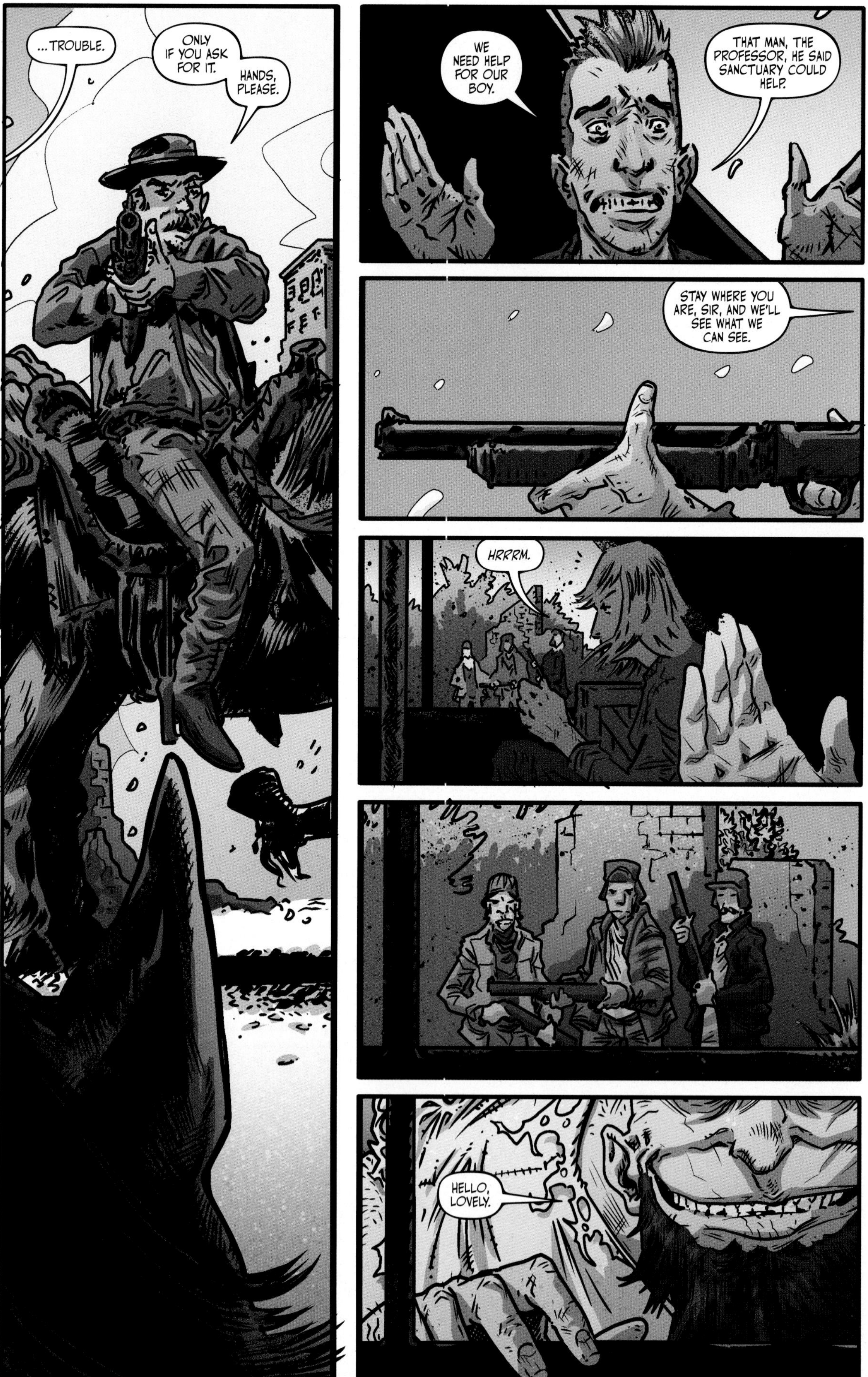
...TROUBLE.
ONLY IF YOU ASK FOR IT.
HANDS, PLEASE.
WE NEED HELP FOR OUR BOY.
THAT MAN, THE PROFESSOR, HE SAID SANCTUARY COULD HELP.
STAY WHERE YOU ARE, SIR, AND WE'LL SEE WHAT WE CAN SEE.
HRRRM.
HELLO, LOVELY.

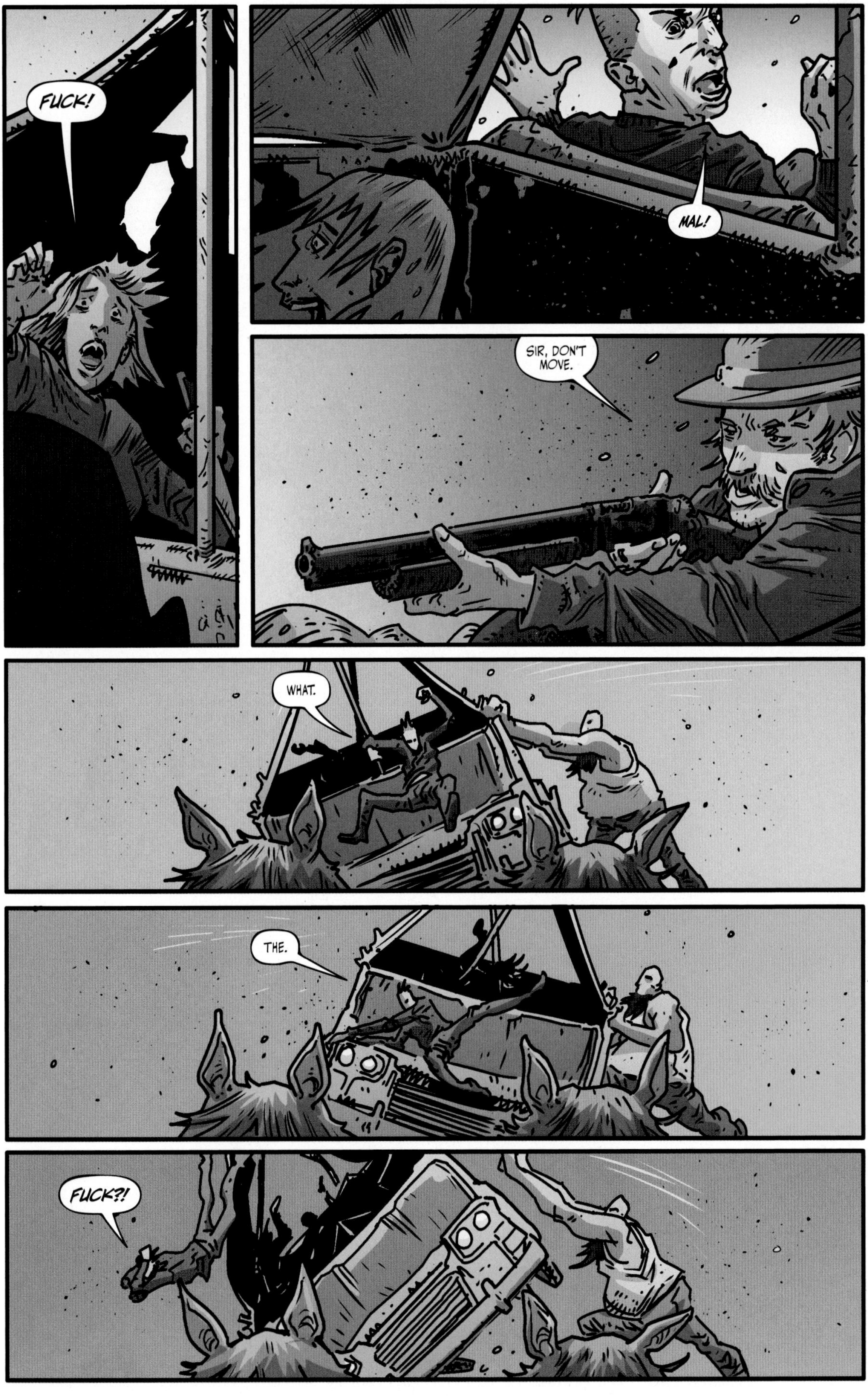
FUCK!
MAL!
SIR, DON'T MOVE.
WHAT.
THE.
FUCK?!

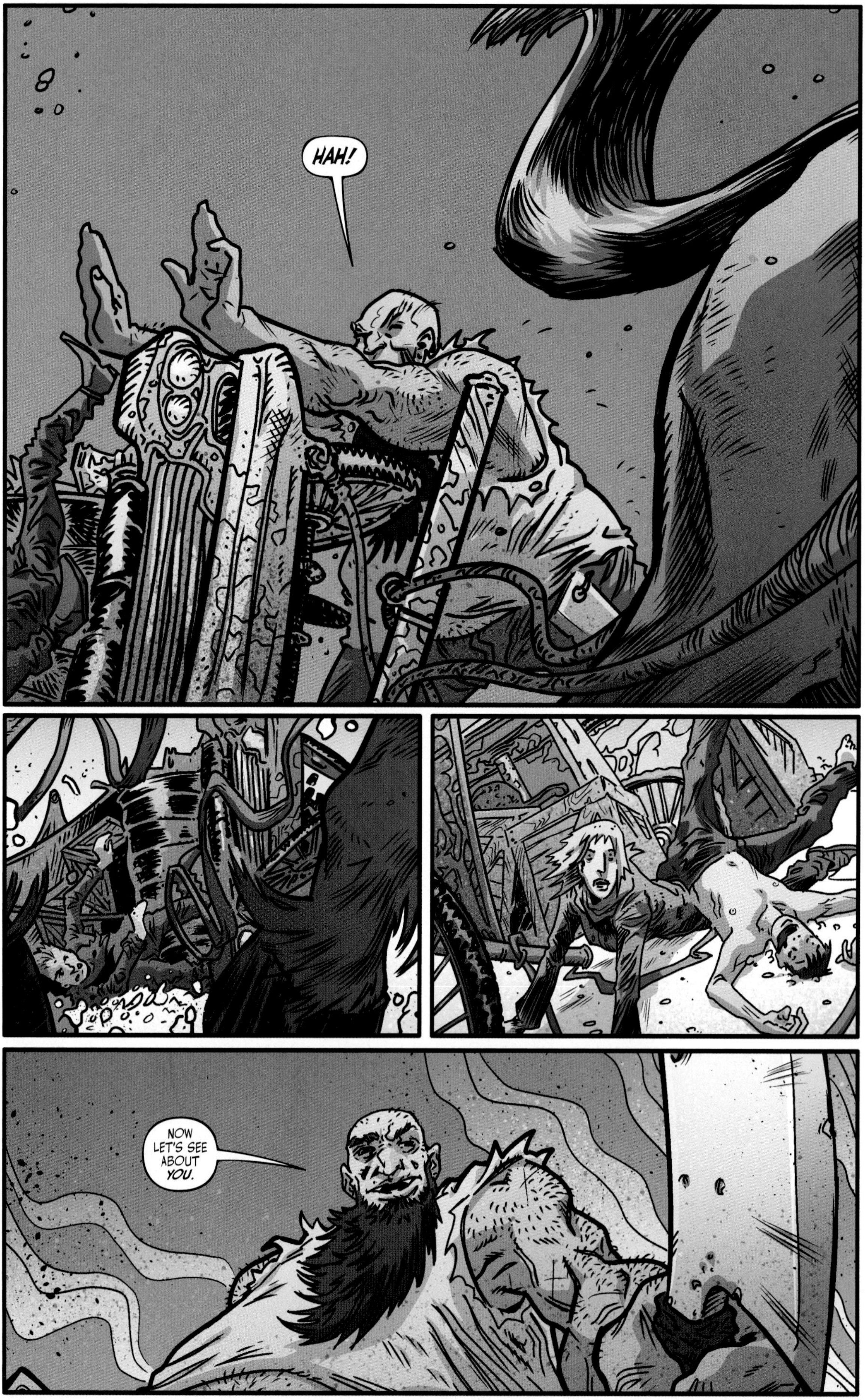
HAH!
NOW LET'S SEE ABOUT YOU.

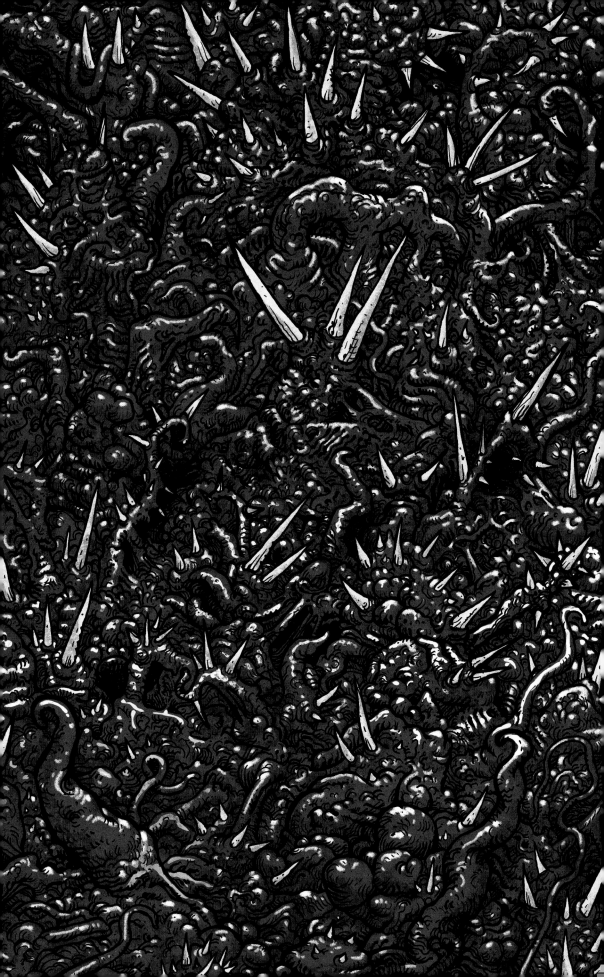

CHAPTER FOUR

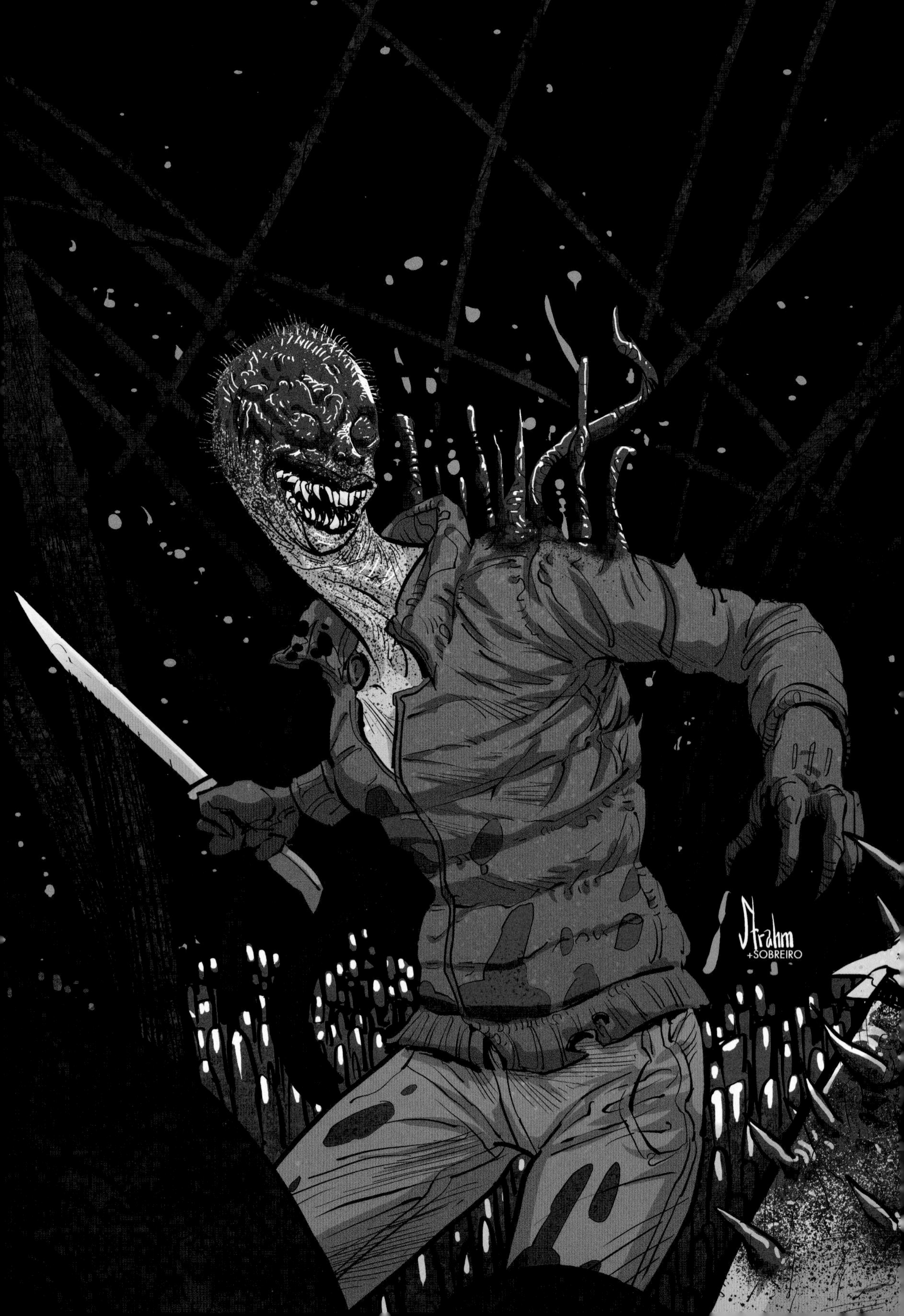
+SOBREIRO

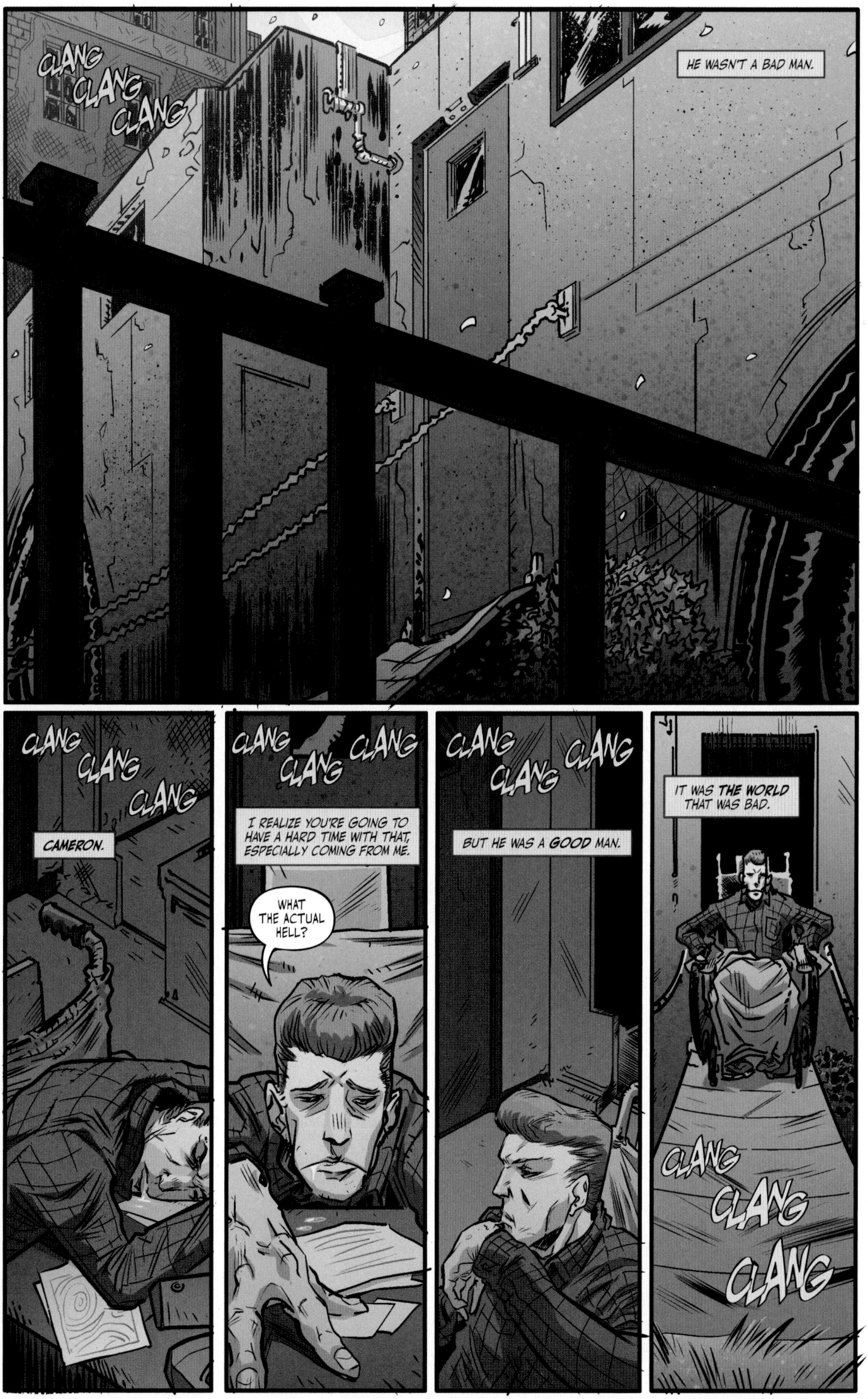
CLANG
CLANG
CLANG
HE WASN'T A BAD MAN.
CLANG
CLANG
CLANG
CAMERON.
CLANG
CLANG
CLANG
I REALIZE YOU'RE GOING TO HAVE A HARD TIME WITH THAT, ESPECIALLY COMING FROM ME.
WHAT THE ACTUAL HELL?
CLANG
CLANG
CLANG
BUT HE WAS A GOOD MAN.
IT WAS THE WORLD THAT WAS BAD.
CLANG
CLANG
CLANG

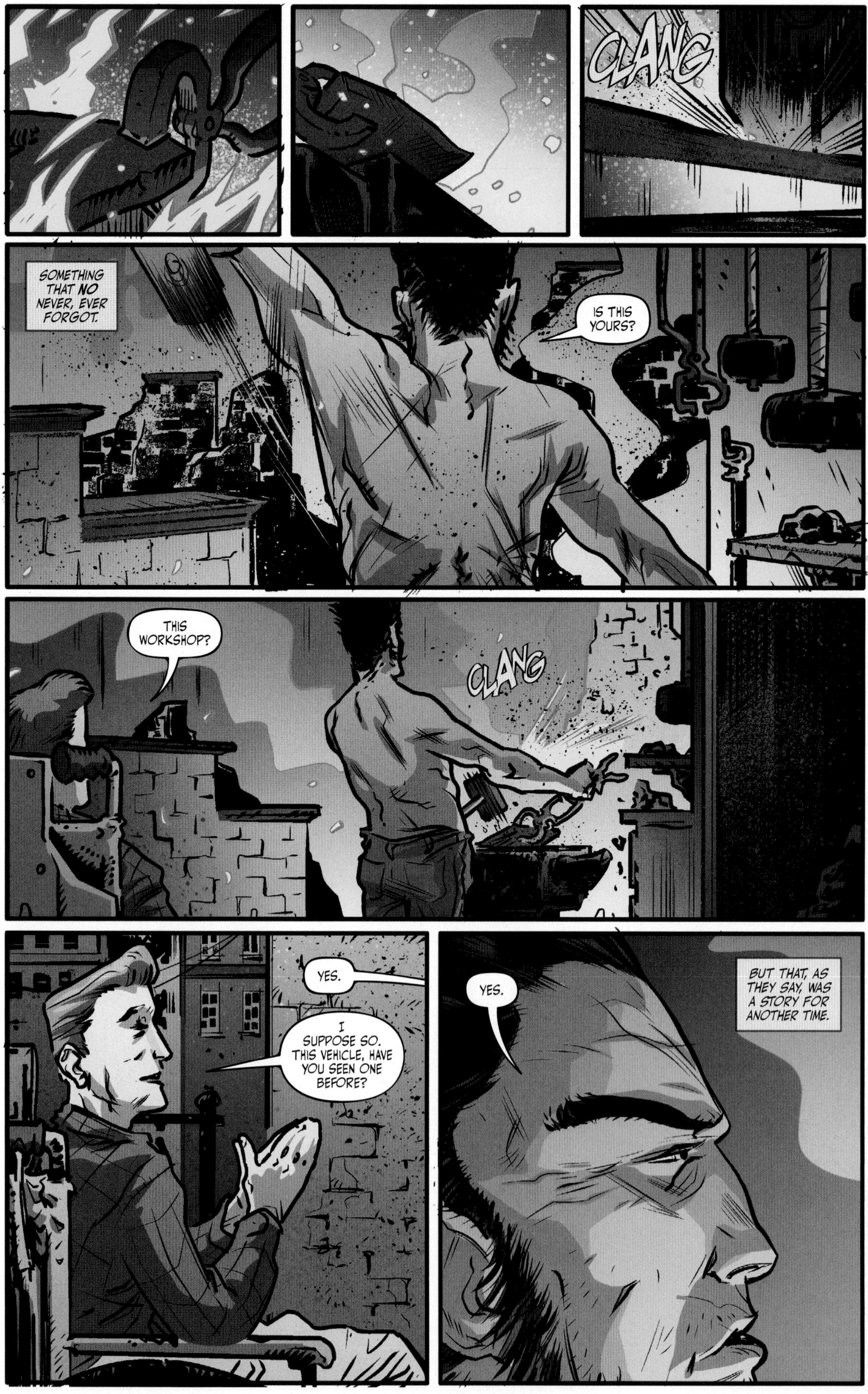
CLANG
SOMETHING THAT NO NEVER, EVER FORGOT.
IS THIS YOURS?
THIS WORKSHOP?
CLANG
YES.
I SUPPOSE SO. THIS VEHICLE, HAVE YOU SEEN ONE BEFORE?
YES.
BUT THAT, AS THEY SAY, WAS A STORY FOR ANOTHER TIME.

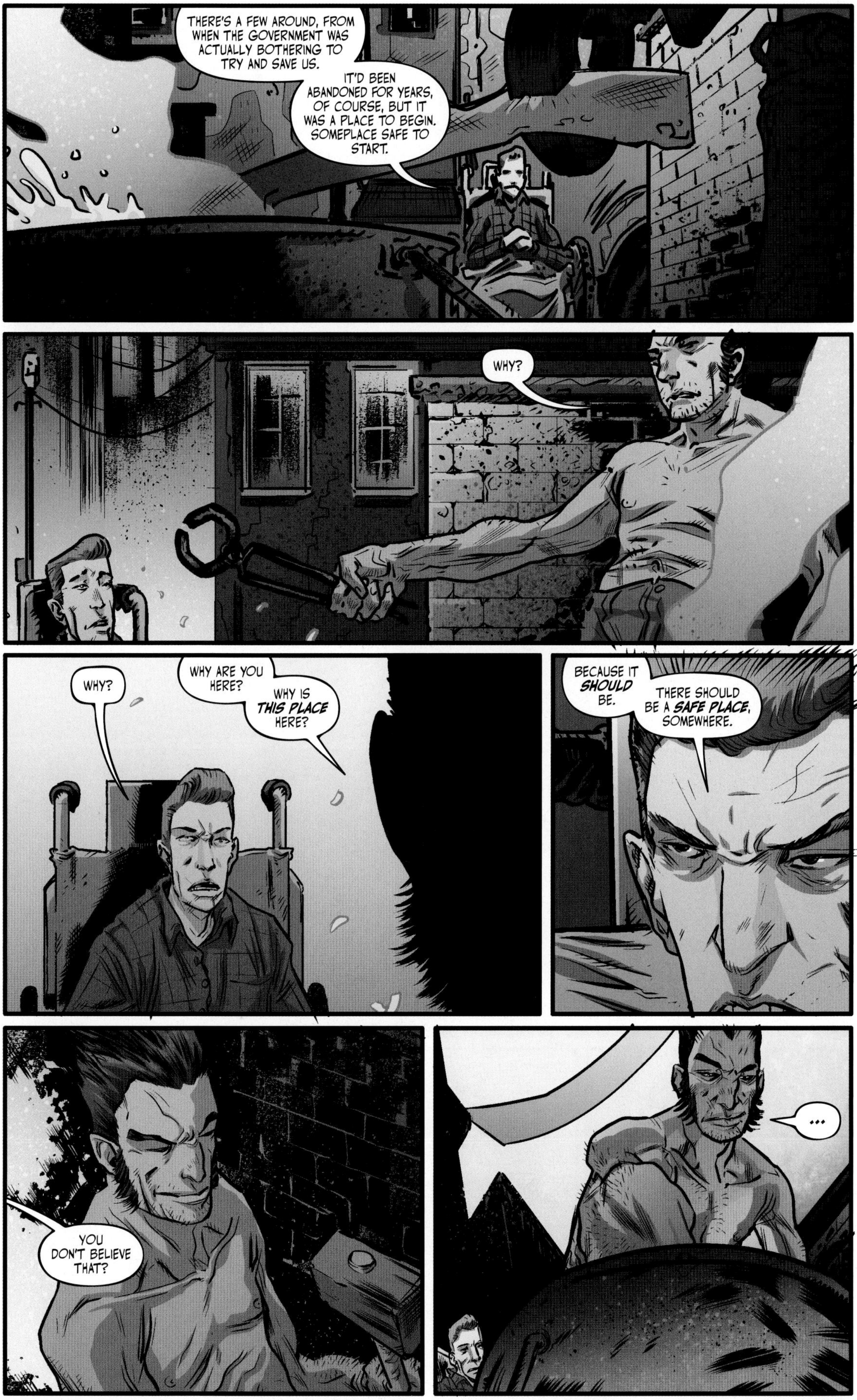
THERE'S A FEW AROUND, FROM WHEN THE GOVERNMENT WAS ACTUALLY BOTHERING TO TRY AND SAVE US.
IT'D BEEN ABANDONED FOR YEARS, OF COURSE, BUT IT WAS A PLACE TO BEGIN. SOMEPLACE SAFE TO START.
WHY?
WHY?
WHY ARE YOU HERE?
WHY IS THIS PLACE HERE?
BECAUSE IT SHOULD BE.
THERE SHOULD BE A SAFE PLACE, SOMEWHERE.
YOU DON'T BELIEVE THAT?
...

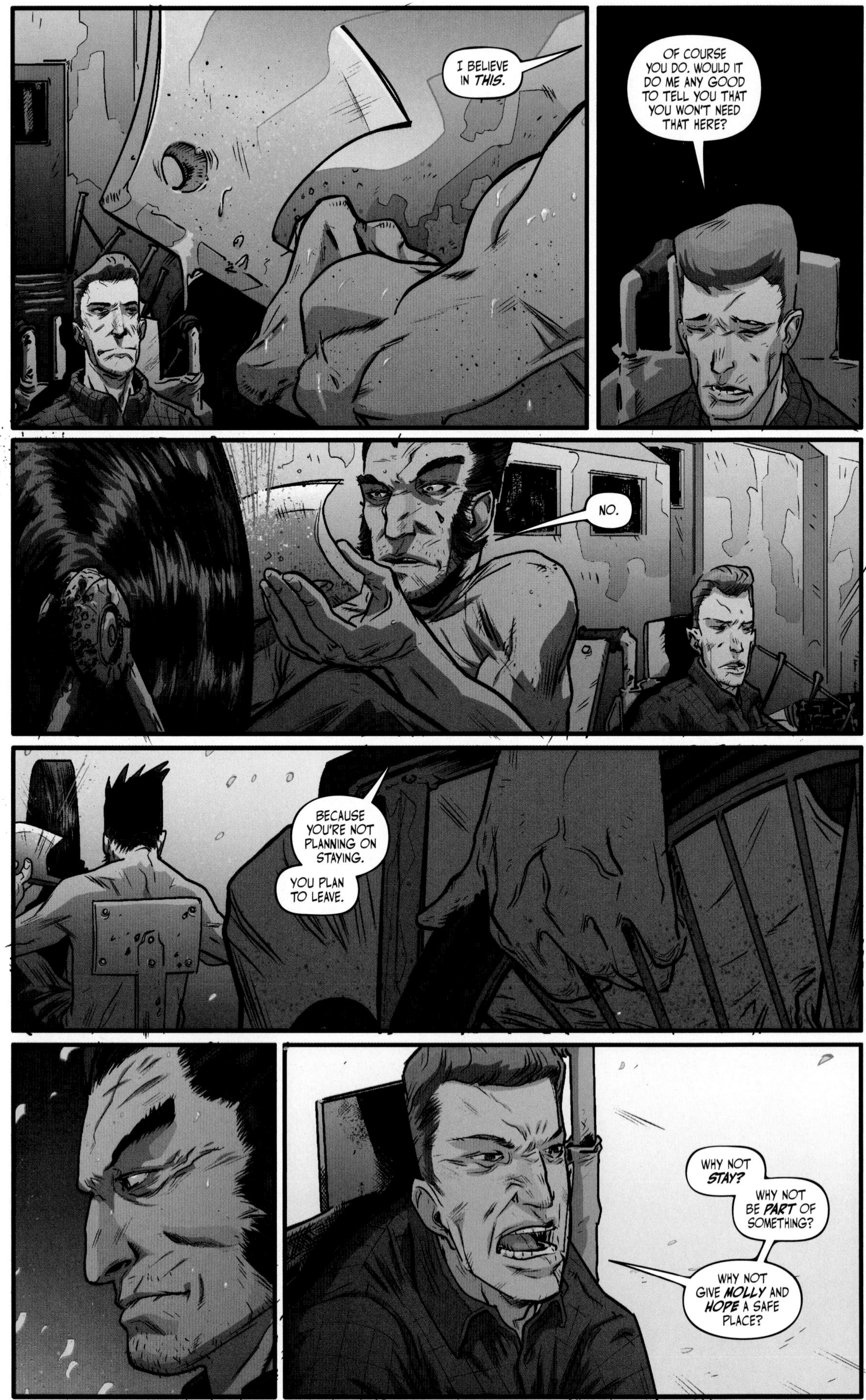
I BELIEVE IN THIS.
OF COURSE YOU DO. WOULD IT DO ME ANY GOOD TO TELL YOU THAT YOU WON'T NEED THAT HERE?
NO.
BECAUSE YOU'RE NOT PLANNING ON STAYING.
YOU PLAN TO LEAVE.
WHY NOT STAY?
WHY NOT BE PART OF SOMETHING?
WHY NOT GIVE MOLLY AND HOPE A SAFE PLACE?

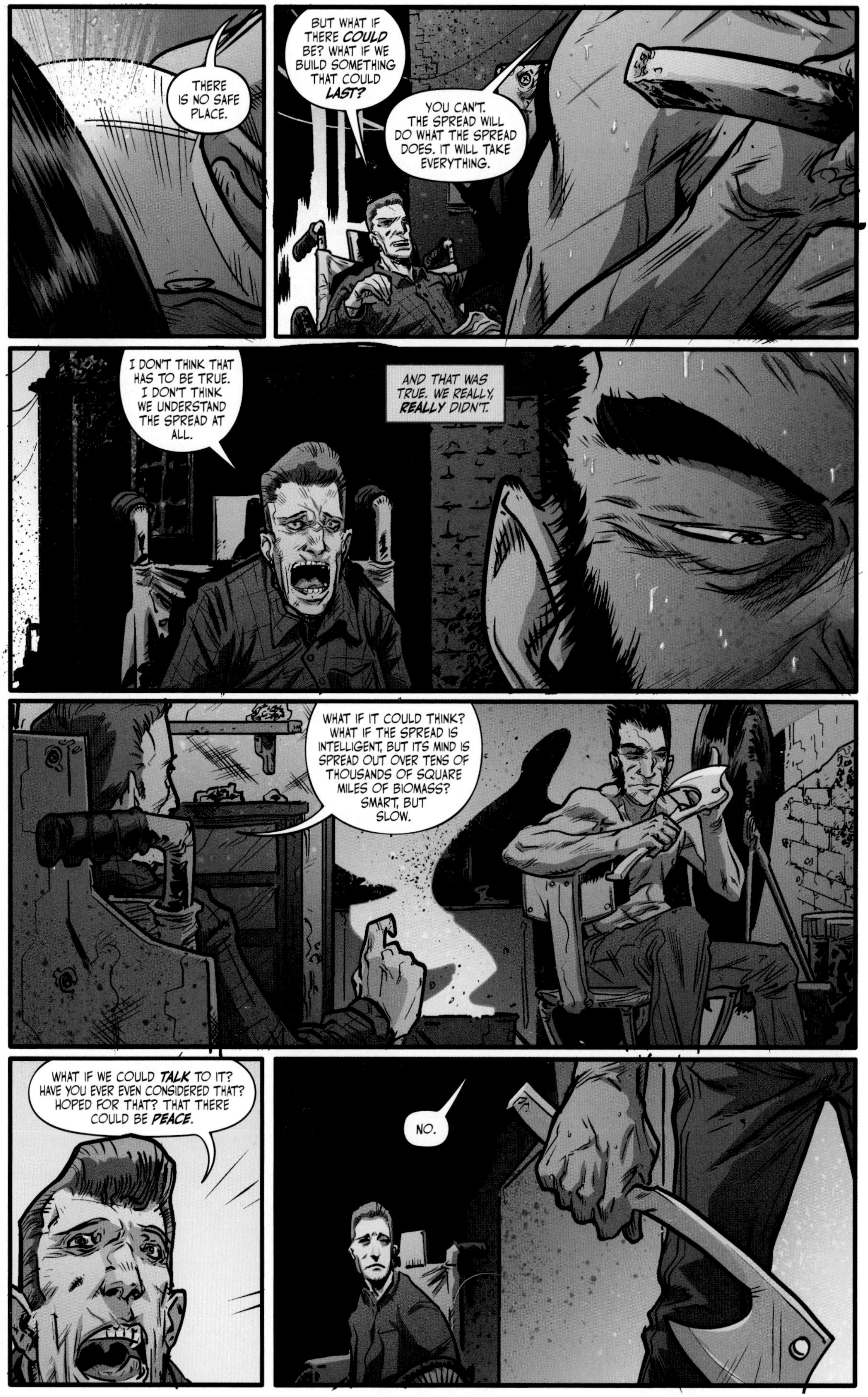
THERE IS NO SAFE PLACE.
BUT WHAT IF THERE COULD BE? WHAT IF WE BUILD SOMETHING THAT COULD LAST?
YOU CAN'T. THE SPREAD WILL DO WHAT THE SPREAD DOES. IT WILL TAKE EVERYTHING.
I DON'T THINK THAT HAS TO BE TRUE. I DON'T THINK WE UNDERSTAND THE SPREAD AT ALL.
AND THAT WAS TRUE. WE REALLY, REALLY DIDN'T.
WHAT IF IT COULD THINK? WHAT IF THE SPREAD IS INTELLIGENT, BUT ITS MIND IS SPREAD OUT OVER TENS OF THOUSANDS OF SQUARE MILES OF BIOMASS? SMART, BUT SLOW.
WHAT IF WE COULD TALK TO IT? HAVE YOU EVER EVEN CONSIDERED THAT? HOPED FOR THAT? THAT THERE COULD BE PEACE.
NO.

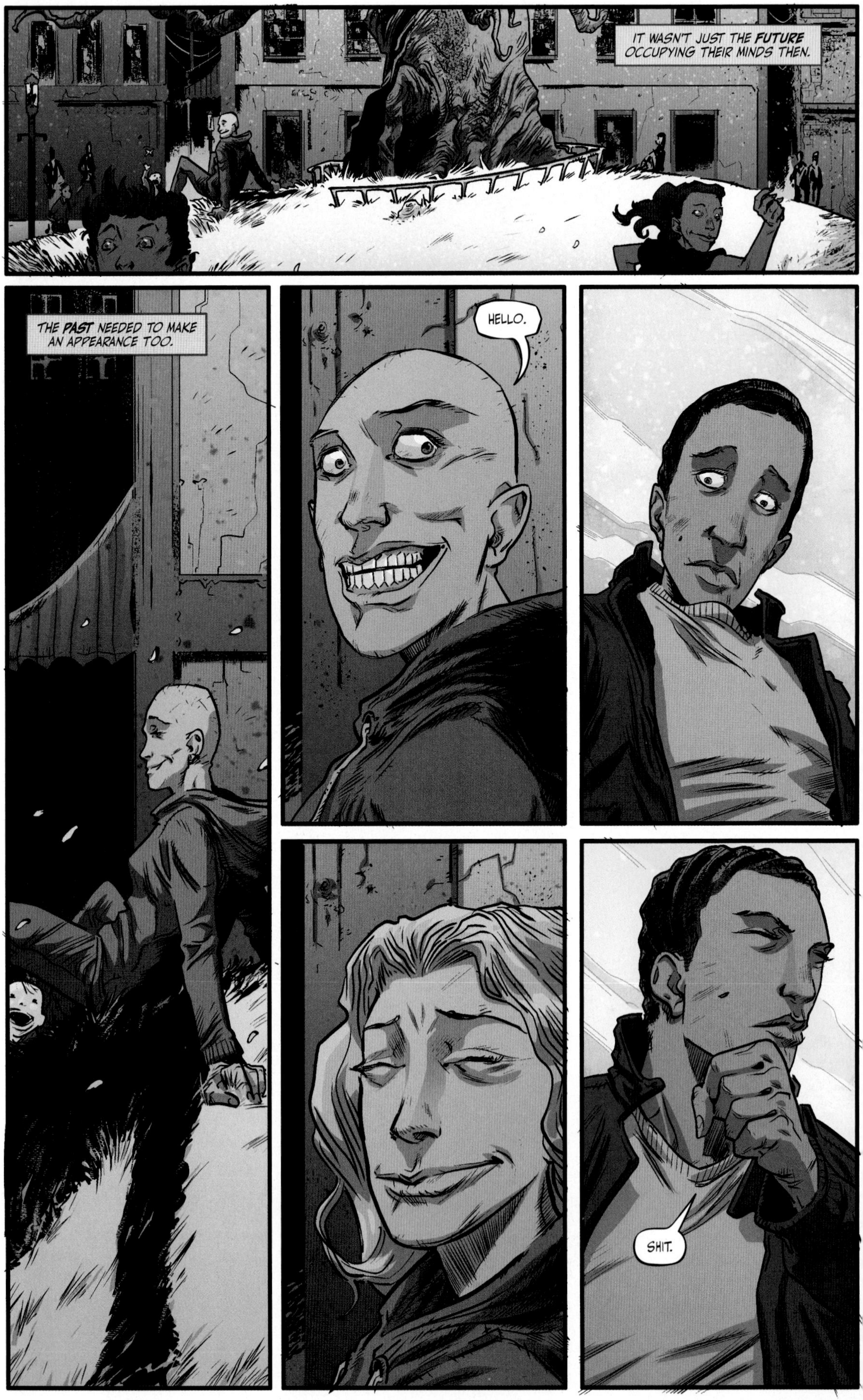
IT WASN'T JUST THE FUTURE OCCUPYING THEIR MINDS THEN.
THE PAST NEEDED TO MAKE AN APPEARANCE TOO.
HELLO.
SHIT.

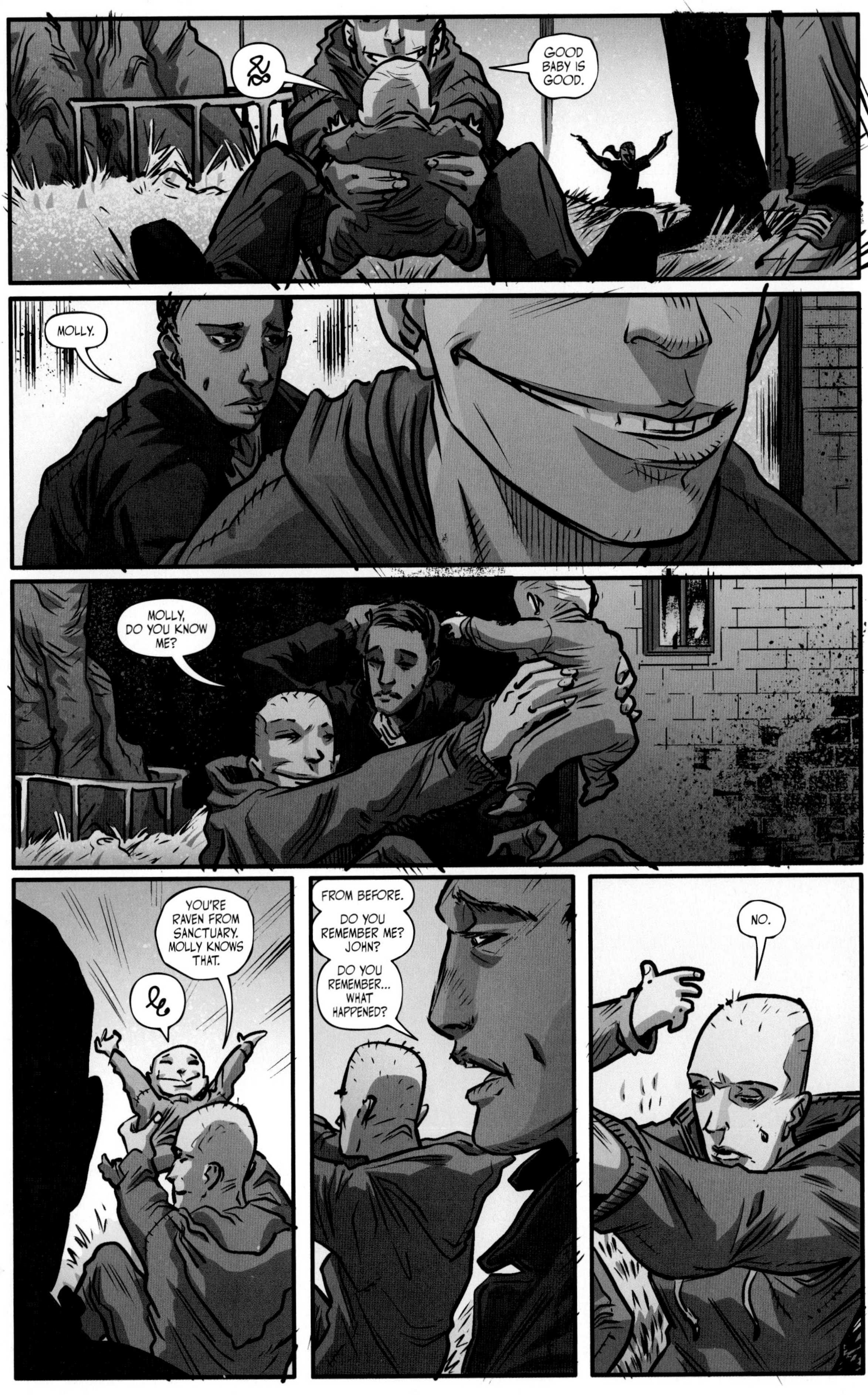
GOOD BABY IS GOOD.
MOLLY.
MOLLY, DO YOU KNOW ME?
YOU'RE RAVEN FROM SANCTUARY. MOLLY KNOWS THAT.
FROM BEFORE.
DO YOU REMEMBER ME? JOHN?
DO YOU REMEMBER... WHAT HAPPENED?
NO.

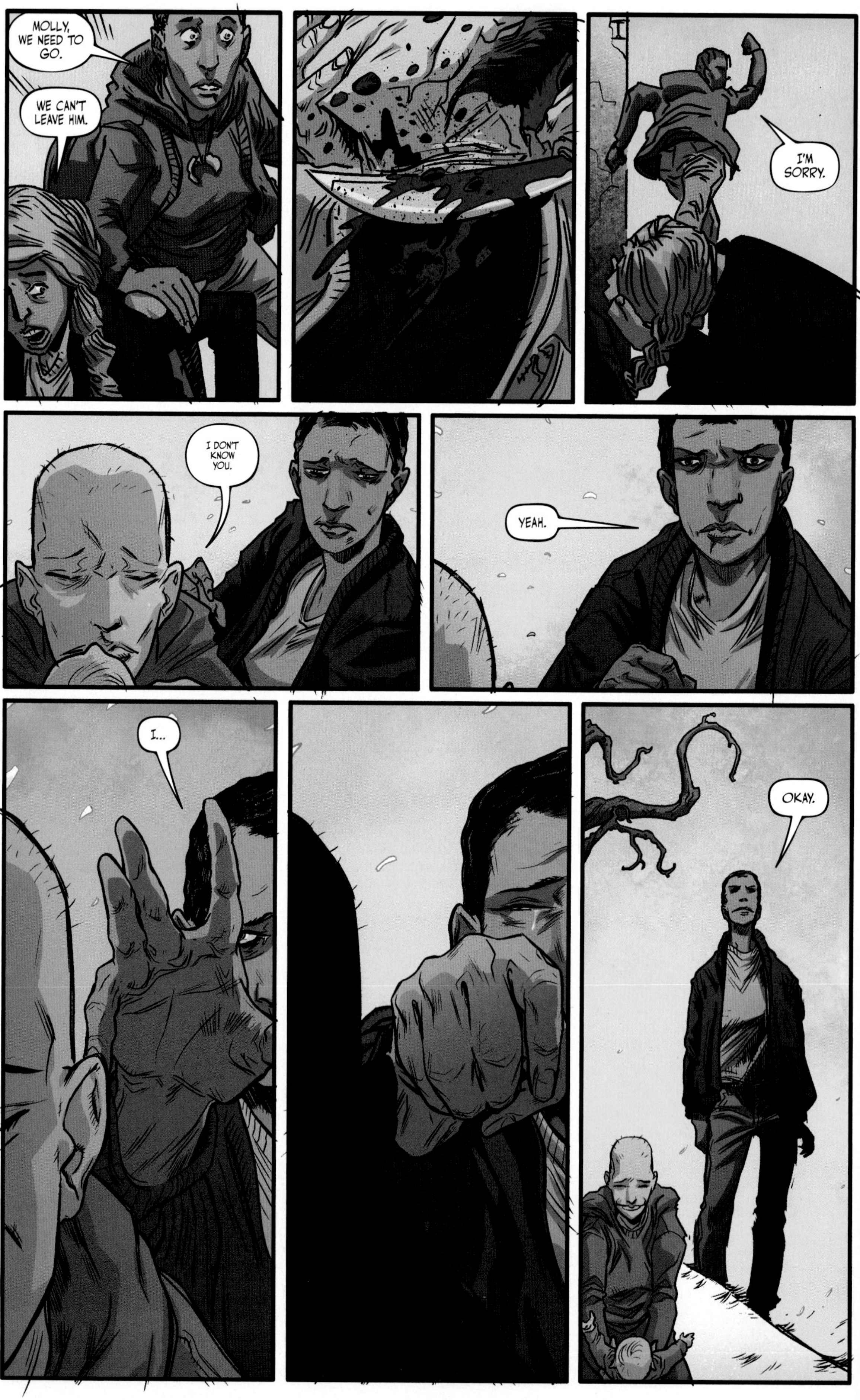
MOLLY, WE NEED TO GO.
WE CAN'T LEAVE HIM.
I'M SORRY.
I DON'T KNOW YOU.
YEAH.
I...
OKAY.

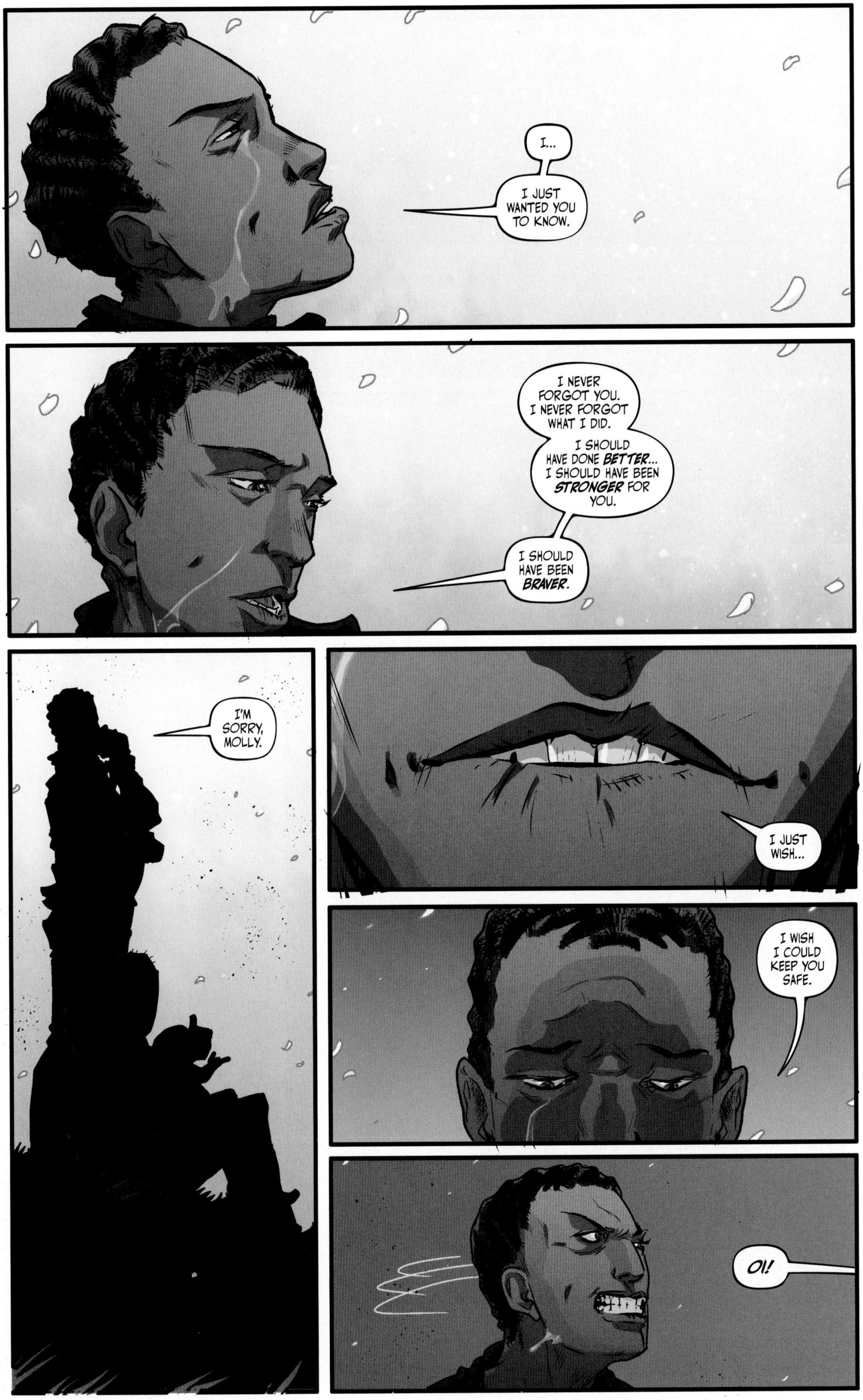
I...
I JUST WANTED YOU TO KNOW.
I NEVER FORGOT YOU. I NEVER FORGOT WHAT I DID.
I SHOULD HAVE DONE BETTER... I SHOULD HAVE BEEN STRONGER FOR YOU.
I SHOULD HAVE BEEN BRAVER.
I'M SORRY, MOLLY.
I JUST WISH...
I WISH I COULD KEEP YOU SAFE.
OI!

FRESH MEAT!
WHAT ARE YOU DOING, JACK?
=UFFFH=
MY JOB, I FEEL FAIRLY SURE. IS THIS NOT WHAT YOU WANTED ME TO DO WHEN YOU ASKED ME TO GO OUTSIDE AND GUARD YOUR PRECIOUS PLACE?
I DON'T BELIEVE IT WAS A REQUEST.
AH, WELL--
AND IN CASE YOU FORGOT, YOU WEREN'T TO BRING THEM THROUGH THE DOOR TRUSSED UP LIKE CHRISTMAS HAMS.

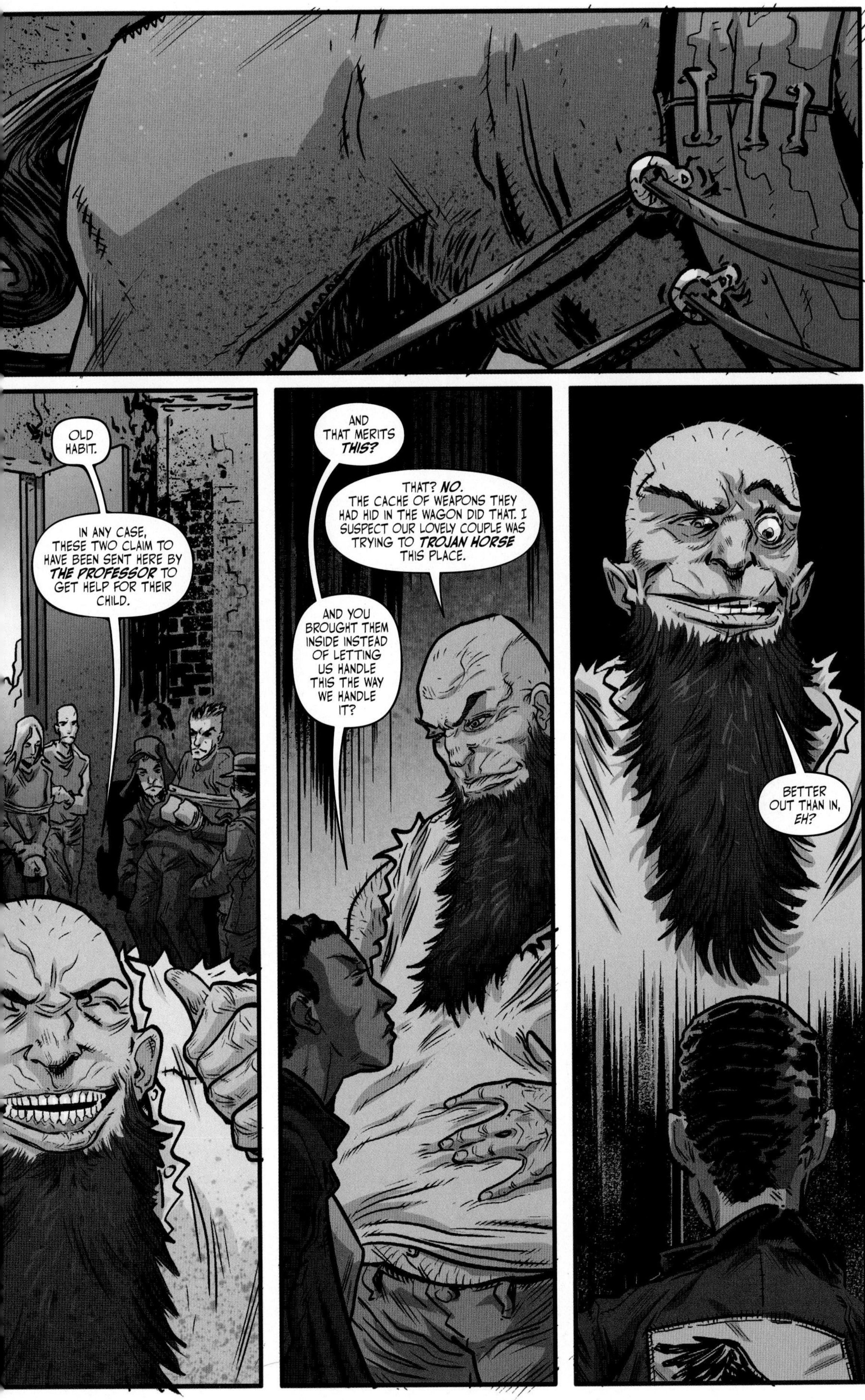
OLD HABIT.
IN ANY CASE, THESE TWO CLAIM TO HAVE BEEN SENT HERE BY THE PROFESSOR TO GET HELP FOR THEIR CHILD.
AND THAT MERITS THIS?
THAT? NO. THE CACHE OF WEAPONS THEY HAD HID IN THE WAGON DID THAT. I SUSPECT OUR LOVELY COUPLE WAS TRYING TO TROJAN HORSE THIS PLACE.
AND YOU BROUGHT THEM INSIDE INSTEAD OF LETTING US HANDLE THIS THE WAY WE HANDLE IT?
BETTER OUT THAN IN, EH?

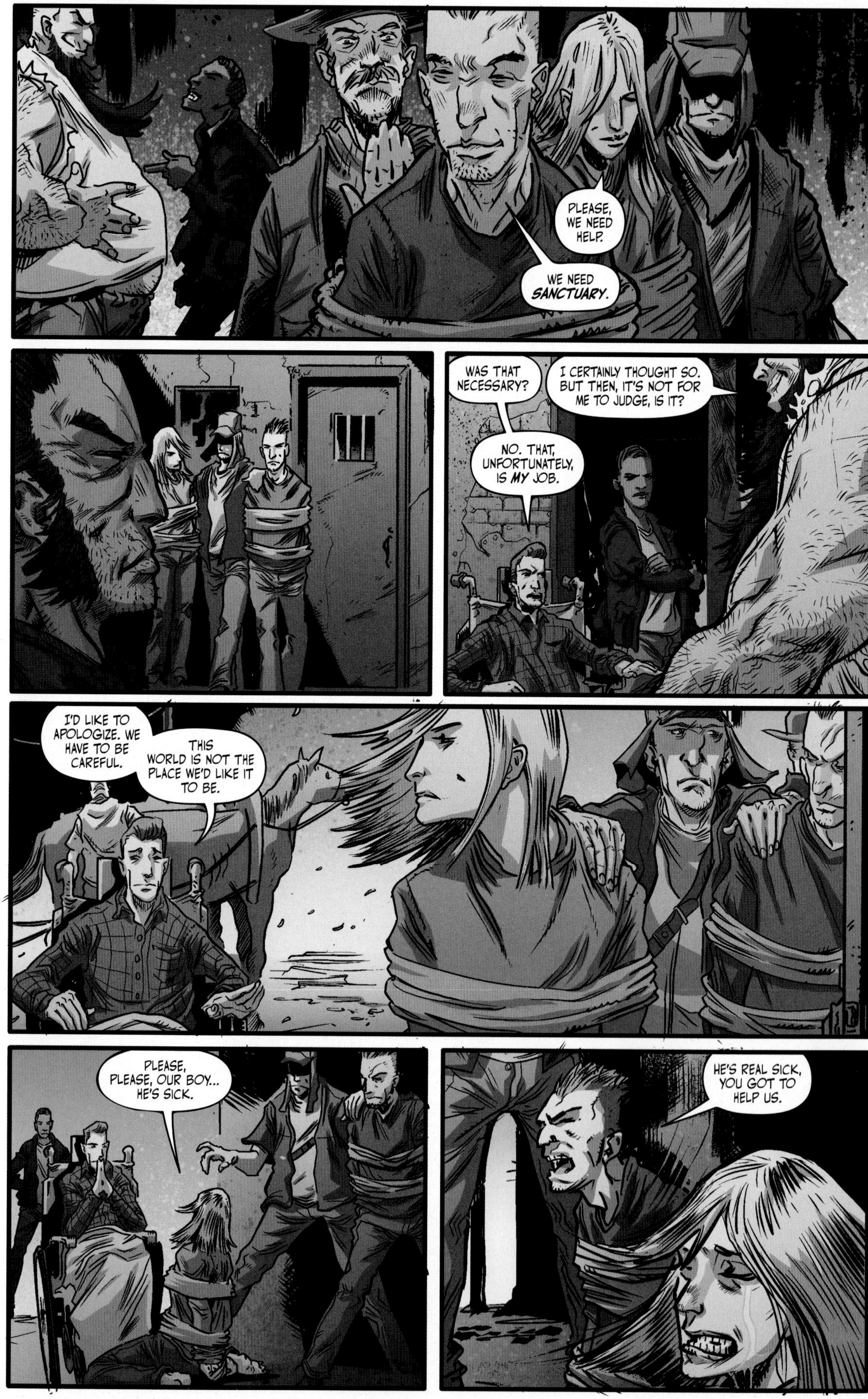
PLEASE, WE NEED HELP.
WE NEED **SANCTUARY**.
WAS THAT NECESSARY?
I CERTAINLY THOUGHT SO. BUT THEN, IT'S NOT FOR ME TO JUDGE, IS IT?
NO. THAT, UNFORTUNATELY, IS **MY** JOB.
I'D LIKE TO APOLOGIZE. WE HAVE TO BE CAREFUL.
THIS WORLD IS NOT THE PLACE WE'D LIKE IT TO BE.
PLEASE, PLEASE, OUR BOY... HE'S SICK.
HE'S REAL SICK, YOU GOT TO HELP US.

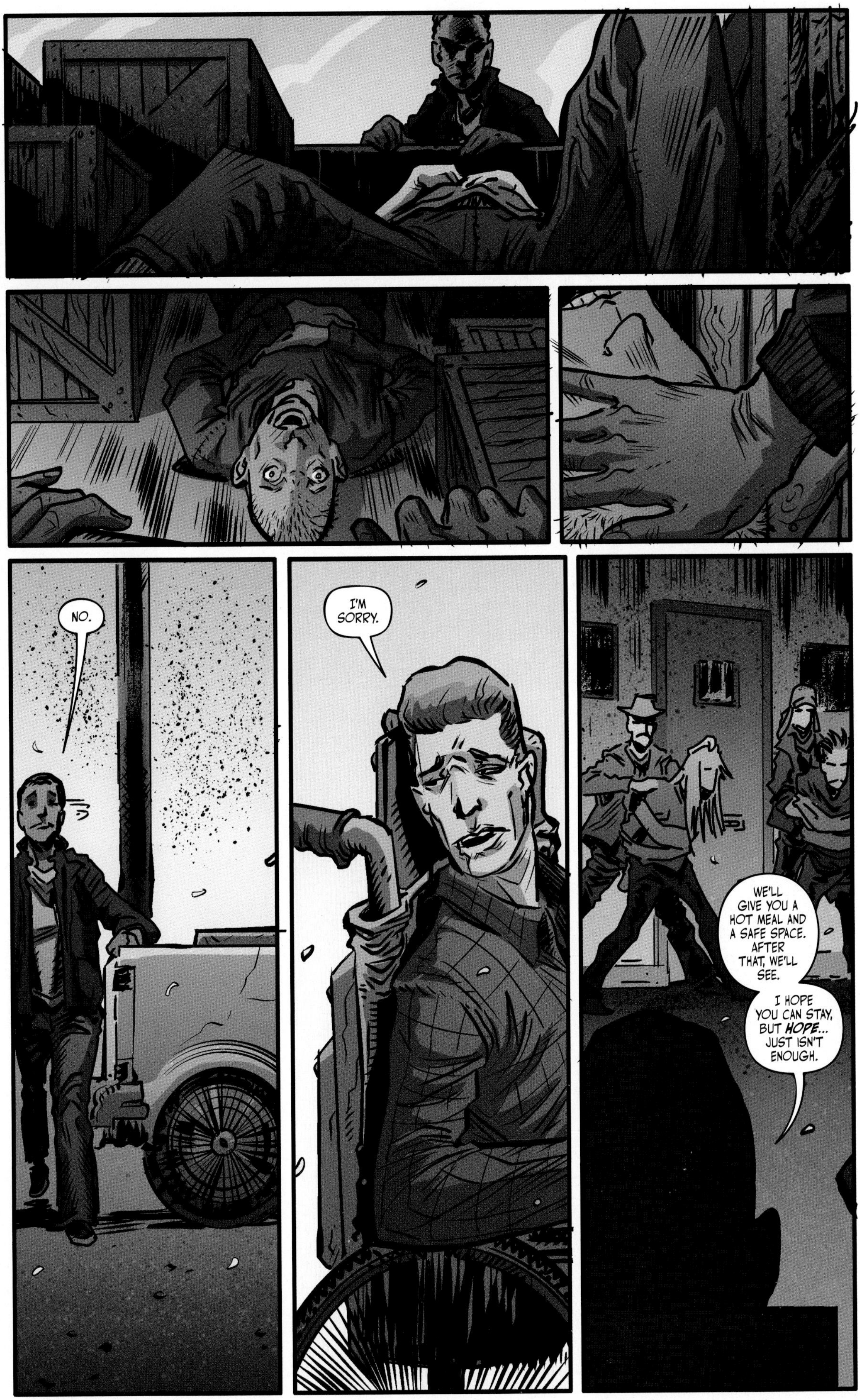
NO.
I'M SORRY.
WE'LL GIVE YOU A HOT MEAL AND A SAFE SPACE. AFTER THAT, WE'LL SEE.
I HOPE YOU CAN STAY, BUT HOPE... JUST ISN'T ENOUGH.

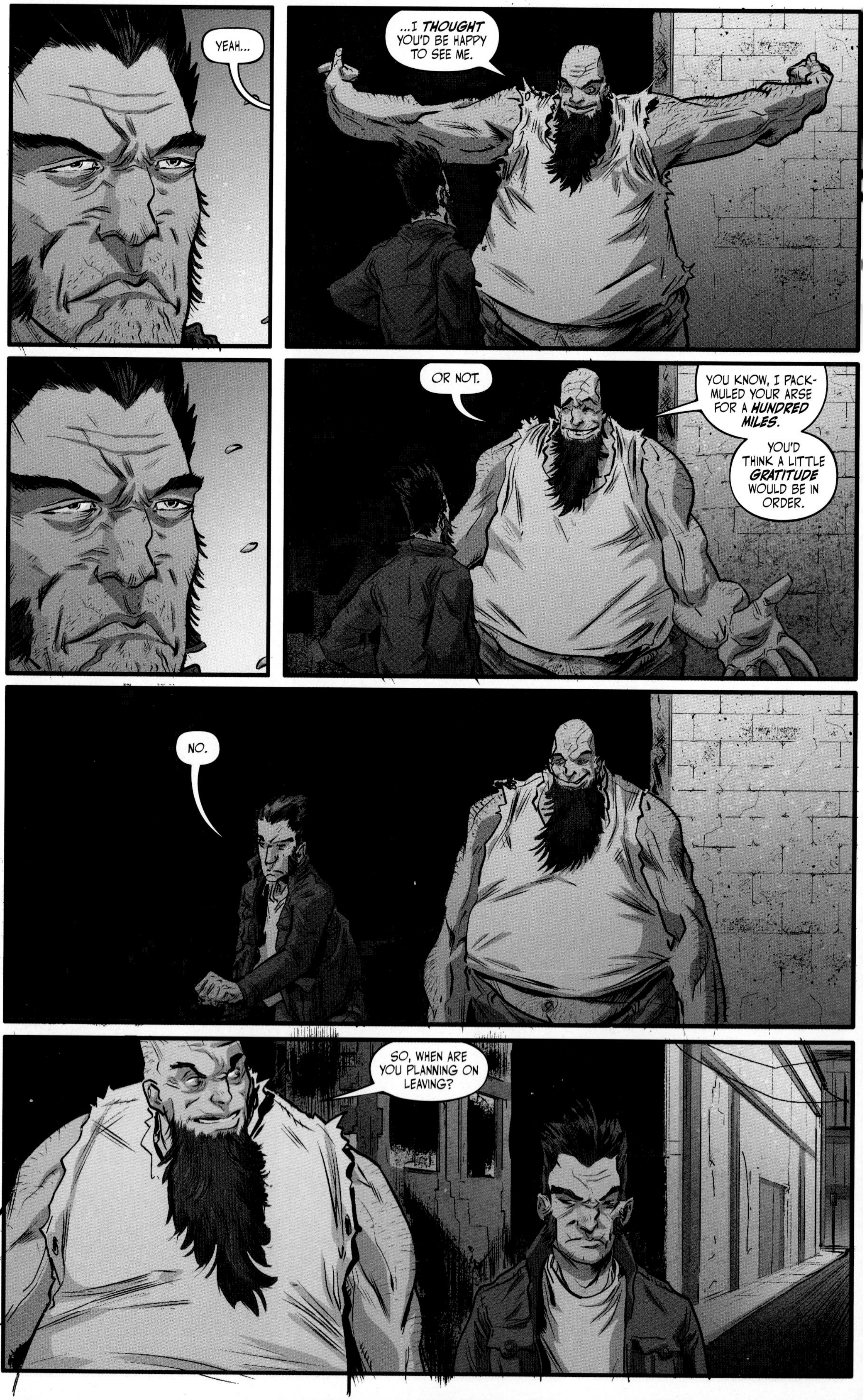
YEAH...
...I THOUGHT YOU'D BE HAPPY TO SEE ME.
OR NOT.
YOU KNOW, I PACK-MULED YOUR ARSE FOR A HUNDRED MILES.
YOU'D THINK A LITTLE GRATITUDE WOULD BE IN ORDER.
NO.
SO, WHEN ARE YOU PLANNING ON LEAVING?

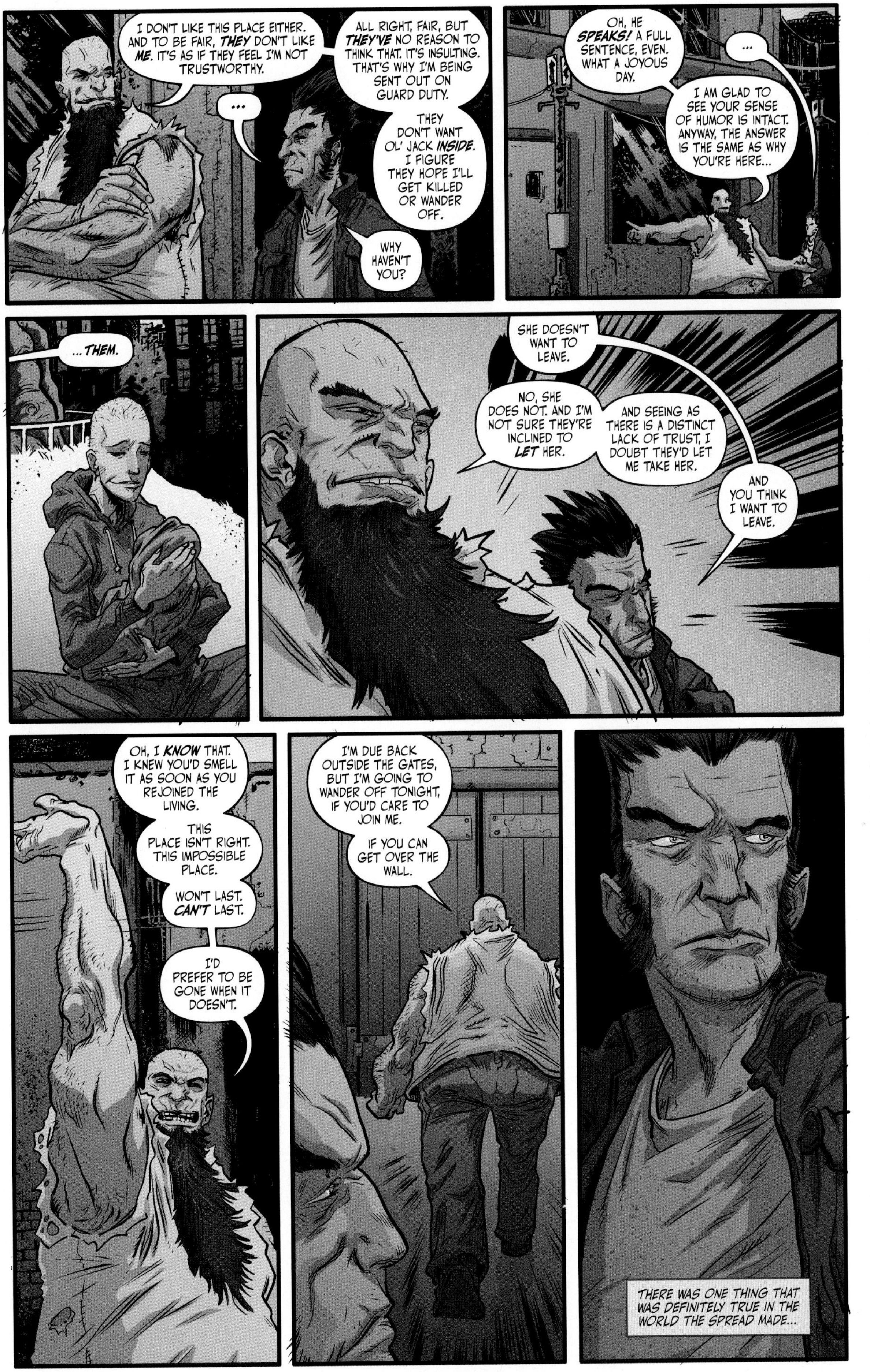
I DON'T LIKE THIS PLACE EITHER. AND TO BE FAIR, THEY DON'T LIKE ME. IT'S AS IF THEY FEEL I'M NOT TRUSTWORTHY.
...
ALL RIGHT, FAIR, BUT THEY'VE NO REASON TO THINK THAT. IT'S INSULTING. THAT'S WHY I'M BEING SENT OUT ON GUARD DUTY.
THEY DON'T WANT OL' JACK INSIDE. I FIGURE THEY HOPE I'LL GET KILLED OR WANDER OFF.
WHY HAVEN'T YOU?
OH, HE SPEAKS! A FULL SENTENCE, EVEN. WHAT A JOYOUS DAY.
...
I AM GLAD TO SEE YOUR SENSE OF HUMOR IS INTACT. ANYWAY, THE ANSWER IS THE SAME AS WHY YOU'RE HERE...
...THEM.
SHE DOESN'T WANT TO LEAVE.
NO, SHE DOES NOT. AND I'M NOT SURE THEY'RE INCLINED TO LET HER.
AND SEEING AS THERE IS A DISTINCT LACK OF TRUST, I DOUBT THEY'D LET ME TAKE HER.
AND YOU THINK I WANT TO LEAVE.
OH, I KNOW THAT. I KNEW YOU'D SMELL IT AS SOON AS YOU REJOINED THE LIVING.
THIS PLACE ISN'T RIGHT. THIS IMPOSSIBLE PLACE.
WON'T LAST. CAN'T LAST.
I'D PREFER TO BE GONE WHEN IT DOESN'T.
I'M DUE BACK OUTSIDE THE GATES, BUT I'M GOING TO WANDER OFF TONIGHT, IF YOU'D CARE TO JOIN ME.
IF YOU CAN GET OVER THE WALL.
THERE WAS ONE THING THAT WAS DEFINITELY TRUE IN THE WORLD THE SPREAD MADE...

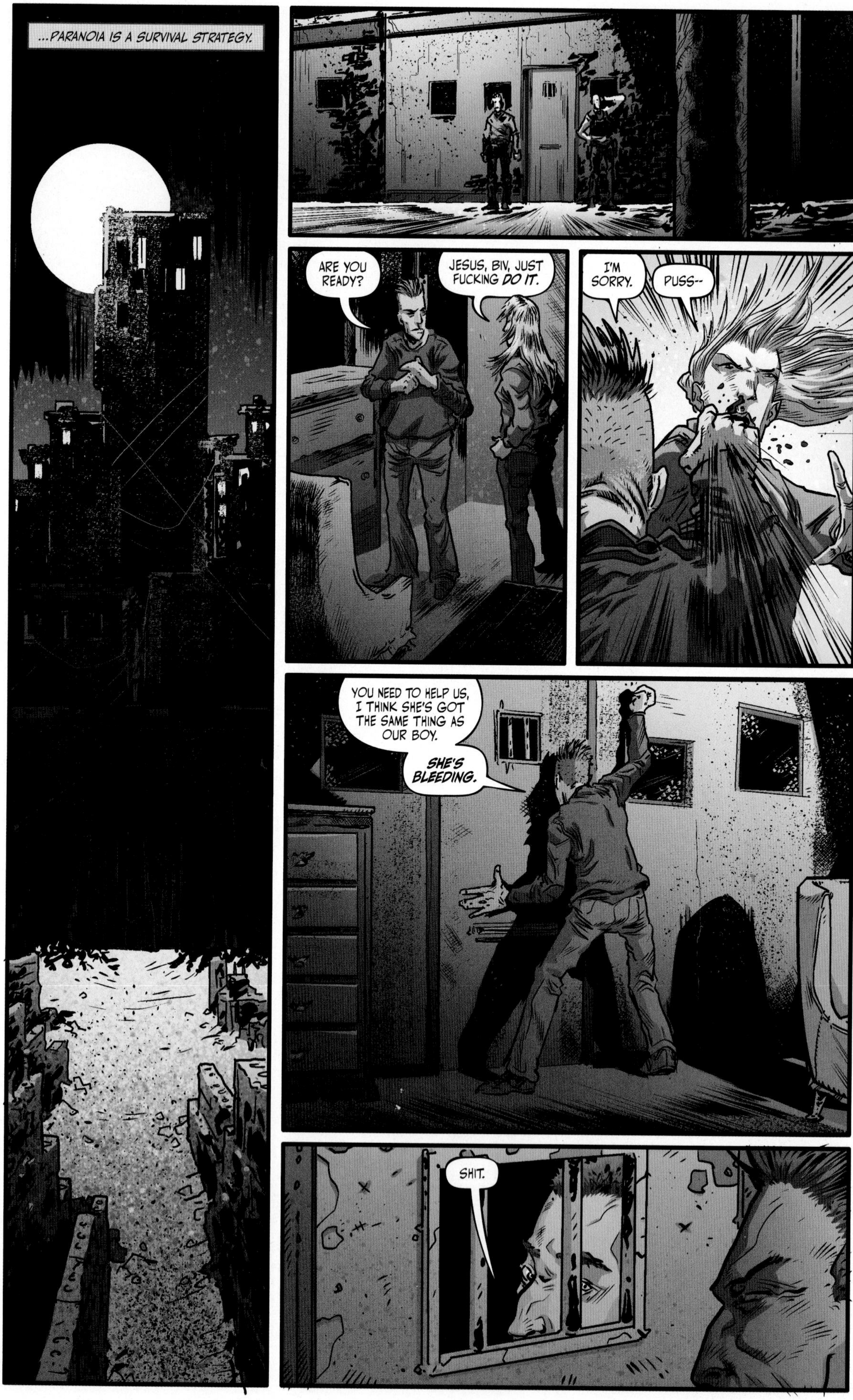
...PARANOIA IS A SURVIVAL STRATEGY.
ARE YOU READY?
JESUS, BIV, JUST FUCKING DO IT.
I'M SORRY.
PUSS--
YOU NEED TO HELP US, I THINK SHE'S GOT THE SAME THING AS OUR BOY.
SHE'S BLEEDING.
SHIT.

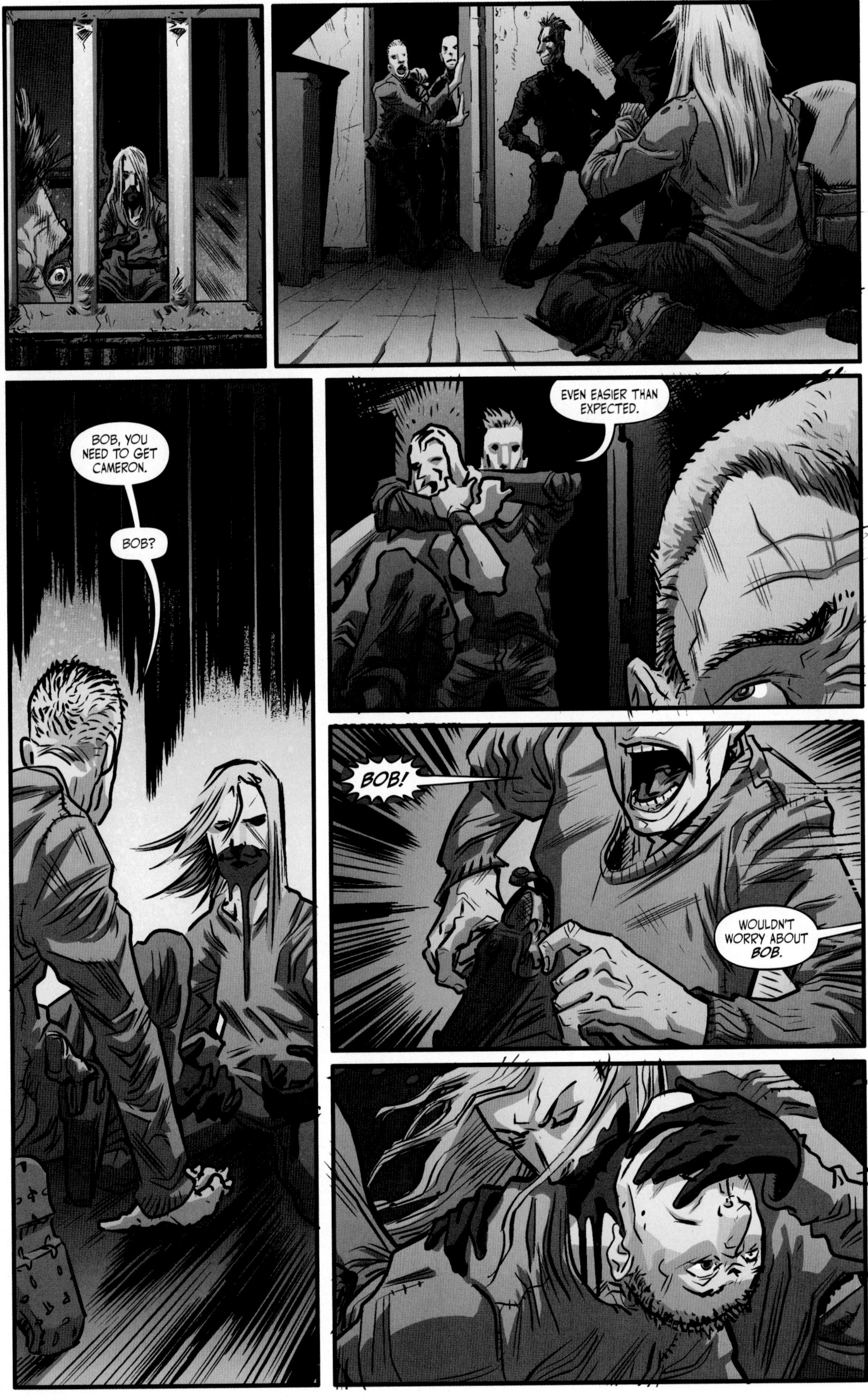
BOB, YOU NEED TO GET CAMERON.
BOB?
EVEN EASIER THAN EXPECTED.
BOB!
WOULDN'T WORRY ABOUT BOB.

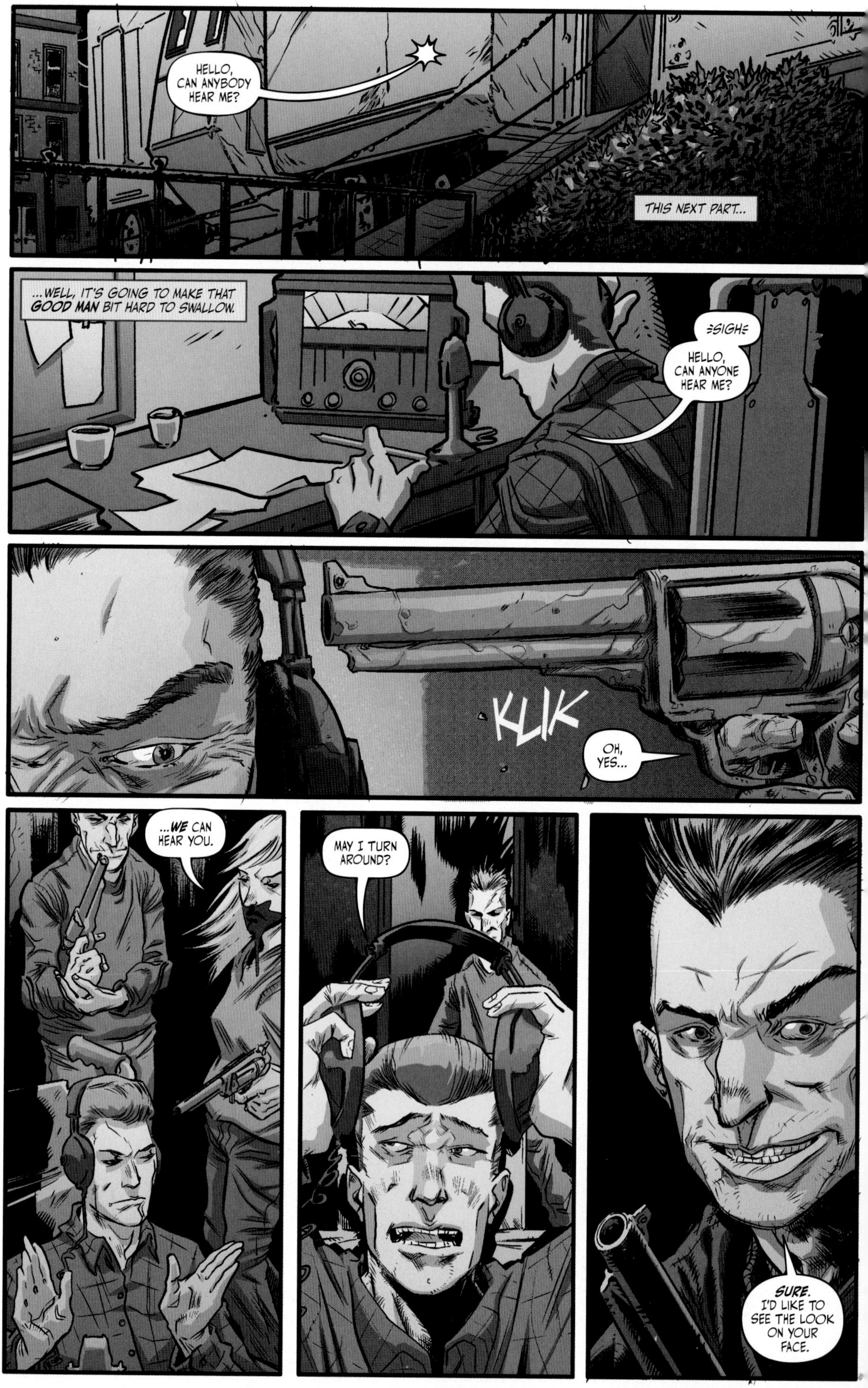
HELLO,
CAN ANYBODY
HEAR ME?
THIS NEXT PART...
...WELL, IT'S GOING TO MAKE THAT
GOOD MAN BIT HARD TO SWALLOW.
=SIGH=
HELLO,
CAN ANYONE
HEAR ME?
KLIK
OH,
YES...
...WE CAN
HEAR YOU.
MAY I TURN
AROUND?
SURE.
I'D LIKE TO
SEE THE LOOK
ON YOUR
FACE.

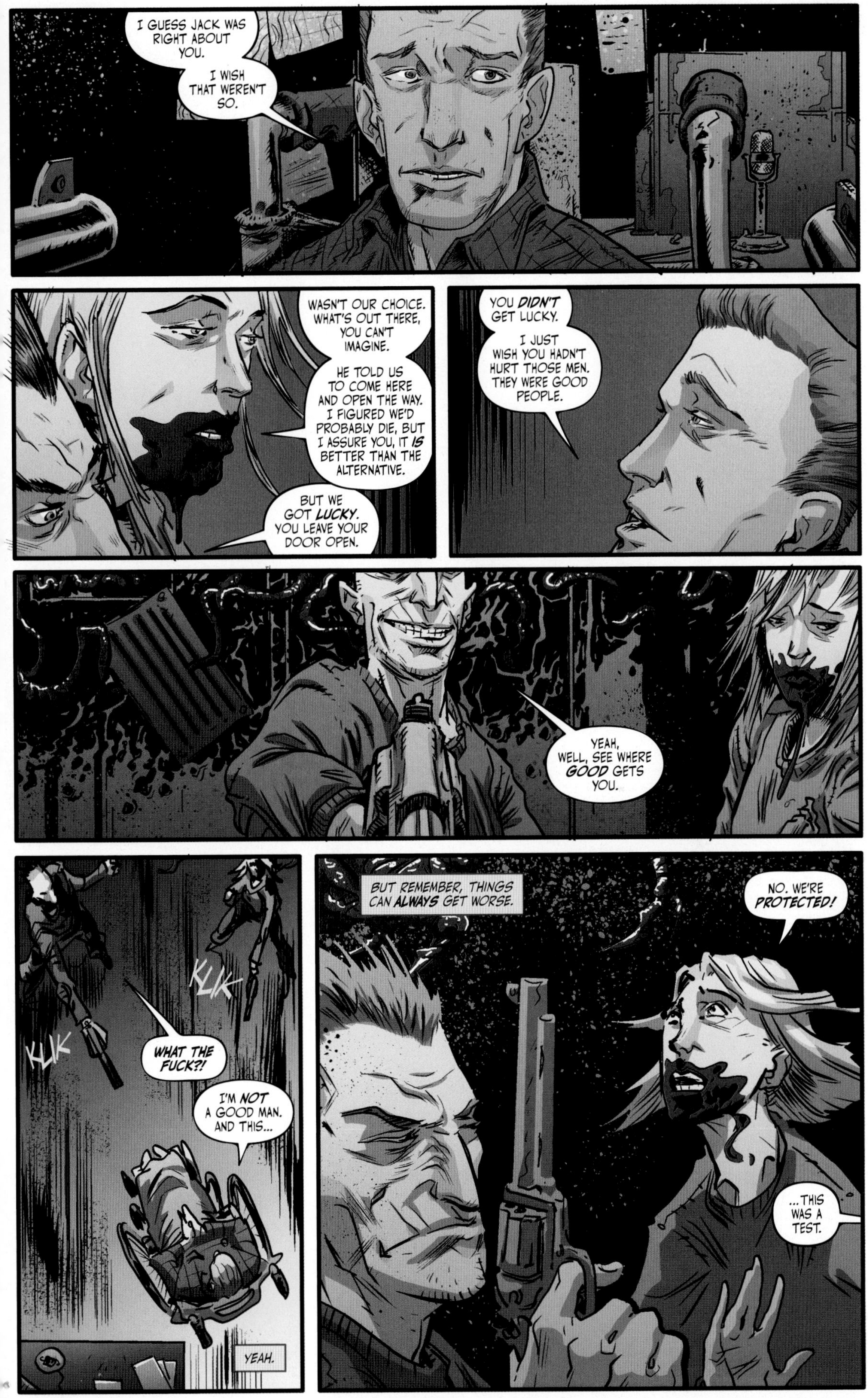
I GUESS JACK WAS RIGHT ABOUT YOU.
I WISH THAT WEREN'T SO.
WASN'T OUR CHOICE. WHAT'S OUT THERE, YOU CAN'T IMAGINE.
HE TOLD US TO COME HERE AND OPEN THE WAY. I FIGURED WE'D PROBABLY DIE, BUT I ASSURE YOU, IT IS BETTER THAN THE ALTERNATIVE.
BUT WE GOT LUCKY. YOU LEAVE YOUR DOOR OPEN.
YOU DIDN'T GET LUCKY.
I JUST WISH YOU HADN'T HURT THOSE MEN. THEY WERE GOOD PEOPLE.
YEAH, WELL, SEE WHERE GOOD GETS YOU.
KLIK
KLIK
WHAT THE FUCK?!
I'M NOT A GOOD MAN. AND THIS...
YEAH.
BUT REMEMBER, THINGS CAN ALWAYS GET WORSE.
NO. WE'RE PROTECTED!
...THIS WAS A TEST.

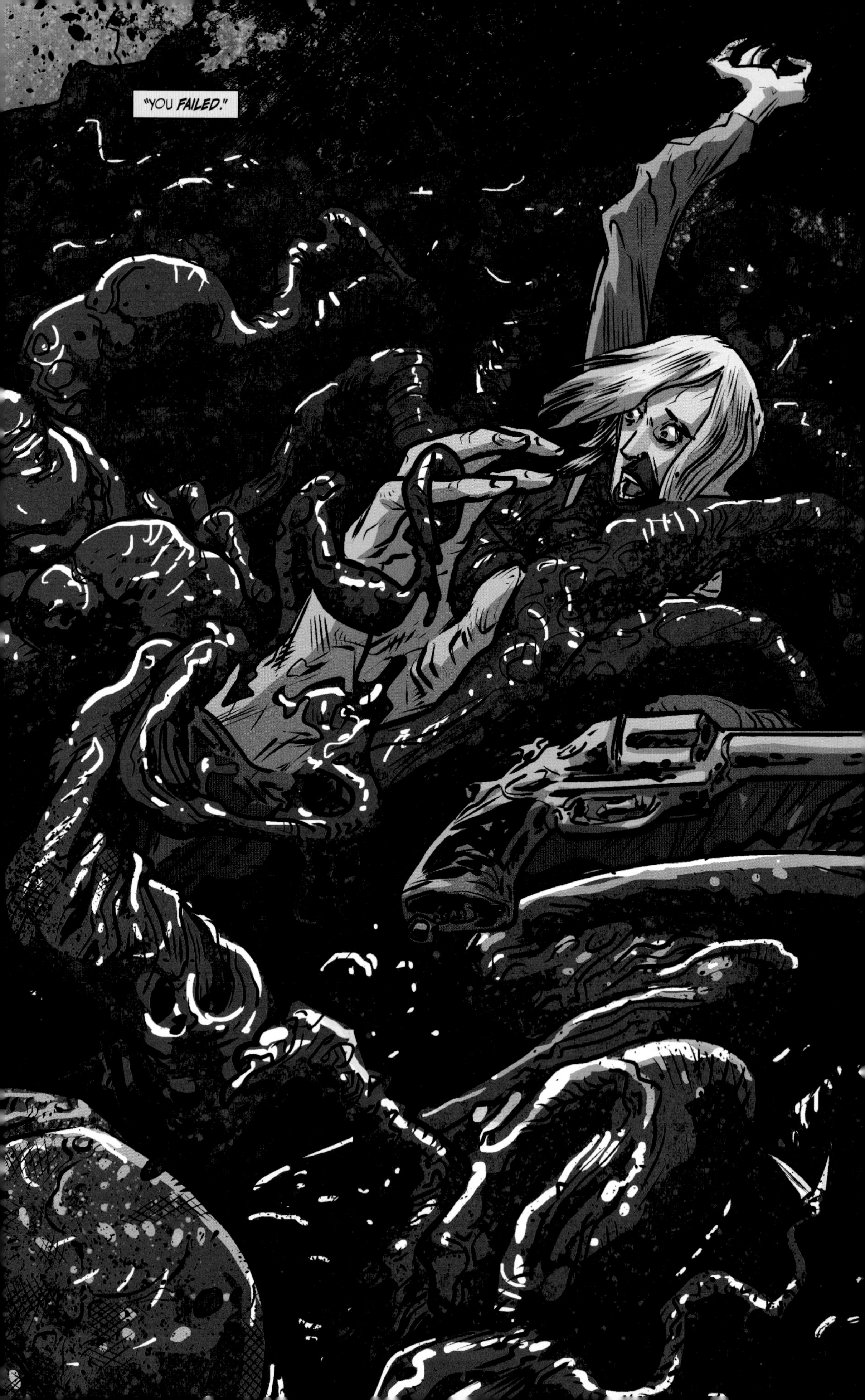
"YOU FAILED."

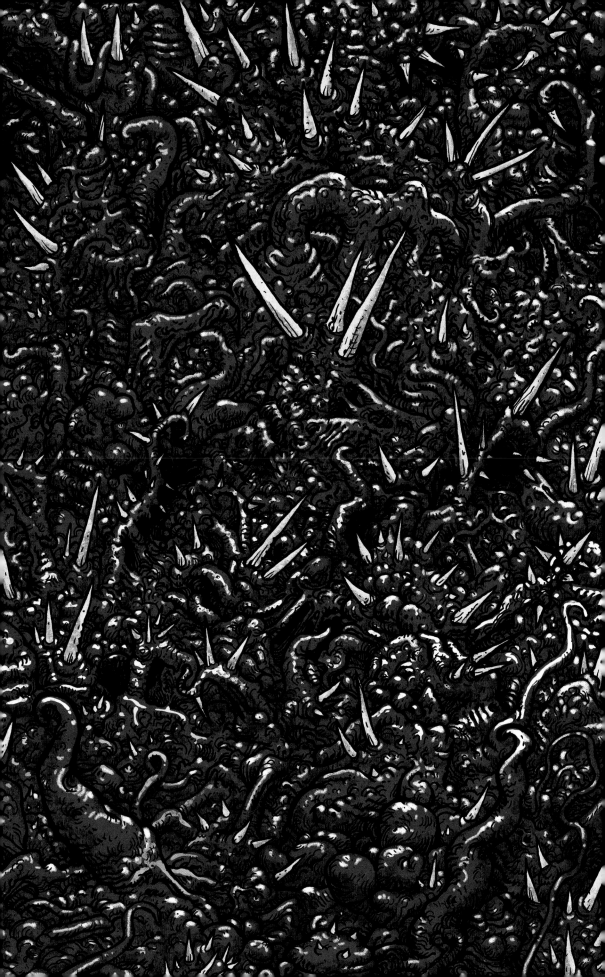

CHAPTER FIVE

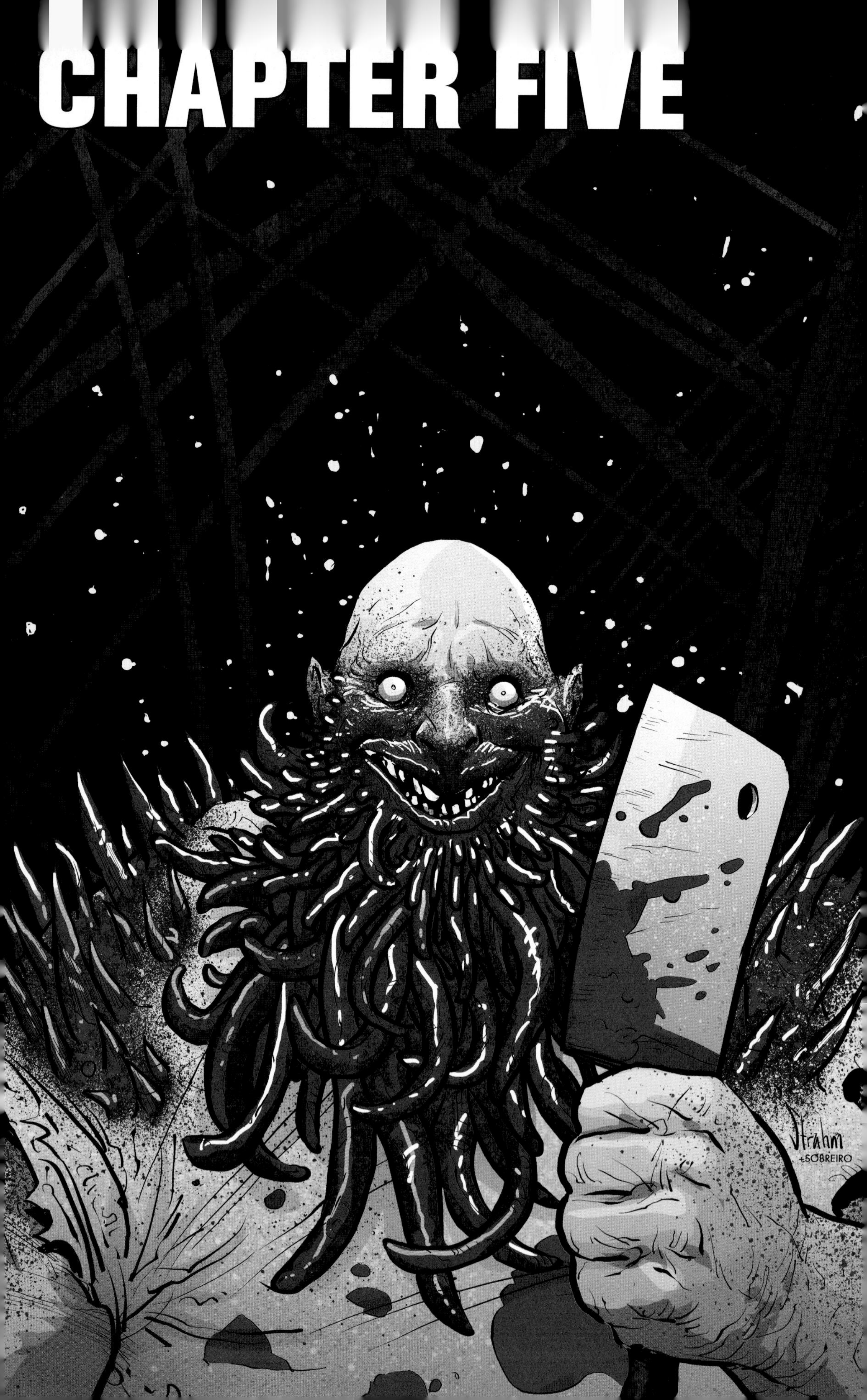

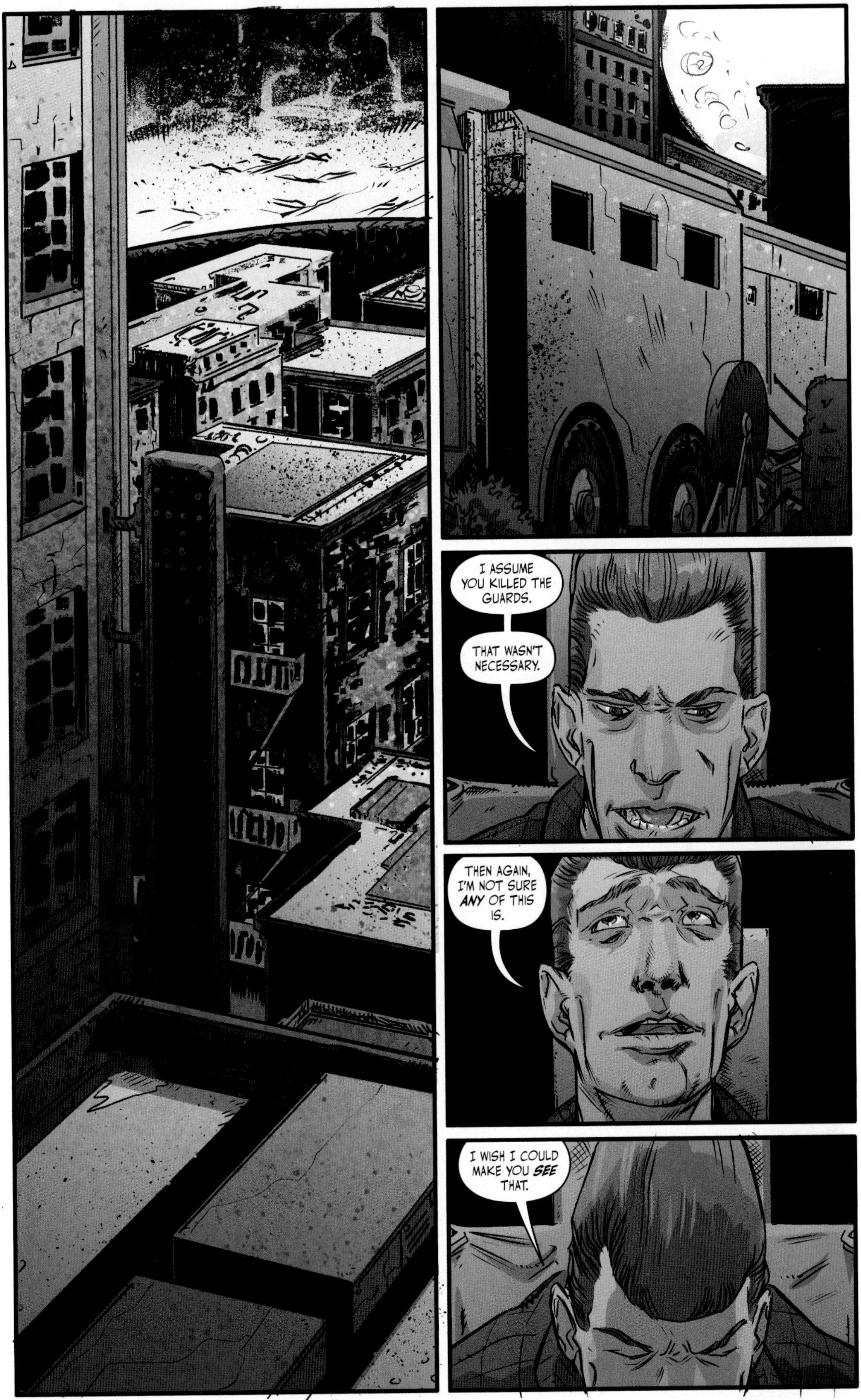
I ASSUME YOU KILLED THE GUARDS.
THAT WASN'T NECESSARY.
THEN AGAIN, I'M NOT SURE ANY OF THIS IS.
I WISH I COULD MAKE YOU SEE THAT.

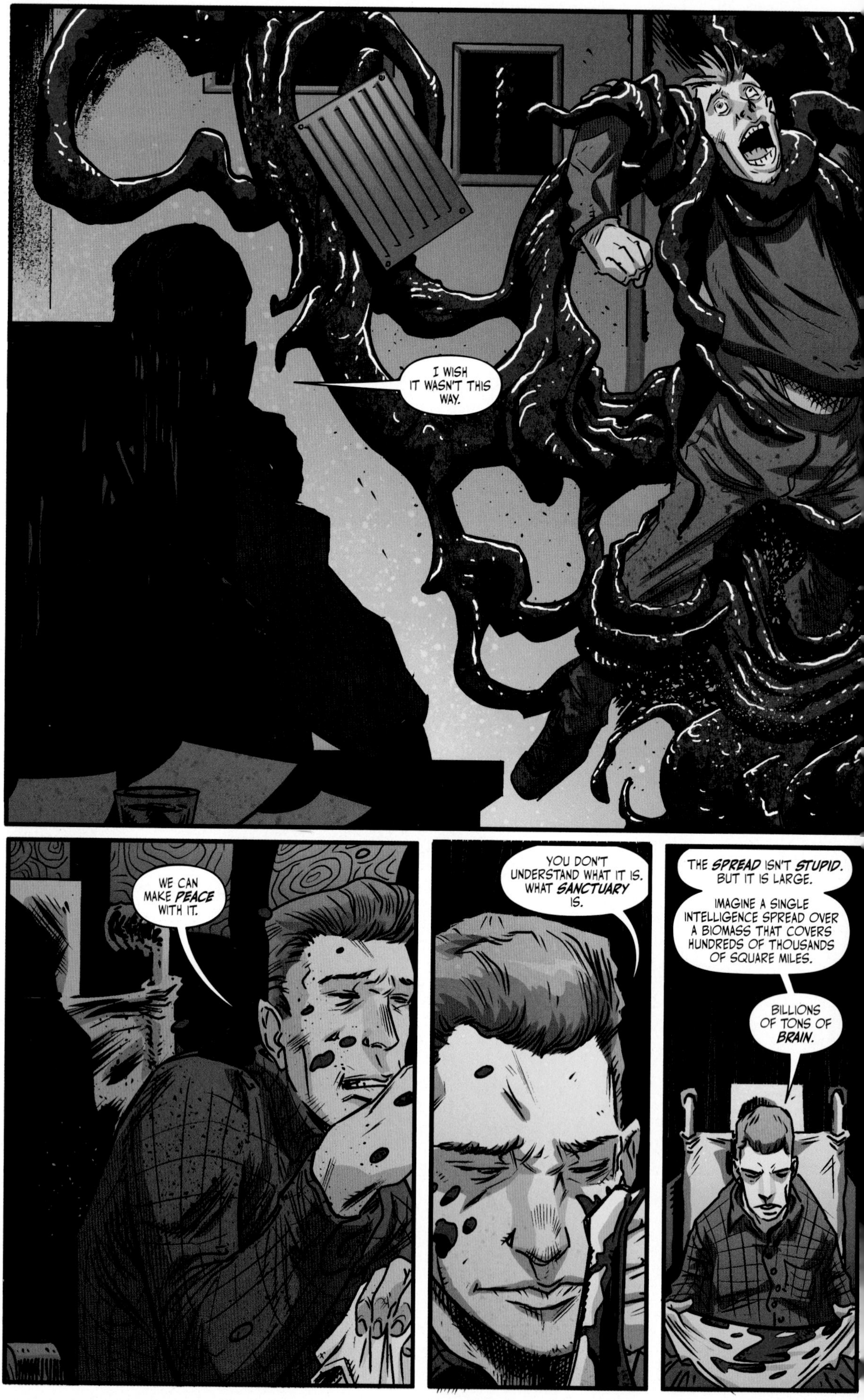
I WISH IT WASN'T THIS WAY.
WE CAN MAKE *PEACE* WITH IT.
YOU DON'T UNDERSTAND WHAT IT IS. WHAT *SANCTUARY* IS.
THE *SPREAD* ISN'T *STUPID*. BUT IT IS LARGE.
IMAGINE A SINGLE INTELLIGENCE SPREAD OVER A BIOMASS THAT COVERS HUNDREDS OF THOUSANDS OF SQUARE MILES.
BILLIONS OF TONS OF *BRAIN*.

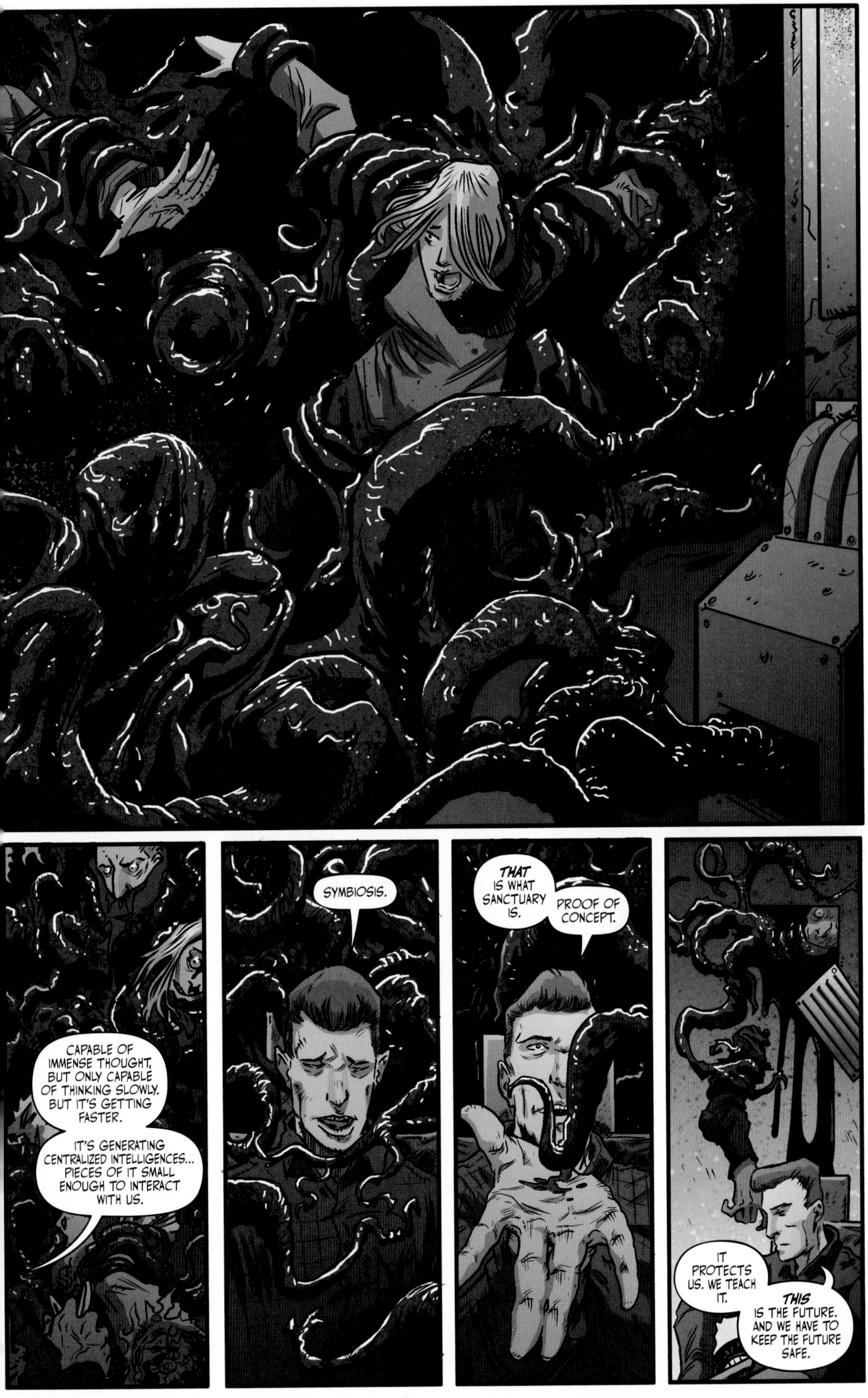
CAPABLE OF IMMENSE THOUGHT, BUT ONLY CAPABLE OF THINKING SLOWLY. BUT IT'S GETTING FASTER.
IT'S GENERATING CENTRALIZED INTELLIGENCES... PIECES OF IT SMALL ENOUGH TO INTERACT WITH US.
SYMBIOSIS.
THAT IS WHAT SANCTUARY IS.
PROOF OF CONCEPT.
IT PROTECTS US. WE TEACH IT.
THIS IS THE FUTURE. AND WE HAVE TO KEEP THE FUTURE SAFE.

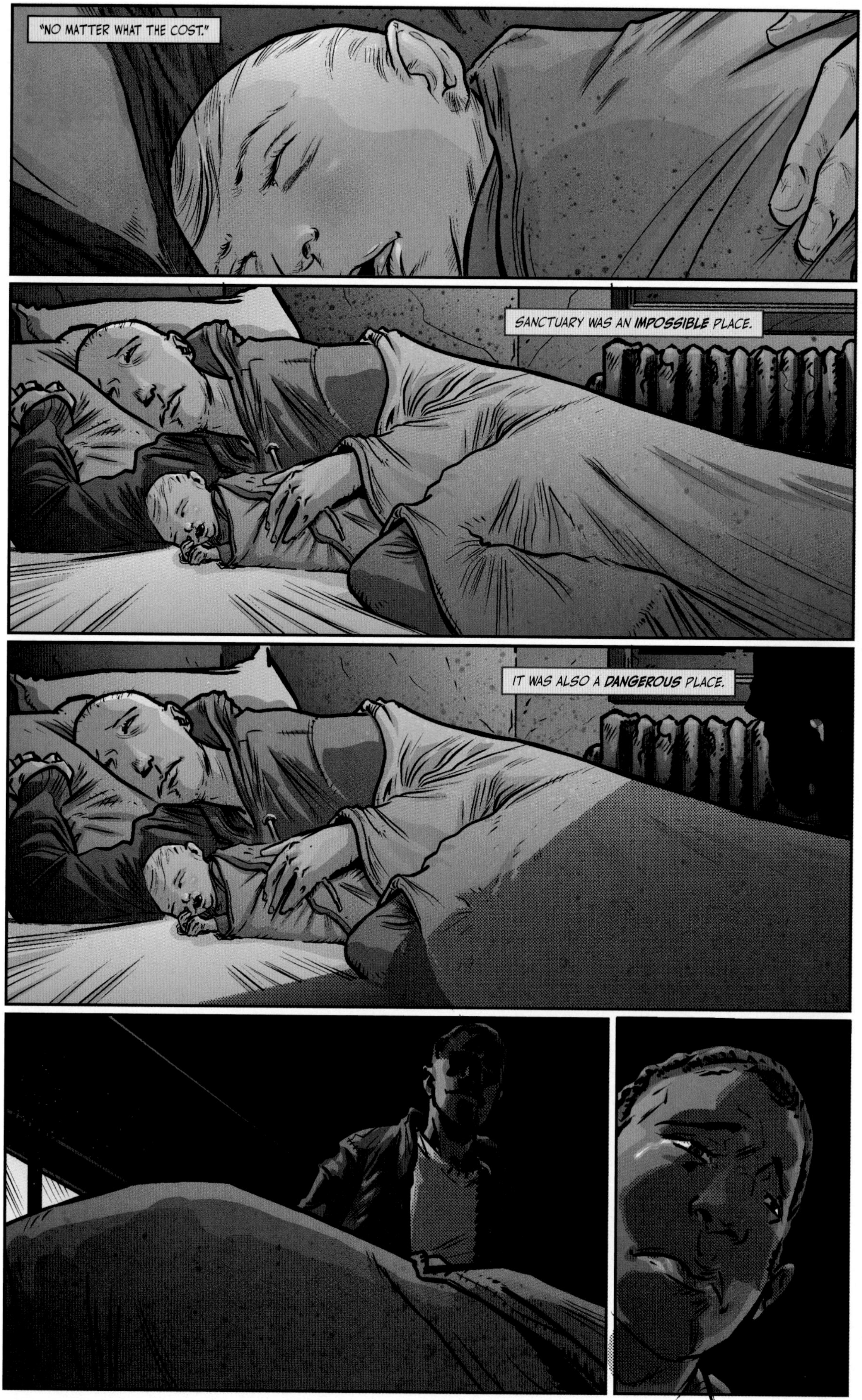
"NO MATTER WHAT THE COST."
SANCTUARY WAS AN IMPOSSIBLE PLACE.
IT WAS ALSO A DANGEROUS PLACE.

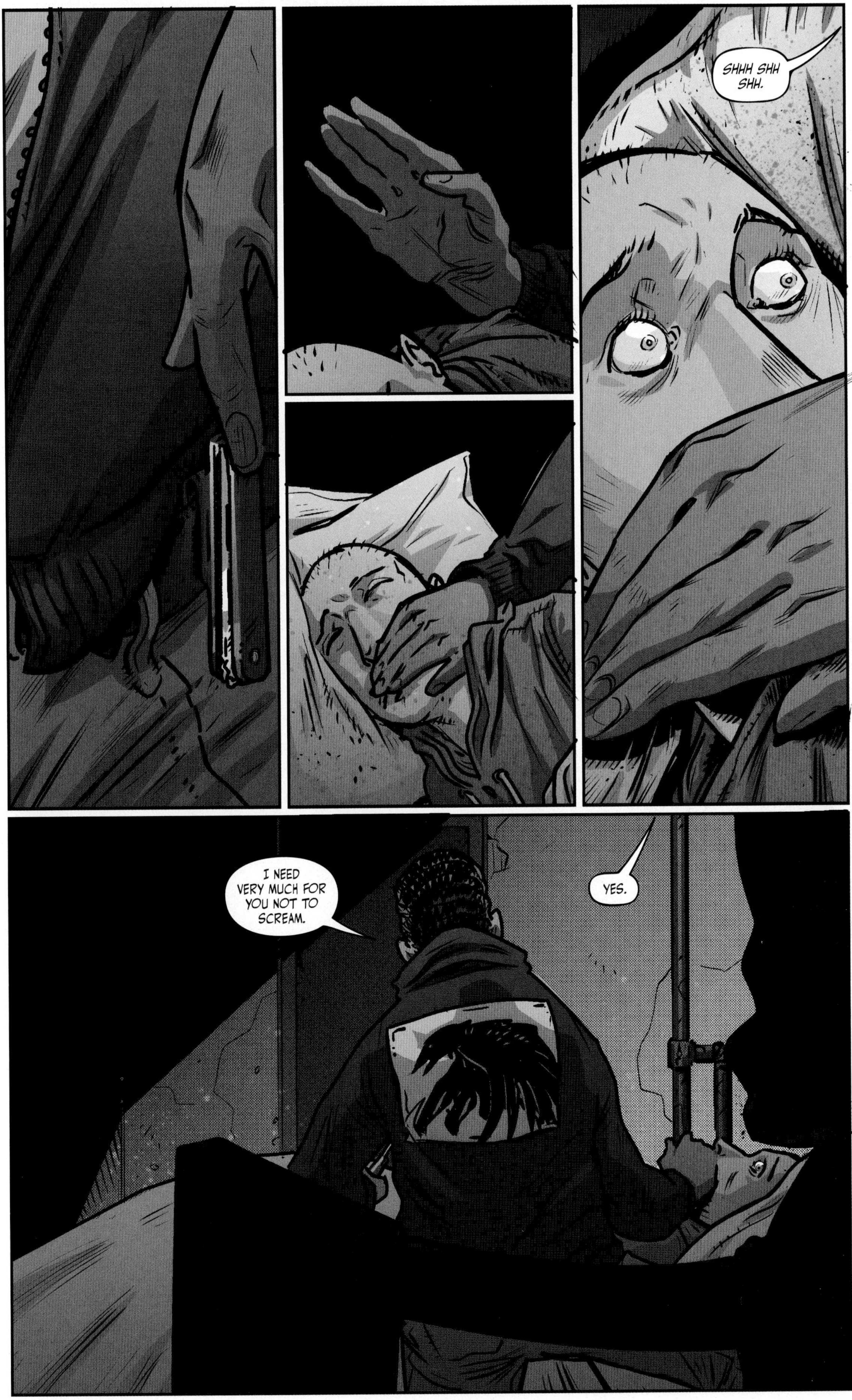
SHHH SHH SHH.
I NEED VERY MUCH FOR YOU NOT TO SCREAM.
YES.

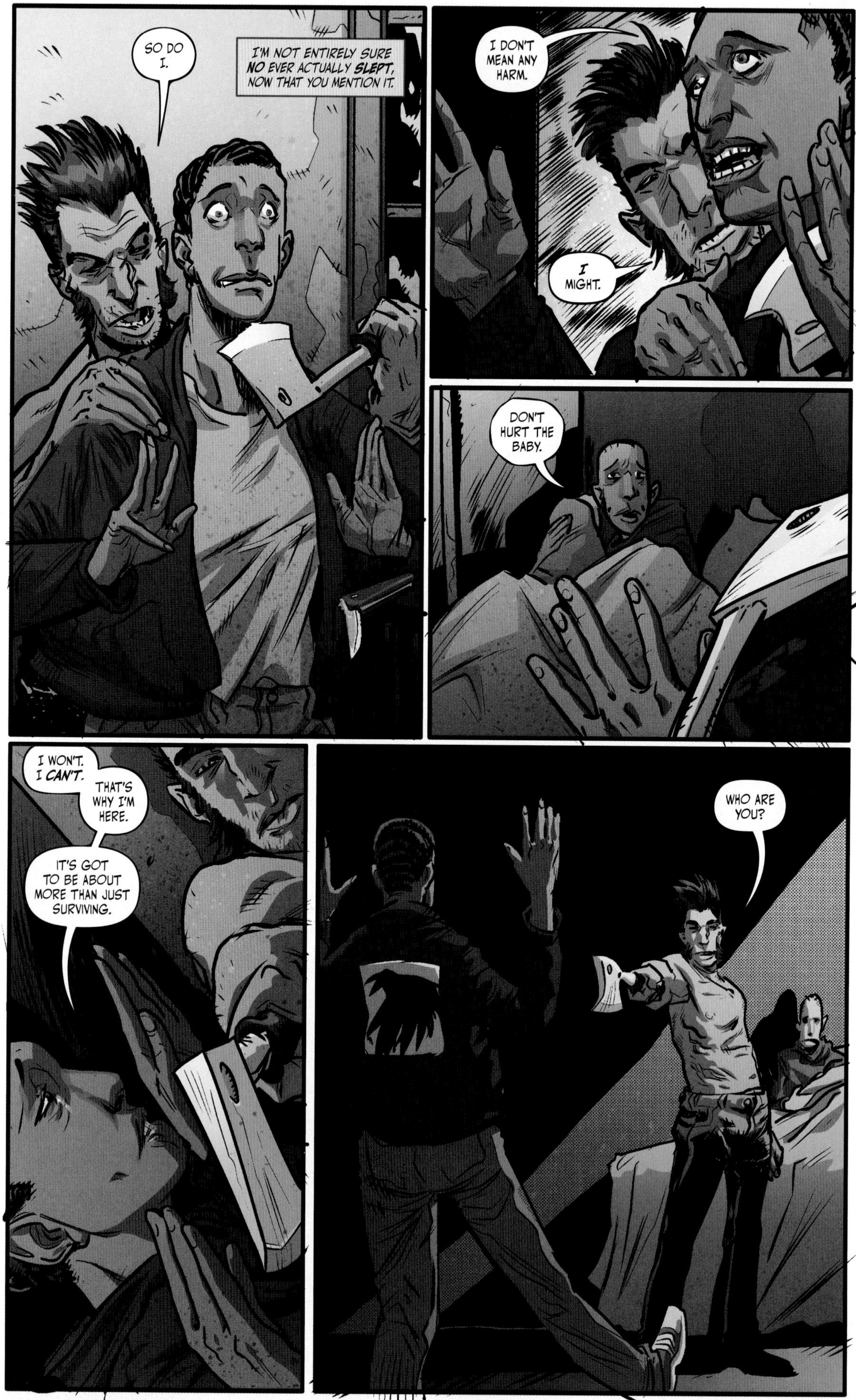
SO DO I.
I'M NOT ENTIRELY SURE NO EVER ACTUALLY SLEPT, NOW THAT YOU MENTION IT.
I DON'T MEAN ANY HARM.
I MIGHT.
DON'T HURT THE BABY.
I WON'T. I CAN'T.
THAT'S WHY I'M HERE.
IT'S GOT TO BE ABOUT MORE THAN JUST SURVIVING.
WHO ARE YOU?

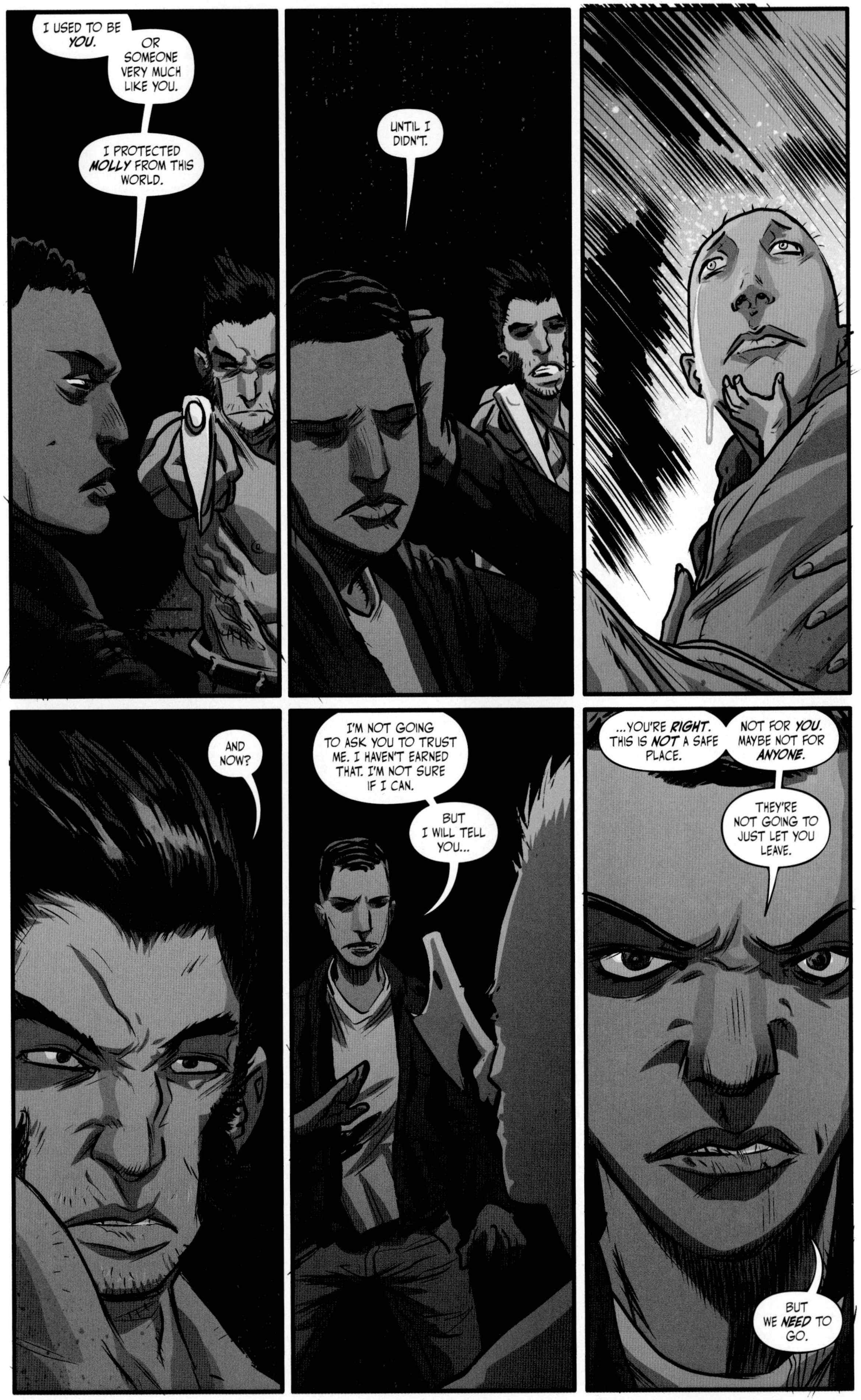
I USED TO BE *YOU*.
OR SOMEONE VERY MUCH LIKE YOU.
I PROTECTED *MOLLY* FROM THIS WORLD.
UNTIL I DIDN'T.
AND NOW?
I'M NOT GOING TO ASK YOU TO TRUST ME. I HAVEN'T EARNED THAT. I'M NOT SURE IF I CAN.
BUT I WILL TELL YOU...
...YOU'RE *RIGHT*. THIS IS *NOT* A SAFE PLACE.
NOT FOR *YOU*. MAYBE NOT FOR *ANYONE*.
THEY'RE NOT GOING TO JUST LET YOU LEAVE.
BUT WE *NEED* TO GO.

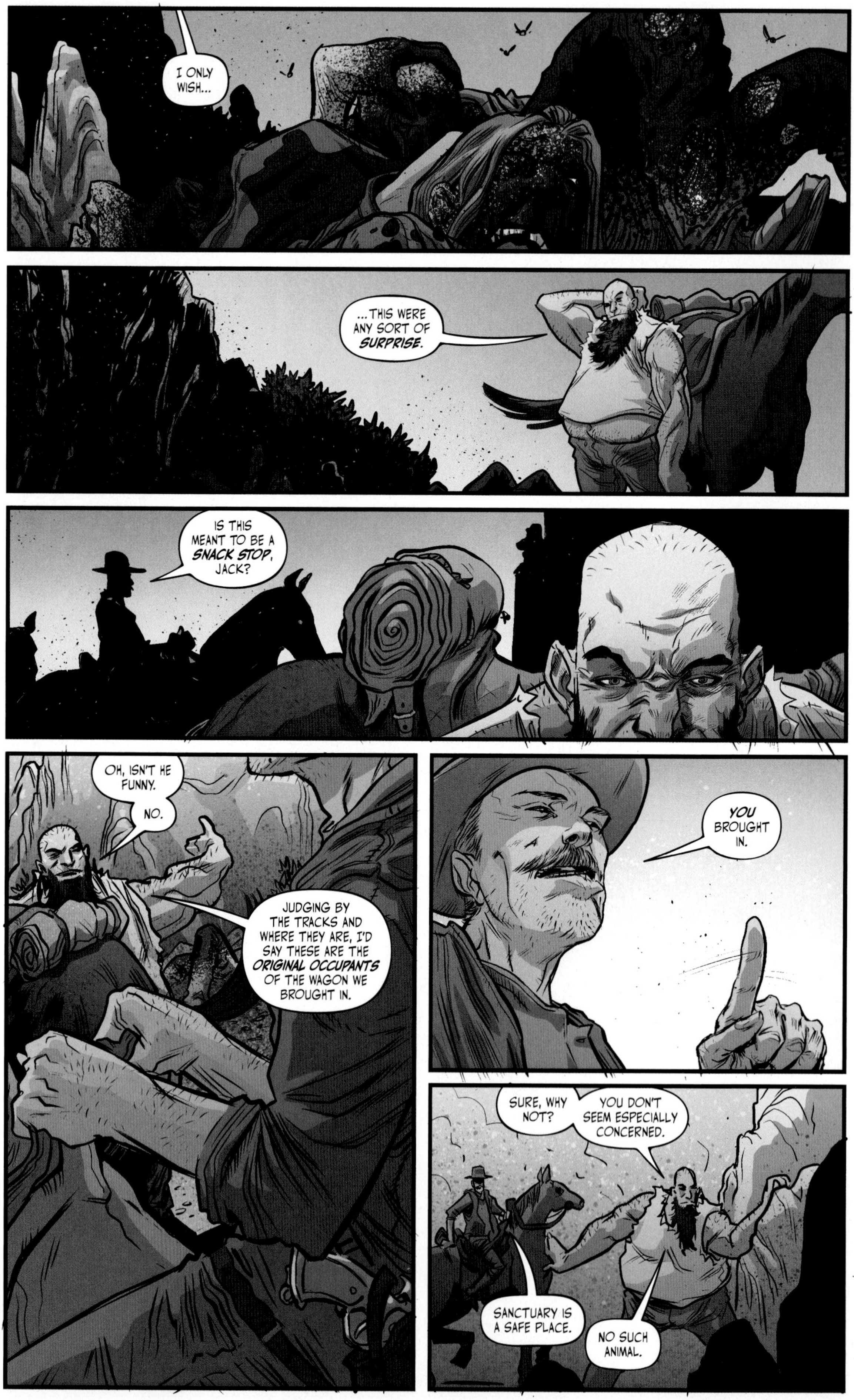

I ONLY WISH...
...THIS WERE ANY SORT OF SURPRISE.
IS THIS MEANT TO BE A SNACK STOP, JACK?
OH, ISN'T HE FUNNY.
NO.
JUDGING BY THE TRACKS AND WHERE THEY ARE, I'D SAY THESE ARE THE ORIGINAL OCCUPANTS OF THE WAGON WE BROUGHT IN.
YOU BROUGHT IN.
...
SURE, WHY NOT?
YOU DON'T SEEM ESPECIALLY CONCERNED.
SANCTUARY IS A SAFE PLACE.
NO SUCH ANIMAL.

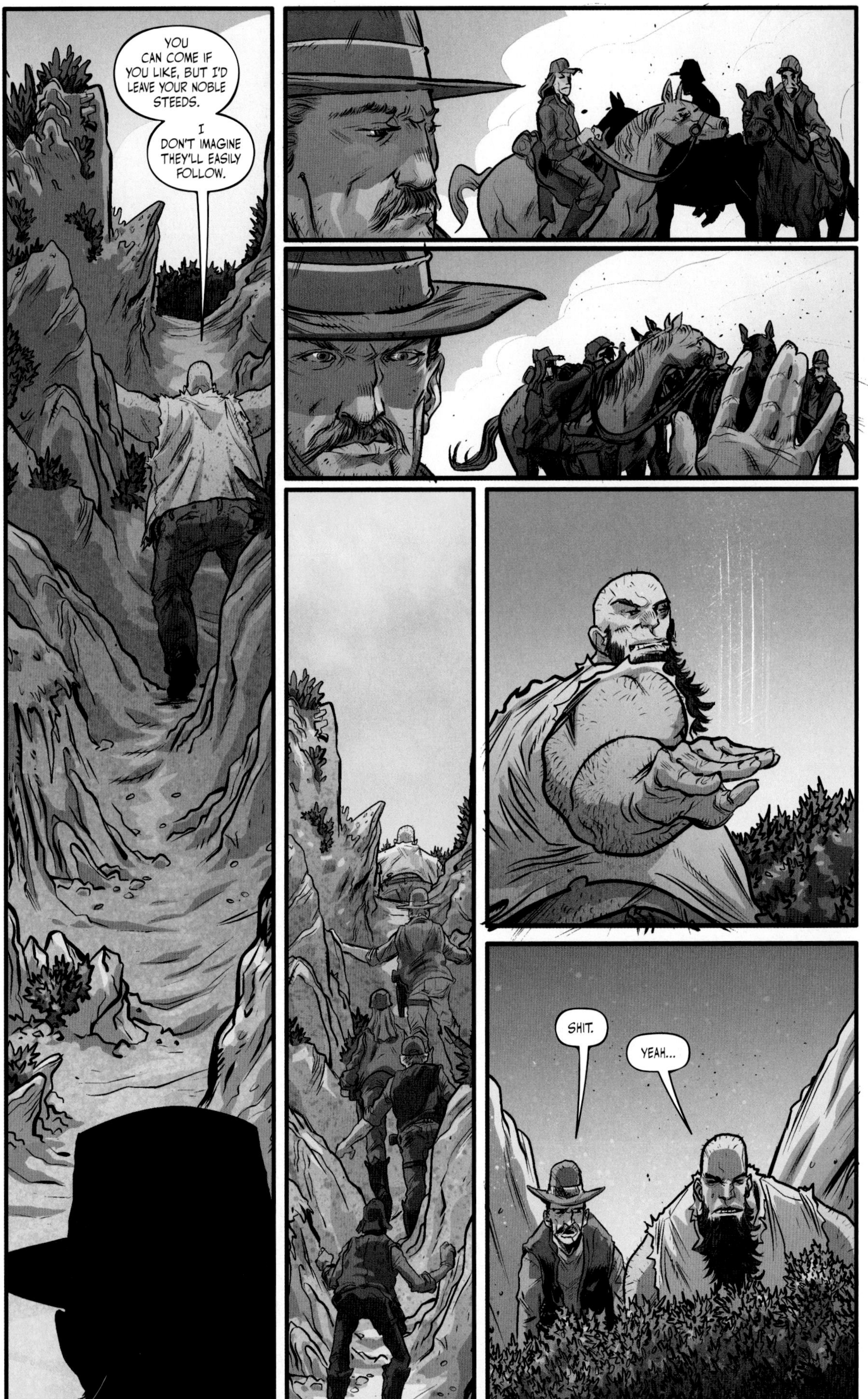
YOU CAN COME IF YOU LIKE, BUT I'D LEAVE YOUR NOBLE STEEDS.
I DON'T IMAGINE THEY'LL EASILY FOLLOW.
SHIT.
YEAH...

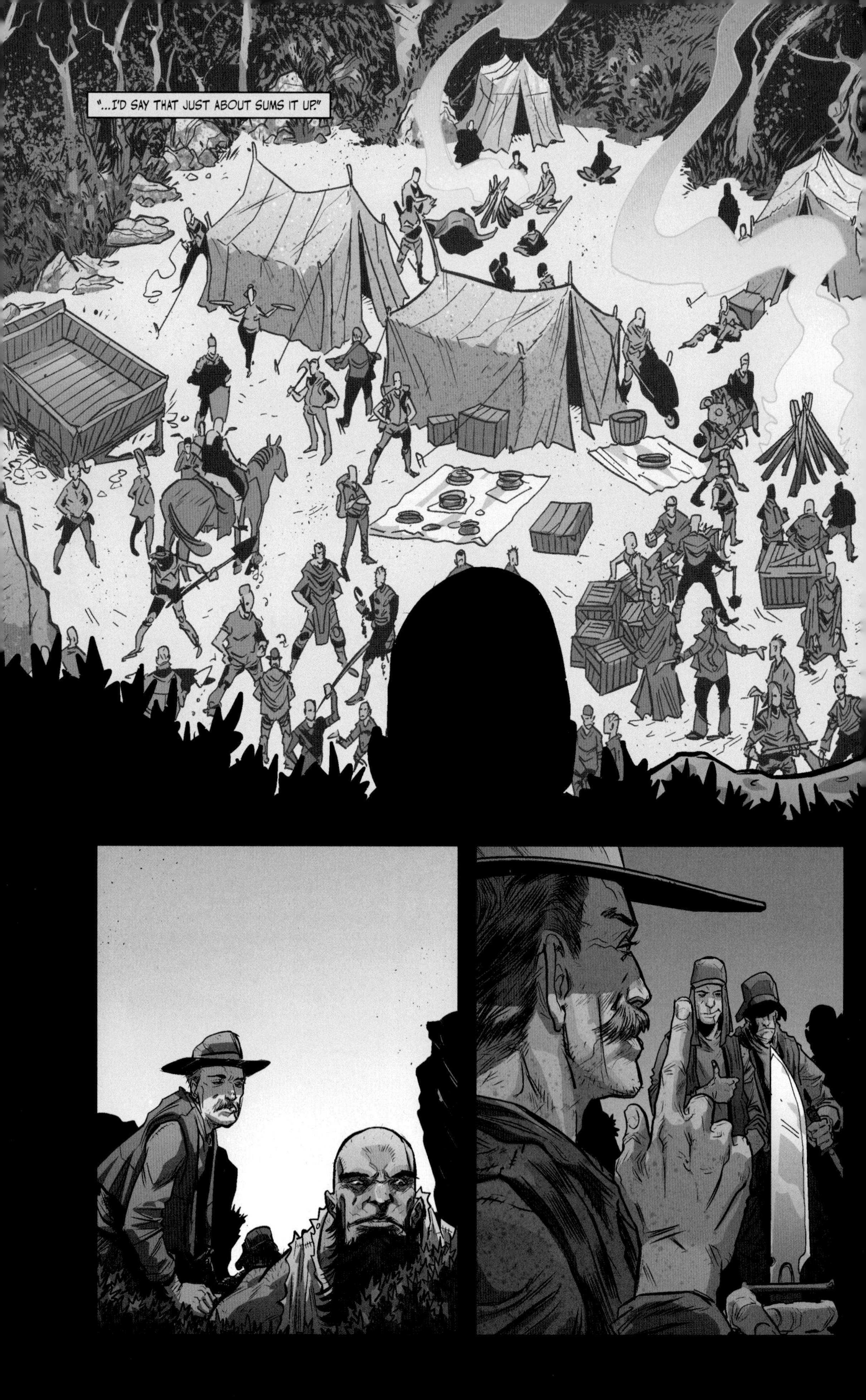
"...I'D SAY THAT JUST ABOUT SUMS IT UP."

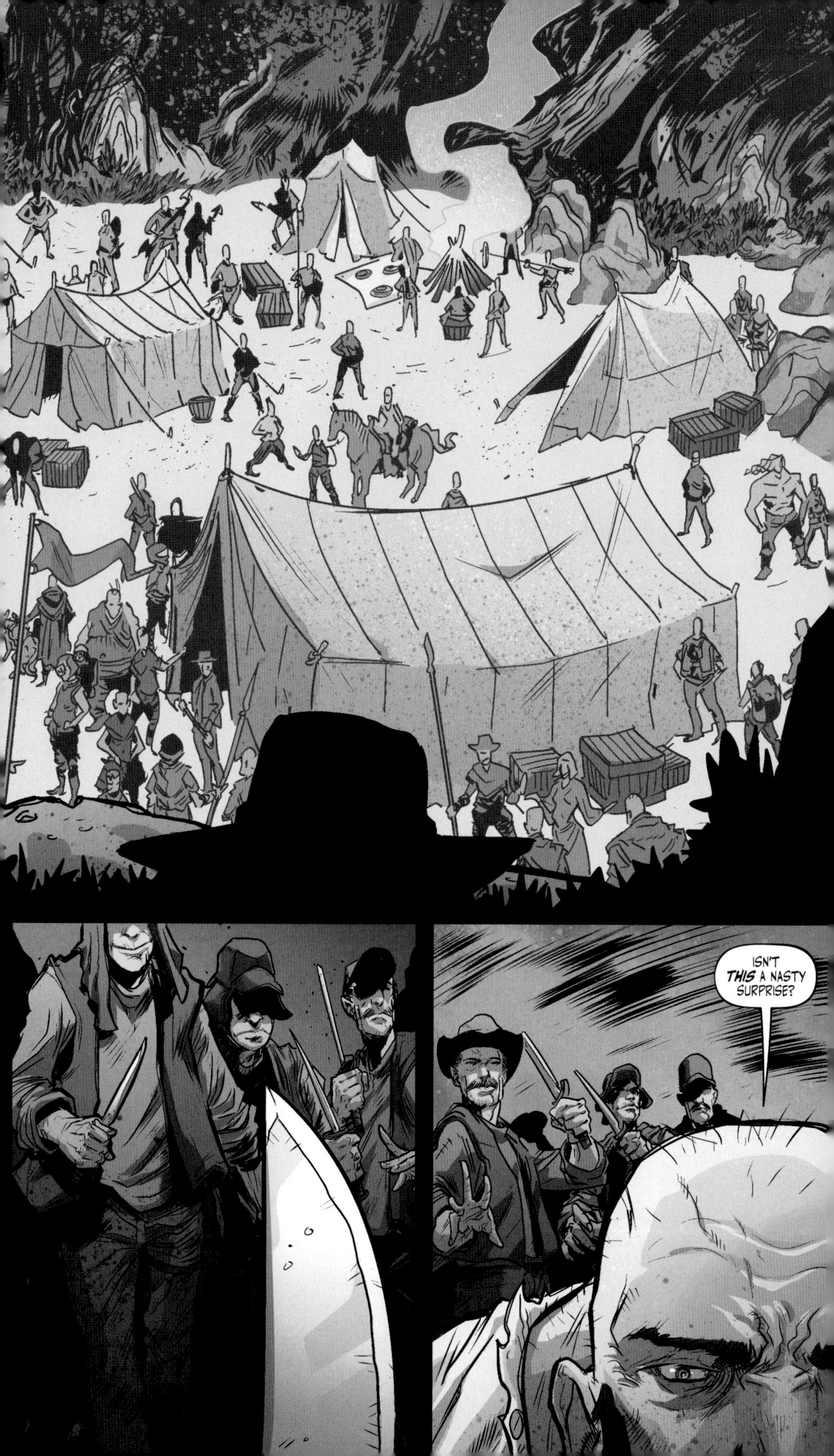
ISN'T *THIS* A NASTY SURPRISE?

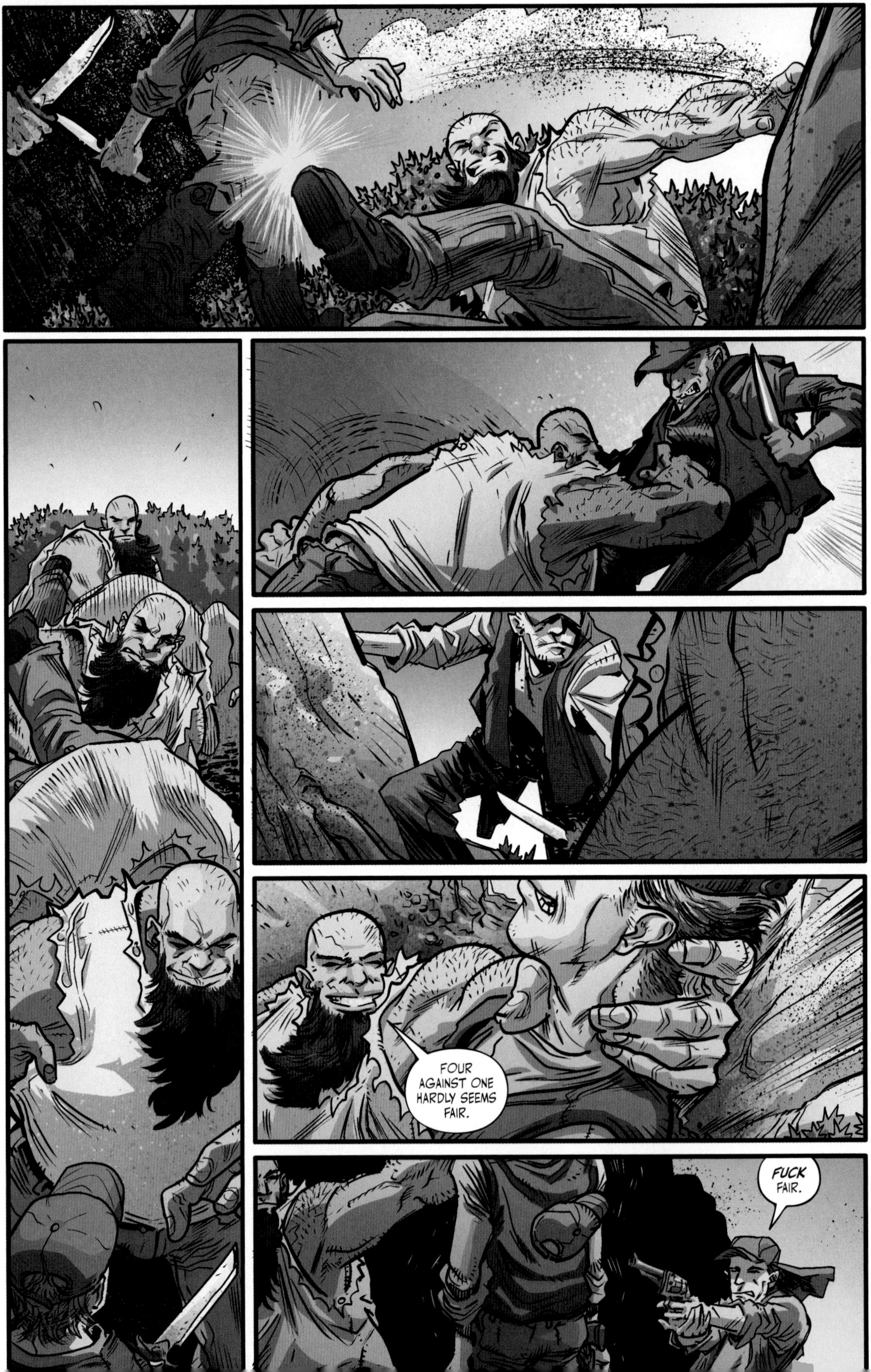
FOUR AGAINST ONE HARDLY SEEMS FAIR.
FUCK FAIR.

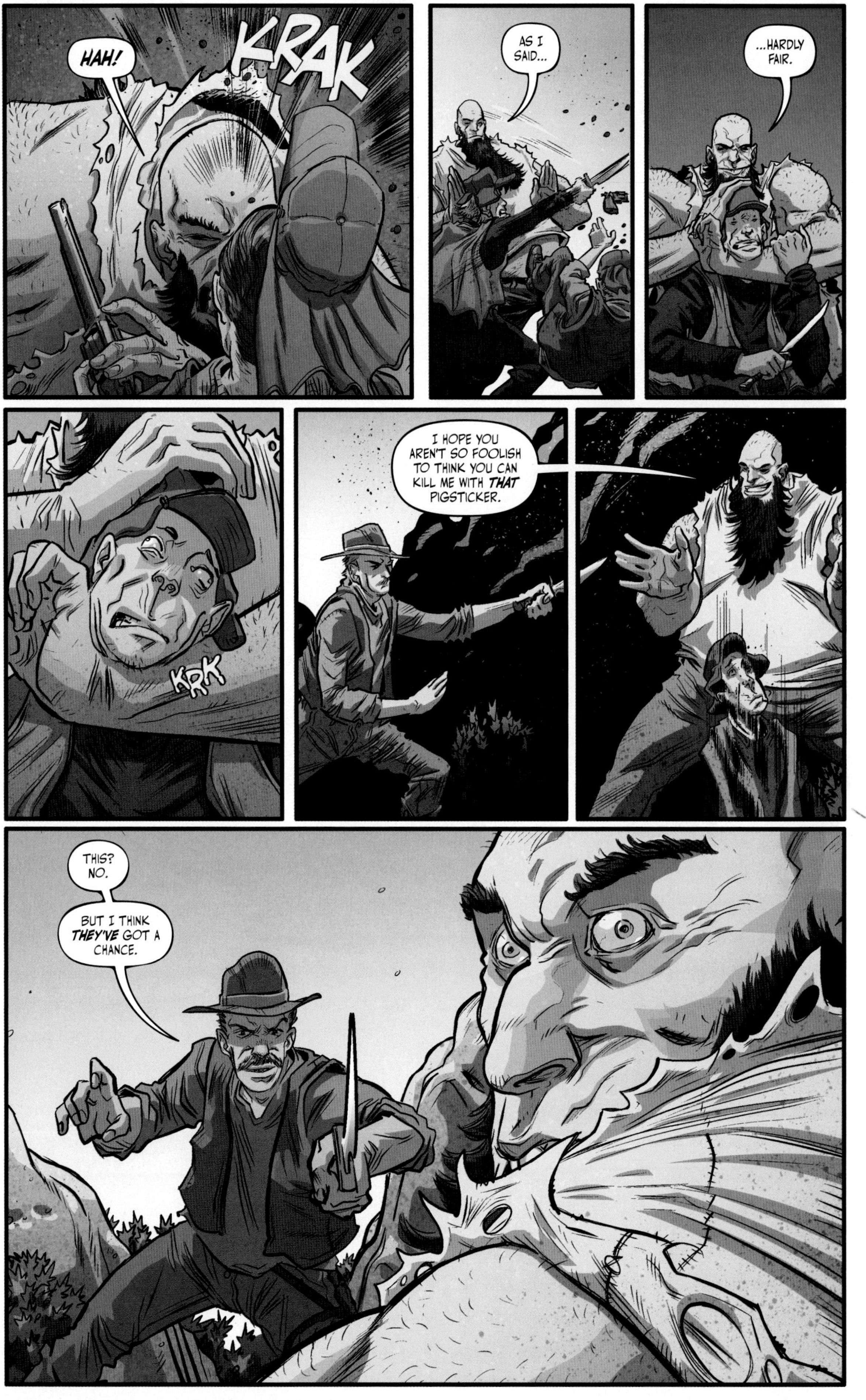
HAH!
KRAK
AS I SAID...
...HARDLY FAIR.
KRK
I HOPE YOU AREN'T SO FOOLISH TO THINK YOU CAN KILL ME WITH *THAT* PIGSTICKER.
THIS? NO.
BUT I THINK *THEY'VE* GOT A CHANCE.

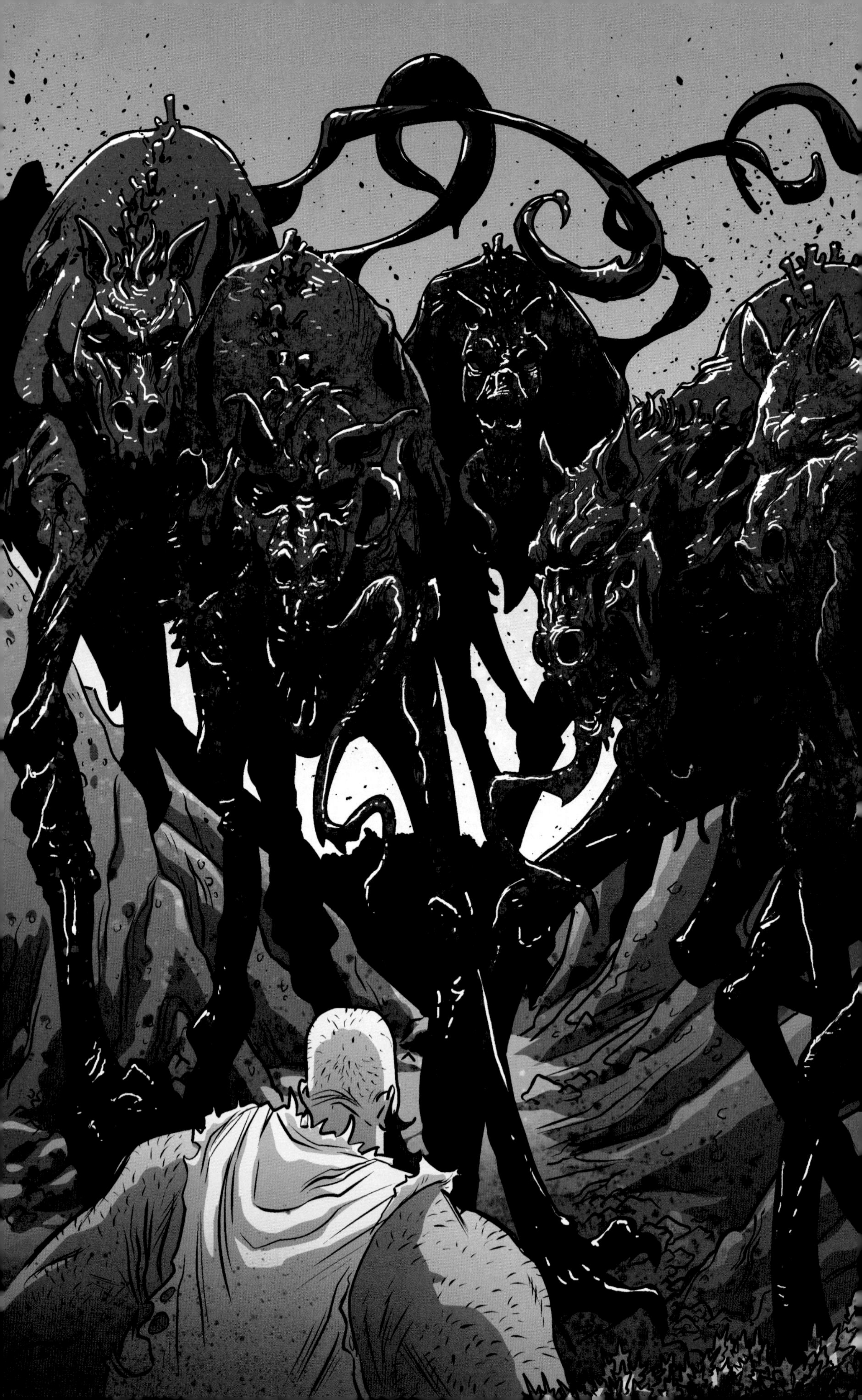

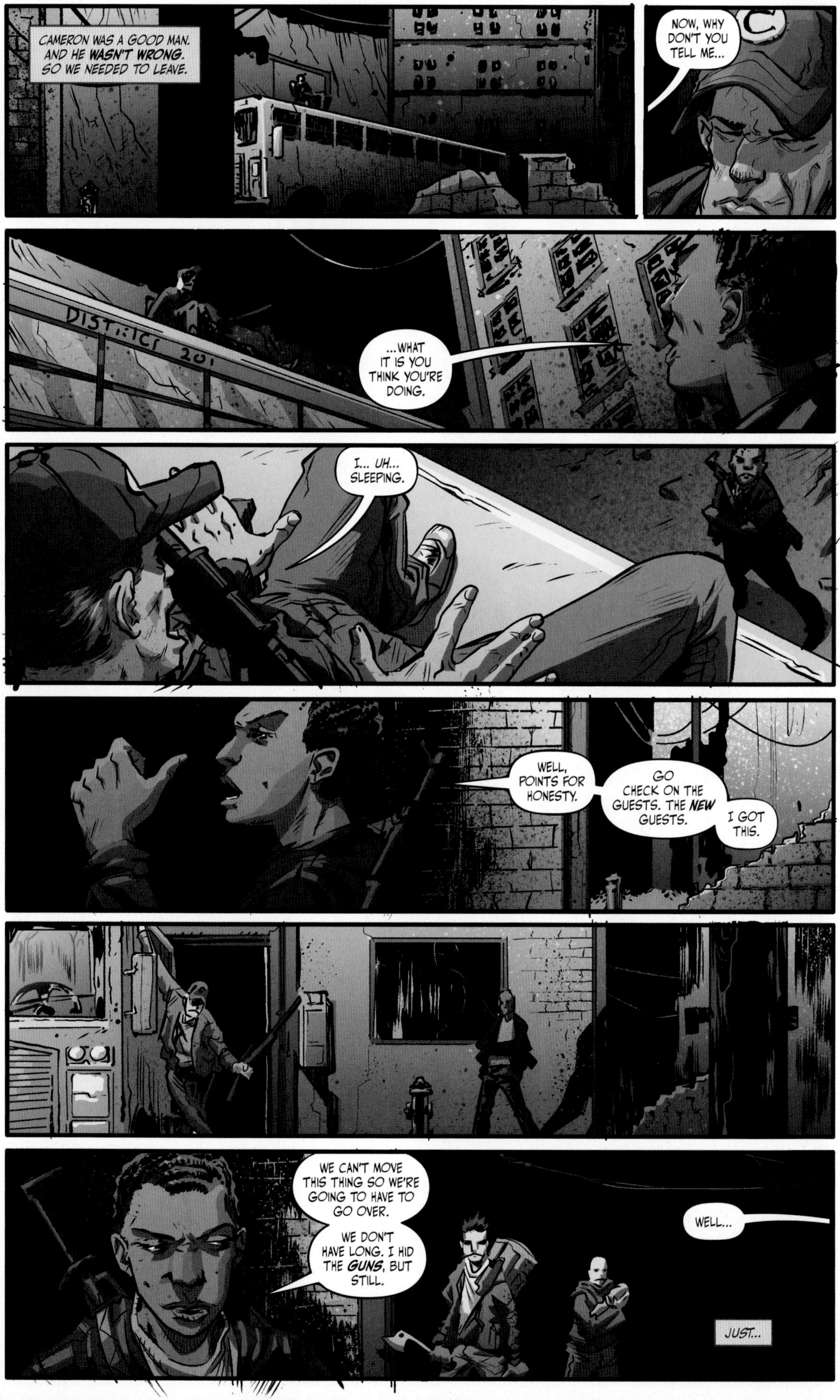
CAMERON WAS A GOOD MAN. AND HE WASN'T WRONG. SO WE NEEDED TO LEAVE.
NOW, WHY DON'T YOU TELL ME...
DISTRICT 201
...WHAT IT IS YOU THINK YOU'RE DOING.
I... UH... SLEEPING.
WELL, POINTS FOR HONESTY.
GO CHECK ON THE GUESTS. THE NEW GUESTS.
I GOT THIS.
WE CAN'T MOVE THIS THING SO WE'RE GOING TO HAVE TO GO OVER.
WE DON'T HAVE LONG. I HID THE GUNS, BUT STILL.
WELL...
JUST...

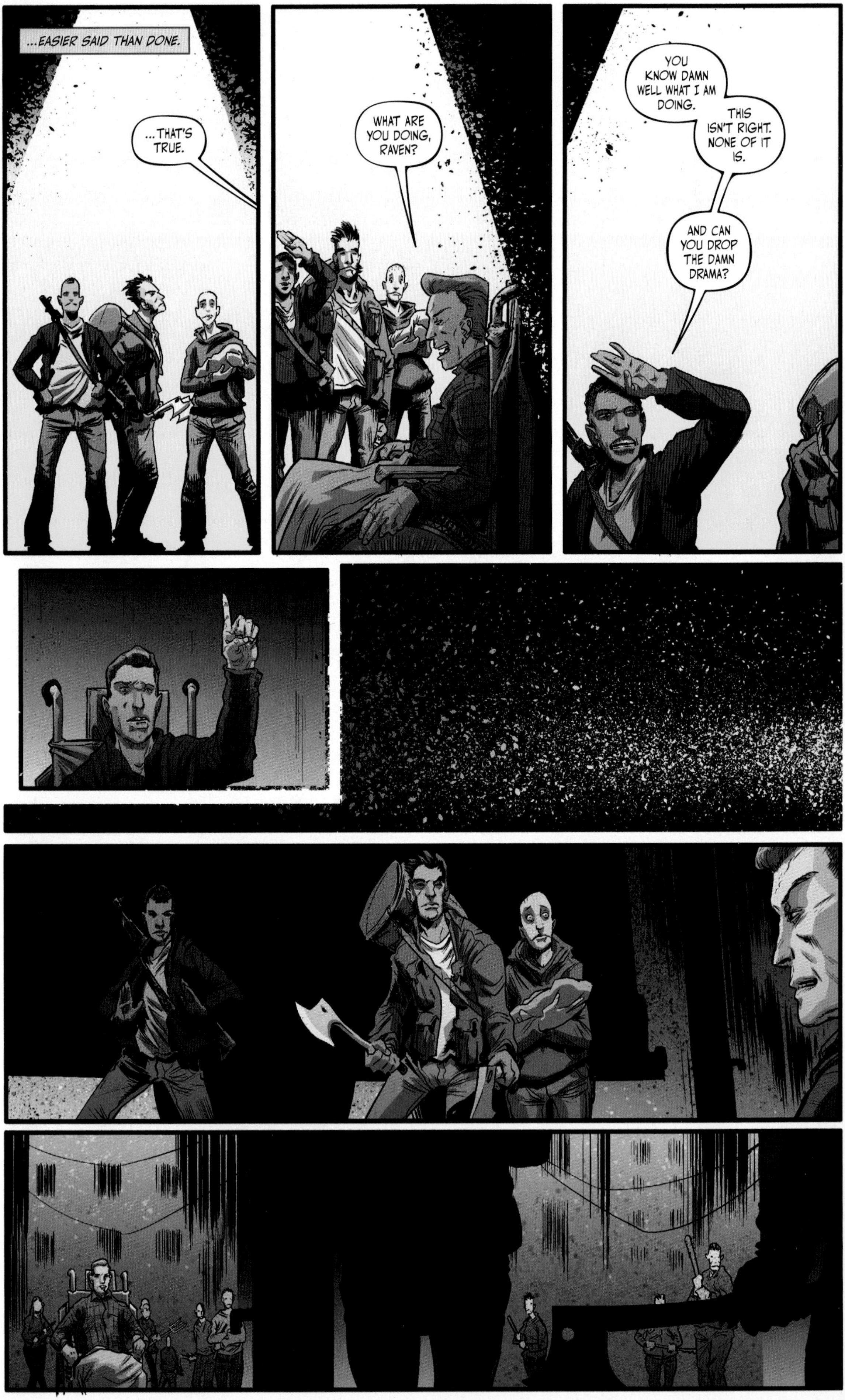
...EASIER SAID THAN DONE.
...THAT'S TRUE.
WHAT ARE YOU DOING, RAVEN?
YOU KNOW DAMN WELL WHAT I AM DOING.
THIS ISN'T RIGHT. NONE OF IT IS.
AND CAN YOU DROP THE DAMN DRAMA?

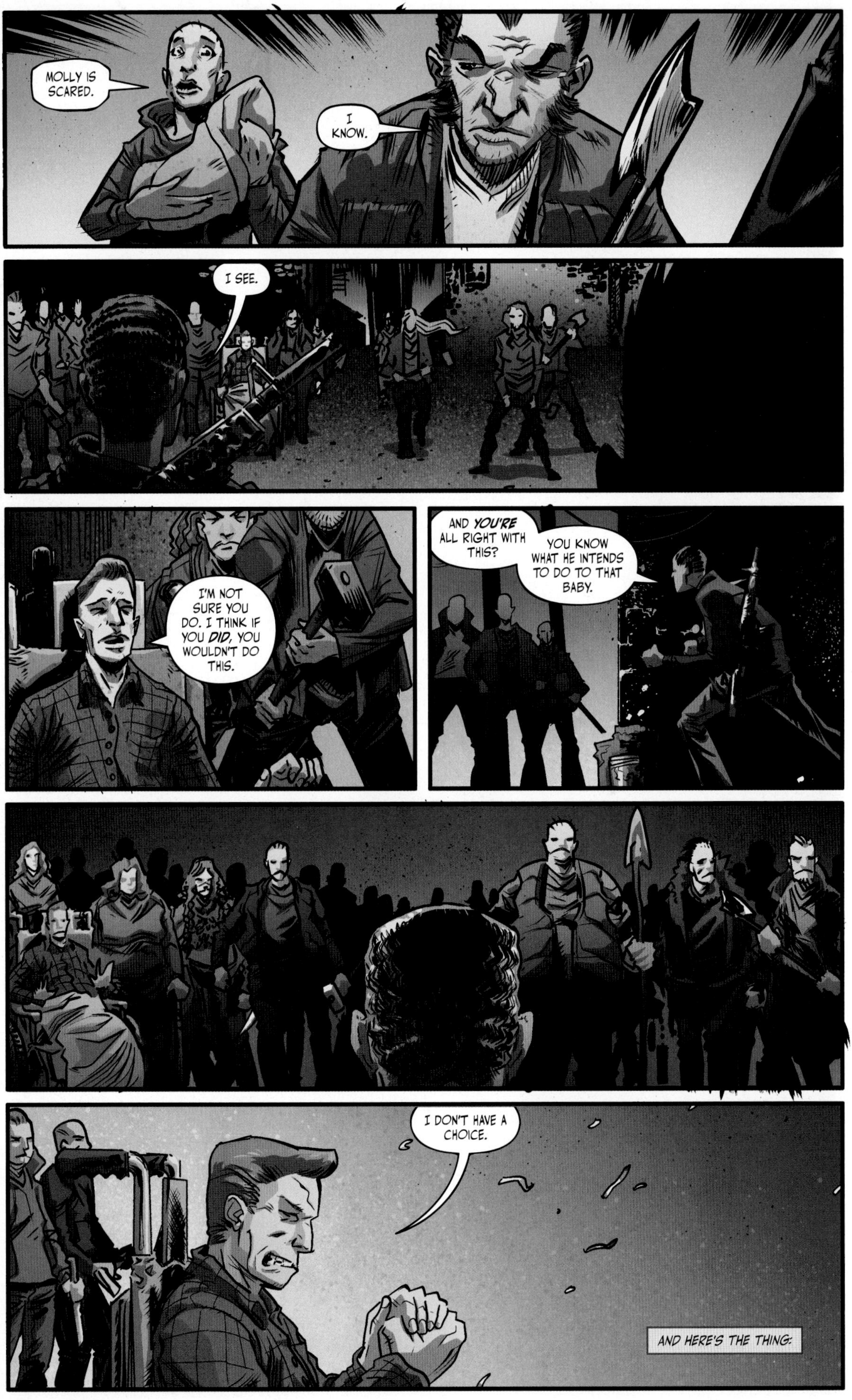
MOLLY IS SCARED.
I KNOW.
I SEE.
I'M NOT SURE YOU DO. I THINK IF YOU *DID*, YOU WOULDN'T DO THIS.
AND *YOU'RE* ALL RIGHT WITH THIS?
YOU KNOW WHAT HE INTENDS TO DO TO THAT BABY.
I DON'T HAVE A CHOICE.
AND HERE'S THE THING:

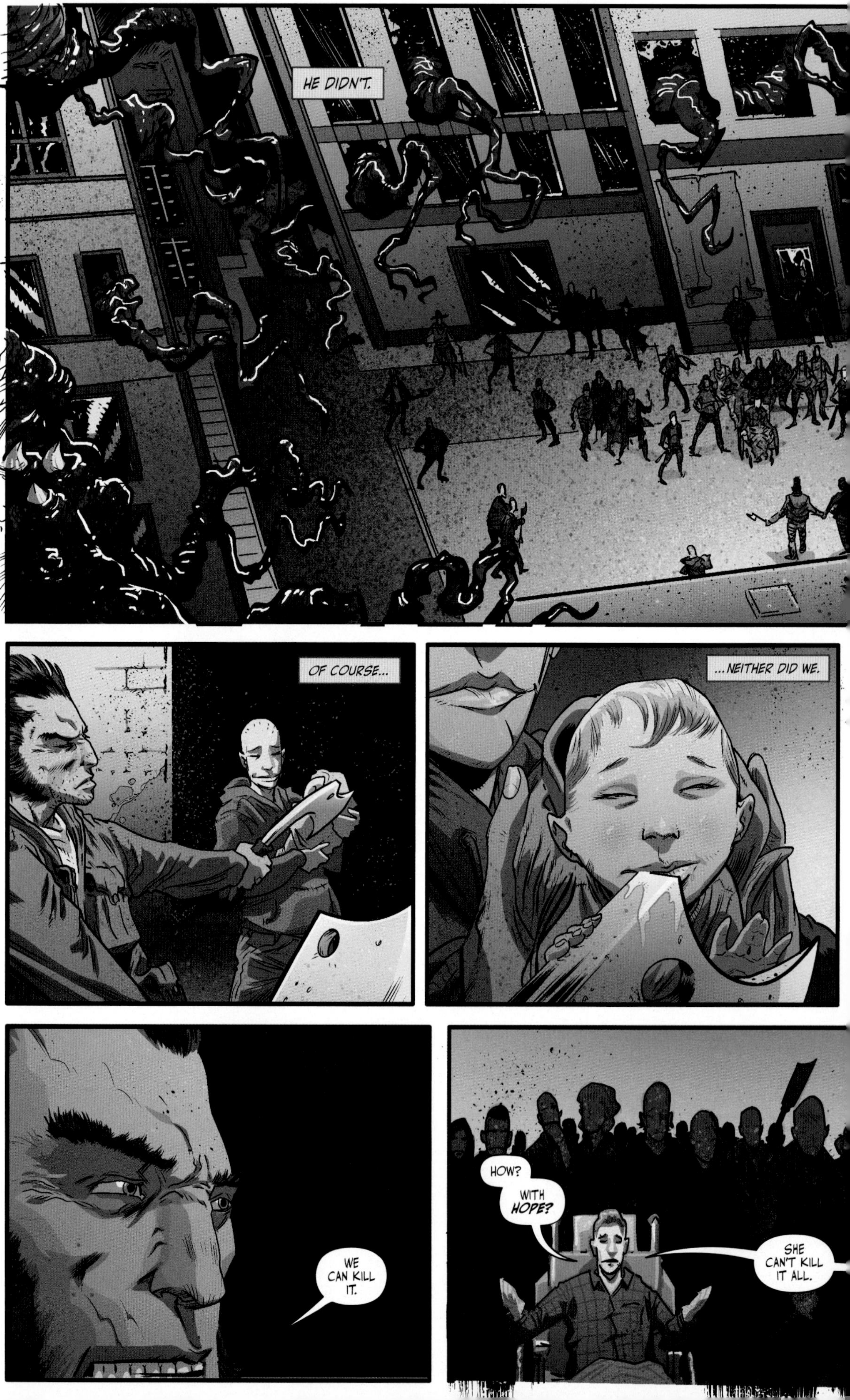
HE DIDN'T.
OF COURSE...
...NEITHER DID WE.
WE CAN KILL IT.
HOW?
WITH HOPE?
SHE CAN'T KILL IT ALL.

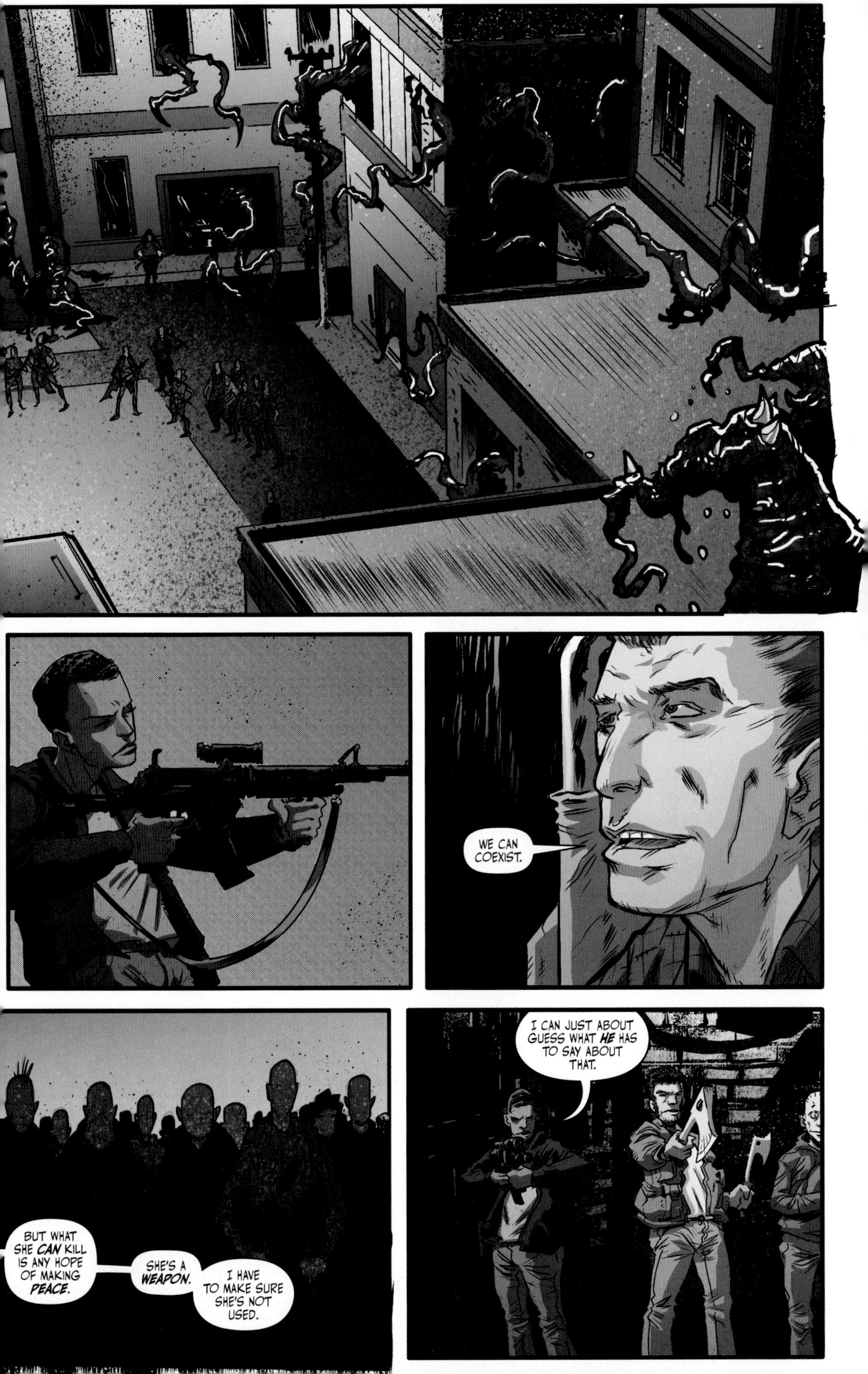
WE CAN COEXIST.
BUT WHAT SHE CAN KILL IS ANY HOPE OF MAKING PEACE.
SHE'S A WEAPON.
I HAVE TO MAKE SURE SHE'S NOT USED.
I CAN JUST ABOUT GUESS WHAT HE HAS TO SAY ABOUT THAT.

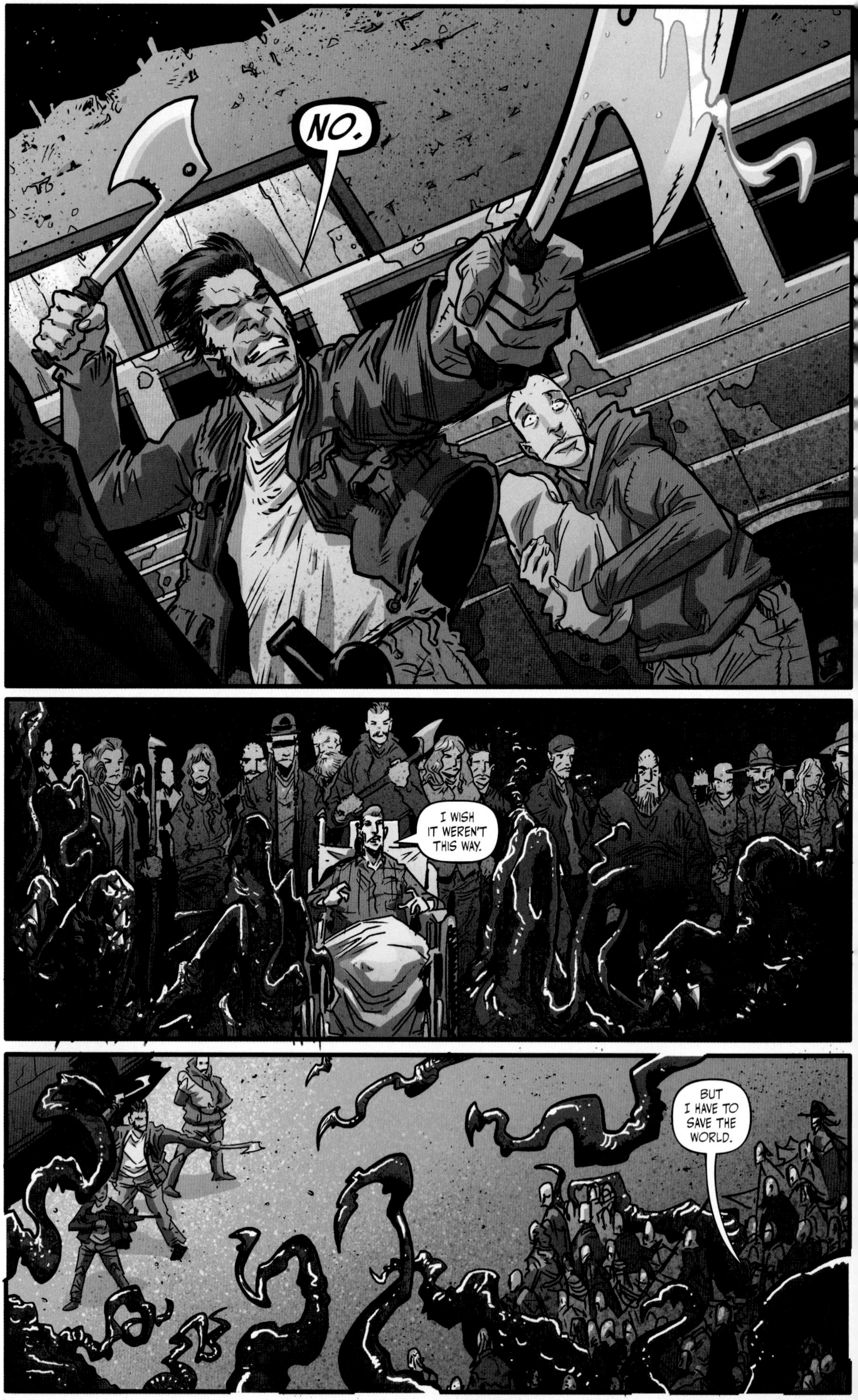
NO.
I WISH IT WEREN'T THIS WAY.
BUT I HAVE TO SAVE THE WORLD.

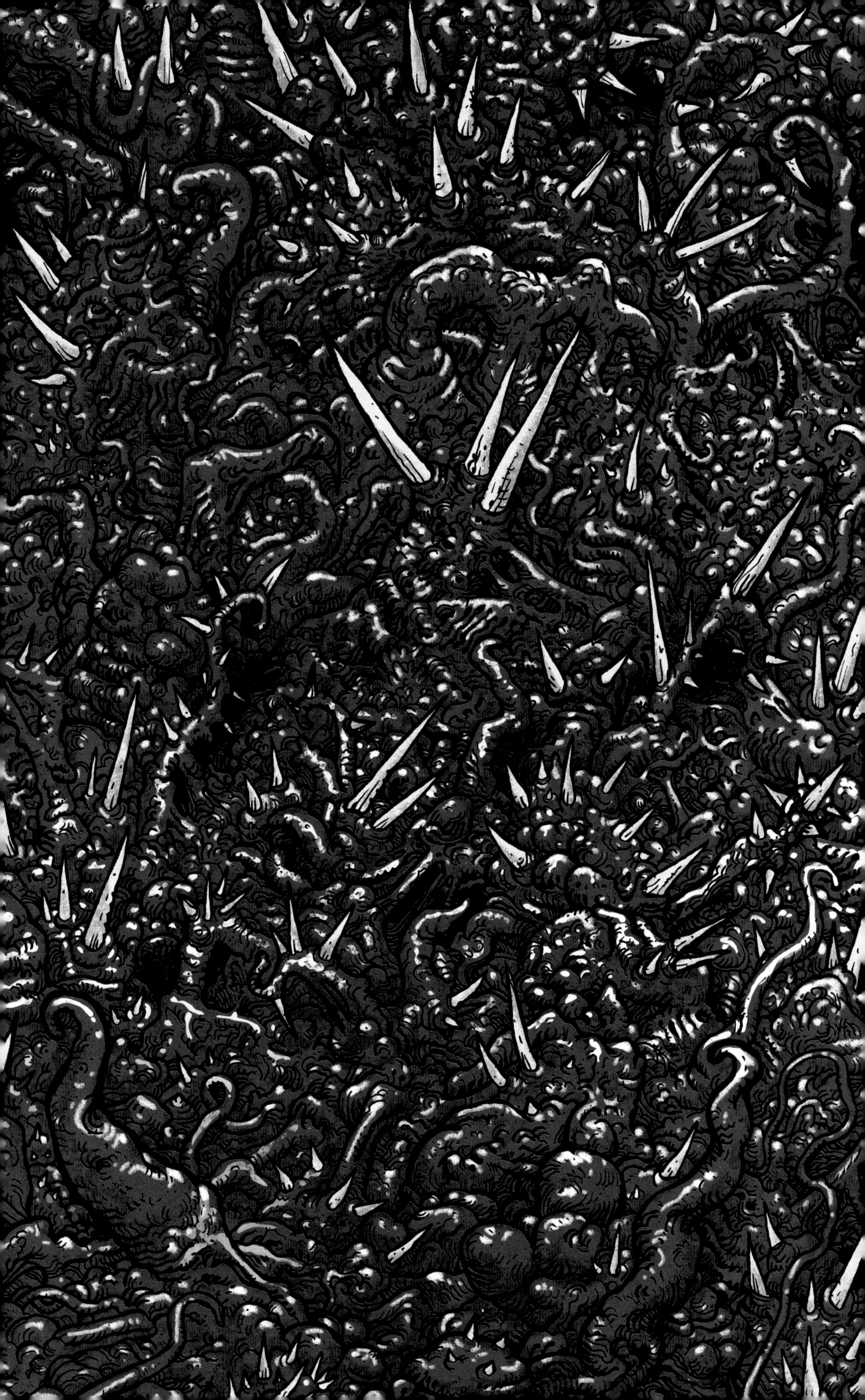

CHAPTER SIX

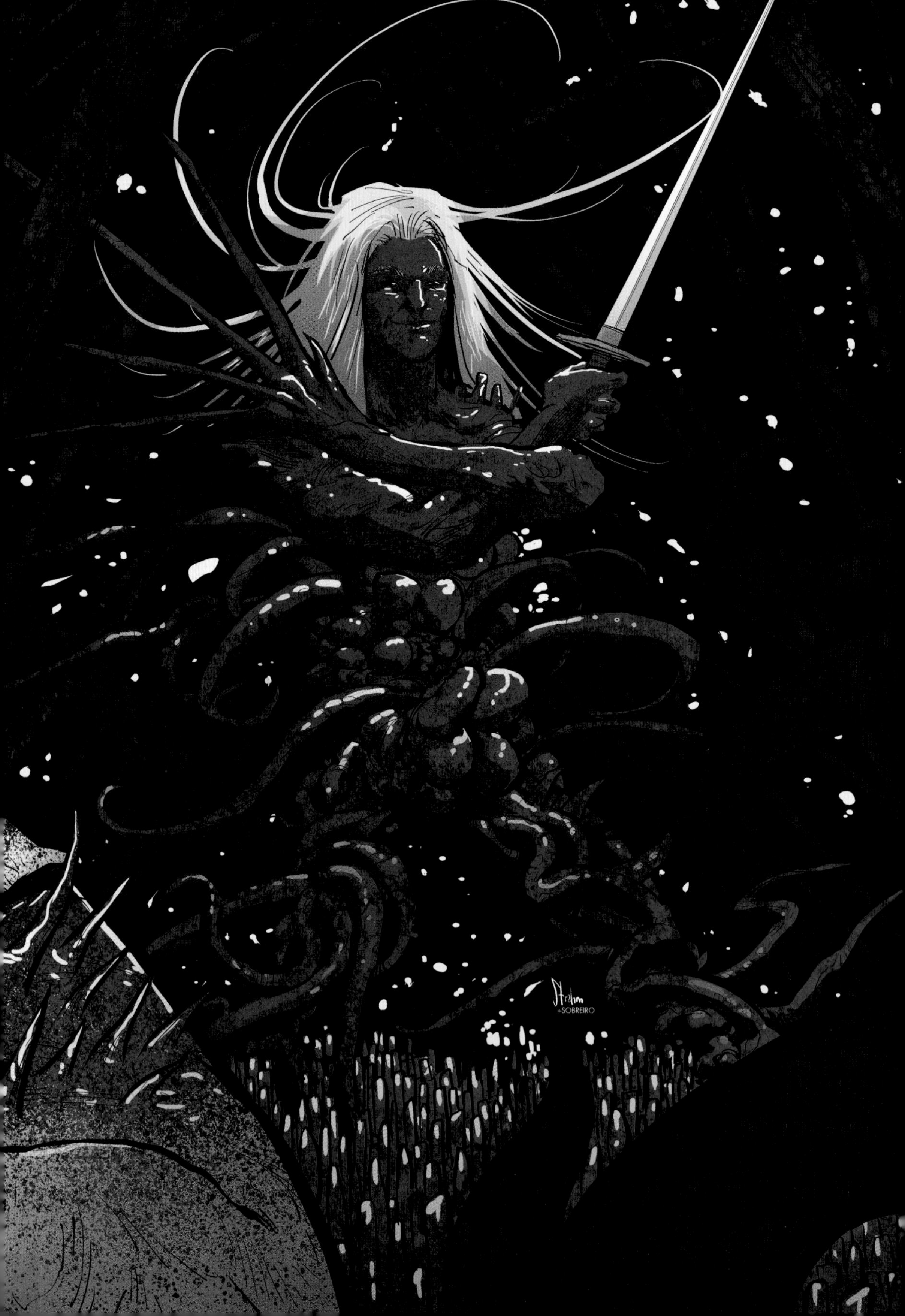
+SOBREIRO

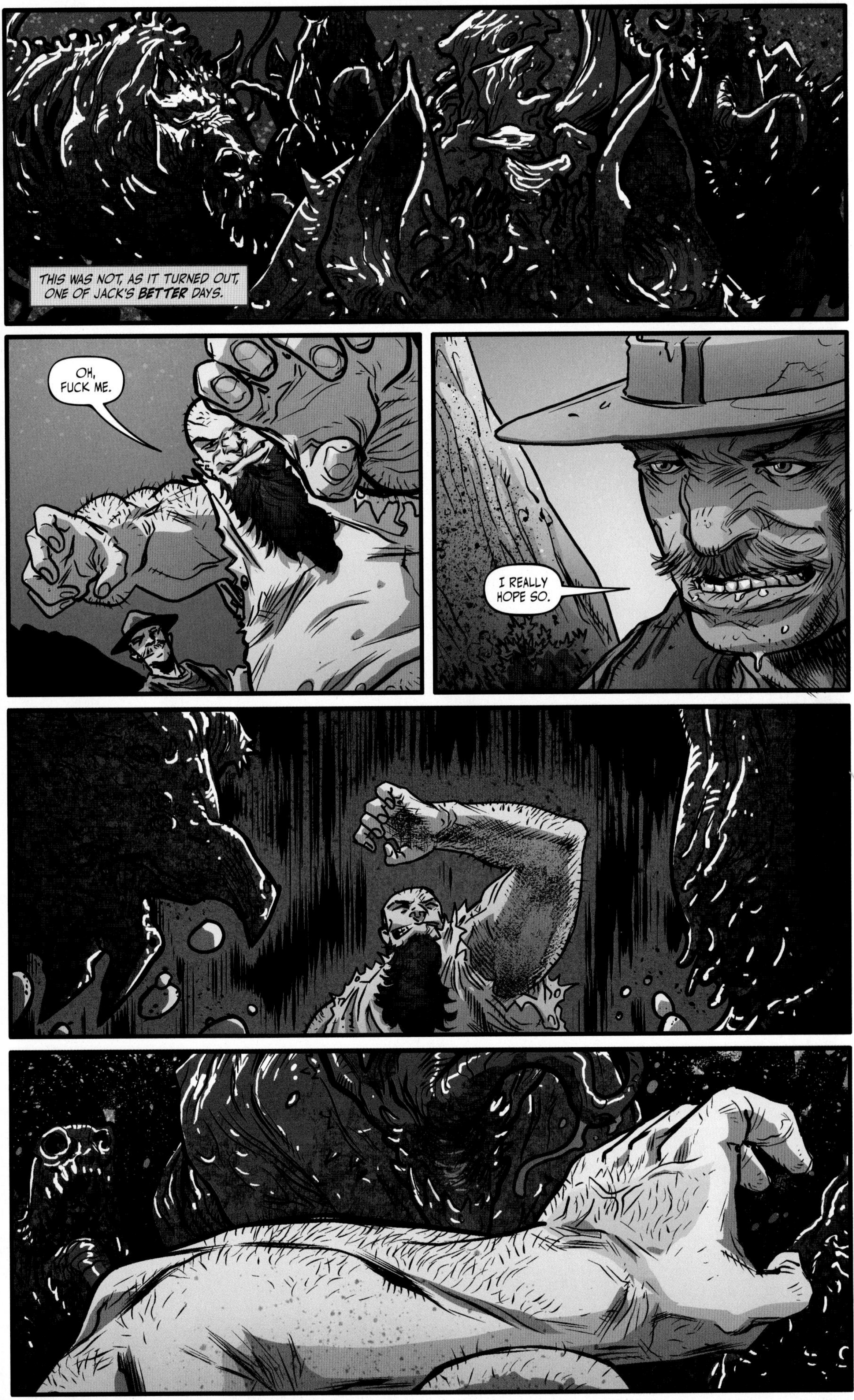
THIS WAS NOT, AS IT TURNED OUT, ONE OF JACK'S **BETTER** DAYS.
OH, FUCK ME.
I REALLY HOPE SO.

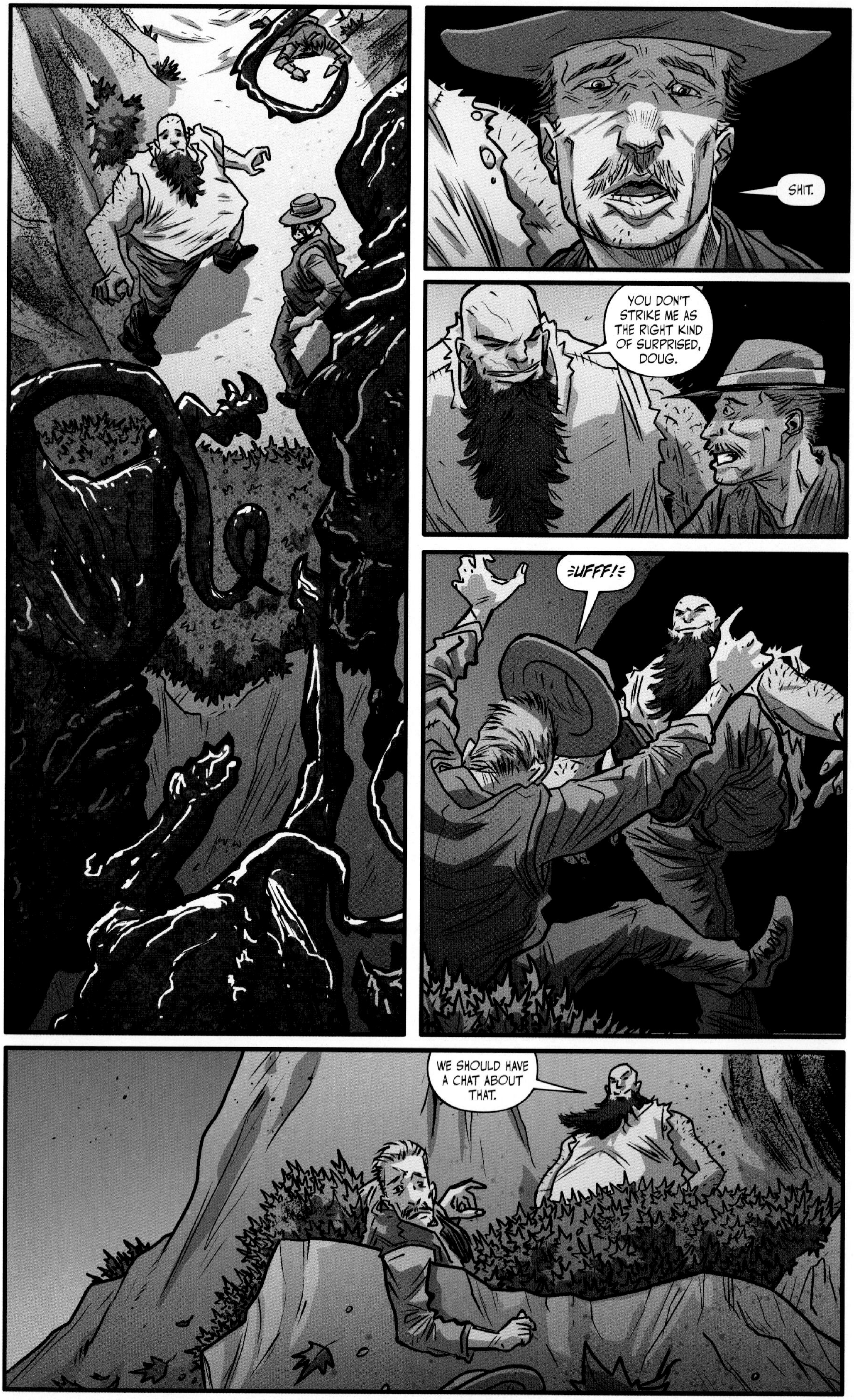
SHIT.
YOU DON'T STRIKE ME AS THE RIGHT KIND OF SURPRISED, DOUG.
UFFF!
WE SHOULD HAVE A CHAT ABOUT THAT.

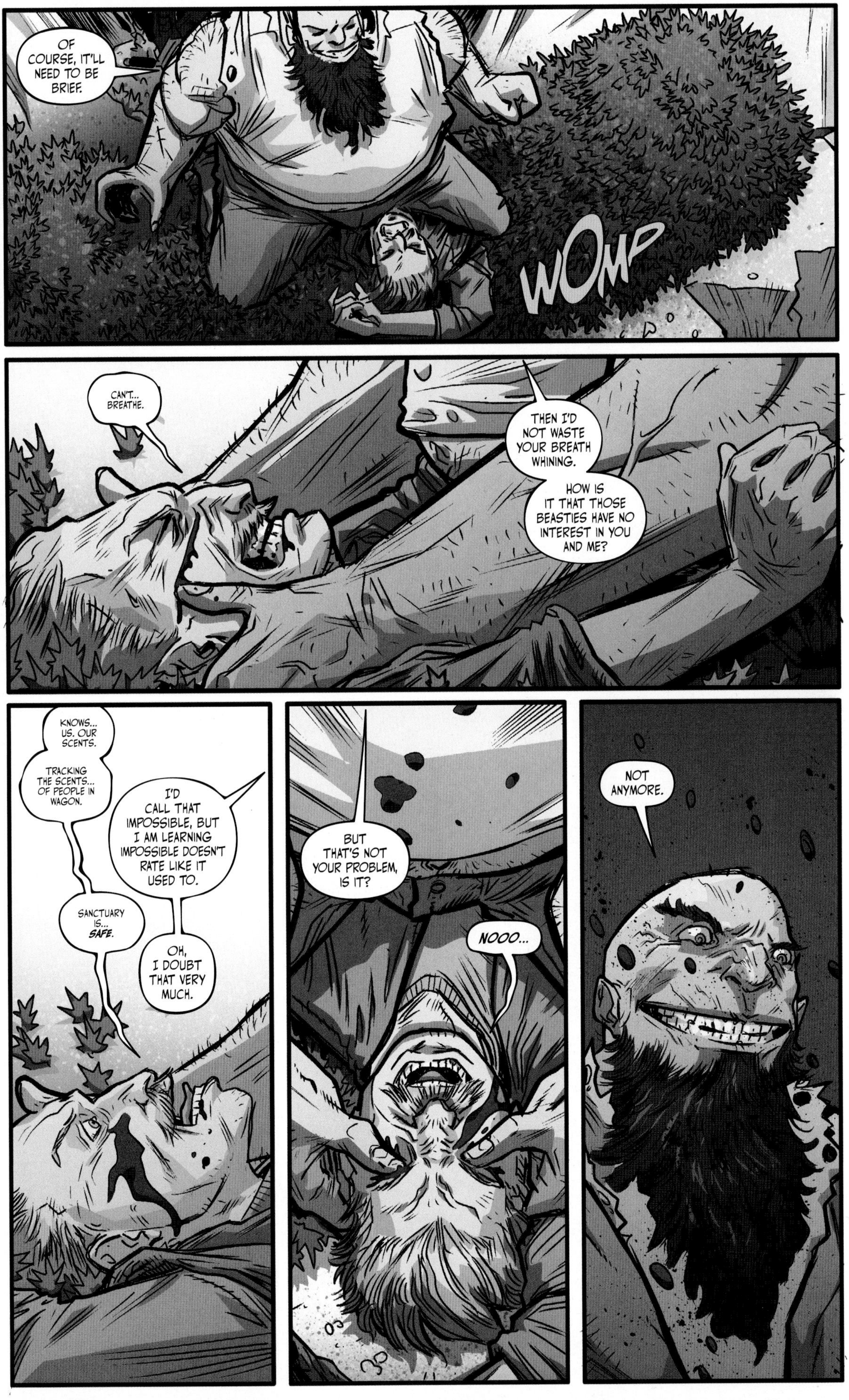
OF COURSE, IT'LL NEED TO BE BRIEF.
WOMP
CAN'T... BREATHE.
THEN I'D NOT WASTE YOUR BREATH WHINING.
HOW IS IT THAT THOSE BEASTIES HAVE NO INTEREST IN YOU AND ME?
KNOWS... US. OUR SCENTS.
TRACKING THE SCENTS... OF PEOPLE IN WAGON.
I'D CALL THAT IMPOSSIBLE, BUT I AM LEARNING IMPOSSIBLE DOESN'T RATE LIKE IT USED TO.
SANCTUARY IS... *SAFE*.
OH, I DOUBT THAT VERY MUCH.
BUT THAT'S NOT YOUR PROBLEM, IS IT?
NOOO...
NOT ANYMORE.

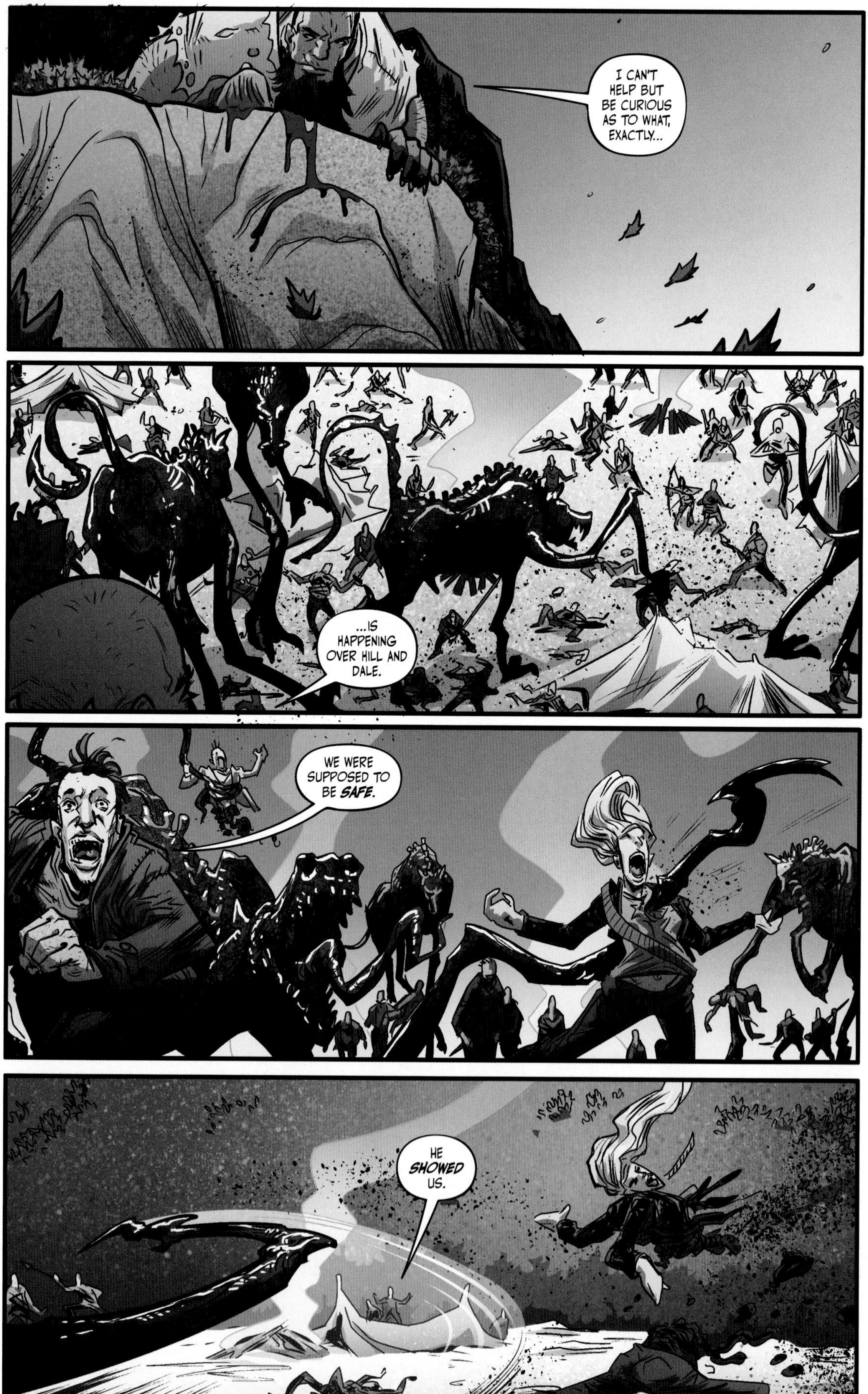
I CAN'T HELP BUT BE CURIOUS AS TO WHAT, EXACTLY...
...IS HAPPENING OVER HILL AND DALE.
WE WERE SUPPOSED TO BE *SAFE*.
HE *SHOWED* US.

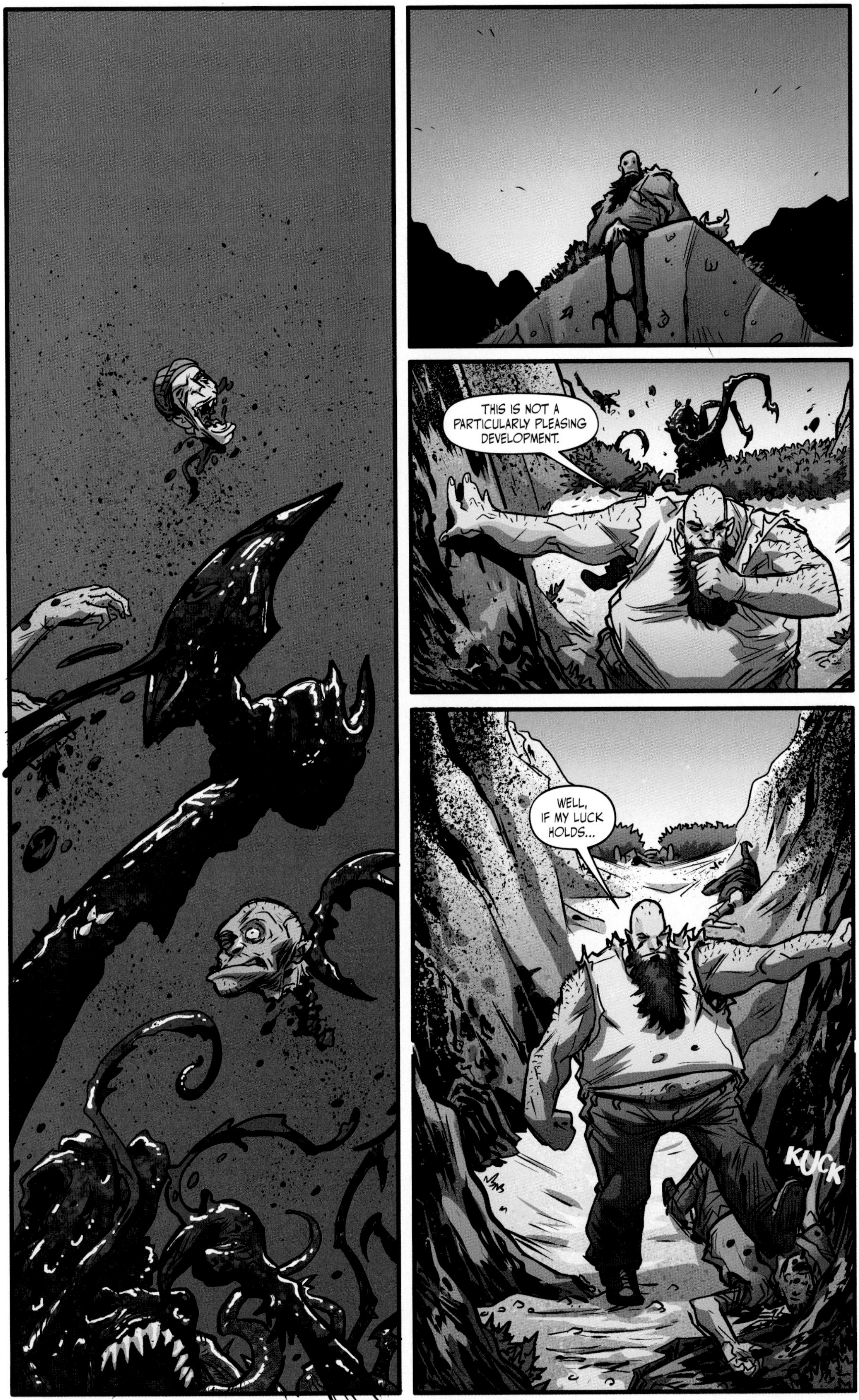
THIS IS NOT A PARTICULARLY PLEASING DEVELOPMENT.
WELL, IF MY LUCK HOLDS...
KUCK

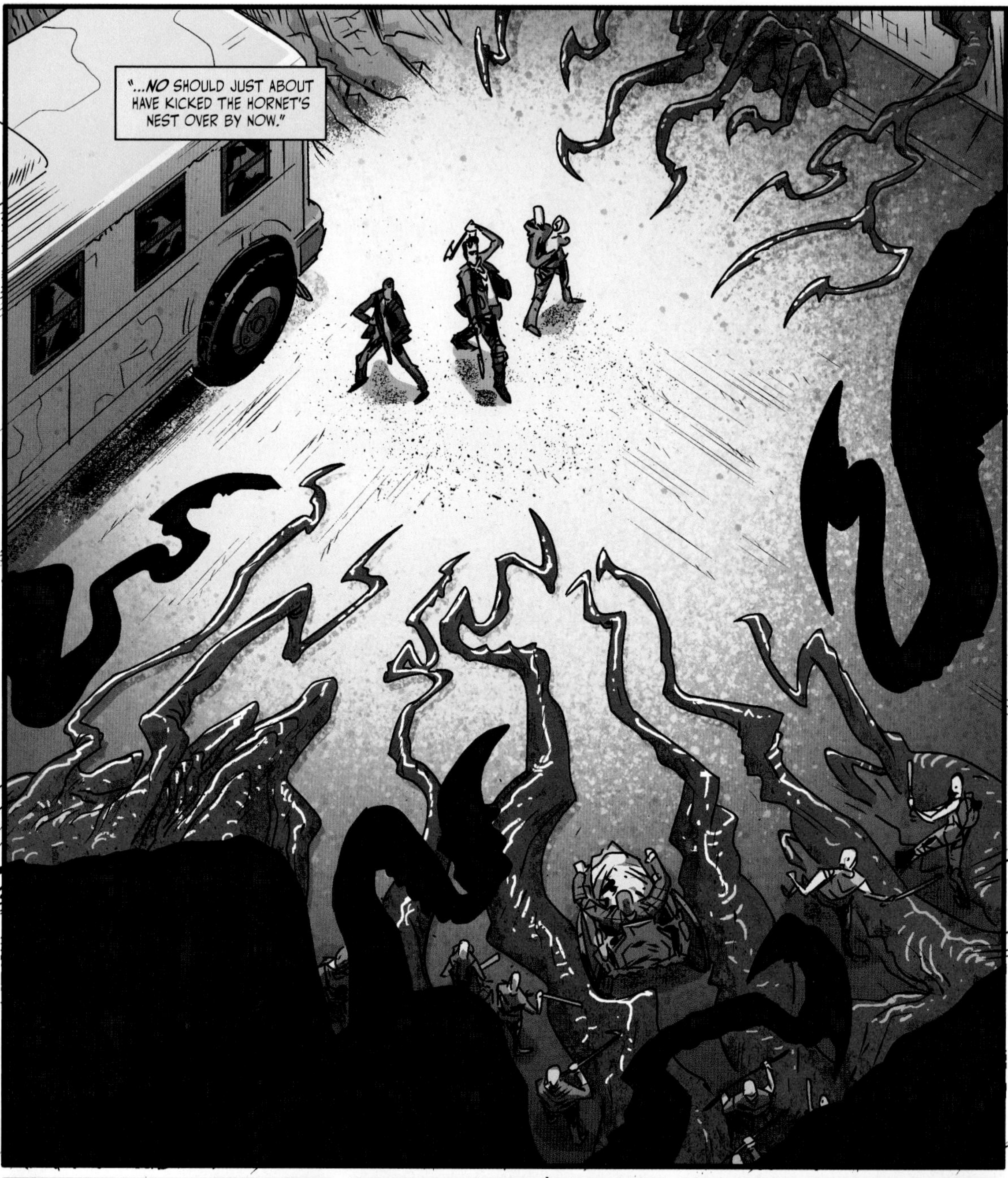
"...NO SHOULD JUST ABOUT HAVE KICKED THE HORNET'S NEST OVER BY NOW."

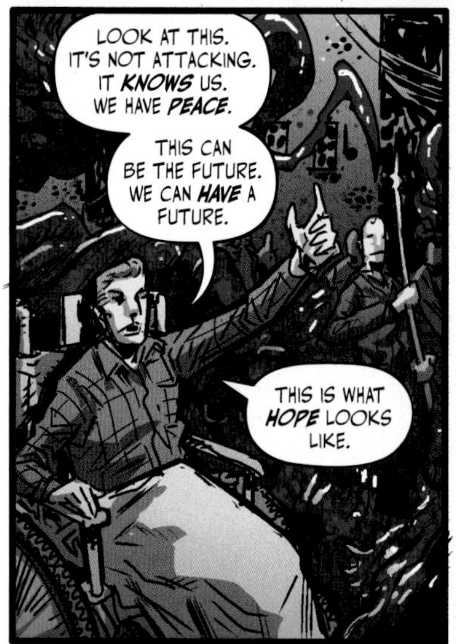
LOOK AT THIS. IT'S NOT ATTACKING. IT KNOWS US. WE HAVE PEACE.
THIS CAN BE THE FUTURE. WE CAN HAVE A FUTURE.
THIS IS WHAT HOPE LOOKS LIKE.

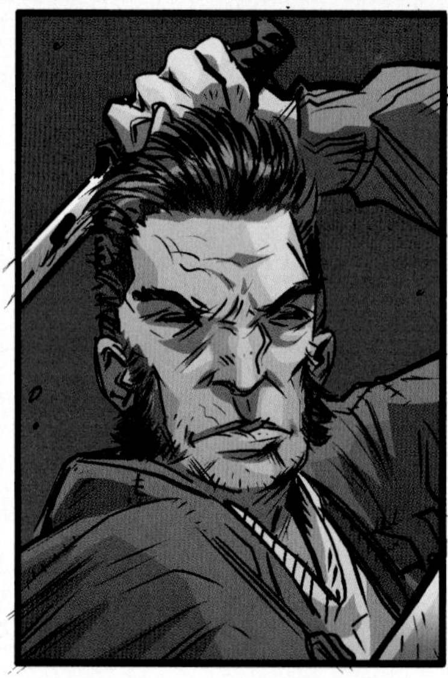

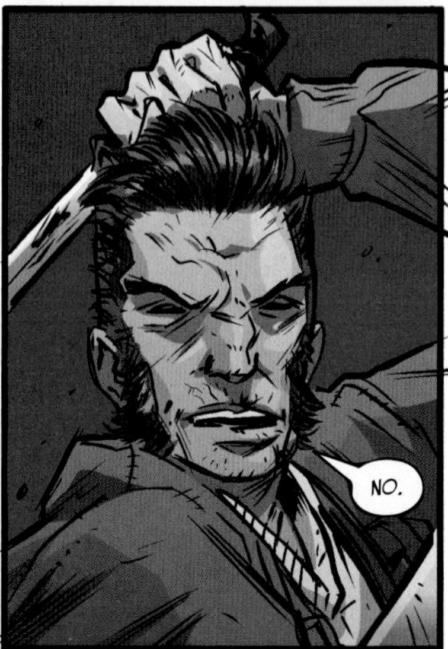
NO.

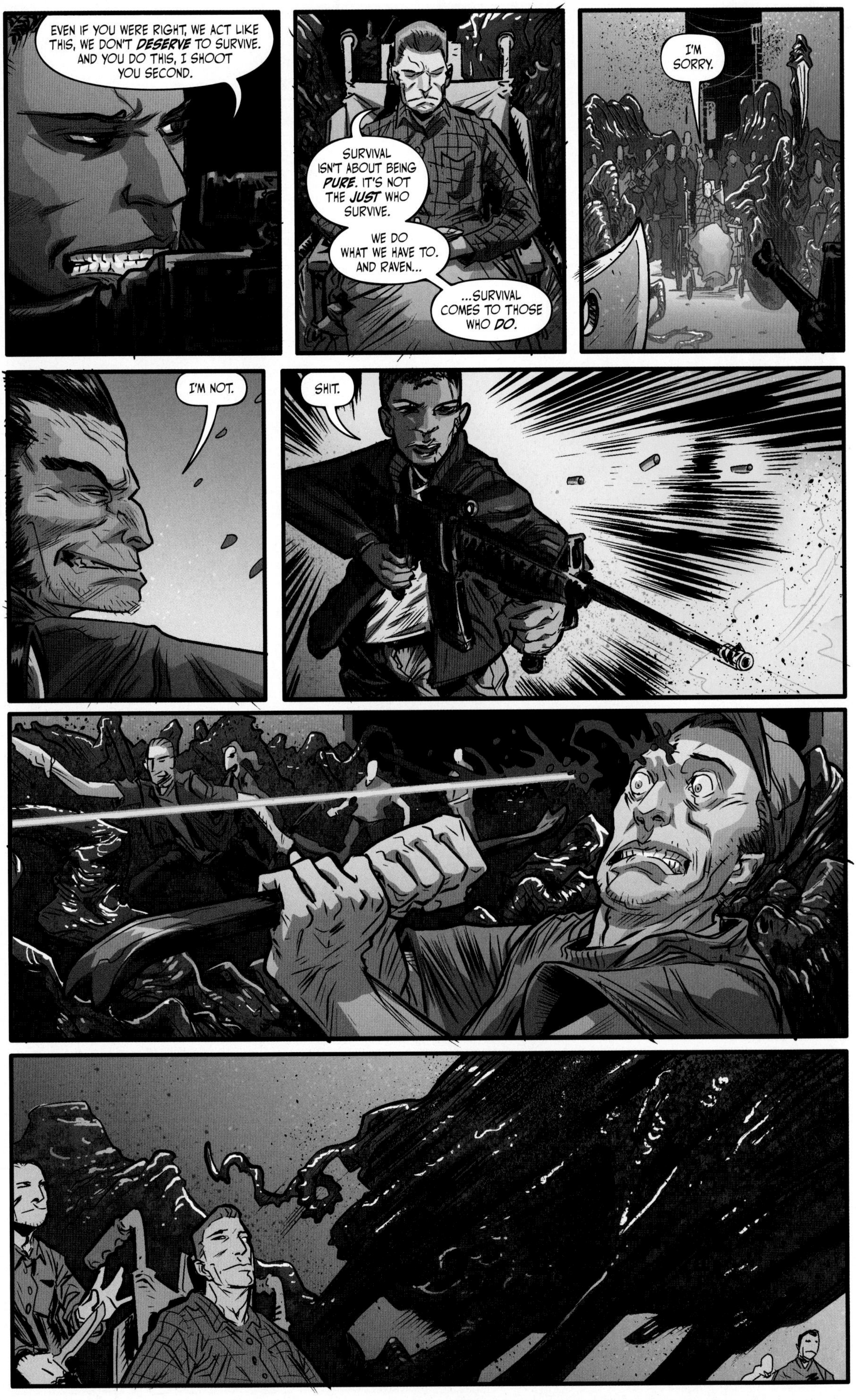
EVEN IF YOU WERE RIGHT, WE ACT LIKE THIS, WE DON'T *DESERVE* TO SURVIVE. AND YOU DO THIS, I SHOOT YOU SECOND.
SURVIVAL ISN'T ABOUT BEING *PURE*. IT'S NOT THE *JUST* WHO SURVIVE.
WE DO WHAT WE HAVE TO. AND RAVEN...
...SURVIVAL COMES TO THOSE WHO *DO*.
I'M SORRY.
I'M NOT.
SHIT.

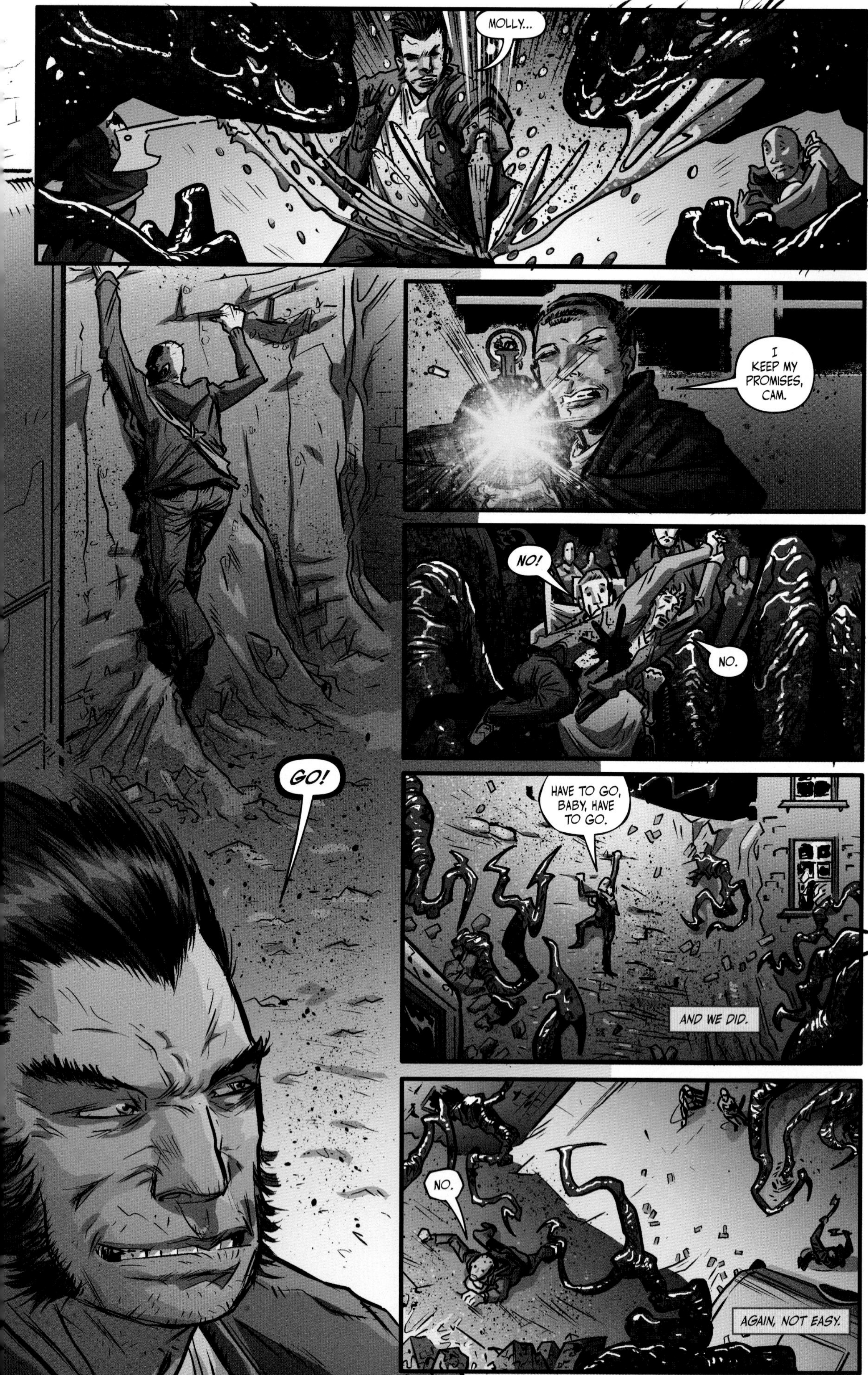
MOLLY...
I KEEP MY PROMISES, CAM.
NO!
NO.
GO!
HAVE TO GO, BABY, HAVE TO GO.
AND WE DID.
NO.
AGAIN, NOT EASY.

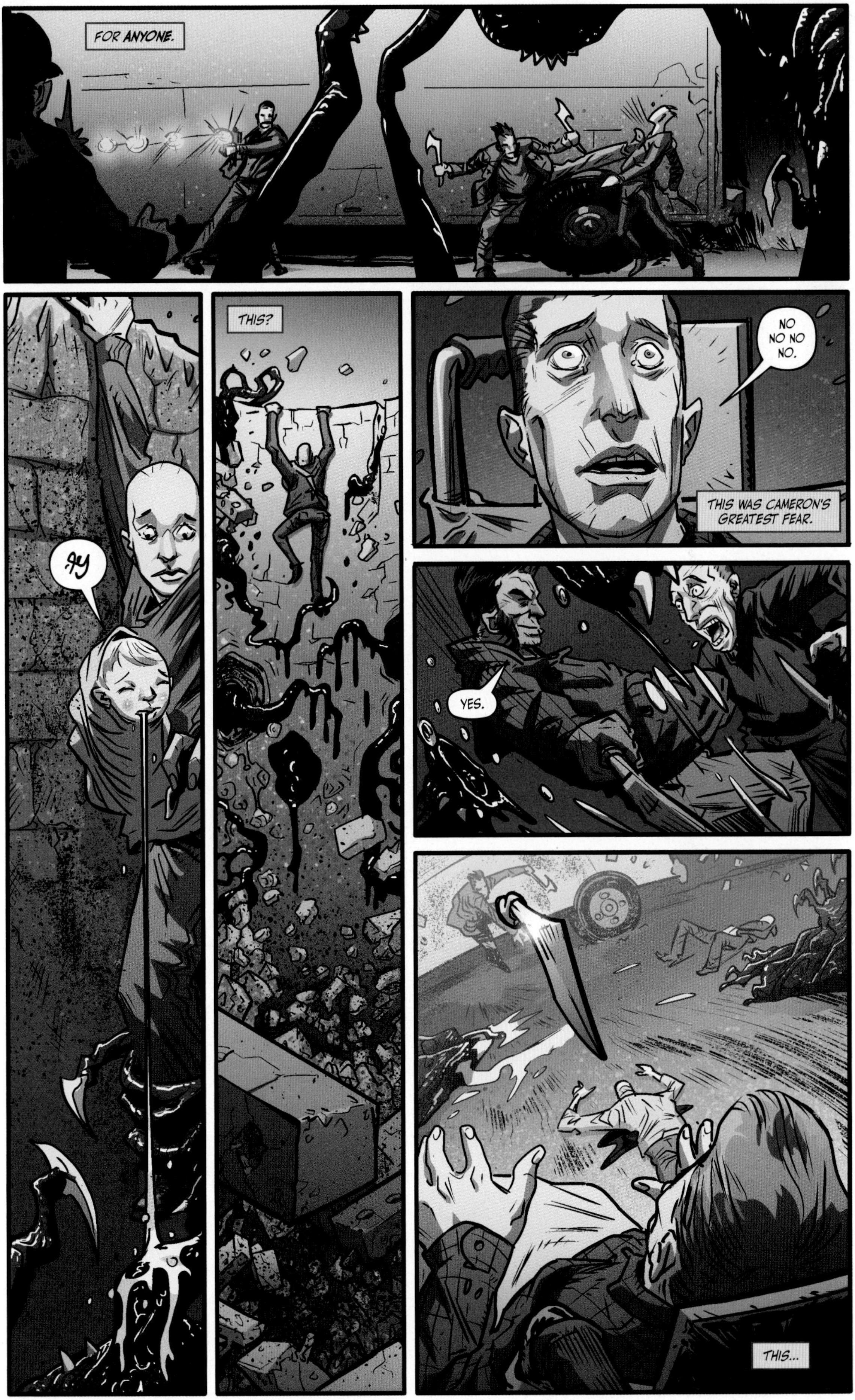
FOR ANYONE.
THIS?
NO NO NO NO.
THIS WAS CAMERON'S GREATEST FEAR.
YES.
THIS...

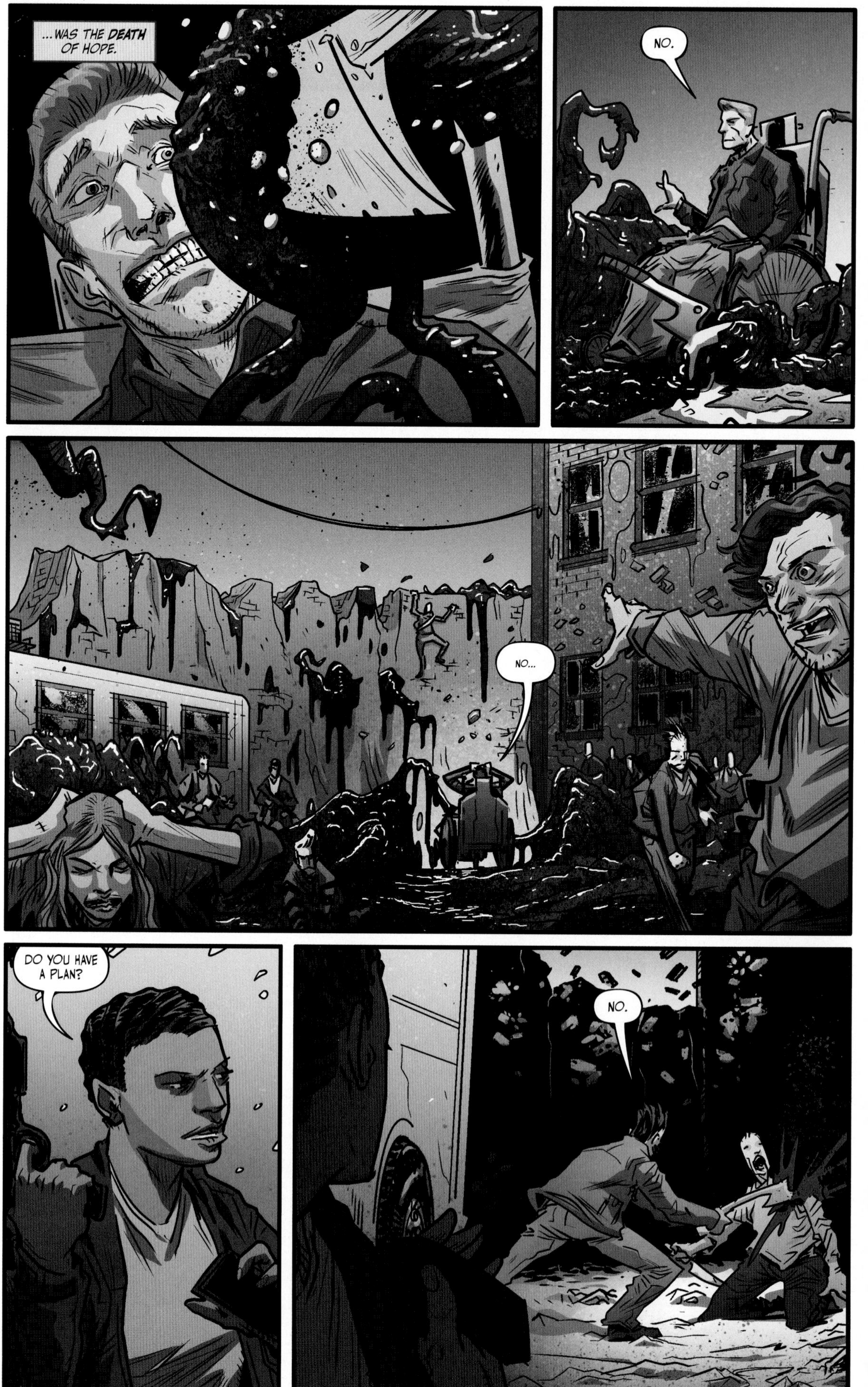
...WAS THE DEATH OF HOPE.
NO.
NO...
DO YOU HAVE A PLAN?
NO.

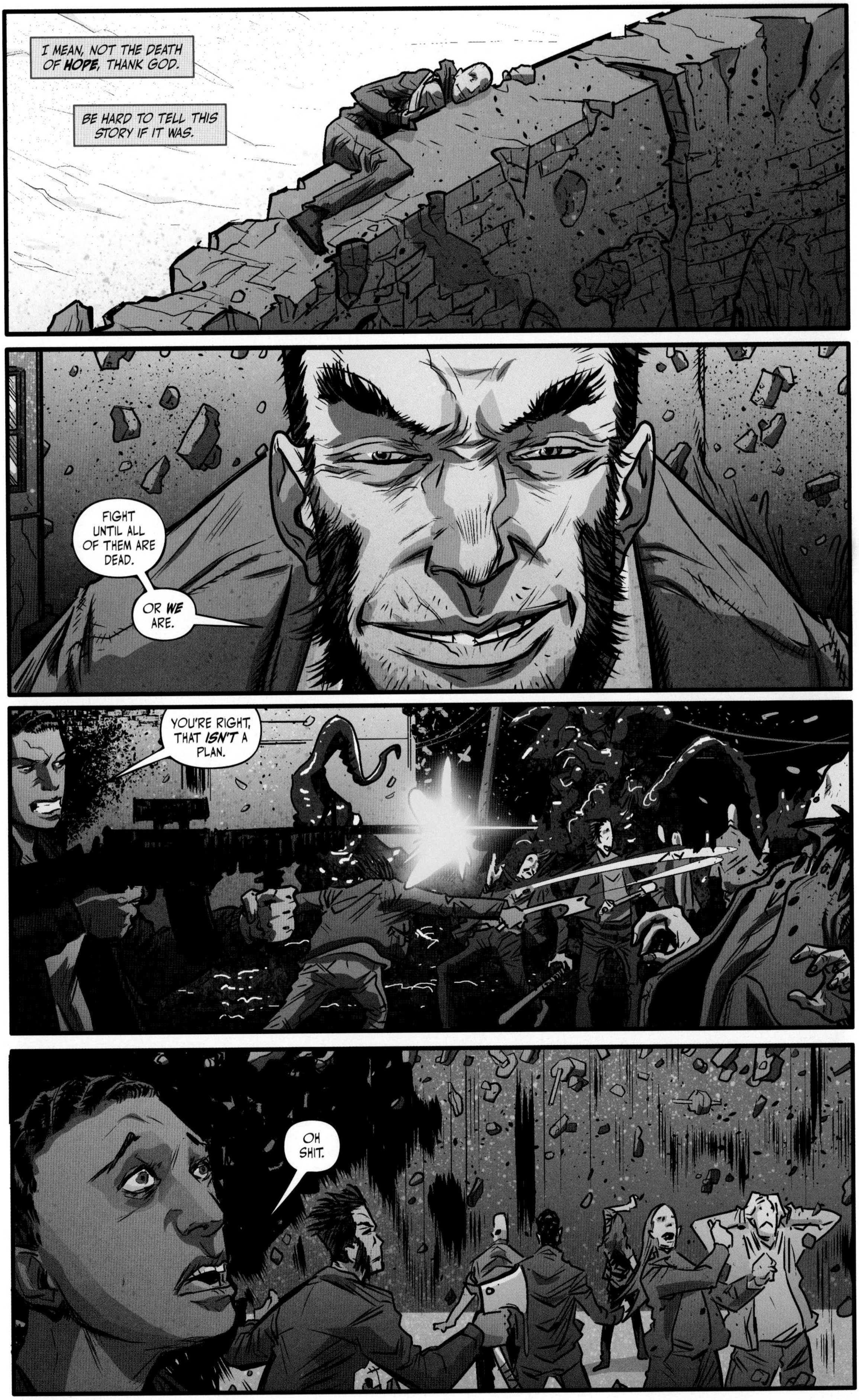
I MEAN, NOT THE DEATH OF HOPE, THANK GOD.
BE HARD TO TELL THIS STORY IF IT WAS.
FIGHT UNTIL ALL OF THEM ARE DEAD.
OR WE ARE.
YOU'RE RIGHT, THAT ISN'T A PLAN.
OH SHIT.

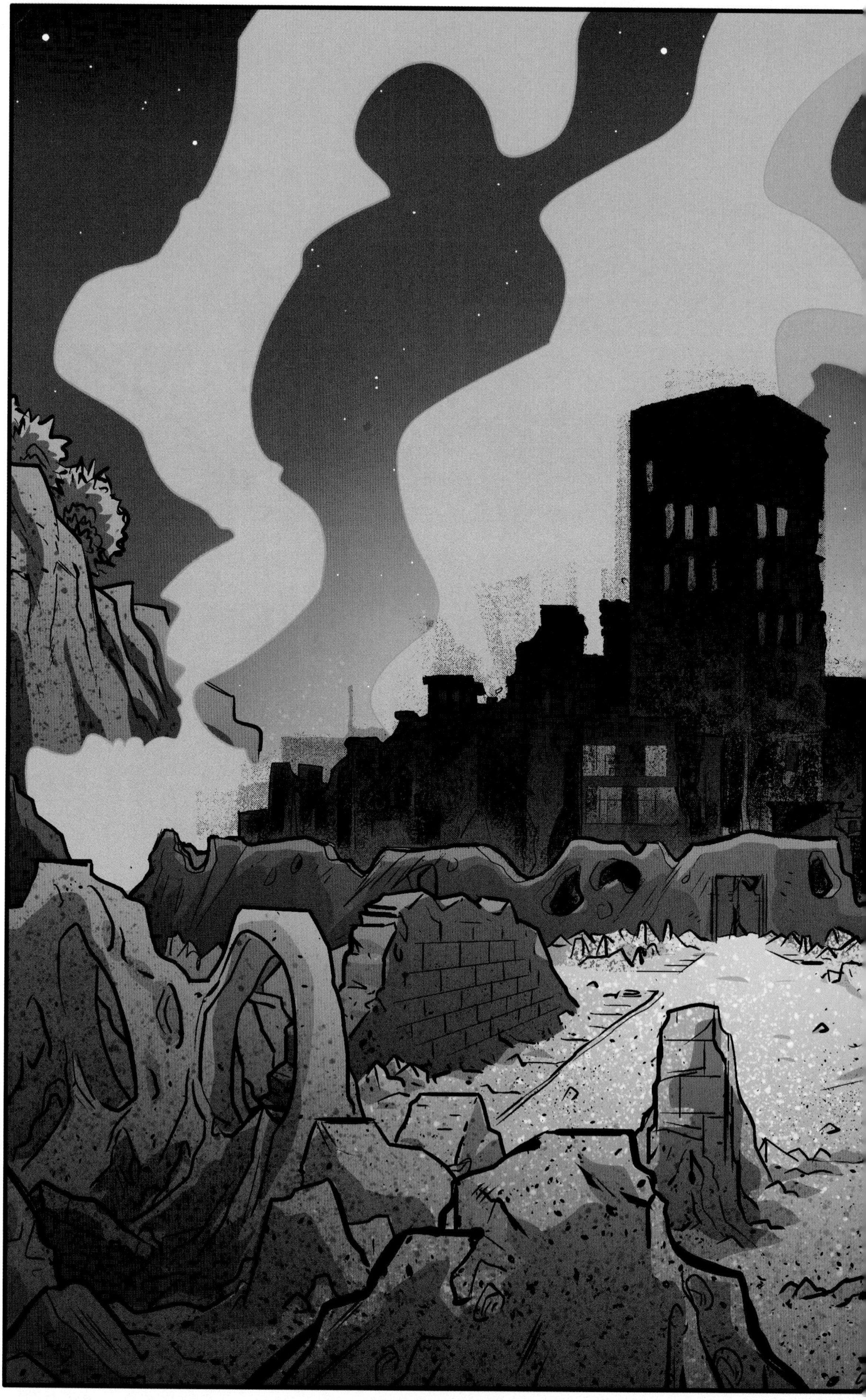

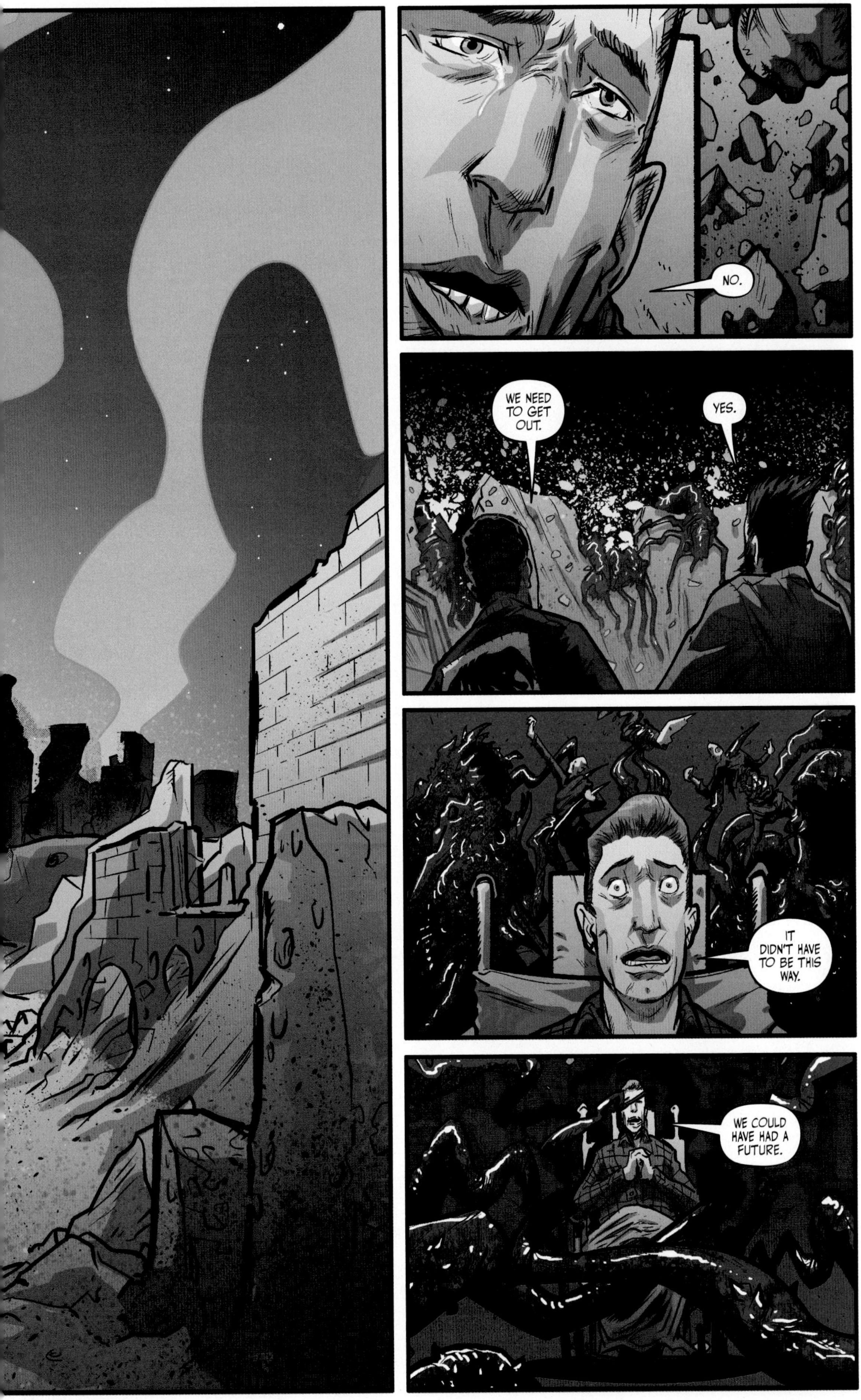
NO.
WE NEED TO GET OUT.
YES.
IT DIDN'T HAVE TO BE THIS WAY.
WE COULD HAVE HAD A FUTURE.

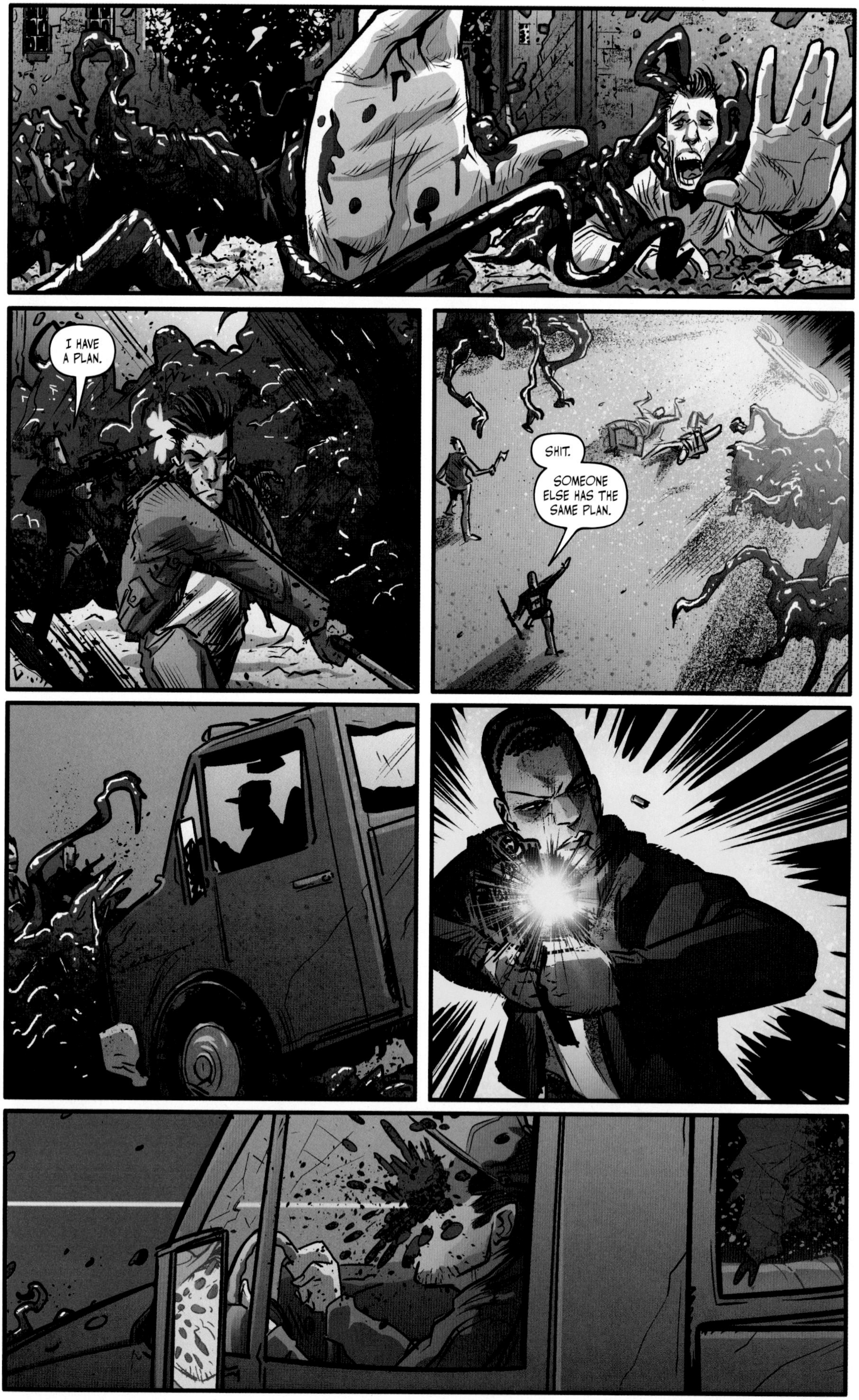
I HAVE A PLAN.
SHIT.
SOMEONE ELSE HAS THE SAME PLAN.

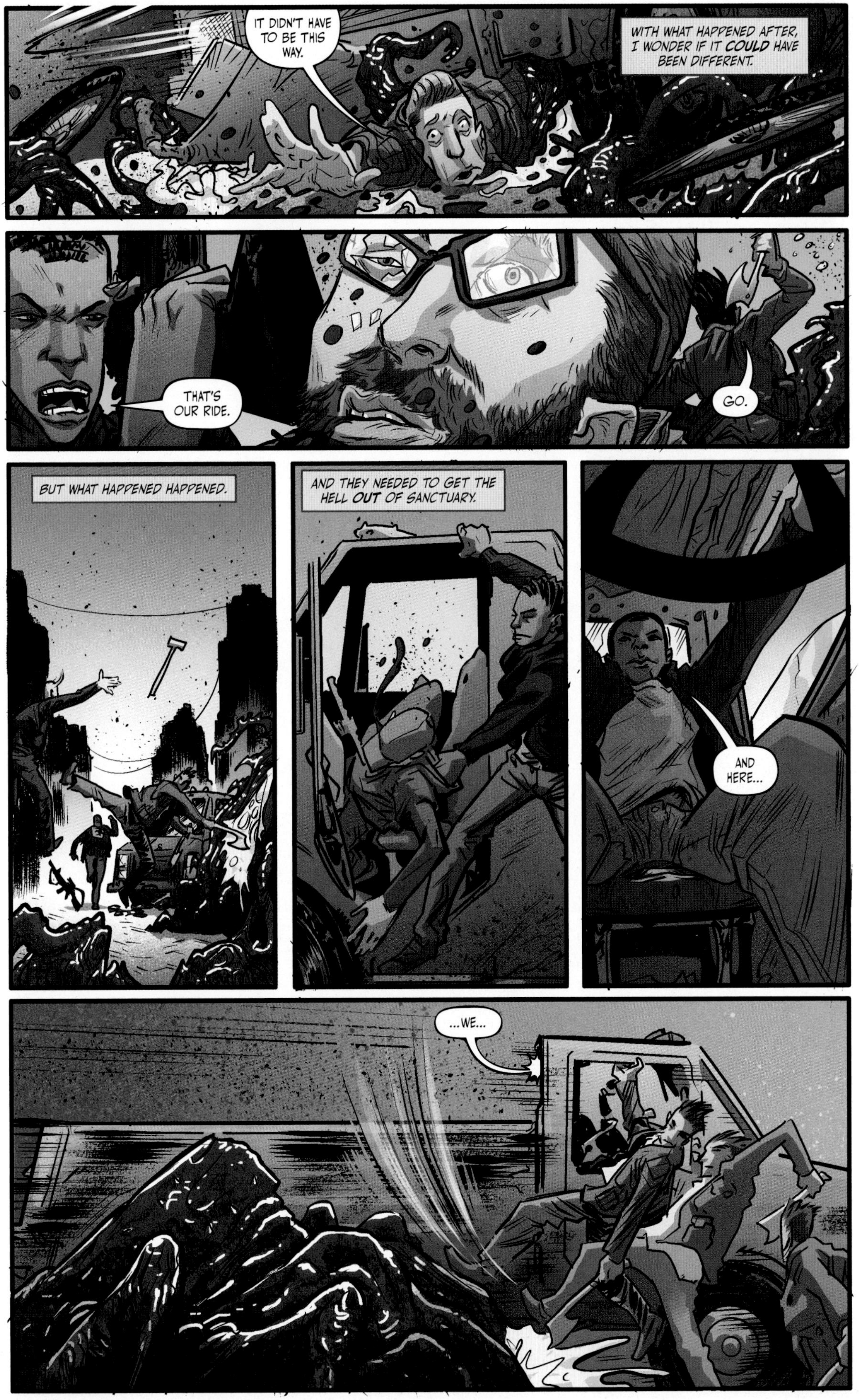
IT DIDN'T HAVE TO BE THIS WAY.
WITH WHAT HAPPENED AFTER, I WONDER IF IT *COULD* HAVE BEEN DIFFERENT.
THAT'S OUR RIDE.
GO.
BUT WHAT HAPPENED HAPPENED.
AND THEY NEEDED TO GET THE HELL *OUT* OF SANCTUARY.
AND HERE...
...WE...

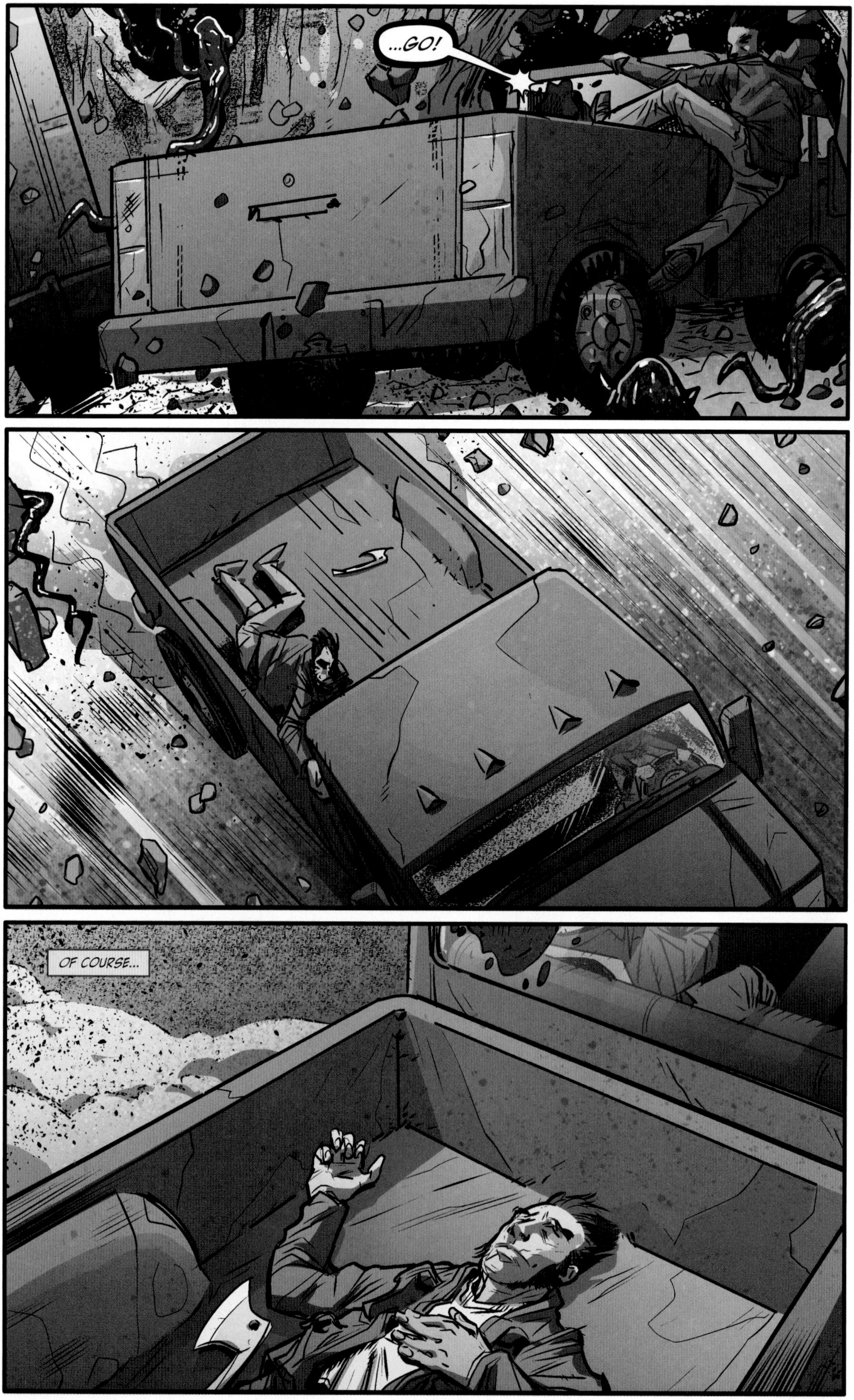
...GO!
OF COURSE...

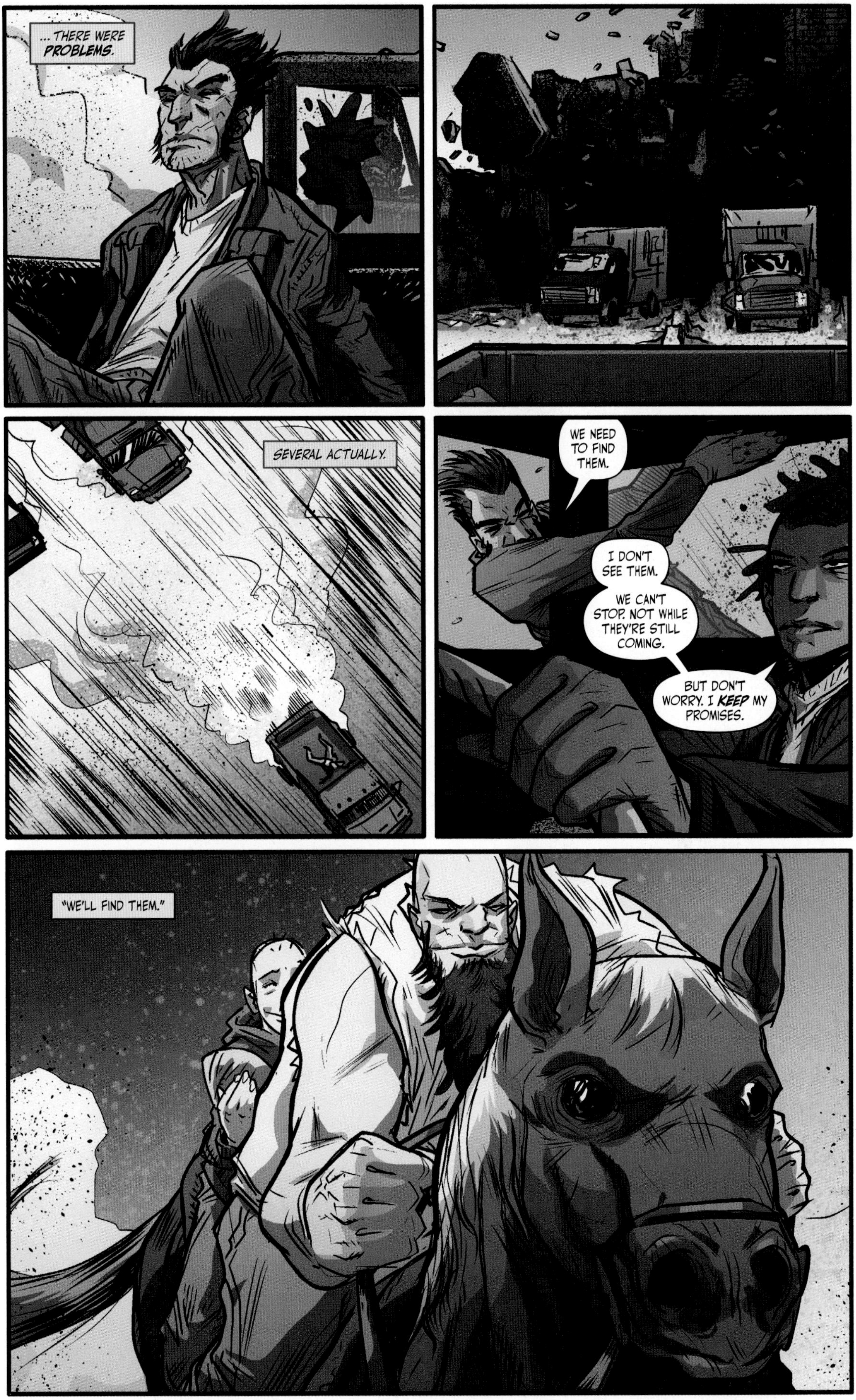
...THERE WERE PROBLEMS.
SEVERAL ACTUALLY.
WE NEED TO FIND THEM.
I DON'T SEE THEM.
WE CAN'T STOP. NOT WHILE THEY'RE STILL COMING.
BUT DON'T WORRY. I KEEP MY PROMISES.
"WE'LL FIND THEM."

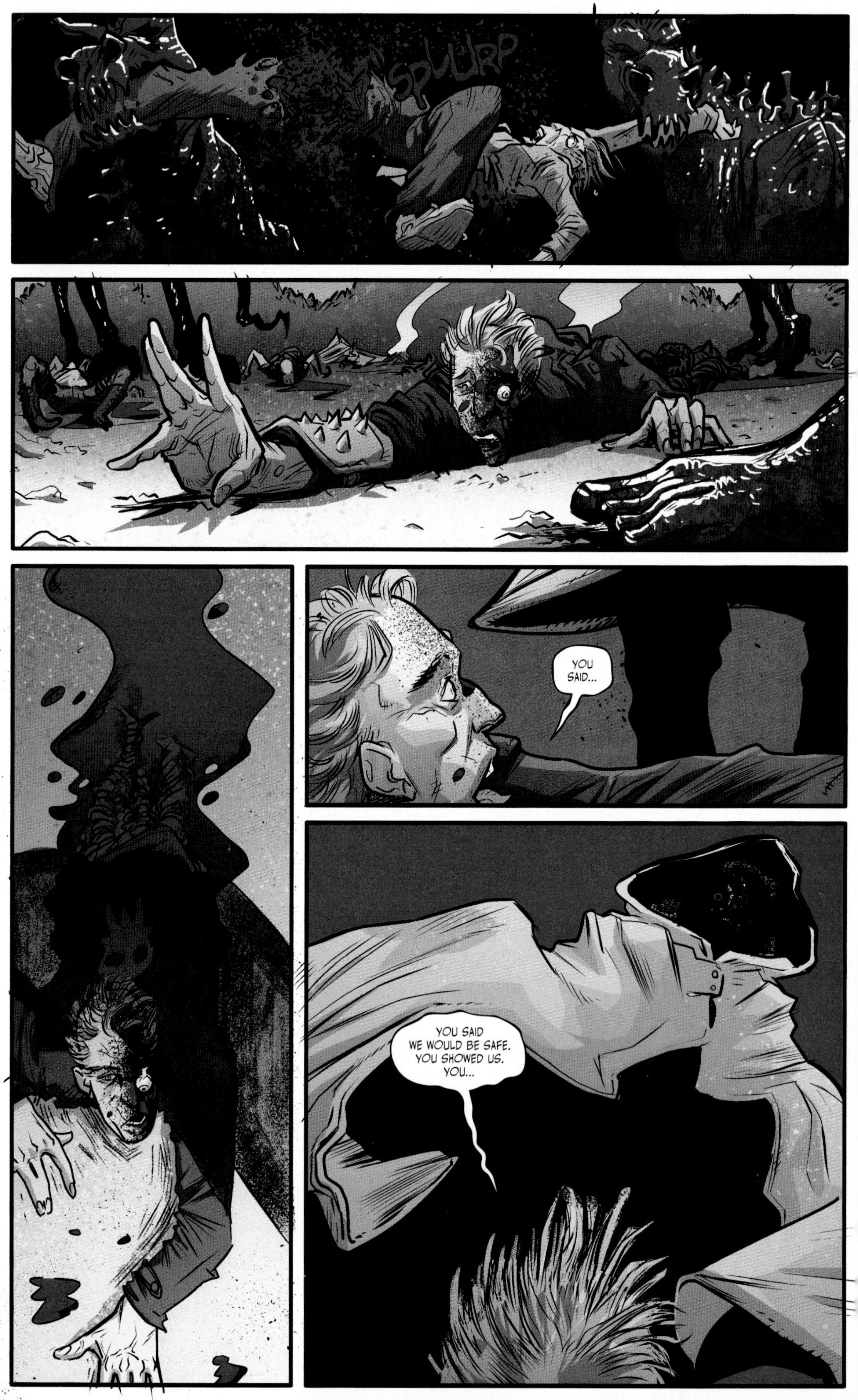
SPLURP
YOU SAID...
YOU SAID WE WOULD BE SAFE. YOU SHOWED US. YOU...

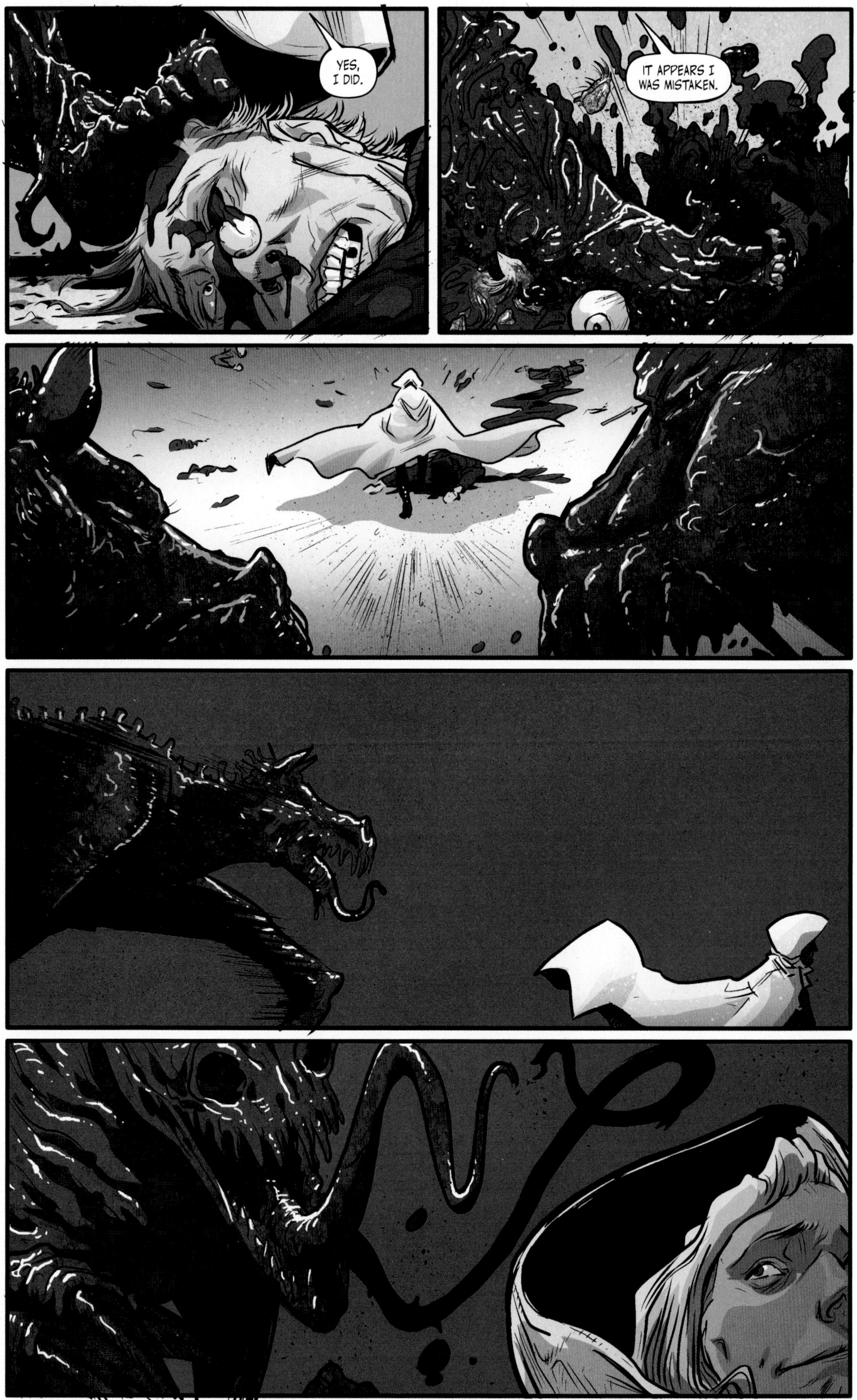
YES, I DID.
IT APPEARS I WAS MISTAKEN.

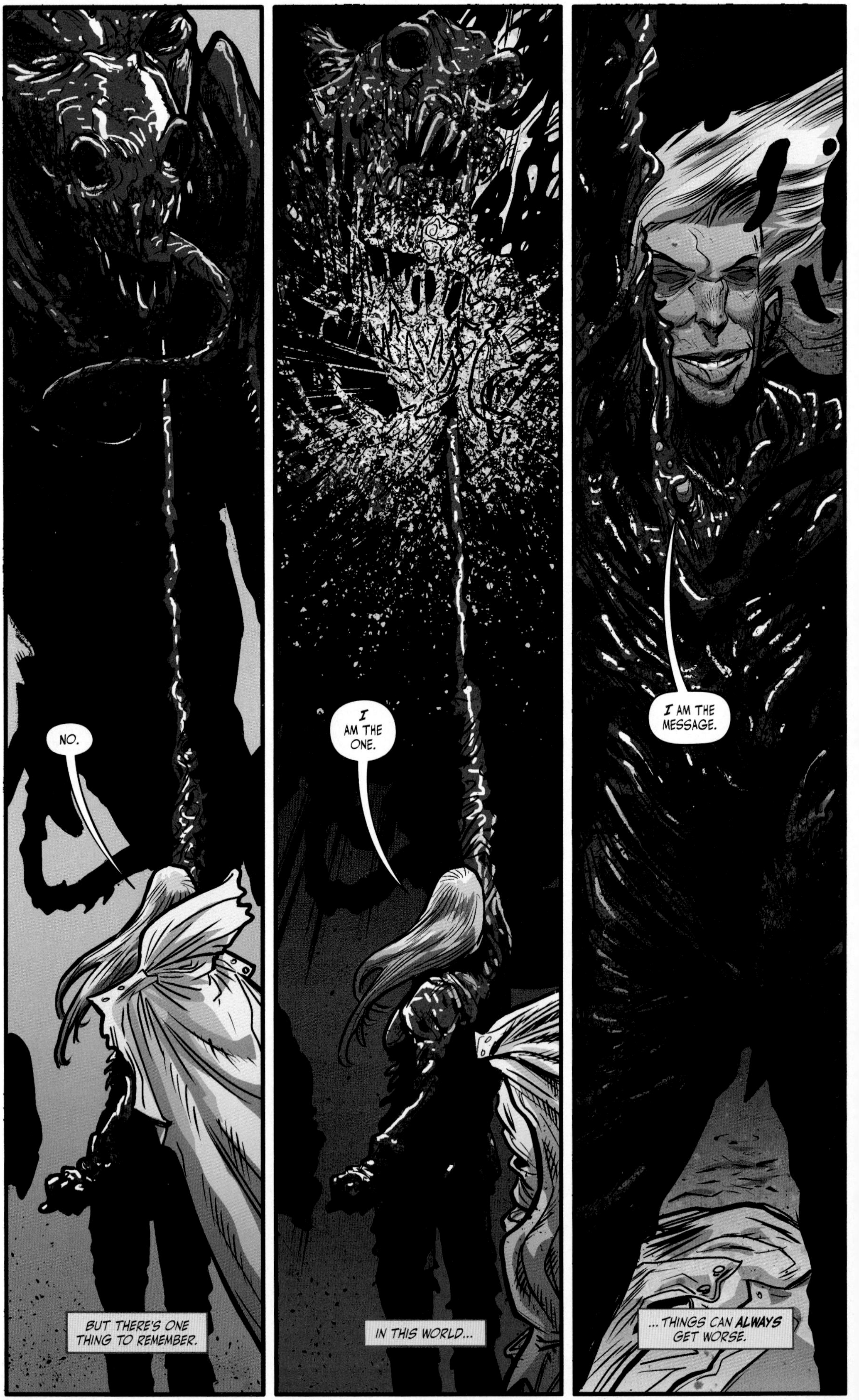
NO.
BUT THERE'S ONE THING TO REMEMBER.
I AM THE ONE.
IN THIS WORLD...
I AM THE MESSAGE.
...THINGS CAN ALWAYS GET WORSE.

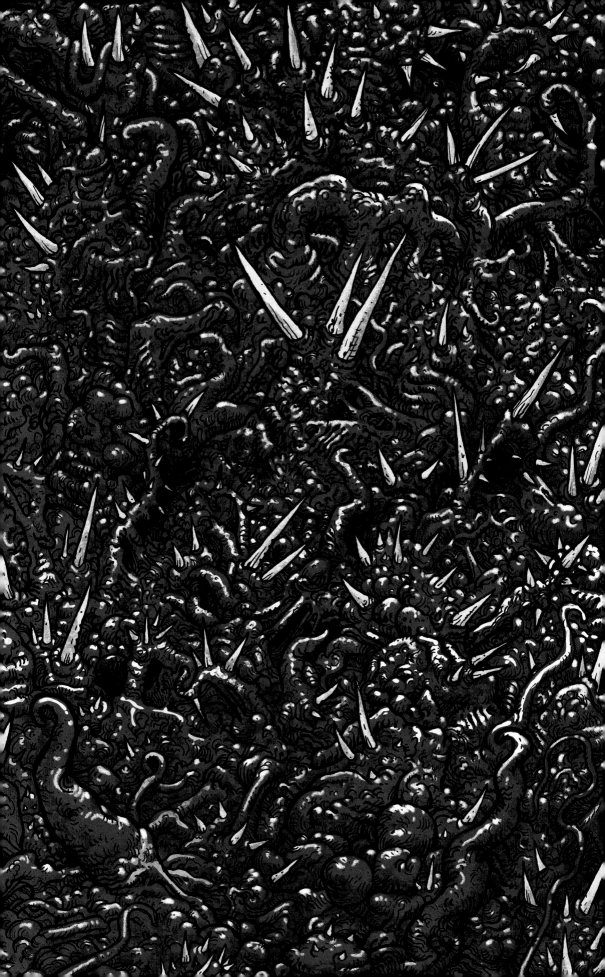

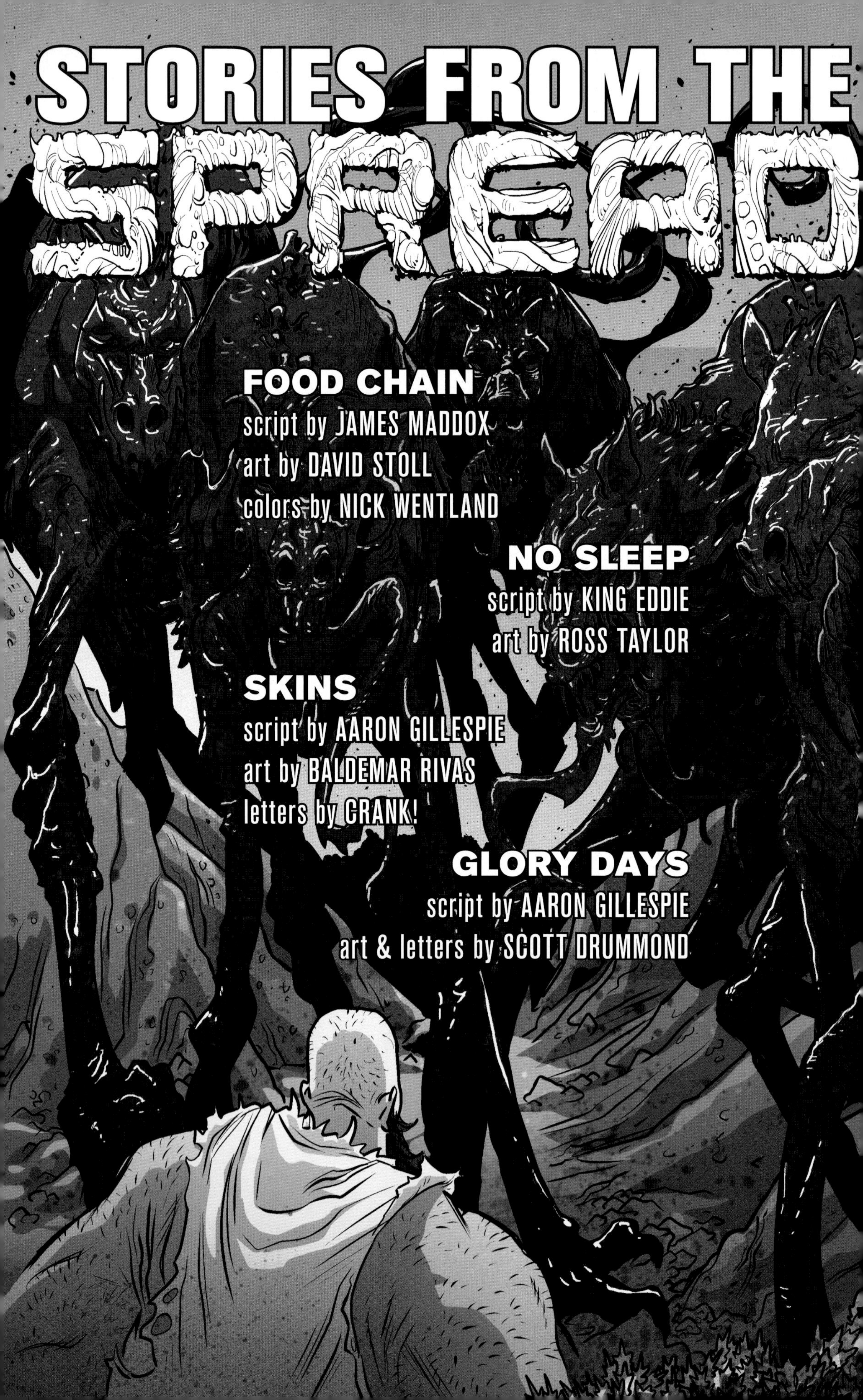
STORIES FROM THE SPREAD
FOOD CHAIN
script by JAMES MADDOX
art by DAVID STOLL
colors by NICK WENTLAND
NO SLEEP
script by KING EDDIE
art by ROSS TAYLOR
SKINS
script by AARON GILLESPIE
art by BALDEMAR RIVAS
letters by CRANK!
GLORY DAYS
script by AARON GILLESPIE
art & letters by SCOTT DRUMMOND

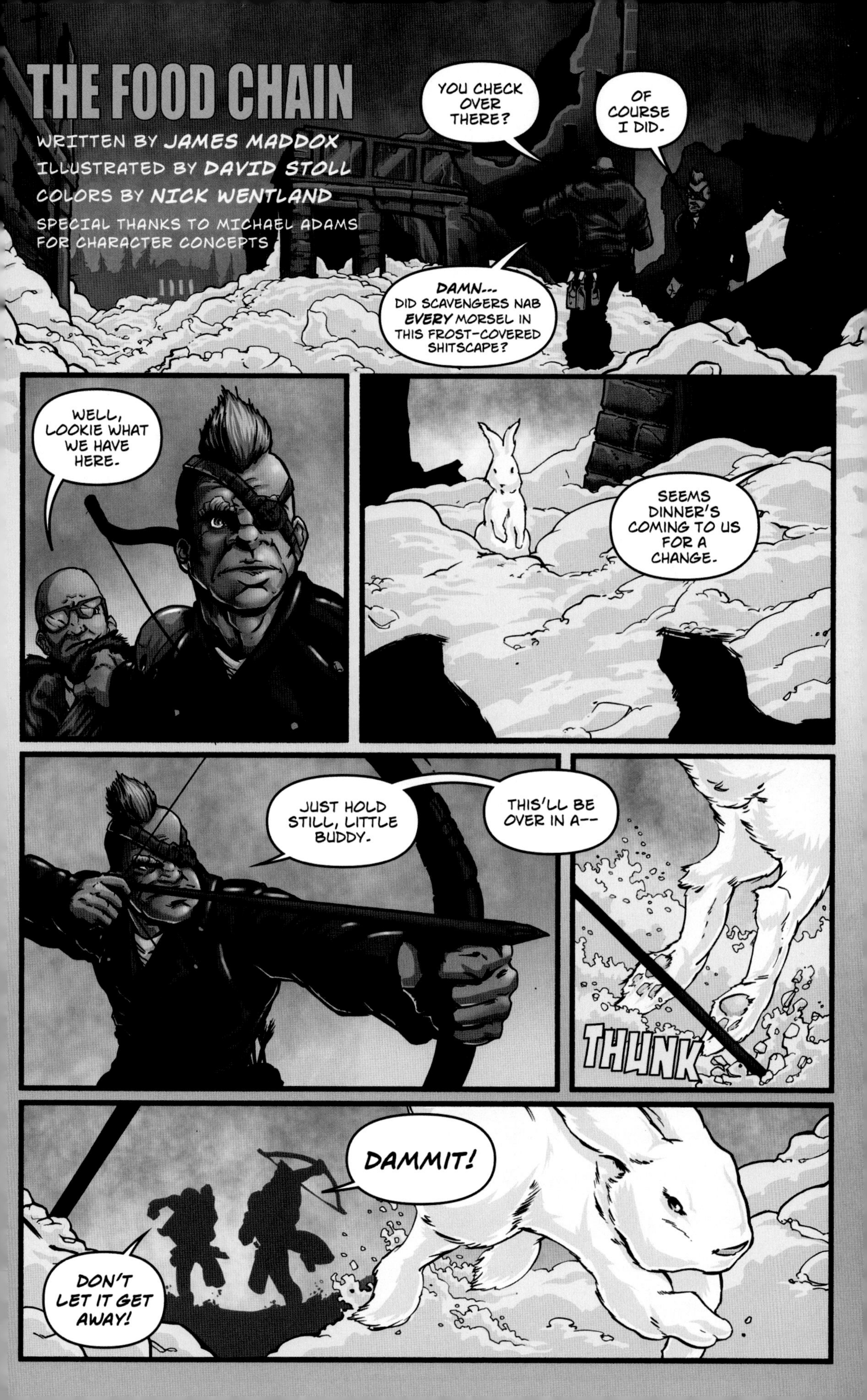
THE FOOD CHAIN
WRITTEN BY JAMES MADDOX
ILLUSTRATED BY DAVID STOLL
COLORS BY NICK WENTLAND
SPECIAL THANKS TO MICHAEL ADAMS FOR CHARACTER CONCEPTS
YOU CHECK OVER THERE?
OF COURSE I DID.
DAMN... DID SCAVENGERS NAB EVERY MORSEL IN THIS FROST-COVERED SHITSCAPE?
WELL, LOOKIE WHAT WE HAVE HERE.
SEEMS DINNER'S COMING TO US FOR A CHANGE.
JUST HOLD STILL, LITTLE BUDDY.
THIS'LL BE OVER IN A--
THUNK
DAMMIT!
DON'T LET IT GET AWAY!

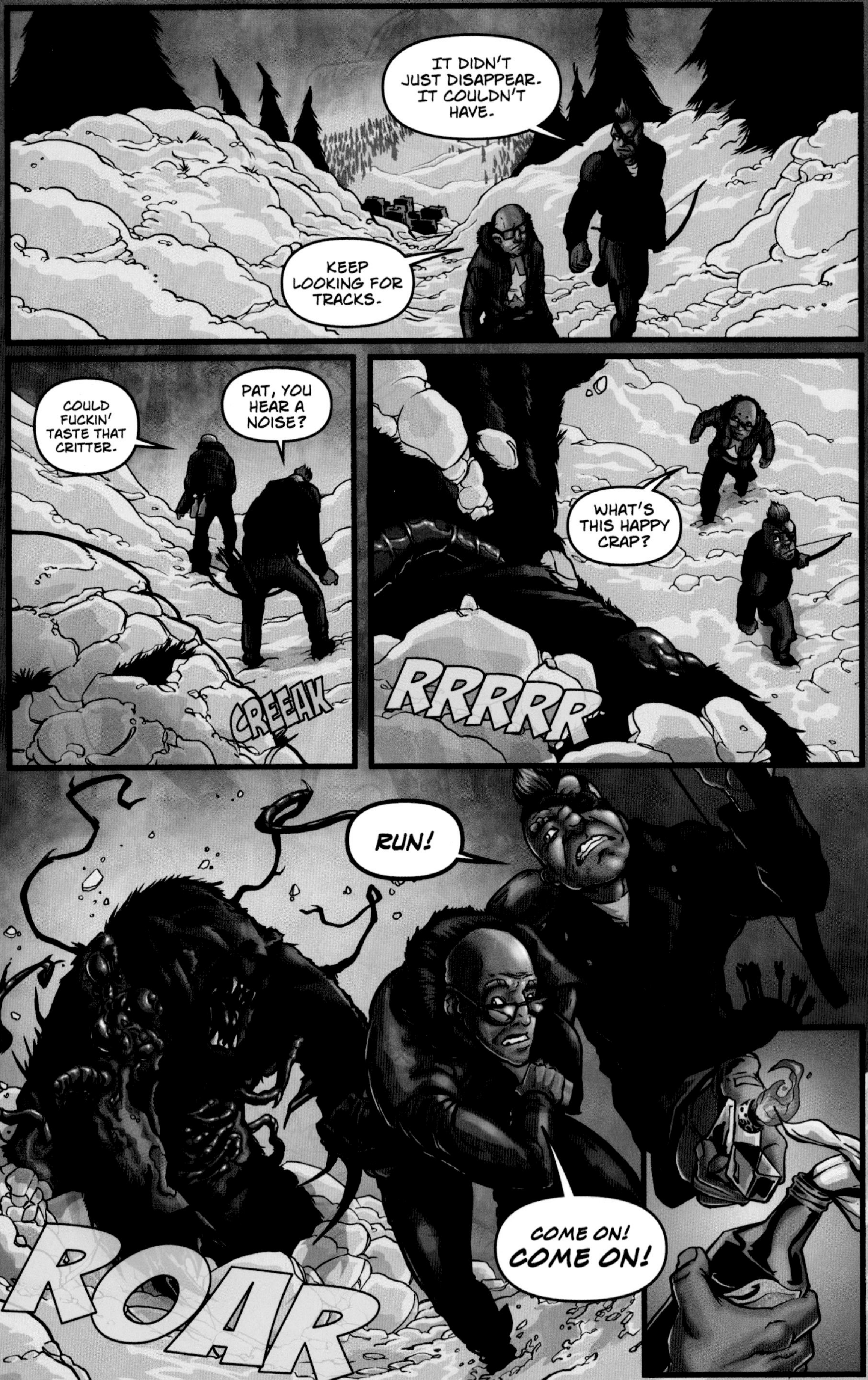
IT DIDN'T JUST DISAPPEAR. IT COULDN'T HAVE.
KEEP LOOKING FOR TRACKS.
COULD FUCKIN' TASTE THAT CRITTER.
PAT, YOU HEAR A NOISE?
CREEAK
WHAT'S THIS HAPPY CRAP?
RRRRRR
RUN!
COME ON! COME ON!
ROAR

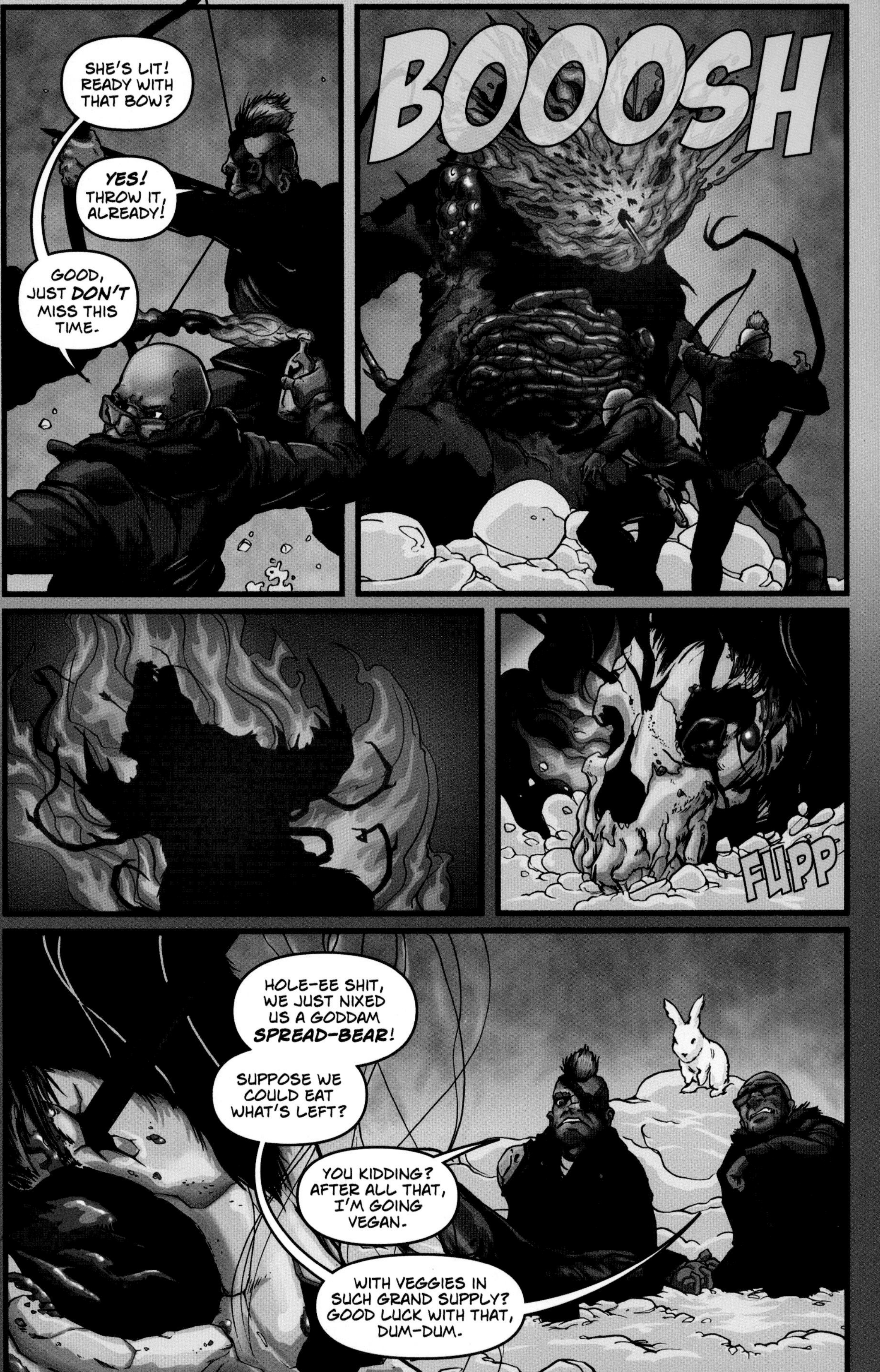
SHE'S LIT! READY WITH THAT BOW?
YES! THROW IT, ALREADY!
GOOD, JUST DON'T MISS THIS TIME.
BOOOSH
FUPP
HOLE-EE SHIT, WE JUST NIXED US A GODDAM SPREAD-BEAR!
SUPPOSE WE COULD EAT WHAT'S LEFT?
YOU KIDDING? AFTER ALL THAT, I'M GOING VEGAN.
WITH VEGGIES IN SUCH GRAND SUPPLY? GOOD LUCK WITH THAT, DUM-DUM.

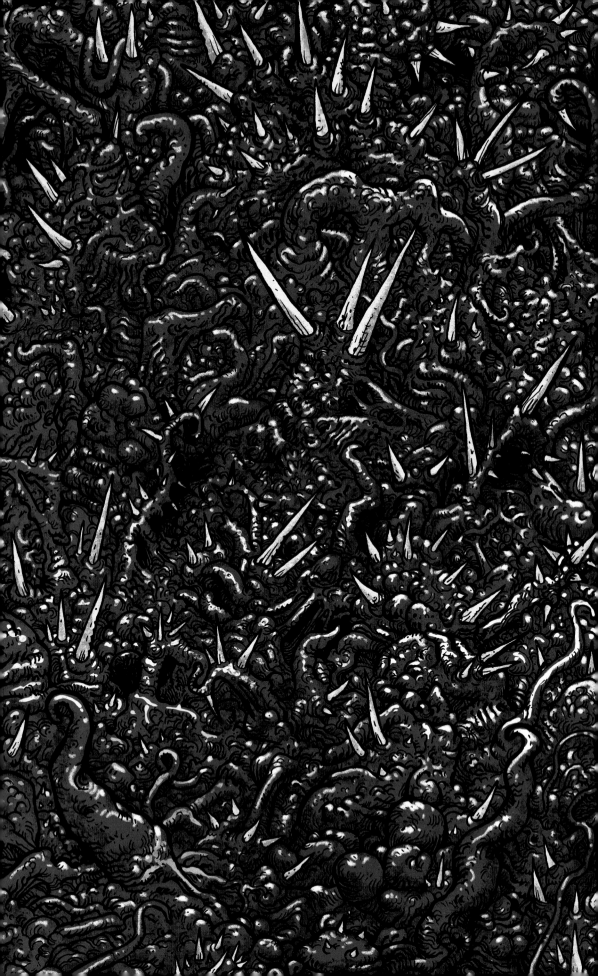

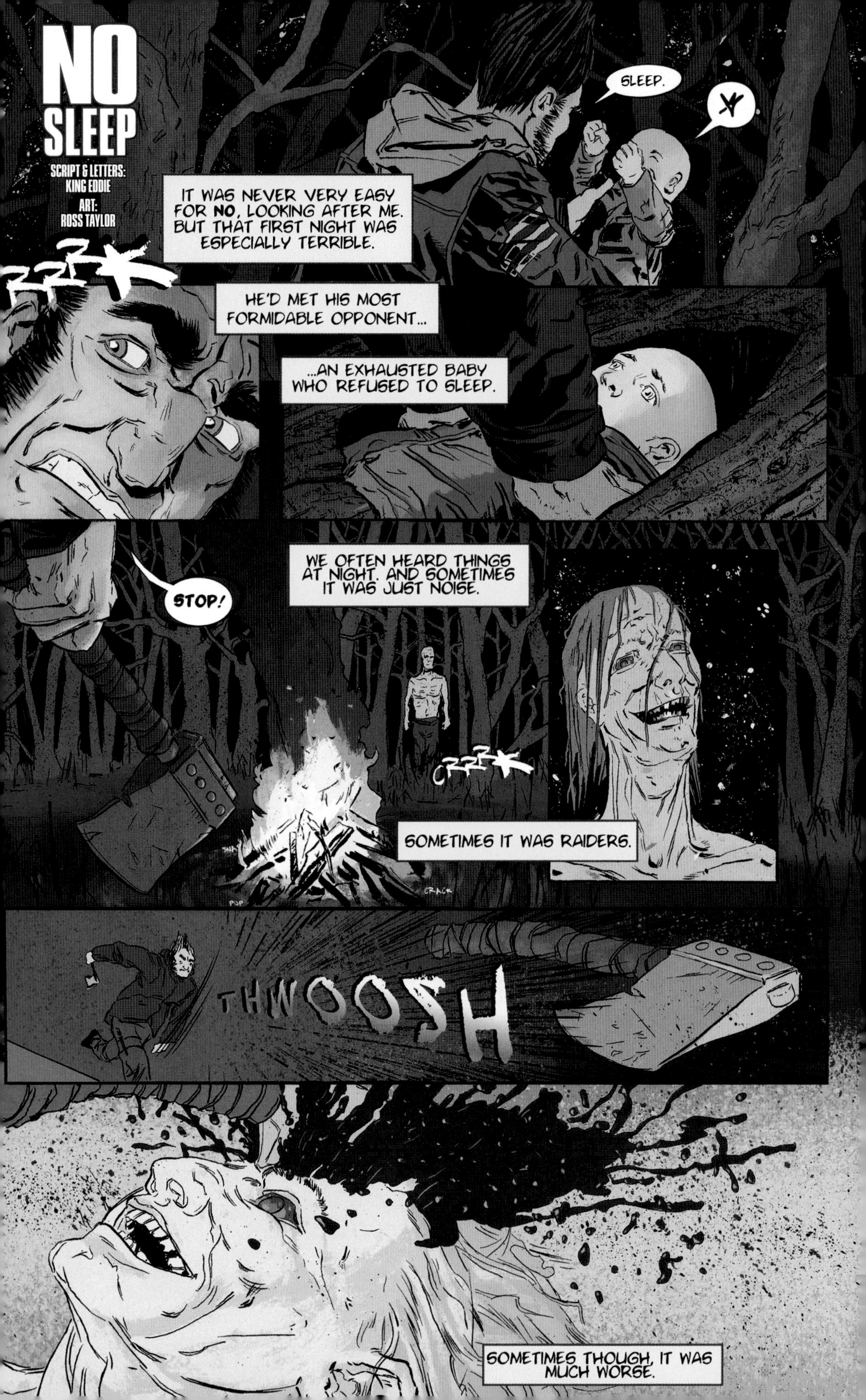
NO SLEEP
SCRIPT & LETTERS: KING EDDIE
ART: ROSS TAYLOR
SLEEP.
IT WAS NEVER VERY EASY FOR NO, LOOKING AFTER ME. BUT THAT FIRST NIGHT WAS ESPECIALLY TERRIBLE.
HE'D MET HIS MOST FORMIDABLE OPPONENT...
...AN EXHAUSTED BABY WHO REFUSED TO SLEEP.
STOP!
WE OFTEN HEARD THINGS AT NIGHT. AND SOMETIMES IT WAS JUST NOISE.
POP
CRACK
SOMETIMES IT WAS RAIDERS.
THWOOSH
SOMETIMES THOUGH, IT WAS MUCH WORSE.

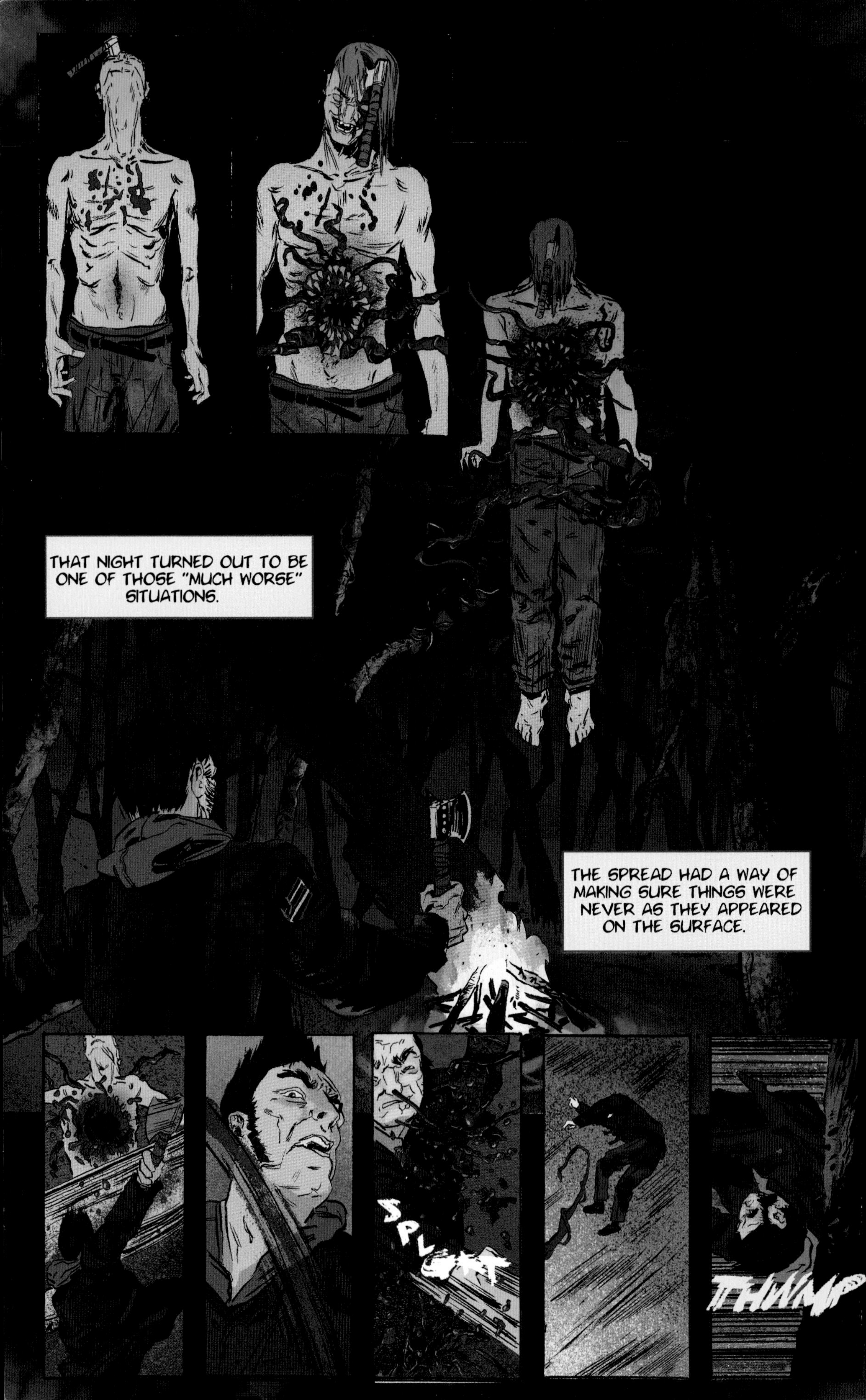
THAT NIGHT TURNED OUT TO BE ONE OF THOSE "MUCH WORSE" SITUATIONS.
THE SPREAD HAD A WAY OF MAKING SURE THINGS WERE NEVER AS THEY APPEARED ON THE SURFACE.
SPLGRT
THWMP

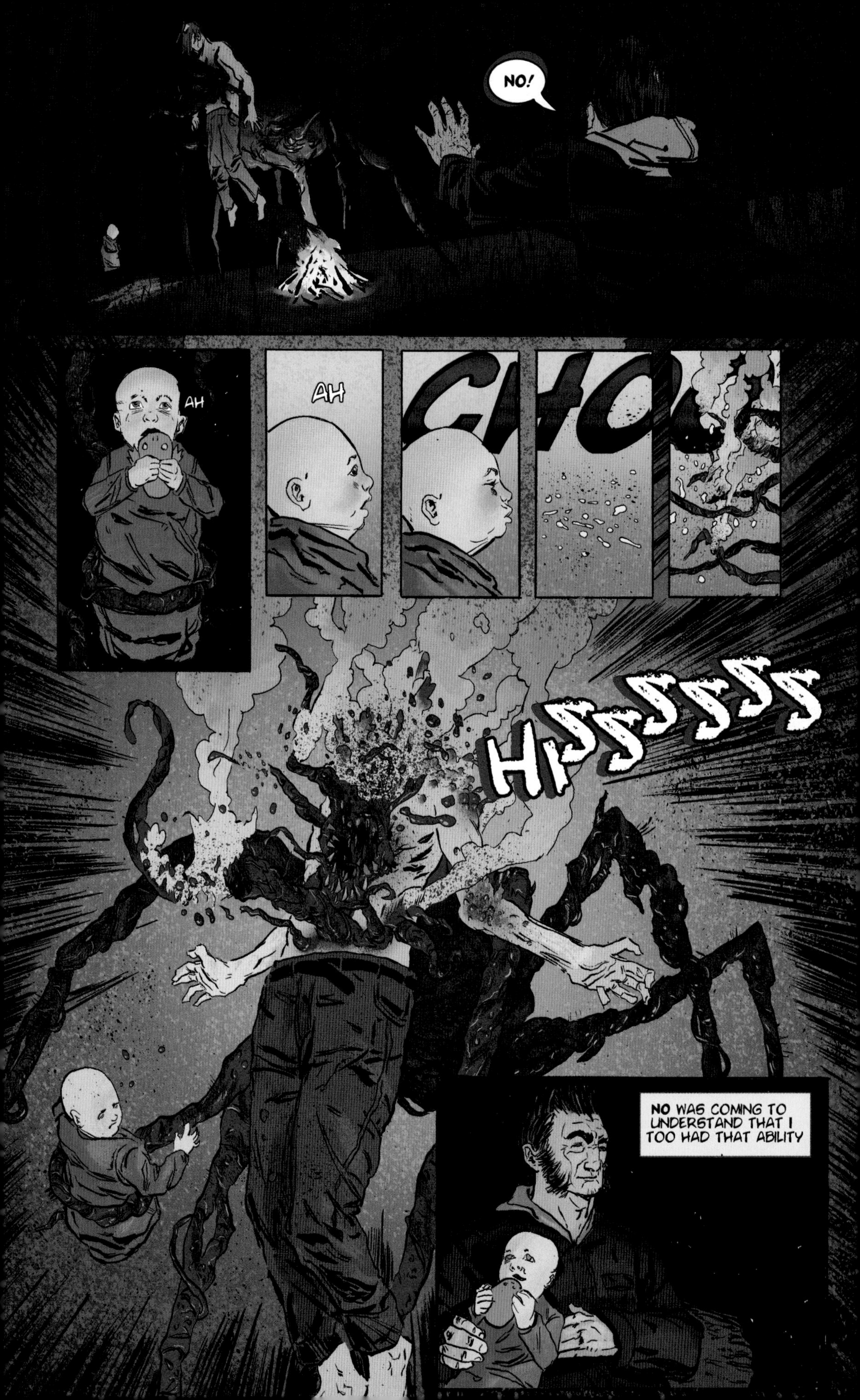
NO!
AH
AH
CHOO
HISSSSSS
NO WAS COMING TO UNDERSTAND THAT I TOO HAD THAT ABILITY

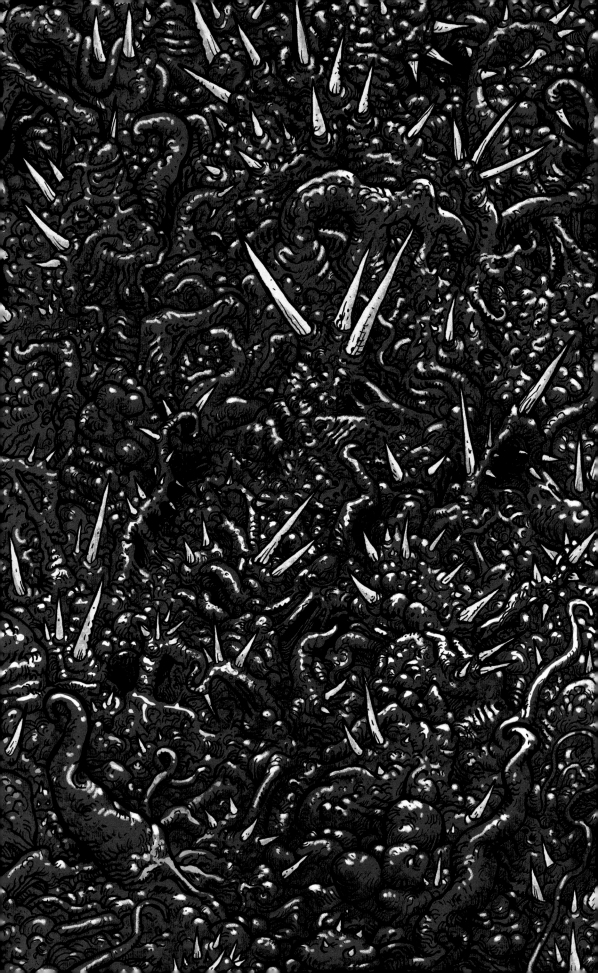

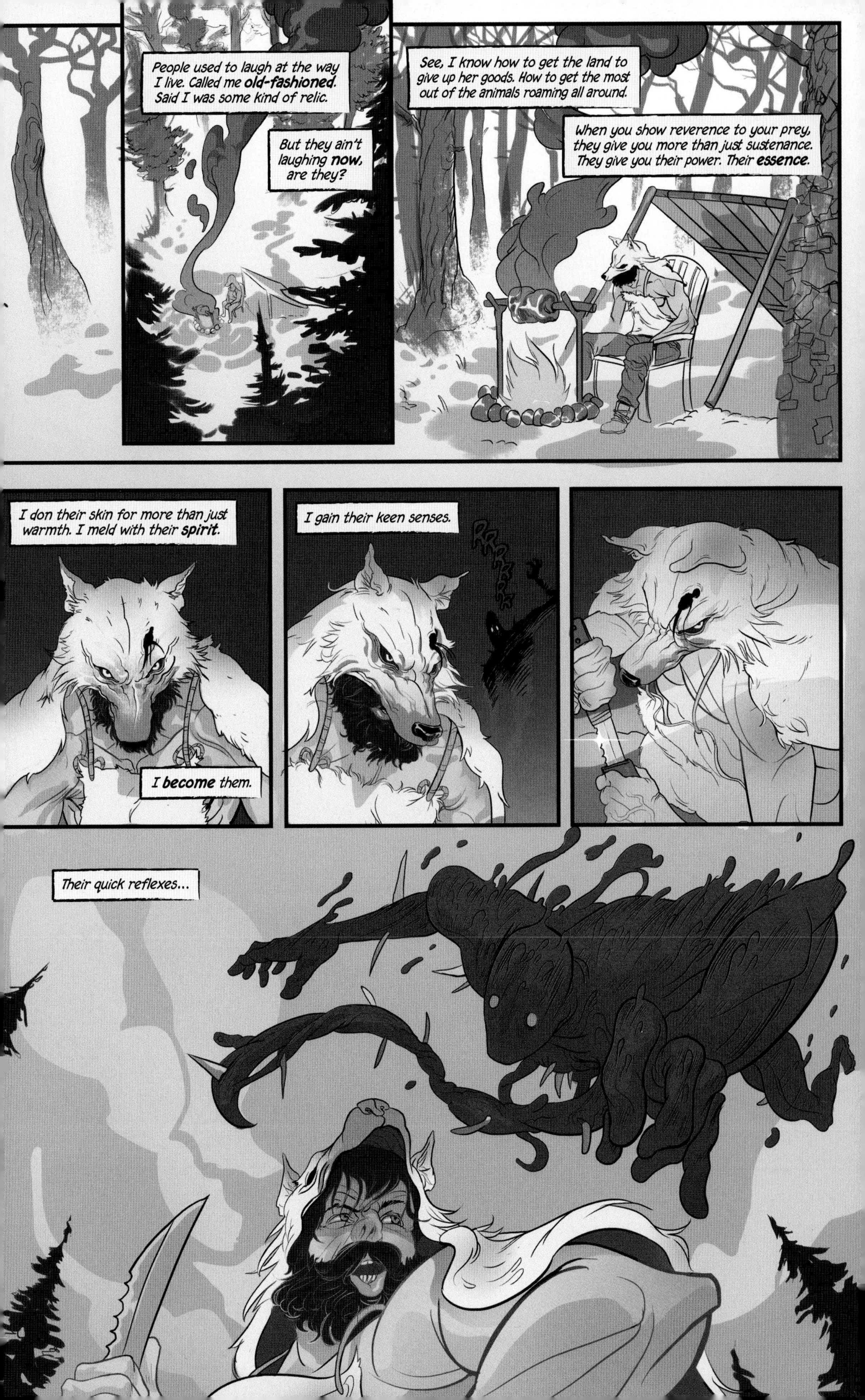

People used to laugh at the way I live. Called me **old-fashioned**. Said I was some kind of relic.
But they ain't laughing **now**, are they?
See, I know how to get the land to give up her goods. How to get the most out of the animals roaming all around.
When you show reverence to your prey, they give you more than just sustenance. They give you their power. Their **essence**.
I don their skin for more than just warmth. I meld with their **spirit**.
I **become** them.
I gain their keen senses.
Their quick reflexes...

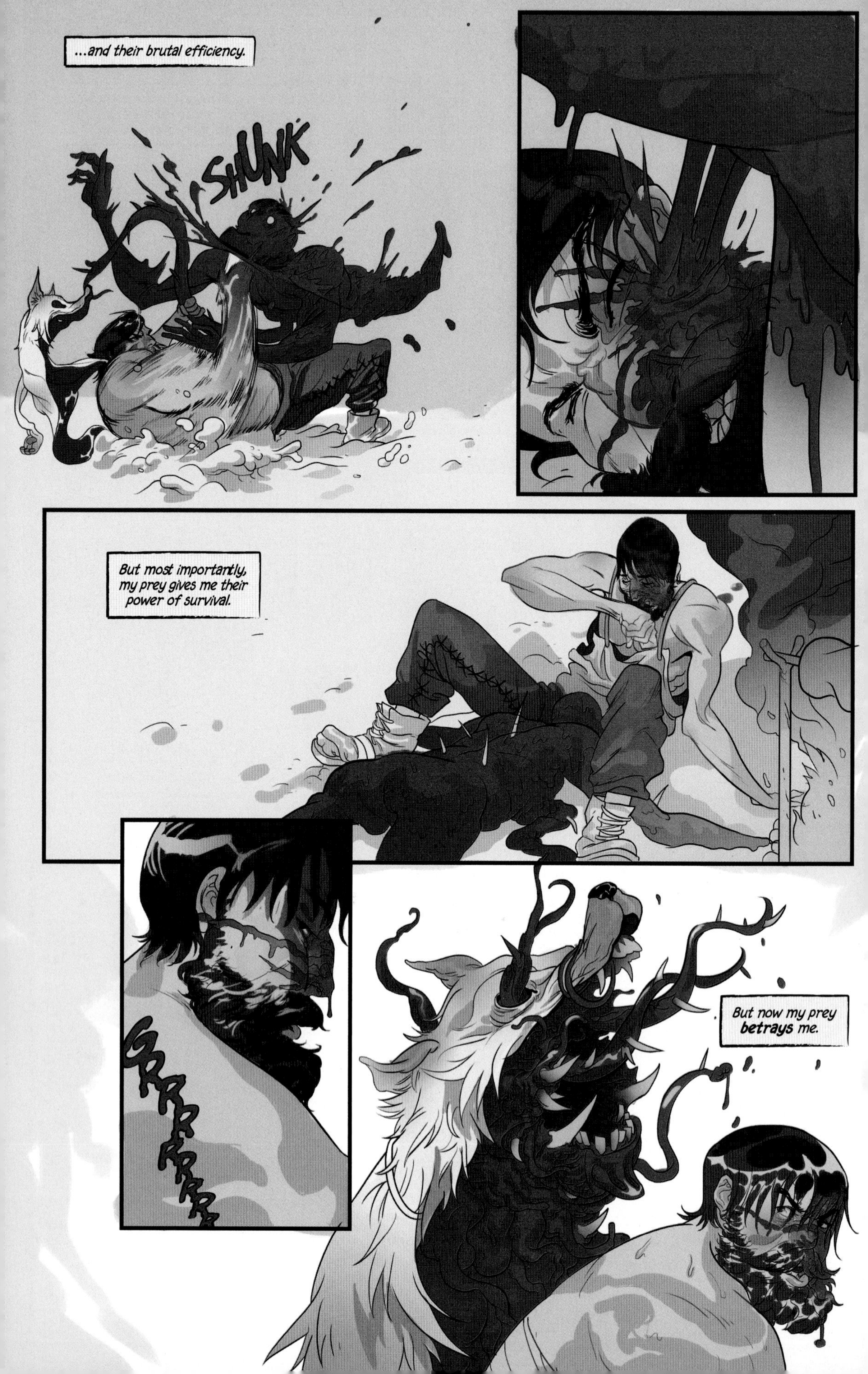
...and their brutal efficiency.
SHUNK
But most importantly, my prey gives me their power of survival.
GRRRRRRRR
But now my prey **betrays** me.

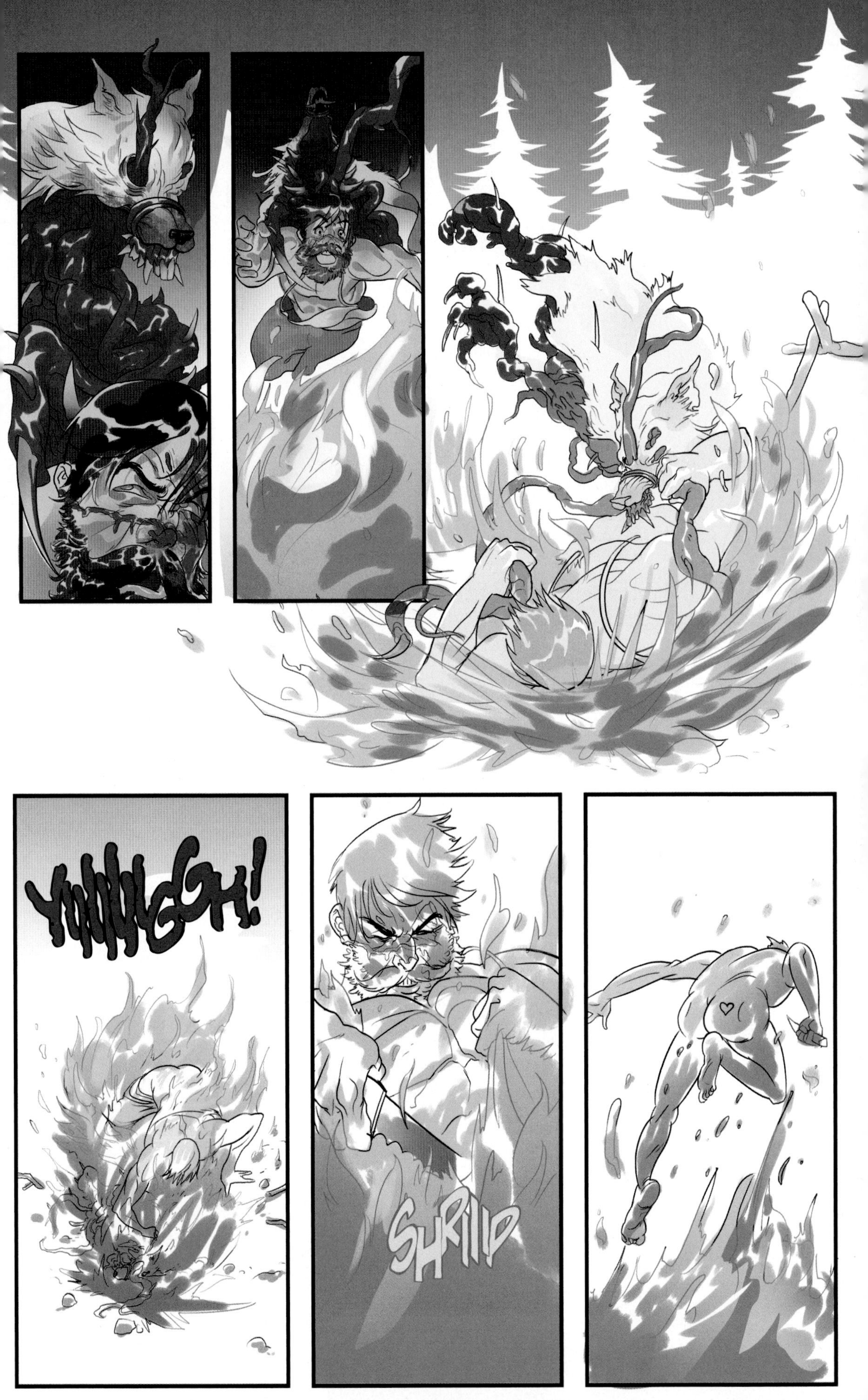
SHRIID

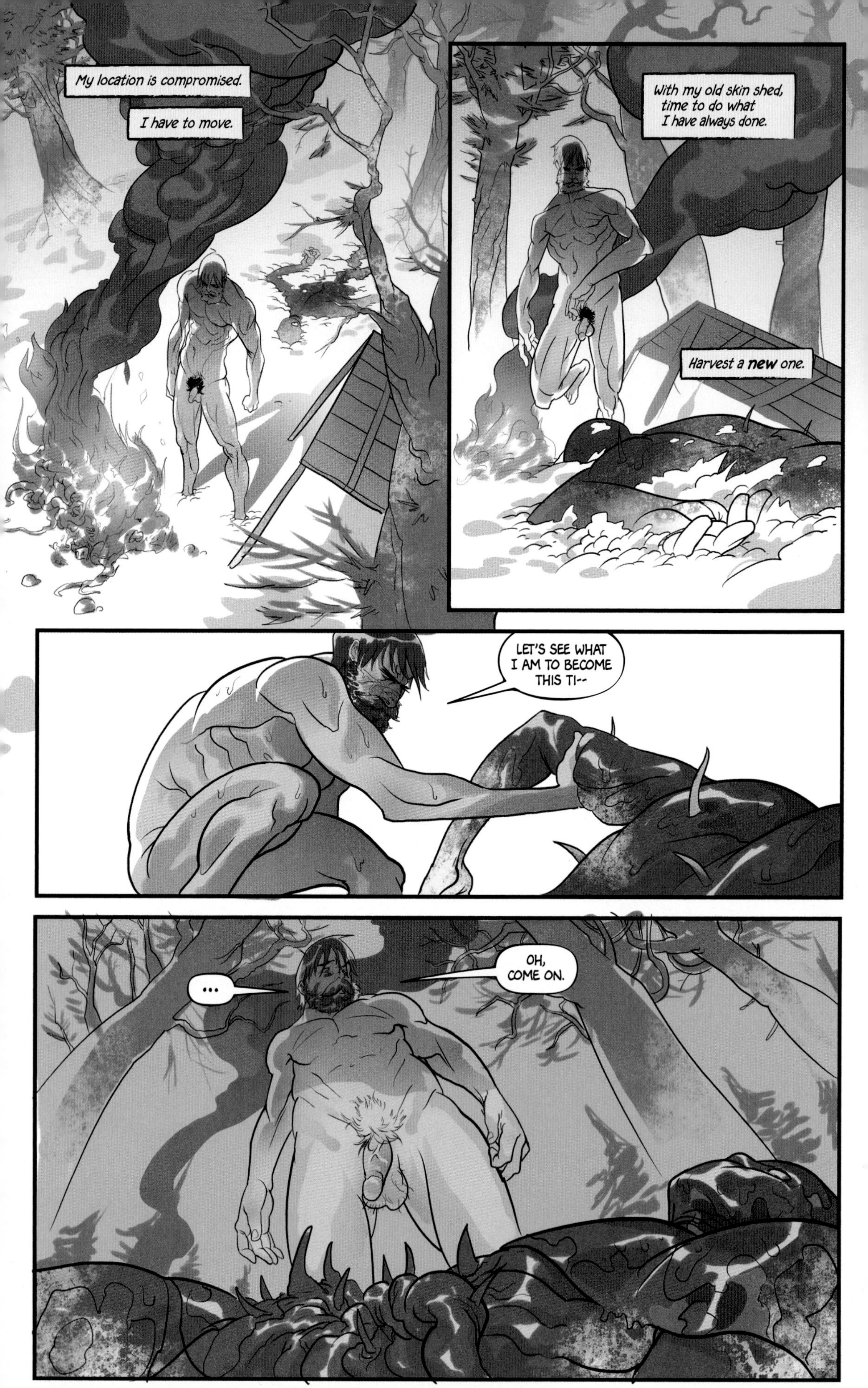
My location is compromised.
I have to move.
With my old skin shed, time to do what I have always done.
Harvest a **new** one.
LET'S SEE WHAT I AM TO BECOME THIS TI--
...
OH, COME ON.

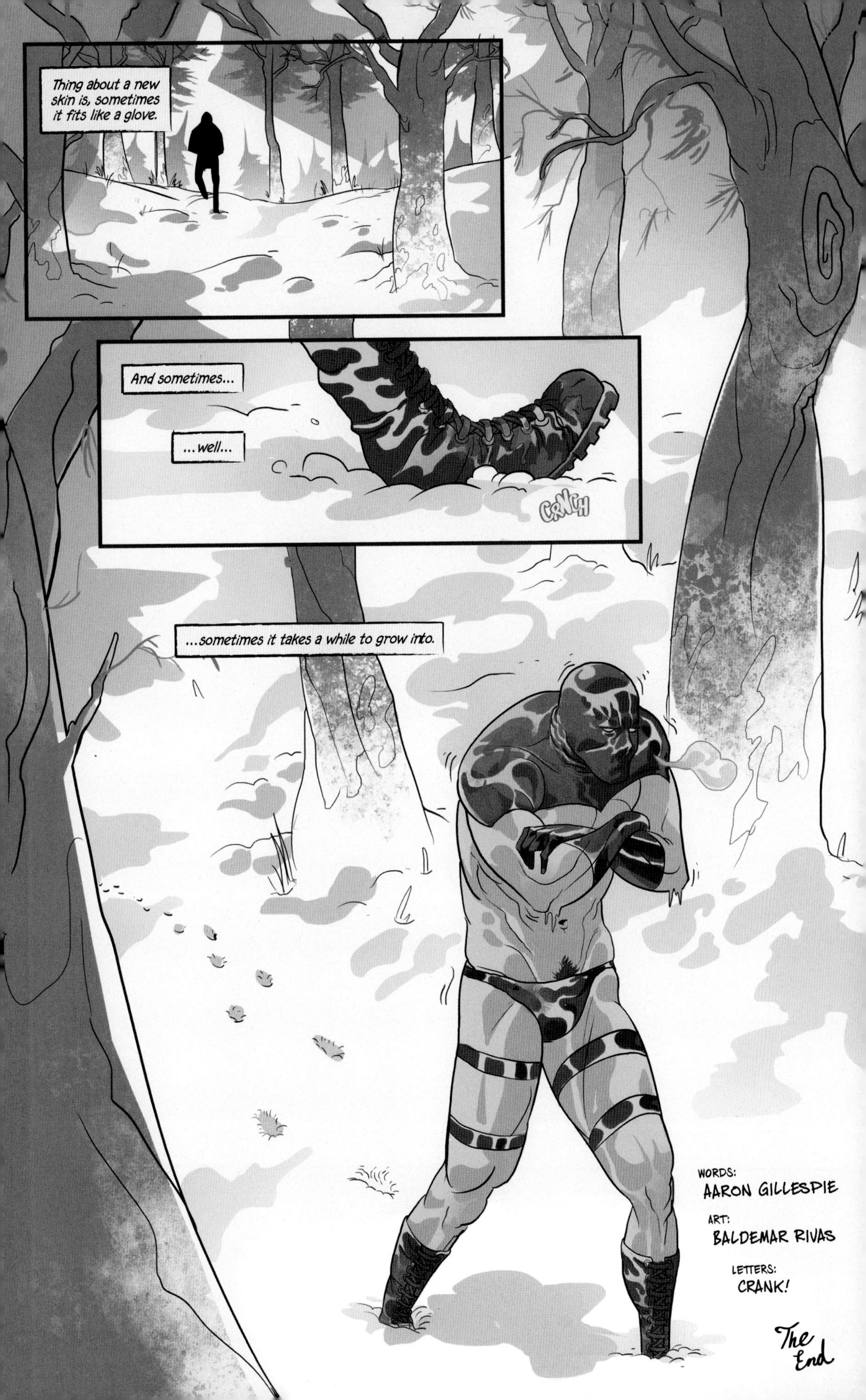
Thing about a new skin is, sometimes it fits like a glove.
And sometimes...
...well...
CRNCH
...sometimes it takes a while to grow into.
WORDS:
AARON GILLESPIE
ART:
BALDEMAR RIVAS
LETTERS:
CRANK!
The End

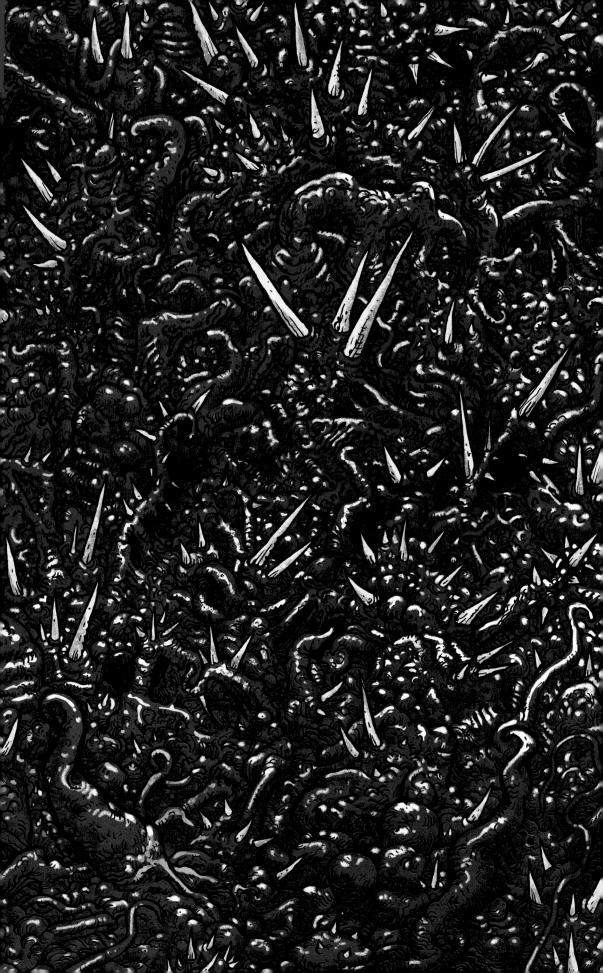

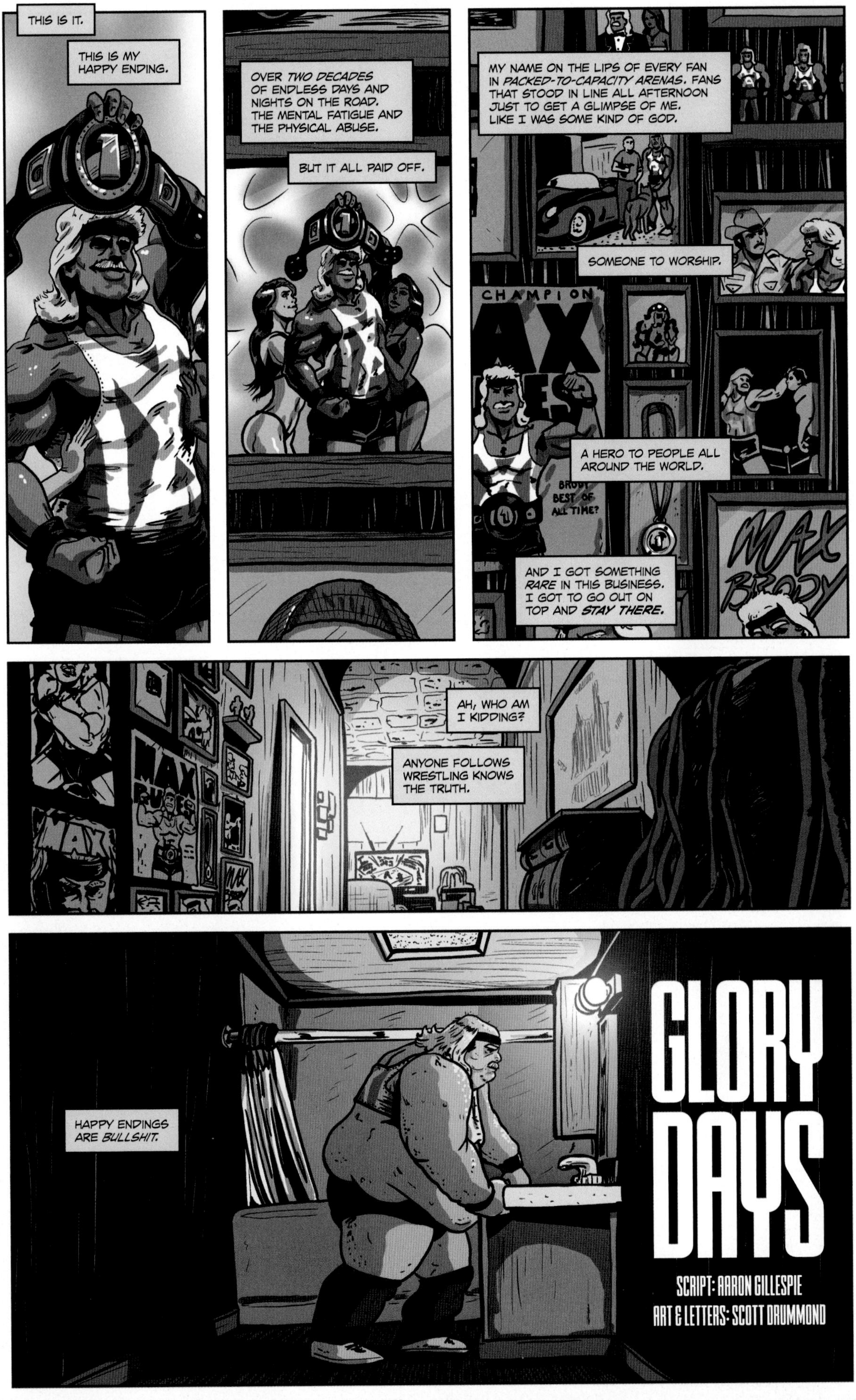
THIS IS IT.
THIS IS MY HAPPY ENDING.
OVER TWO DECADES OF ENDLESS DAYS AND NIGHTS ON THE ROAD. THE MENTAL FATIGUE AND THE PHYSICAL ABUSE.
BUT IT ALL PAID OFF.
MY NAME ON THE LIPS OF EVERY FAN IN PACKED-TO-CAPACITY ARENAS. FANS THAT STOOD IN LINE ALL AFTERNOON JUST TO GET A GLIMPSE OF ME. LIKE I WAS SOME KIND OF GOD.
SOMEONE TO WORSHIP.
CHAMPION
A HERO TO PEOPLE ALL AROUND THE WORLD.
BRODY BEST OF ALL TIME?
AND I GOT SOMETHING RARE IN THIS BUSINESS. I GOT TO GO OUT ON TOP AND STAY THERE.
AH, WHO AM I KIDDING?
ANYONE FOLLOWS WRESTLING KNOWS THE TRUTH.
HAPPY ENDINGS ARE BULLSHIT.
GLORY DAYS
SCRIPT: AARON GILLESPIE
ART & LETTERS: SCOTT DRUMMOND

A'WRIGHT, BIG DADDY, LISTEN UP...

'CUZ I AIN'T REPEATING MYSELF.

I BEEN AT THIS GAME A LONG DAMN TIME. FACED DOWN A LOT GOOD MEN.

TITO CRANE, BRIAN ASH, THE MAD HILLBILLY CLEM PUTNEY...

WAS A TIME I'D'VE TOLD YOU THOSE WERE MY TOUGHEST OPPONENTS.

BUT NOT NO MORE.

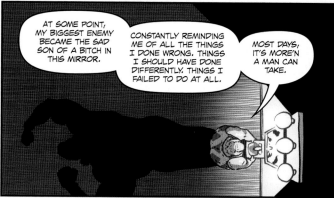

AT SOME POINT, MY BIGGEST ENEMY BECAME THE SAD SON OF A BITCH IN THIS MIRROR.

CONSTANTLY REMINDING ME OF ALL THE THINGS I DONE WRONG. THINGS I SHOULD HAVE DONE DIFFERENTLY. THINGS I FAILED TO DO AT ALL.

MOST DAYS, IT'S MORE'N A MAN CAN TAKE.

BUT THEN CAME THE DAY YOU FOUND ME, BIG DADDY.

YOU SAW DEEP INSIDE ME, PAST ALL THE PAIN AND THE BULLSHIT. ALL THE WAY DOWN TO THE *TRUTH*.

YOU KNEW THERE WAS STILL SOME GRIT LEFT IN THIS BROKEN-DOWN OLD MAN!

YOU ISSUED THE CHALLENGE AND I ACCEPT!

SO NOW IT'S TIME TO SHOW THE WORLD WHAT YOU SAW, BIG DADDY!

WRESTLING'S ABOUT ONE THING: FIGHTING THE GOOD FIGHT!

AND AIN'T NO ONE DOES THAT BETTER THAN...

MAX GODDAMN BRODY!

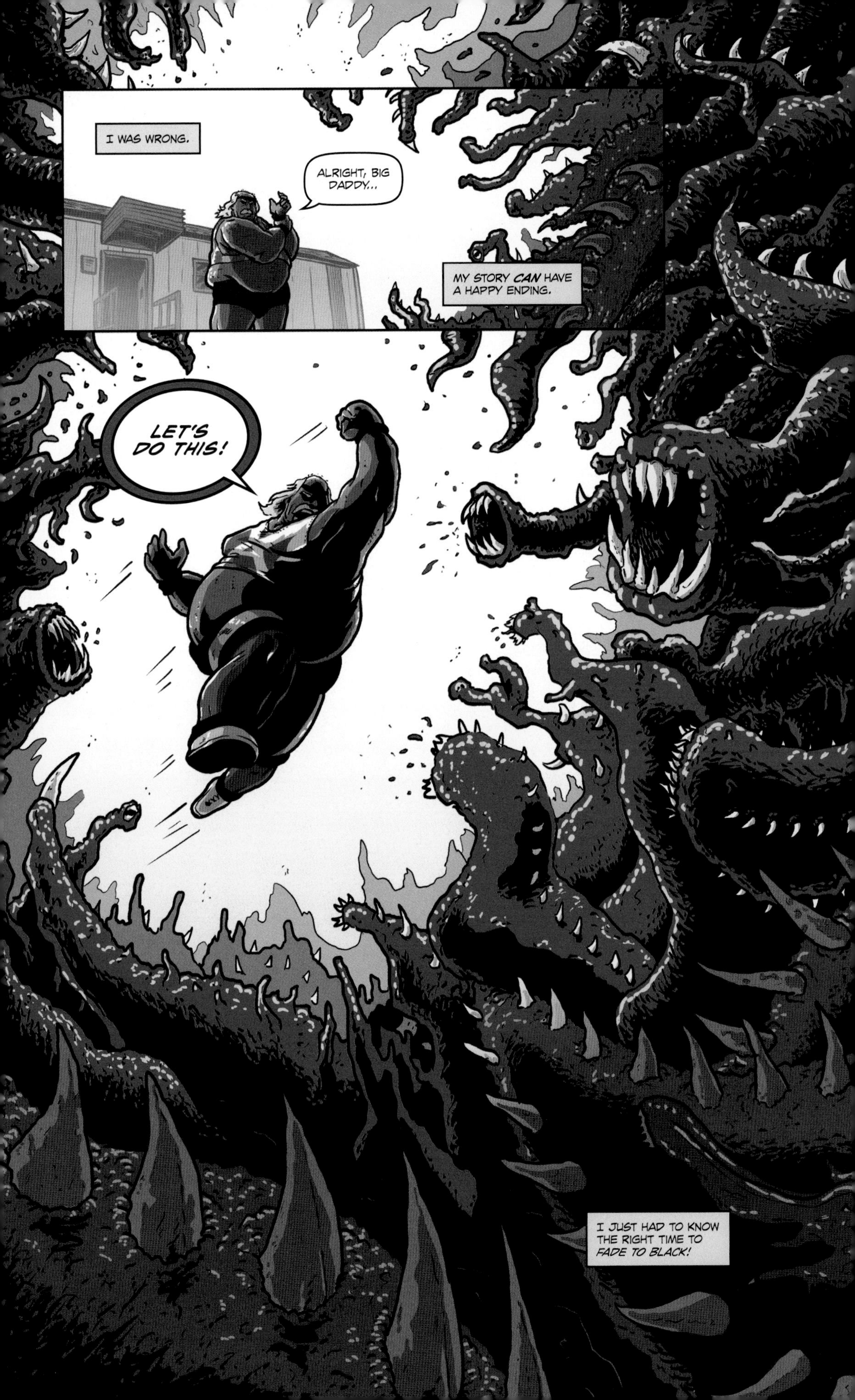
I WAS WRONG.
ALRIGHT, BIG DADDY...
MY STORY *CAN* HAVE A HAPPY ENDING.
LET'S DO THIS!
I JUST HAD TO KNOW THE RIGHT TIME TO *FADE TO BLACK!*

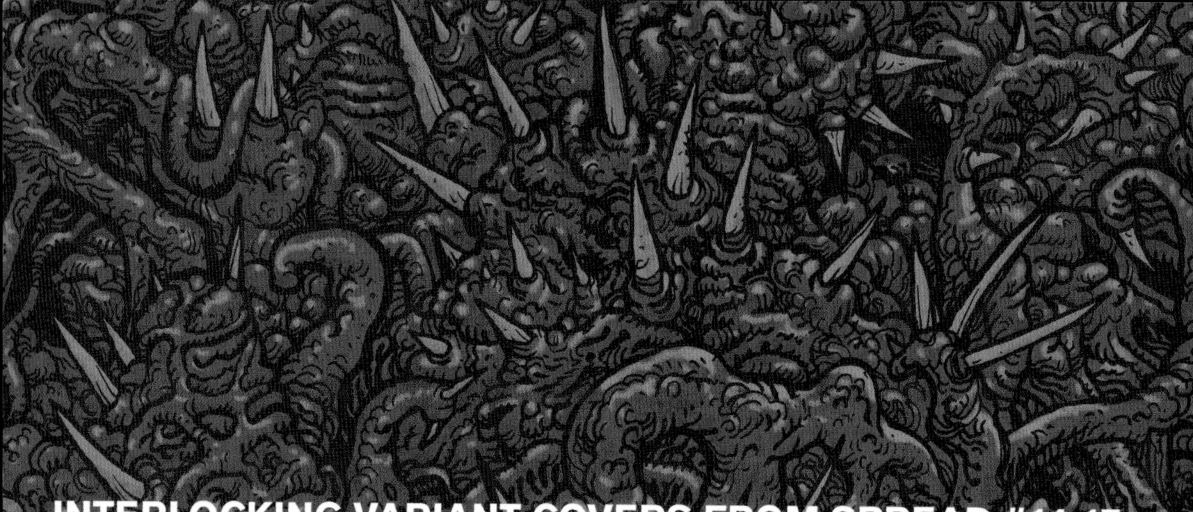

INTERLOCKING VARIANT COVERS FROM SPREAD #14-17

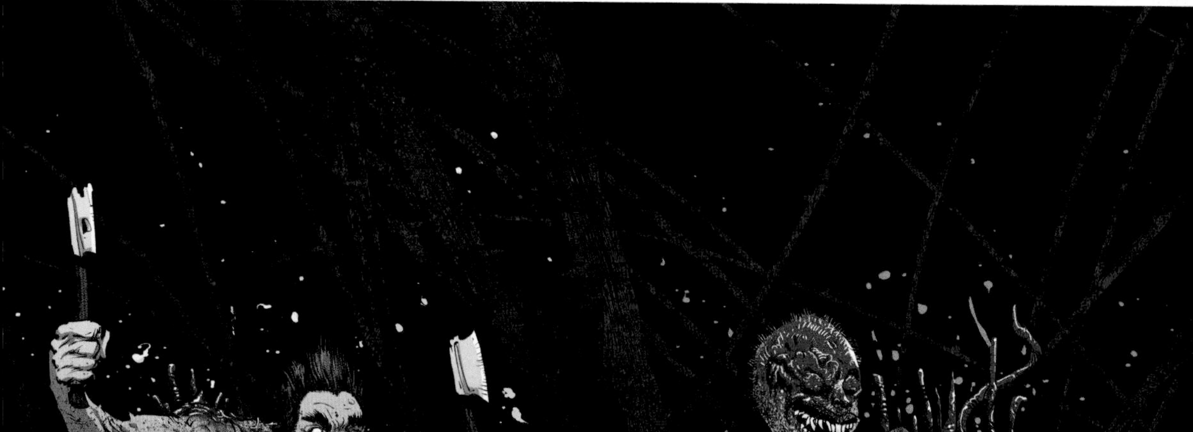

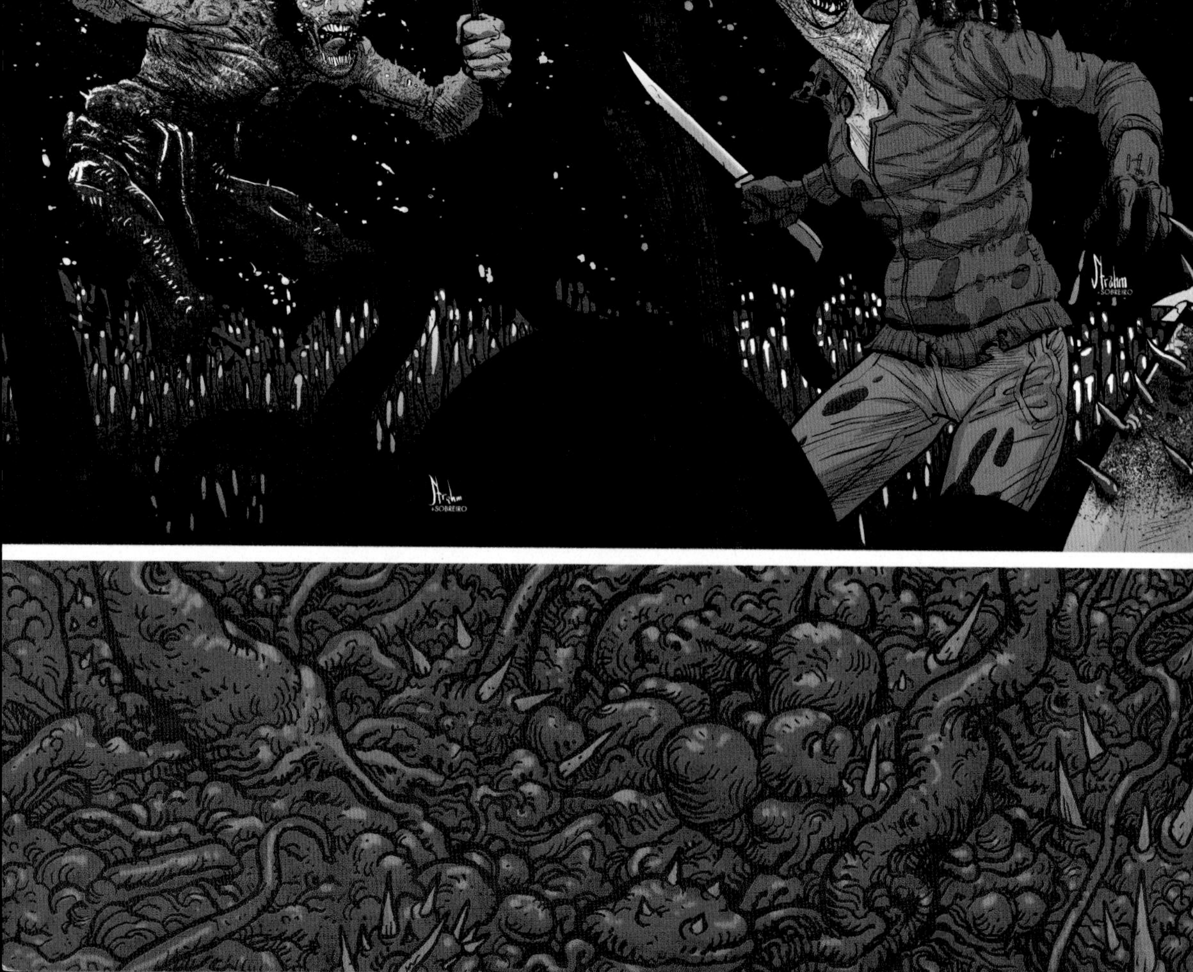

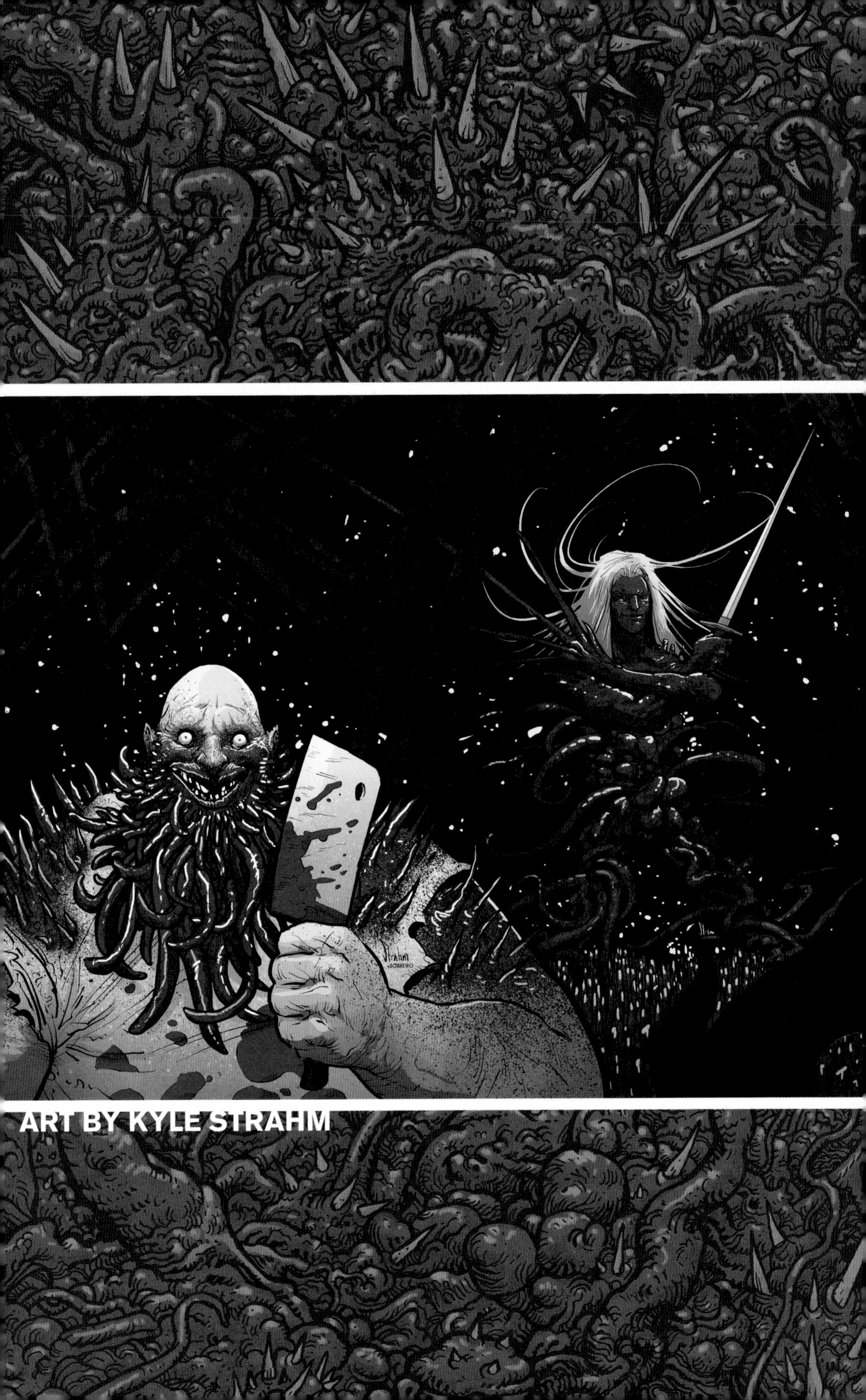

ART BY KYLE STRAHM

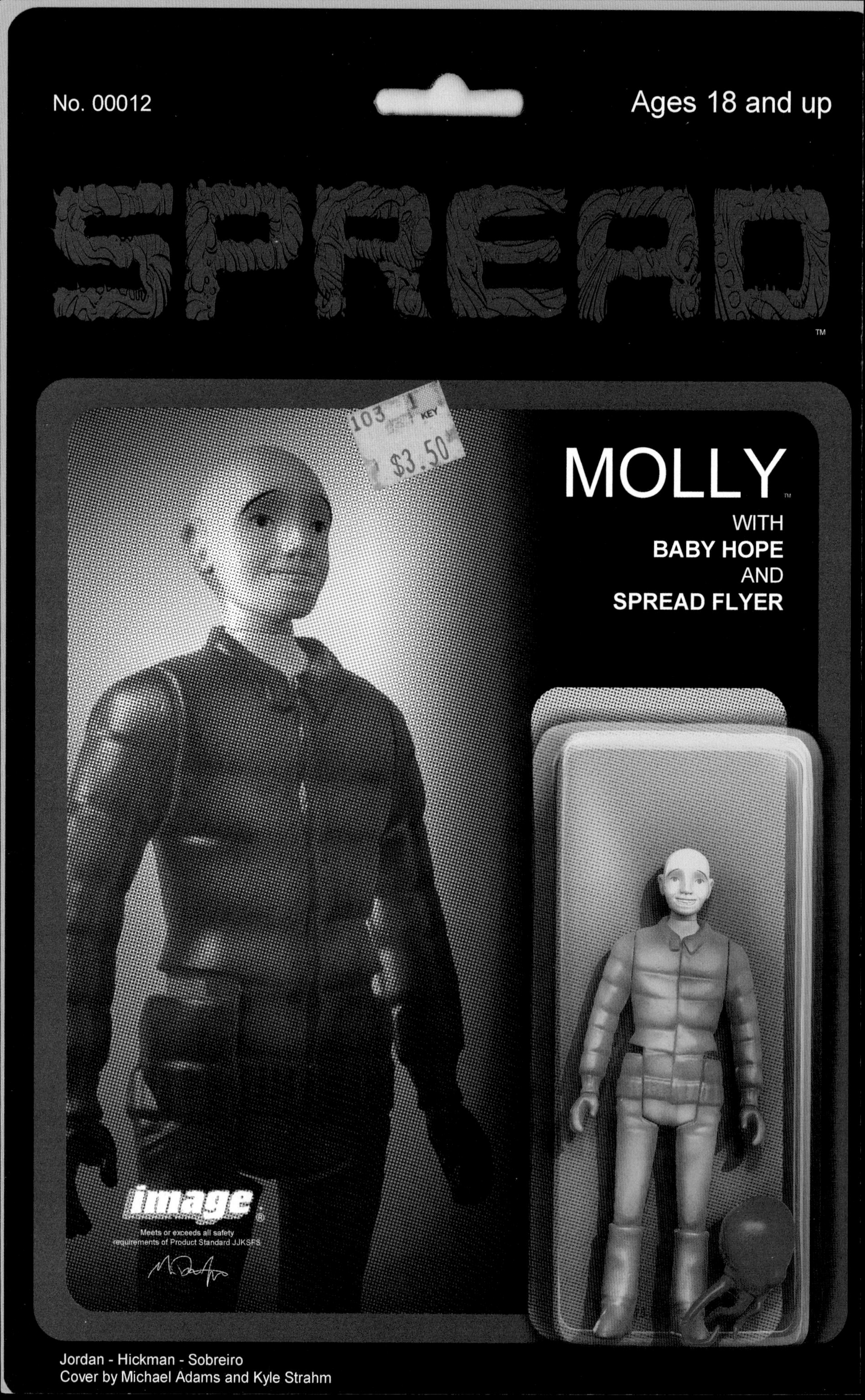
No. 00012
Ages 18 and up
SPREAD
TM
MOLLY
TM
WITH
BABY HOPE
AND
SPREAD FLYER
image
Meets or exceeds all safety requirements of Product Standard JJKSFS
Jordan - Hickman - Sobreiro
Cover by Michael Adams and Kyle Strahm

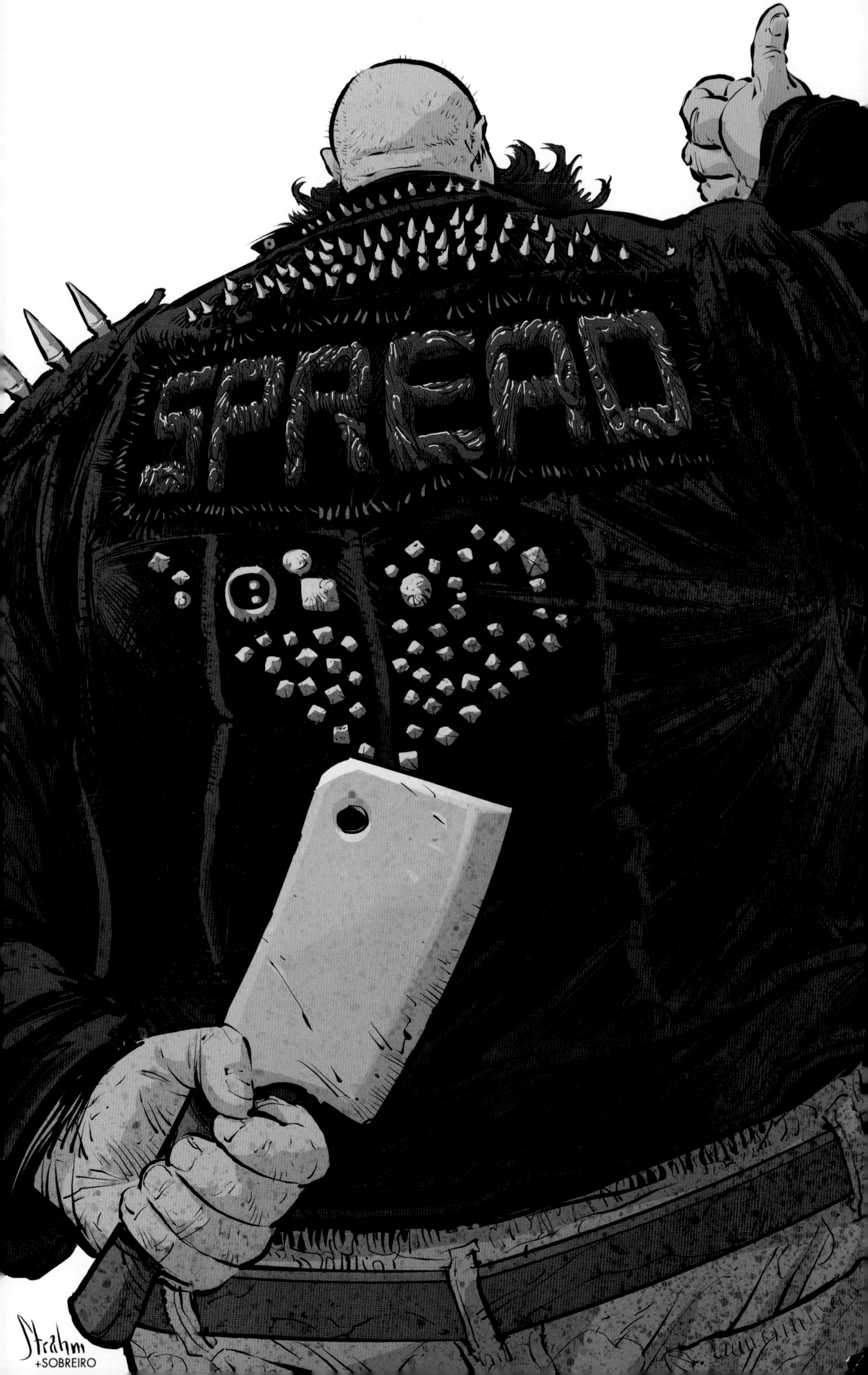
SPREAD
Strahm
+SOBREIRO

SPREAD

™

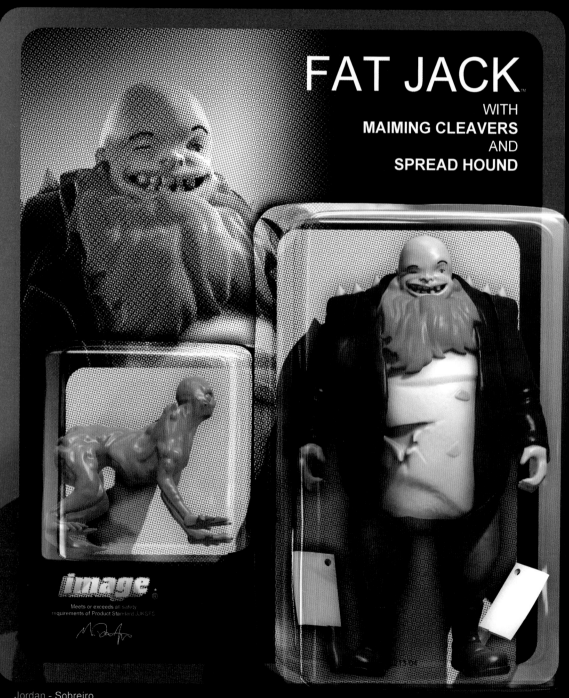

FAT JACK™

WITH
MAIMING CLEAVERS
AND
SPREAD HOUND

image®

Meets or exceeds all safety
requirements of Product Standard JJKGPS

Jordan - Sobreiro
Cover by Michael Adams and Kyle Strahm

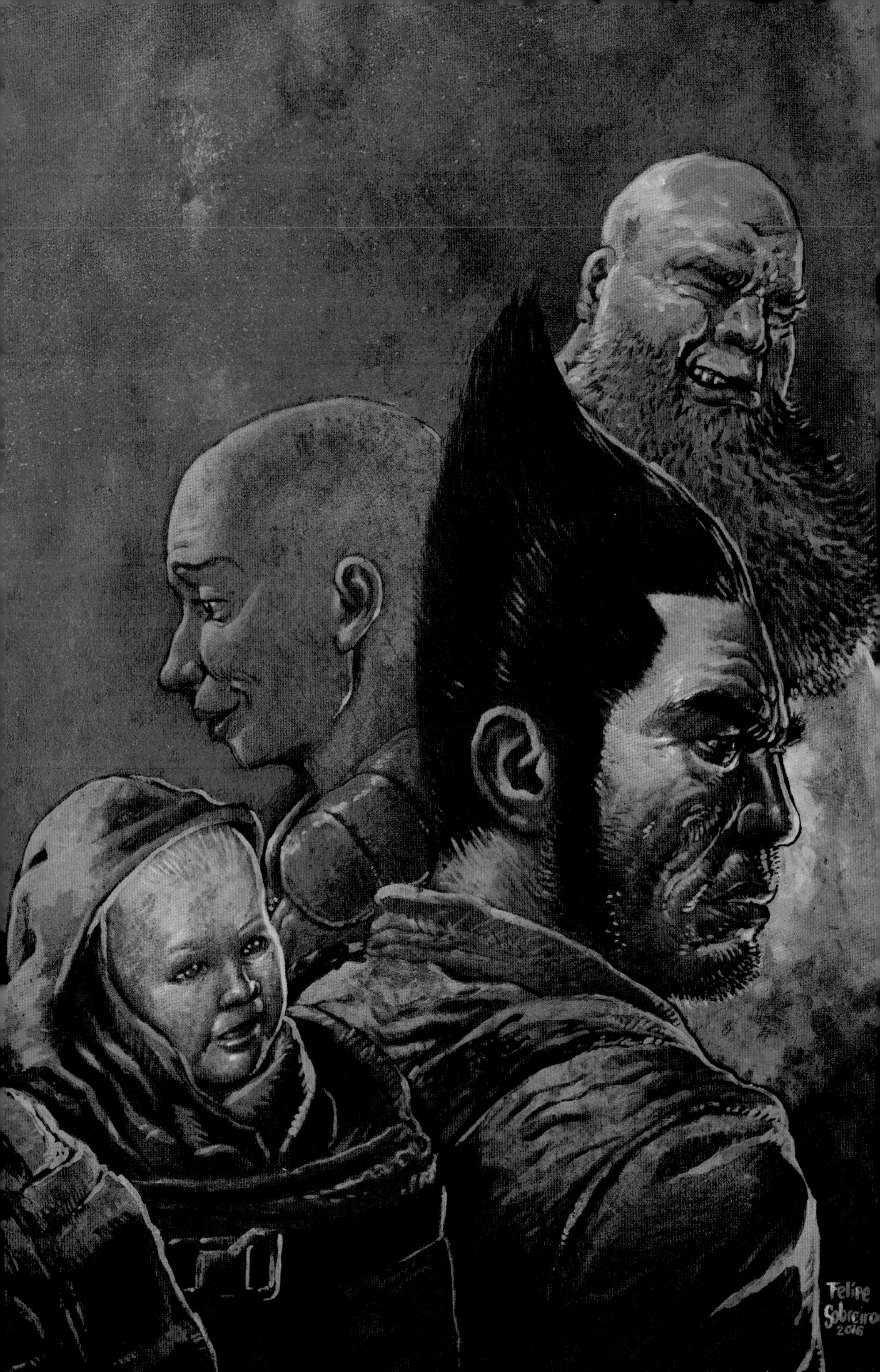
Felipe
Sobreiro
2016

FELIPE SOBREIRO

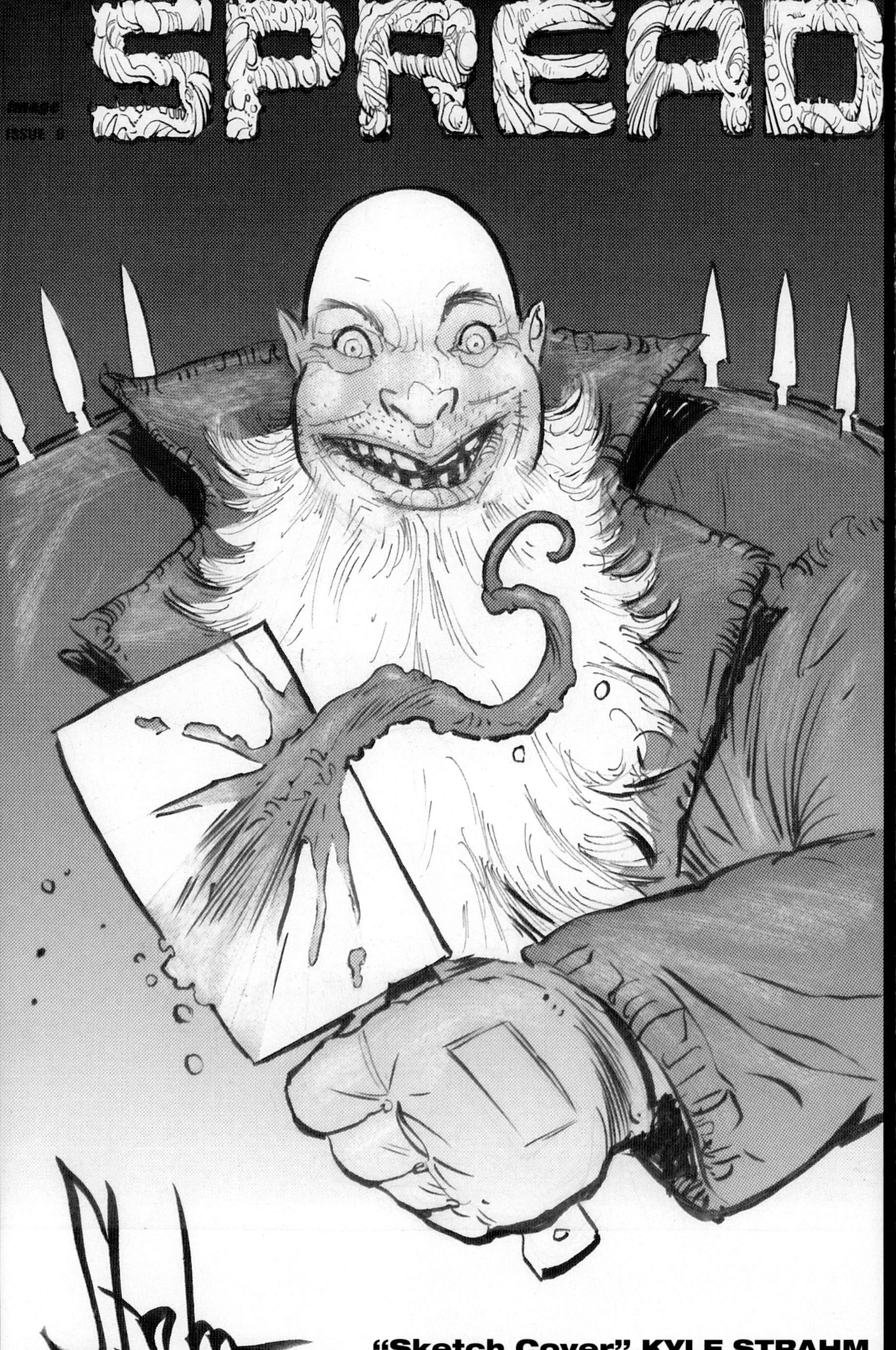
SPREAD

“Sketch Cover” KYLE STRAHM

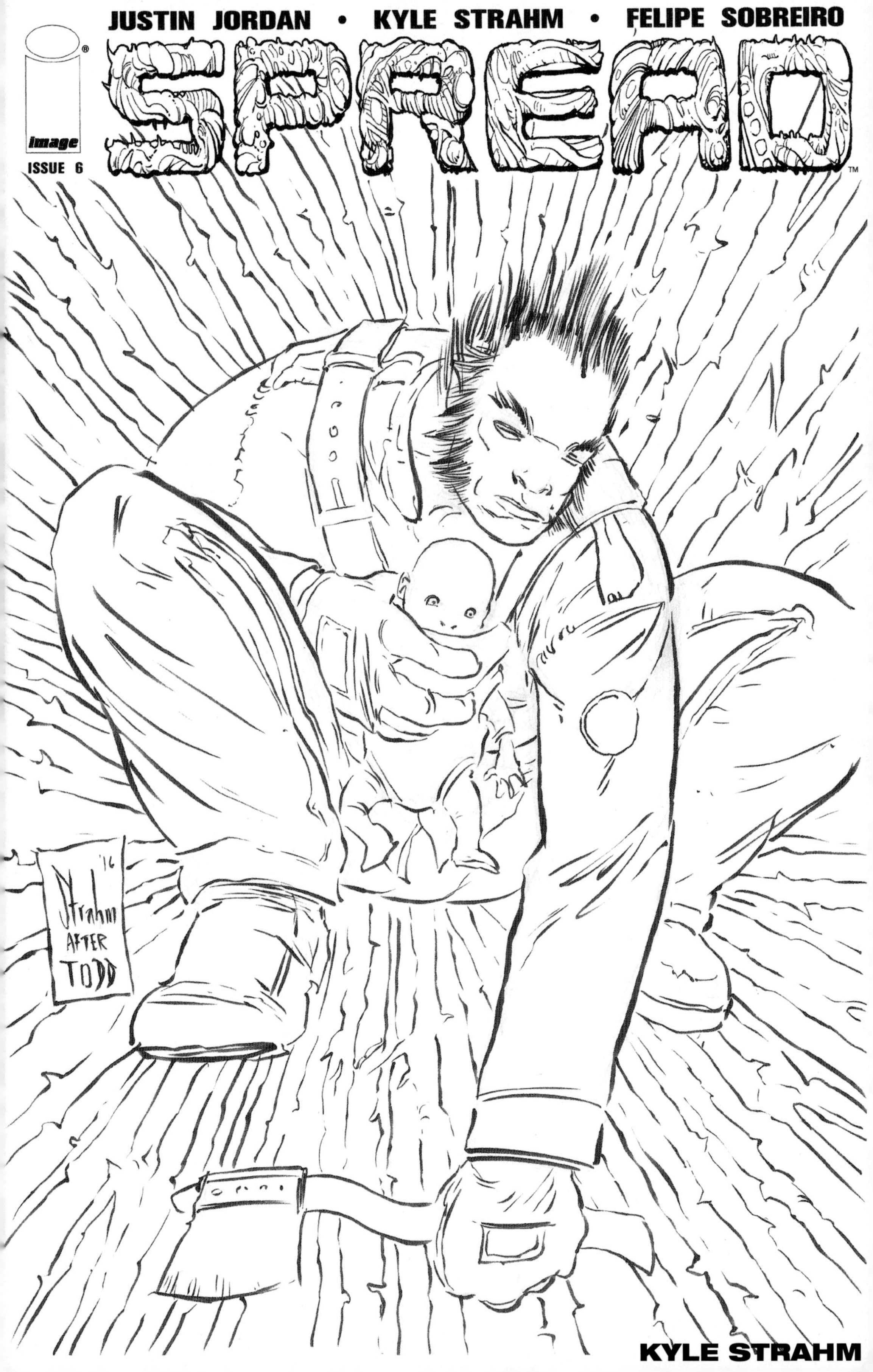
JUSTIN JORDAN • KYLE STRAHM • FELIPE SOBREIRO
image
ISSUE 6
SPREAD
Strahm '16 AFTER TODD
KYLE STRAHM

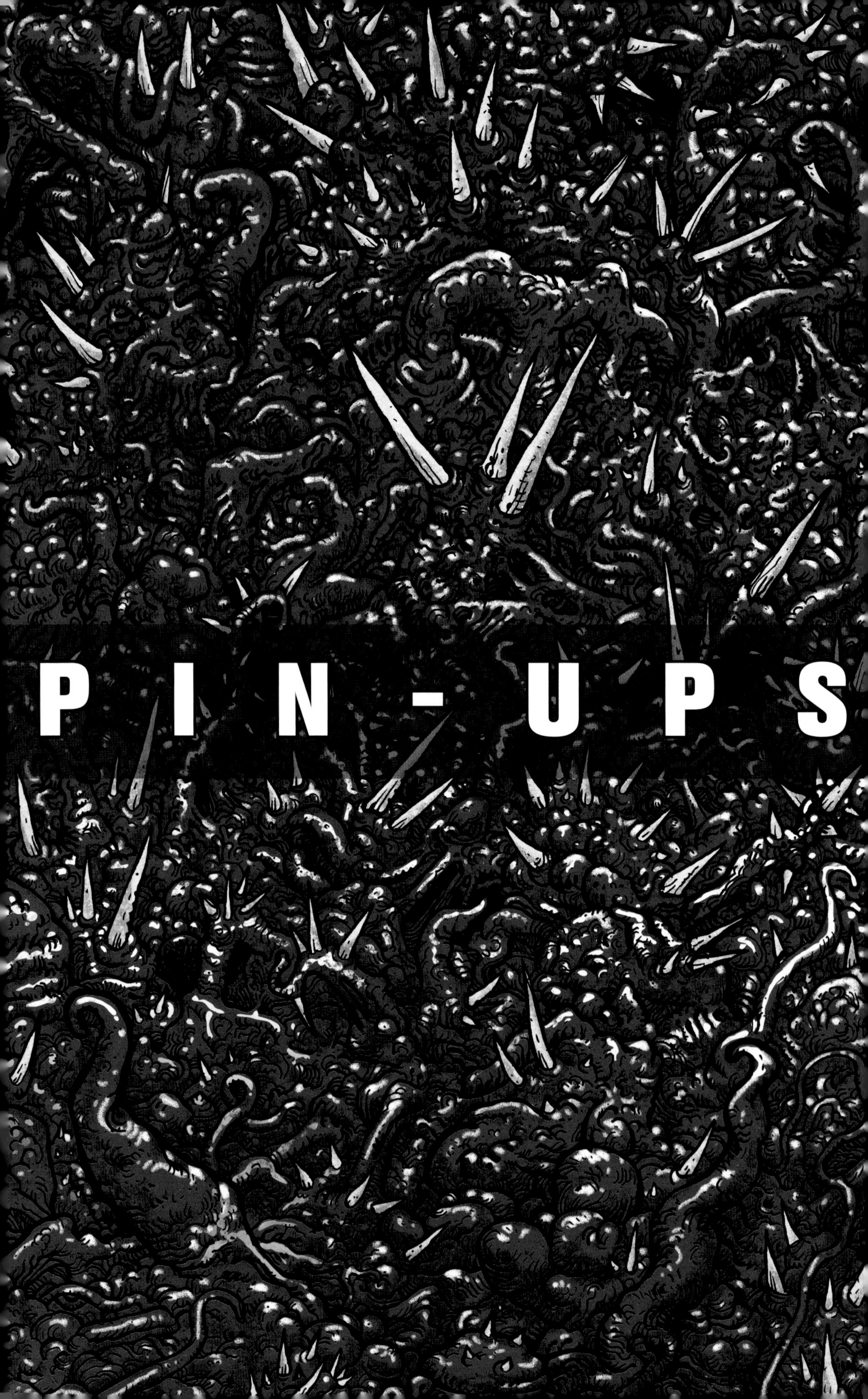
PIN-UPS

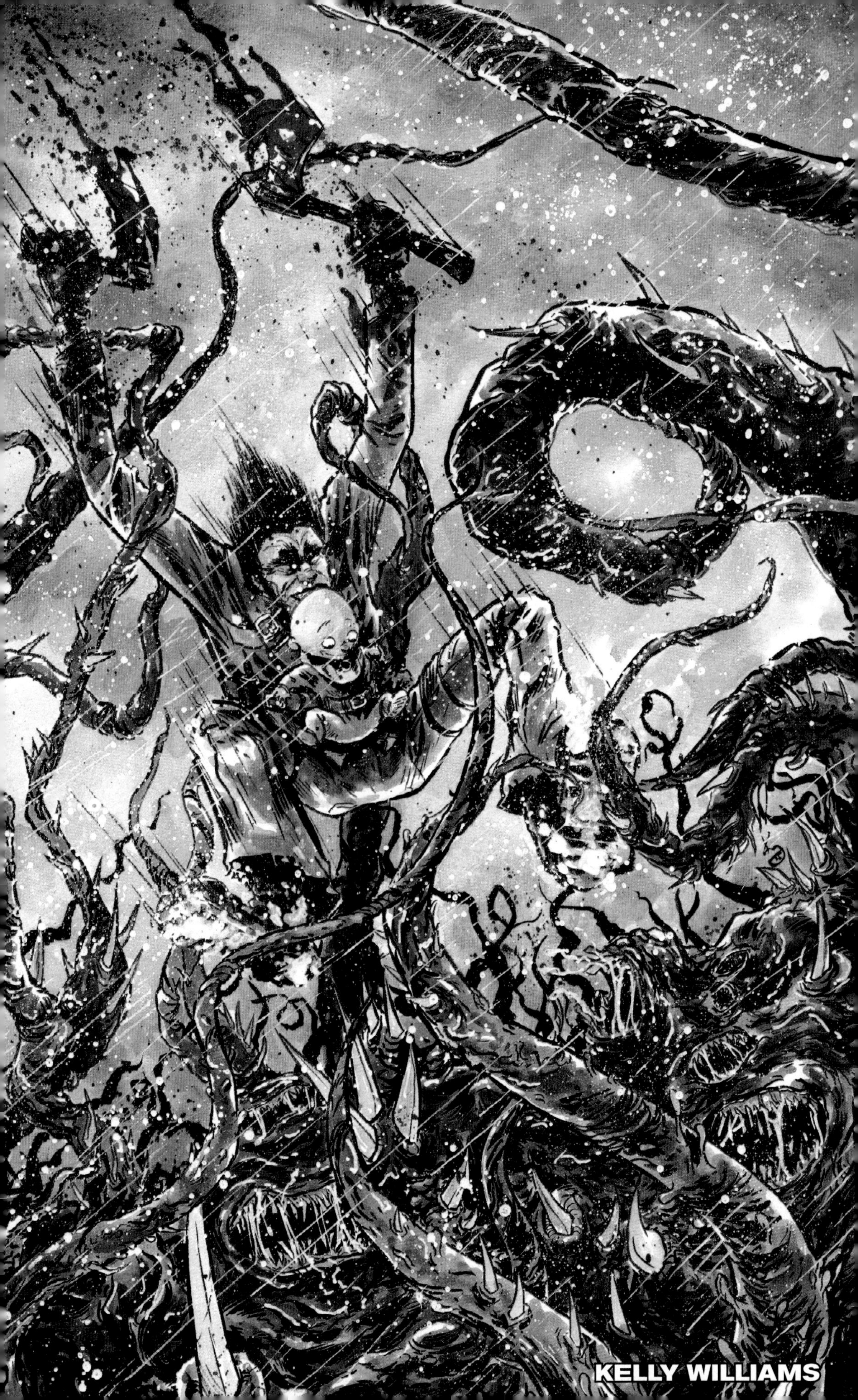
KELLY WILLIAMS

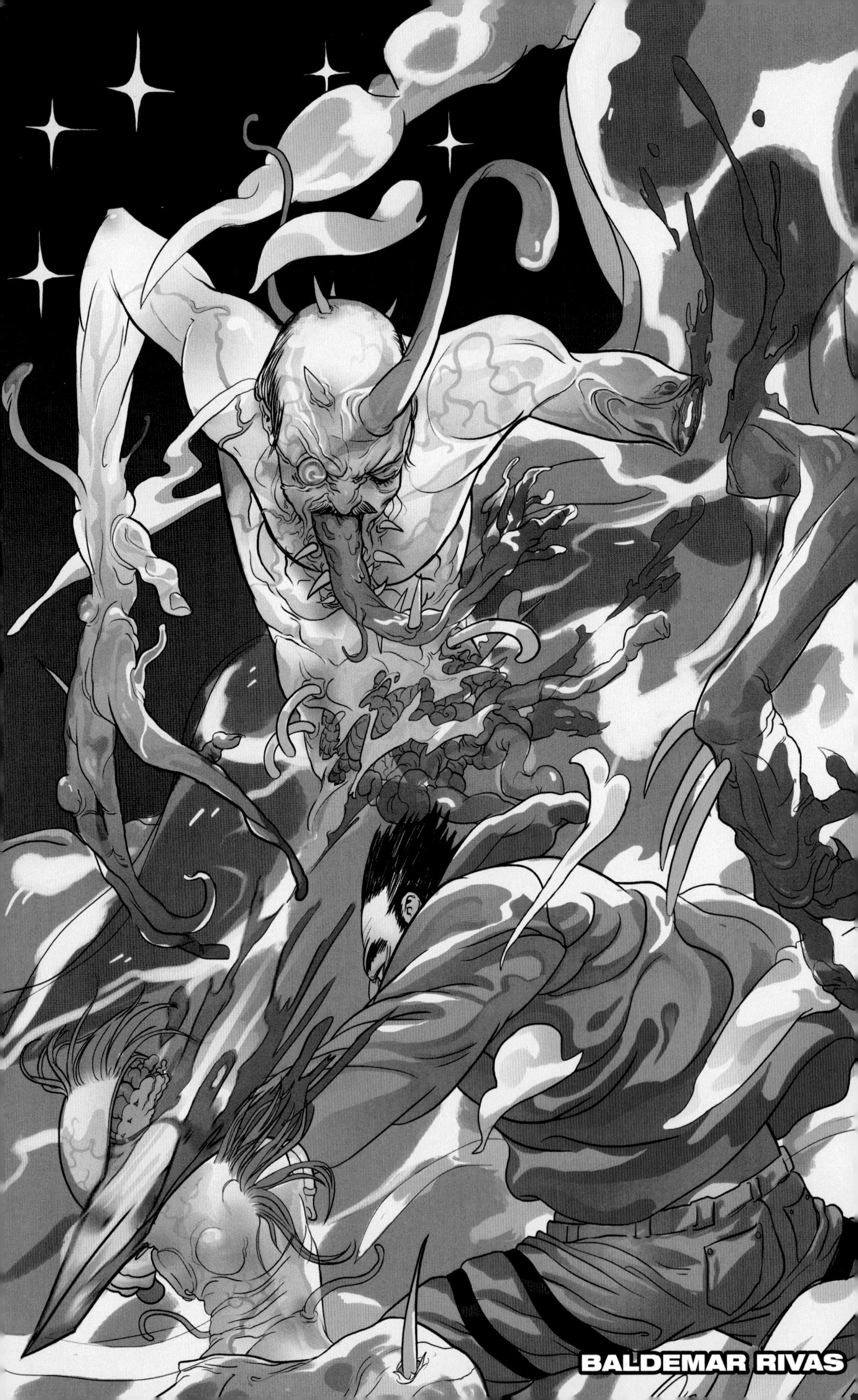

BALDEMAR RIVAS

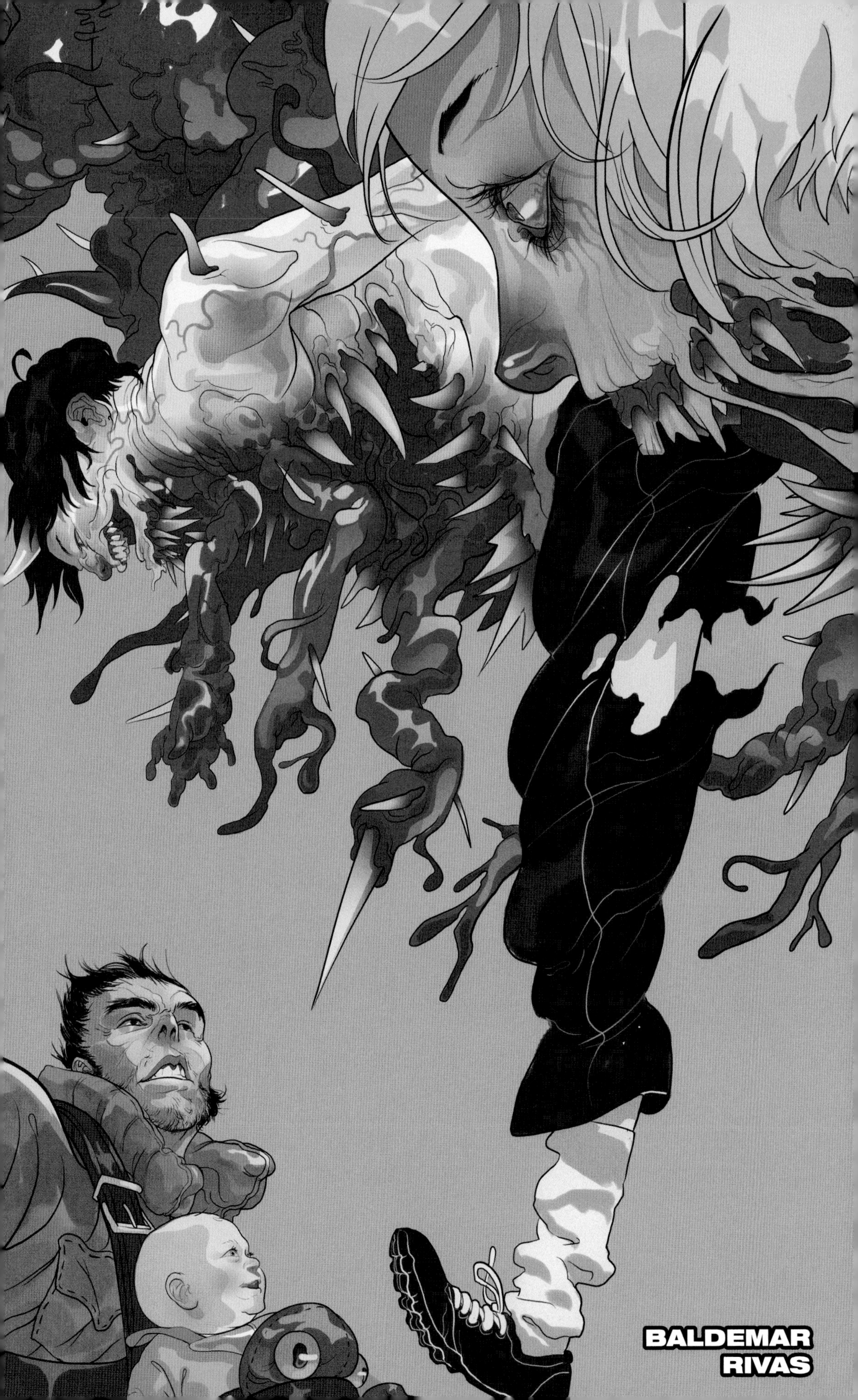
BALDEMAR
RIVAS

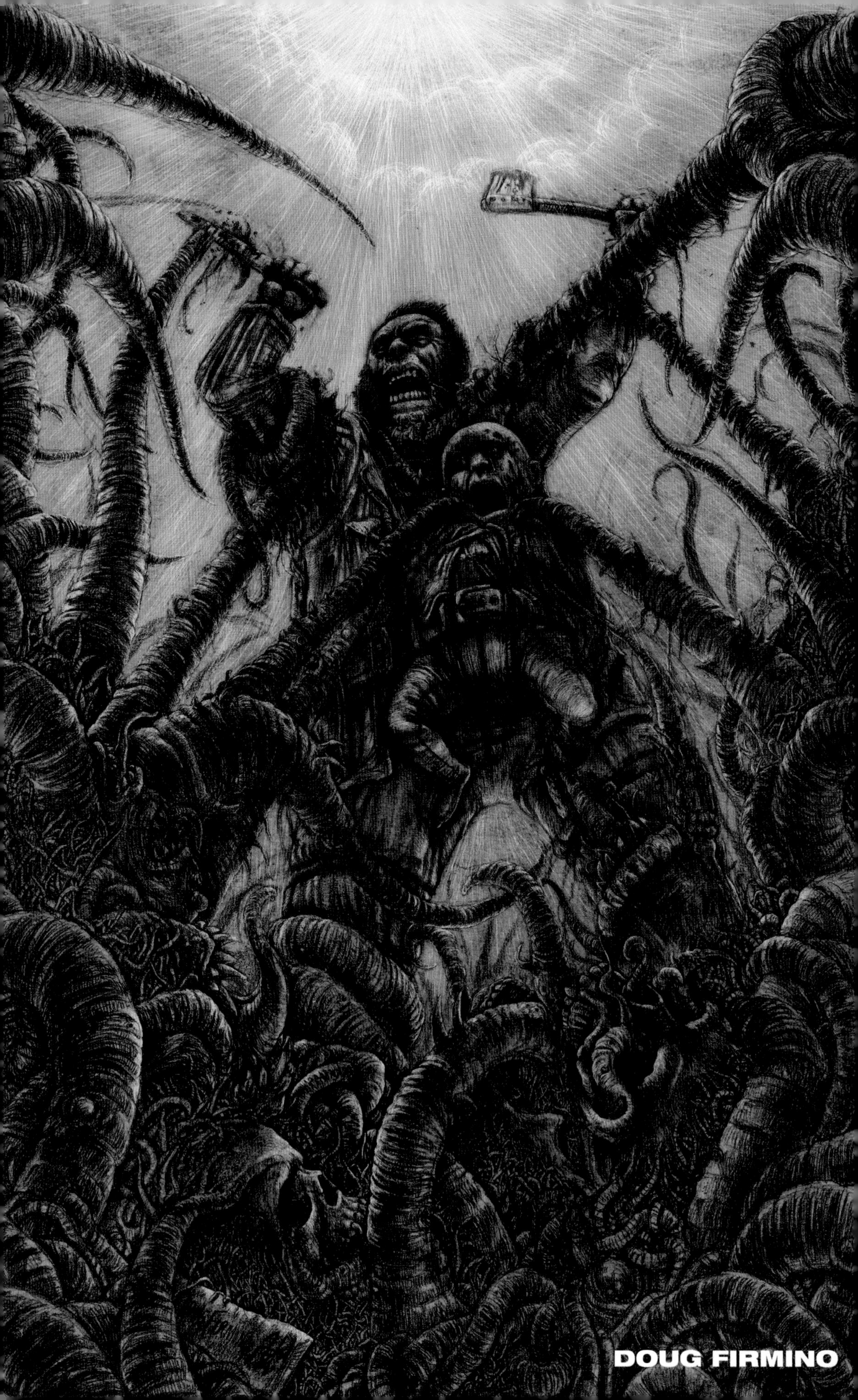
DOUG FIRMINO

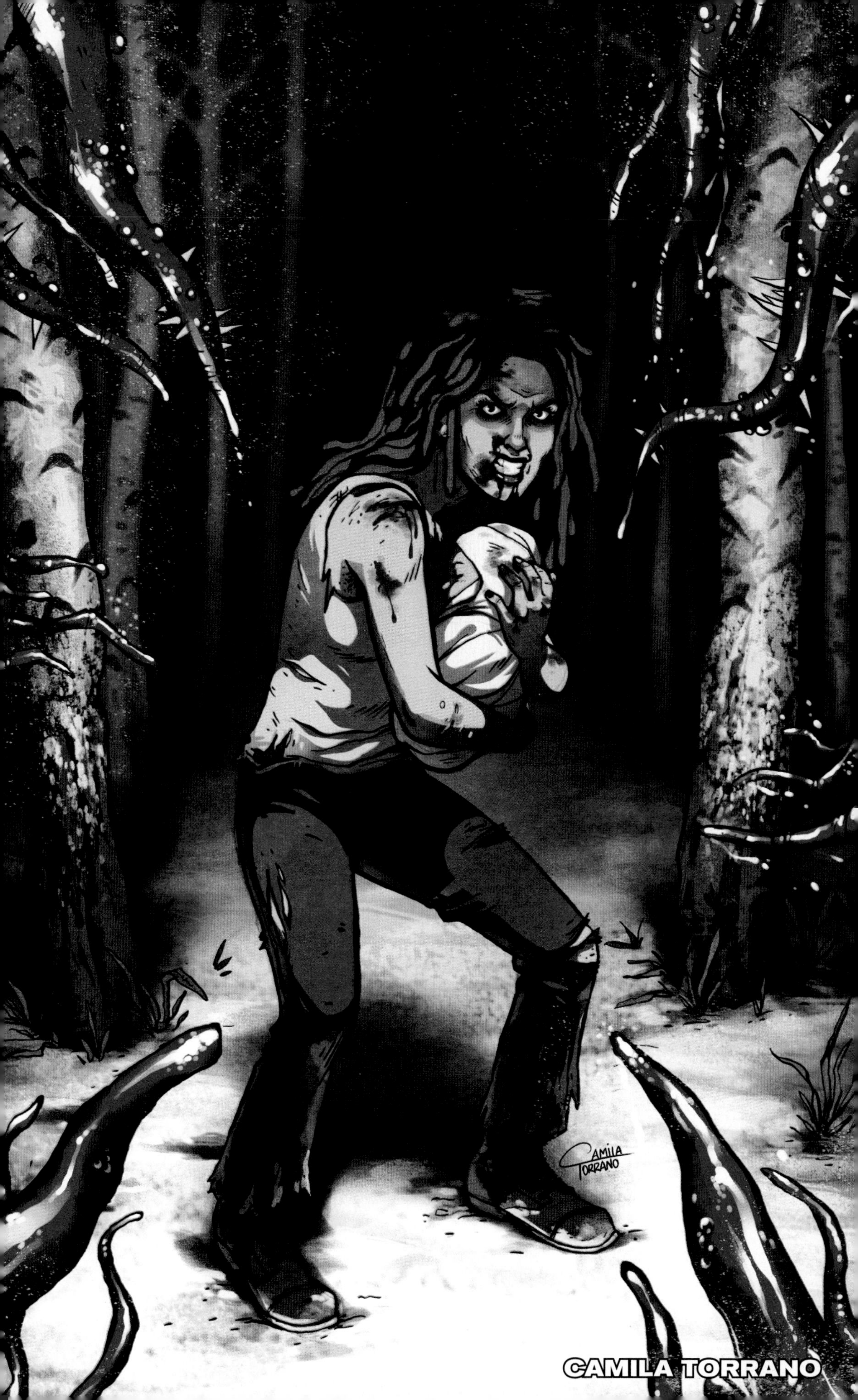
CAMILA TORRANO
CAMILA TORRANO

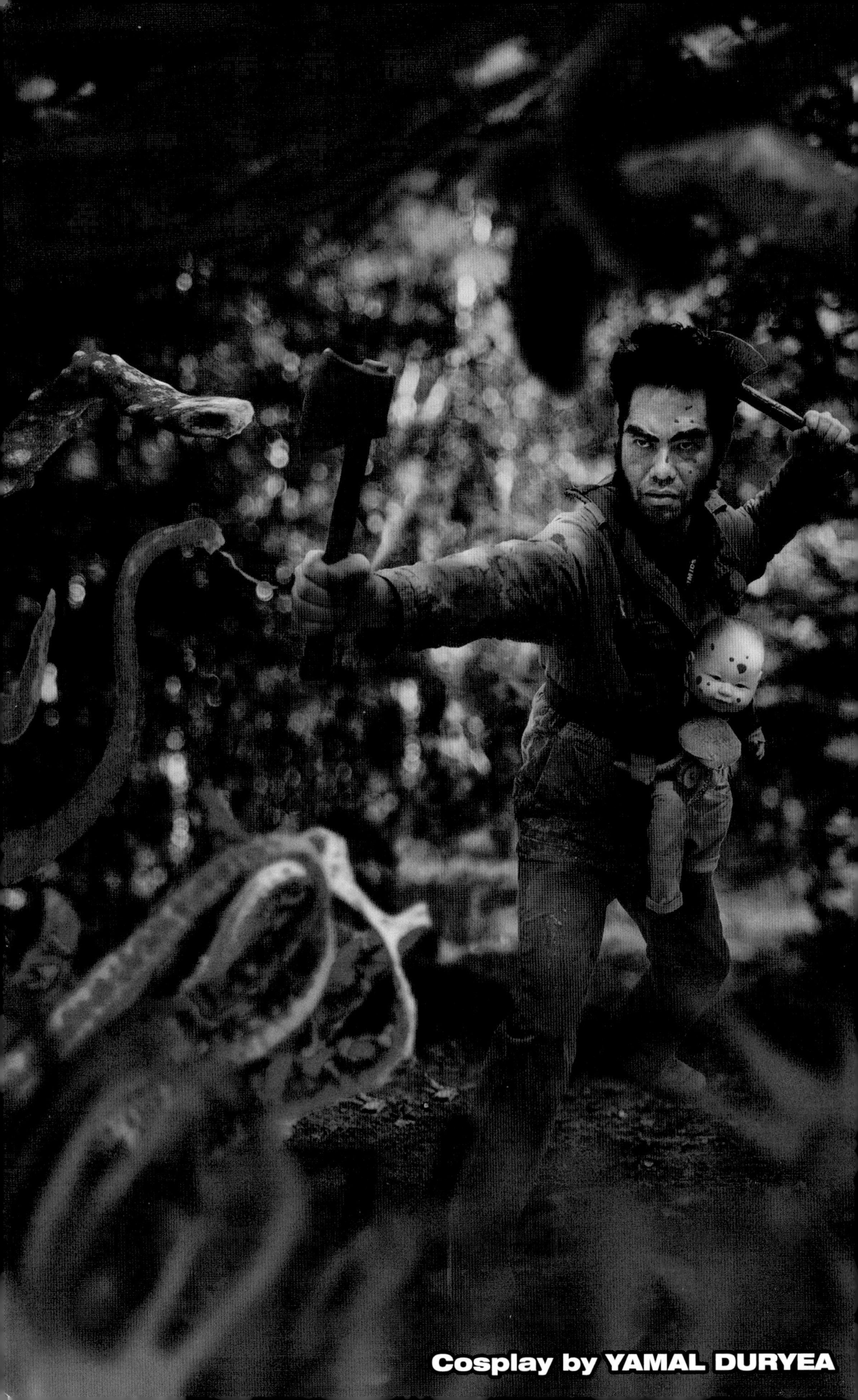

Cosplay by YAMAL DURYEA

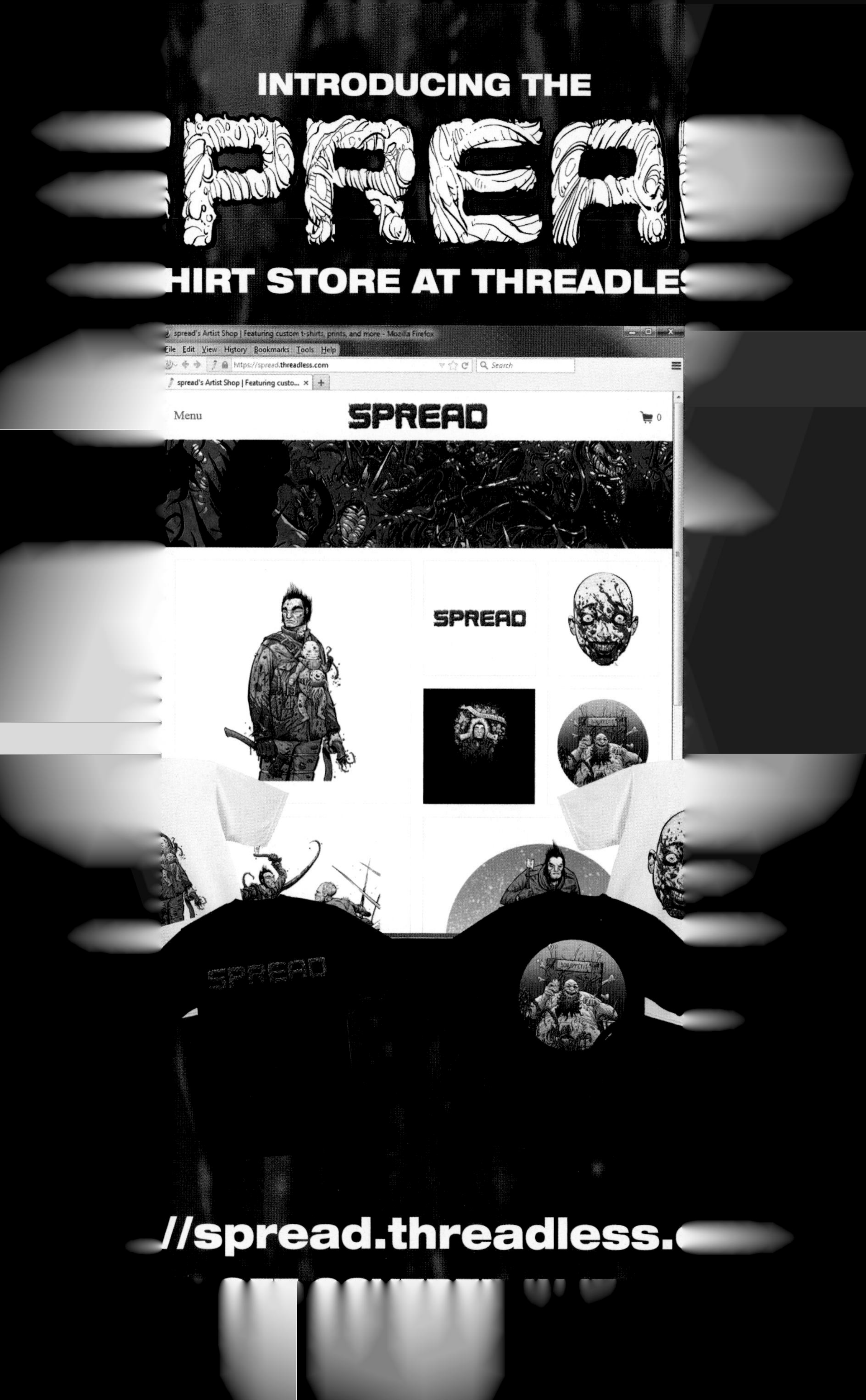
INTRODUCING THE
HIRT STORE AT THREADLES
spread's Artist Shop | Featuring custom t-shirts, prints, and more - Mozilla Firefox
File Edit View History Bookmarks Tools Help
https://spread.threadless.com
Search
spread's Artist Shop | Featuring custo...
Menu
SPREAD
0
SPREAD
SPREAD
//spread.threadless.

JUSTIN JORDAN

Justin Jordan lives in the wilds of Pennsylvania and writes comics. Lots of comics. Most notably the *Luther Strode* saga and *Dead Body Road* for Image.

Twitter: @Justin_Jordan
Email: JustinJordan@gmail.com
Facebook: www.facebook.com/JustinJordanComics/

KYLE STRAHM

Kyle Strahm lives and works in a house in Kansas City, Missouri where he watches tv shows from back when they did it right and he rearranges old toys like a crazy person. You might have seen his work published by Marvel, DC, Dark Horse, IDW, Todd McFarlane Productions and various others.

Website: www.kylestrahm.com
Instagram: kylestrahm_art
Twitter: @kstrahm
Facebook: www.facebook.com/krstrahm

JOHN BIVENS

John draws stuff. Examples of this include the book you are holding now, *Dark Engine* (Image Comics), *Old Wounds* (Pop Goes the Icon), and multiple anthologies and such. He lives in Minneapolis.

Website: www.john-bivens.com
Instagram: bivensjohn
Twitter: @John_Bivens
Facebook: www.facebook.com/ArtOfJohnThomasBivens
Tumblr: johnbivens.tumblr.com

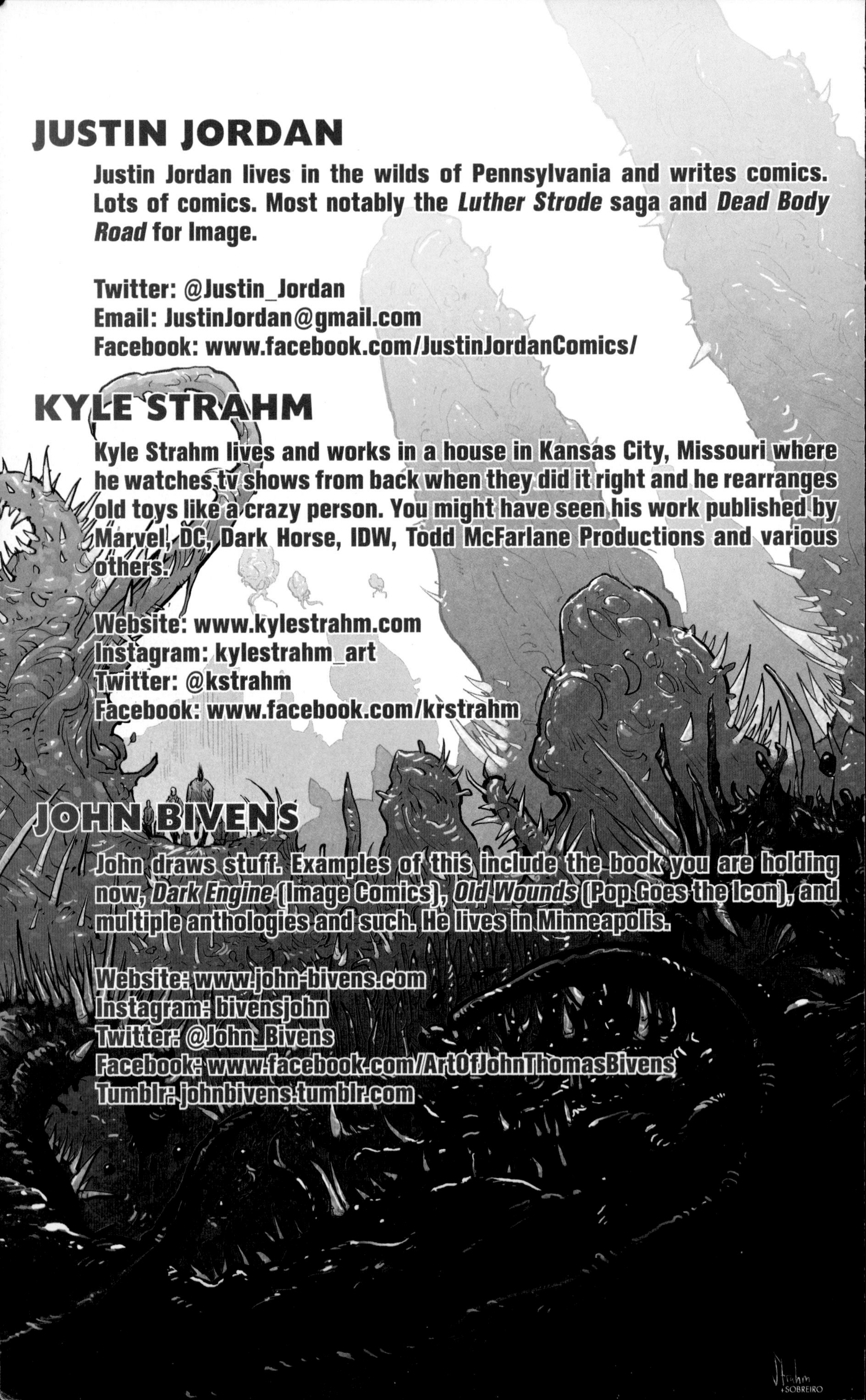

FELIPE SOBREIRO

Felipe Sobreiro is an artist and colorist from Brazil. His work has been published, among others, by Image, Marvel, DC, BOOM! Studios and Dark Horse. He's the colorist of the *Luther Strode* saga.

Website: www.sobreiro.com
Instagram: sobreiro
Twitter: @therealsobreiro
Facebook: www.facebook.com/fsobreiro

CRANK!

Crank! letters a bunch of books put out by Image, Dark Horse and Oni Press. He also has a podcast with Mike Norton (www.crankcast.net) and he makes music (www.sonomorti.bandcamp.com).

Twitter: @ccrank

SEBASTIAN GIRNER

Sebastian Girner is a freelance editor and writer who has helped creatively guide and produce comics for such publishers as Marvel Entertainment, Image Comics, VIZ Media and Random House. He lives and works in Brooklyn.

Website: www.sebastiangirner.com
Twitter: @SGirner

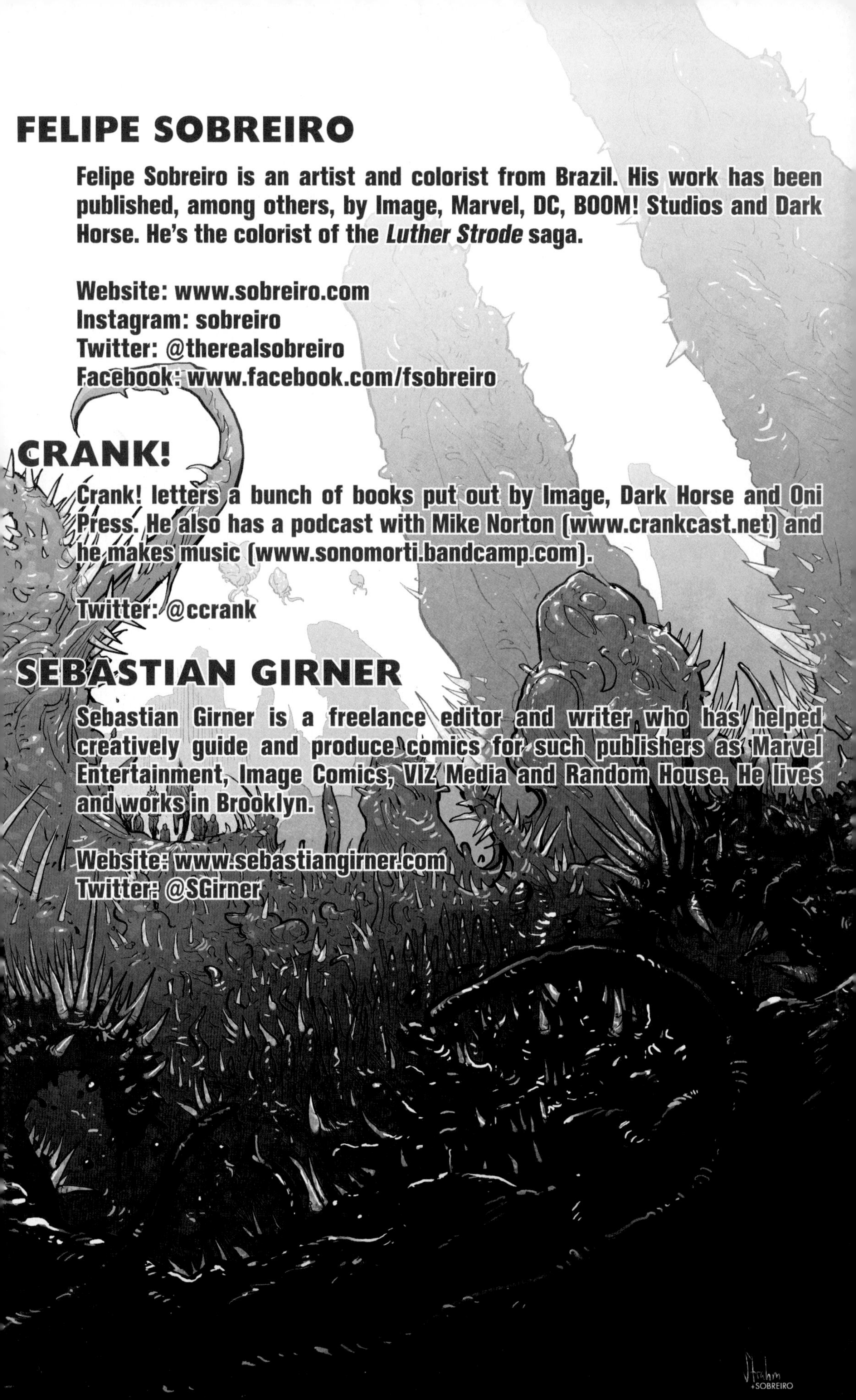

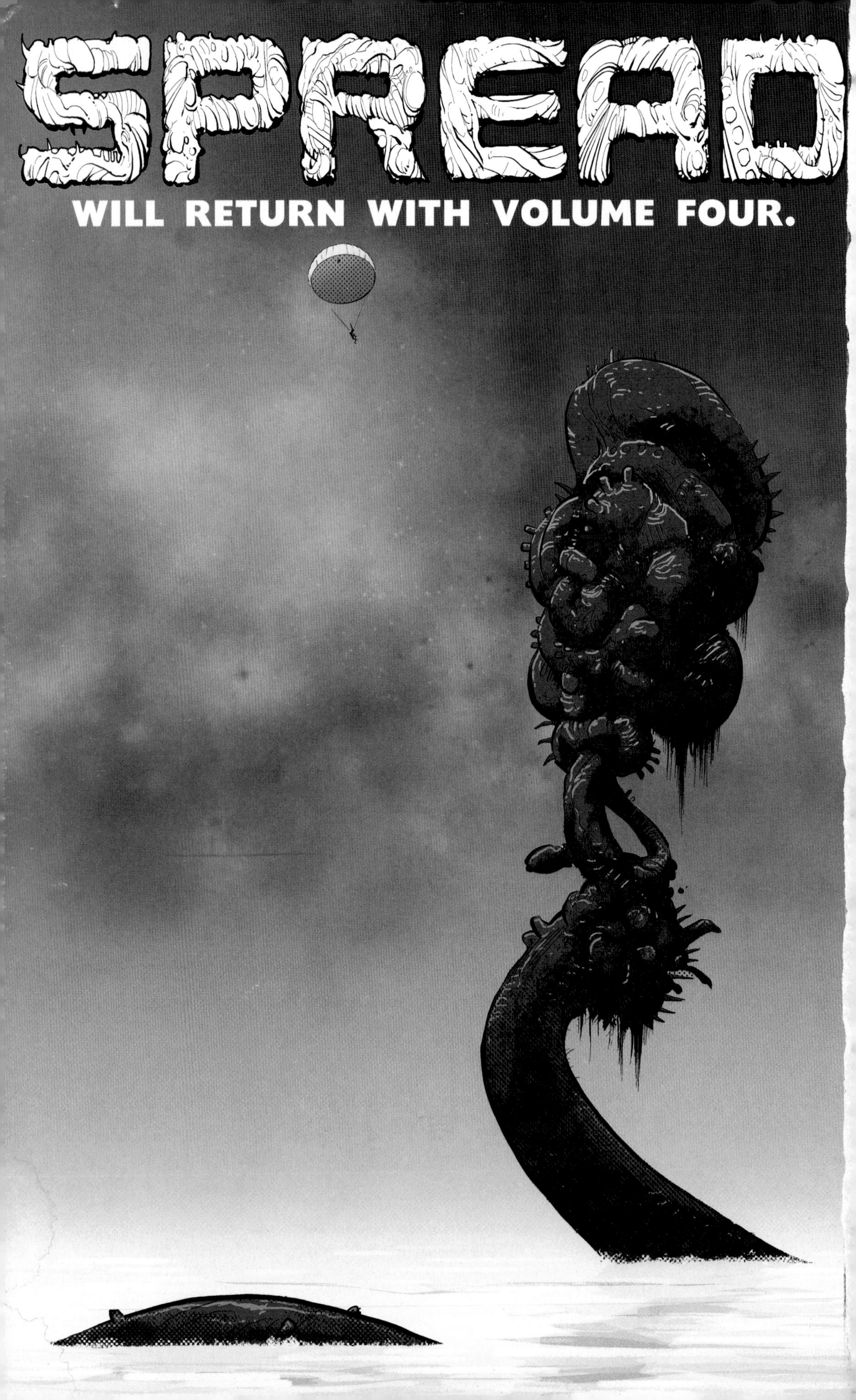
SPREAD
WILL RETURN WITH VOLUME FOUR.